The Viana Memoirs
Vol. I

The Navigator

by

L. Katherine Dailey

The Navigator *is wholly and completely a work of
fiction. Any similarity between characters and persons
living or dead is purely coincidental. While some locations
are real, they are used fictionally within this context.*

Cover Photo by L. Katherine Dailey
Taken from Cape Disappointment Lighthouse, Washington, USA
Cover Design: Linda Lane

ISBN: 0-9746122-9-4

Publisher: Edit et Cetera Ltd.

www.denvereditor.com

Dedicated to my fun-loving sister, Christine Phillips,
my very first reader. Thanks for urging me on
to chapter two and for naming this novel.
With you—my model for the character of
Jessica—life is always an adventure!

Other books by L. Katherine Dailey

Fruits of the Famine
The Journey

ACKNOWLEDGMENTS

With special thanks to my editor, Linda Lane. Your devotion to excellence and professionalism is truly inspiring!

To my husband, Michael: There must be a word to describe my appreciation for your understanding and patience. I have yet to discover it.

The sincerest of gratitude to my parents, Lois and Neil Dailey and Charles and Mary Jo Betts, for your loving support.

But most of all, thank you, all my readers. Without your enthusiasm for my stories, this book would never have been printed.

Chapter One

"So, you thought you could hide from me..."

John Viana's voice came soft and deep after he stepped into the darkness to gaze at a veiled glow near the horizon. The crescent moon hid behind a cloak of heavy clouds and drizzling rain.

"...But if you're there, I'll find you."

He clutched his oilskin coat below the collar, shivering in the piercing dampness of the night. Moving to the railing of the tower's crown, he scanned the heavens high above a restless sea. A penetrating white beam passed above his head and reached far out across the water, piercing the silvery fog and dismissing it in one easy swoop. Moments later a red beam of equal intensity followed.

His hand slipped into his pocket, his fingers settling around his watch, but he let it go. He did not have to look—he knew the hands rested on the ten o'clock hour—the same time he had gazed into the night sky in search of the familiar luminary every night for fifteen years.

Leaning forward onto the railing, he strained to see the elusive moon. At times he could almost envision her face in its carved surface—the soft lines of her cheeks, the arch of each delicate brow, eyes as blue and deep as the sea itself, crimson lips that curved upward to one side when she would tease a smile from his own, the fine nose that crinkled when she laughed, even the smooth caramel tone of her skin.

John's drenched head dropped. His eyes closed, beads of rain dripping from his hair to trickle over his brow and cheeks.

Would he ever escape her memory? Would he one day find freedom from the torment that besieged him night after night, year after year? Perhaps his choice to man the lighthouse had been an unwise one, for the sea and the nights alone fed his anguish.

Their final moments together echoed through his mind like a melody, a cherished song burned long ago into his soul...

"Don't look at me that way," she had said then. "You'll make me cry."

The small child in his arms reached out to her mother, wailing, tears smudged over her rosy cheeks.

"Are you sure about this, John?" she said in that soft Spanish accent.

"Go. She needs you. We'll be all right."

"But in eight years, John, we've been apart only once."

He cupped one hand around the head of the four-year-old, their middle daughter, and felt the fingers of their oldest grip the hem of his coat. Glancing toward the ship, he blinked so she would not notice the mist in his eyes.

She touched his arm. "Every night at ten o'clock, look out at the moon and know that I, too, am gazing at it." She kissed the head of each daughter before her lips met her husband's one last time.

The youngest cried for her departing mother, pulling his attention back, but he could still feel the gentle stroke of his wife's hand on his cheek...

When he emerged from the memory, it was the wind caressing his face. His eyes opened, focusing again upon the ashen glow low in the sky. The question that haunted him every night came again.

"Why?" he cried out to the fading luminary. "*Why* did I let you go?"

Chapter Two

A warm July breeze billowed the heavy velvet drapes hanging on either side of several tall windows, carrying the soft fragrance of roses and lavender from the gardens outside.

William Sutton had arrived late. He stood in the large archway that opened into the spacious ballroom and watched several couples swirling about.

The women's flounced gowns of taffeta, lace, or tarlatan floated across the polished floor, their ruffles cascading into lagging trains. Dressed in black double-breasted tail coats and white gloves, the men guided their ladies in graceful, synchronized motions, their eyes attentive and their postures rigid.

After a few moments, the late arrival weaved along the perimeter of the dance floor, nodding at chatting couples and men with top hats in hand.

A flash of copper blazing forth from across the room caught his attention—the curls of a young woman dressed in a gown of royal blue. The unusual color nagged at his memory. Where had he seen that hair before? No...it could not be. *Could it?*

"Mr. Sutton!" a woman called out, approaching him from behind.

He turned to find his hostess. A plan began to form. His family had been acquainted with the Boswells for decades, and he had thought the white-haired baron and his pretentious wife old when *he* was a child. Now forty-five, William wondered at her antiquity. Just how old *could* she be by now?

"I'd like to say how delighted Lord Boswell and I are that you were able to attend our gathering," she squawked. The insincerity in her voice made him wonder what had prompted the invitation. "We know your work does not allow you to escape often. I believe it has been several years since our last meeting."

"Indeed, I think you're correct," he replied.

Something inside him recoiled. Her plumage in full display, Lady Boswell resembled an old peacock. Even more pompous than her lofty peers, she no doubt allowed this evening's event to further inflate her ego. He feared contact with a sharp object could send her airborne into an adjoining room. Only the weight of the extravagant sapphire pendant draped about her neck, encircled with a full complement of diamonds, held her earthbound. It pressed against her ample bosom, tugging the crepe skin of her throat downward.

"I trust your family is well." He forced his mind back to the conversation, lest he laugh out loud at the mental pictures he was conjuring up. "I congratulate you on the upcoming nuptials of your youngest. I spied her on the dance floor with the young man I assume to be her fiancé. She looks stunning for tonight's engagement ball."

"Thank you." She sniffed.

An uncomfortable lull in the conversation followed despite the manor and the grand hall's filling with cheerful music coming from an ensemble of flutes and violins.

Grumbling began in his belly as delightful aromas of the upcoming feast wafted about them. White soup, boiled salmon, and dressed cucumber, according to his menu card, would introduce the meal. Sweetbreads and roast fillet of veal would follow, garnished with mashed turnips. One of his favorites, spinach with croutons, would be served as the third course, among other delicacies. And his most treasured treat of all, brandied pudding, would seal the feast. Anticipating the meal to come, he almost forgot the presence of his hostess.

His thoughts of culinary delights were shattered by her voice. "I do believe you were well acquainted with the Everett family at one time."

"Yes, my lady."

"I was sorry to hear of Margaret Everett's passing last year—infamous though she was. At least she was able to survive her husband by several years. I assume her estate was handled by your firm?"

"Correct again." Ah, *now* it became clear—the single reason a woman of her stature would condescend to mingle with him, a mere barrister. He was quite certain this was also the explanation for his invitation to the gala affair. The fate of an estate the size of the Everett fortune was of great interest to the wealthy landowners and nobility across the country, and Lady Boswell's curiosity regarding the business of others was legendary. He wondered whether she were also reminding him that the Boswells would *never* consider placing *their* estate in the care of his firm.

"Young Lord Everett is a very wealthy man now." Her obvious eagerness to draw from him any interesting tidbit hung from every word. "I am certain we have not seen the last of him."

He drew a heavy breath and focused again on the flame-haired girl across the room. His reason for continuing this distasteful conversation shot a surge of guilt through him. He, too, harbored the hope of uncovering a piece of information.

"My lady," he said, "I was noticing how this society has changed since I was last associated. There are many new faces." He watched her take the bait, her attention diverted by the opportunity to gossip—a subject that rivaled the aristocracy's esteem for money. "Who are the two gentlemen standing there by the entrance?"

"One is a nephew of Lord Boswell, who has recently moved into the county. The other is his business partner."

"And what of the older couple across the room, there by the hearth?"

"They are Sir Thompson and his wife from the western coast, Cornwall County, in the Land's End area. They are associates of Lord Boswell's cousin and are here on holiday for a few months."

"And the young lady with them is their daughter?"

"No, no. She was introduced to me as a traveling companion from their town. I do not recall her name at the moment. Often they bring along one or two less-fortunates on their holidays. They are indeed charitable that way. However, in my opinion, they should leave such gestures of generosity to the squire. After all, it is his duty to handle the needs of the lower classes."

"Pardon me," another guest interrupted.

"Lovely party, my lady," William said, grasping the opportunity to escape. Satisfied with the information she had shared, he bowed his head to their hostess. "You'll excuse me," he stated as he moved away, his eyes fixed on the Thompsons' young female traveling companion.

Despite a few curves, her willowy shape did not quite fill the satin gown. Her bronze tresses spun into loose spirals that lay atop her head. In the soft light of the candelabras, she seemed to be wearing a copper crown. Ringlet wisps framed her fair face.

For a brief moment their eyes met, and although he was too far away to tell, he knew hers were blue.

She turned in haste, leaving the ballroom.

Brentwood House, a cozy stone structure, sat atop a small hillside, its back tucked into the woods surrounding the knoll. The only home Jessica Viana remembered, it was almost as precious to her as was her beloved family.

She watched from the window of her second-story bed-chamber while her father disappeared into the forest below. She knew his routine by heart. He would follow the footpath that stretched from their whitewashed porch through the forest toward a rocky beach. A small wooden rowboat waited to carry him to Brentwood Lighthouse—'Old Stormy' her father had dubbed it. Standing about a half mile out in the ocean, its crown could often be seen above the forest canopy from the large window in her room. But such was not always the case on this temperamental English coast. Many times she had seen her father engulfed by fog or driving rain before reaching the cover of the trees, the light from his lantern disappearing from view.

This evening, however, the weather was perfect. A contented sigh escaped her lips. Watching the sun drop toward the quiet summer sea, she anticipated the approaching sunset, when the horizon would exchange its dusty blue for a dramatic golden blanket.

She often found herself deep in thought about the lands that lay beyond that horizon. More than once she had promised herself that someday she would venture far beyond her present world. But when, if ever, would her dread of the sea be rooted from her heart?

Turning from the window, she snuggled into a wingback chair to read for the second time the letter that had arrived the previous week from Kent, where her sister, Grace, had spent the last three months.

Dear Jessie,

How I long to be home with you again. Although I have so enjoyed the outings with the Thompsons, I am growing weary. Kent is a magnificent county, the likes of which I have never seen before. If beauty were the single consideration, I should be content to stay here forever. I have heard this part of the country called the Garden of England, and no wonder, for the forest floor is so covered with ferns and mosses that the only earth to be seen is the winding of an occasional footpath leading to a wildflower meadow or quiet lake. The countryside is breathtaking—tiny cottages nestled into the hillsides, lazy brooks tumbling over the rocks, quaint village window boxes brimming with the pinks and blues of summer flowers. Oh, Jess, you must see for yourself!

I am writing to you from London now. The endless activities of the city seem to captivate the ladies and gentlemen who live in great abundance here. They have many dances and gatherings and seem to enjoy the companions within their circles.

However, I find myself perplexed by one matter: how a marriage can ever take place among them. You know how I am always careful to keep a watchful eye for the ideal man for my sisters, but, Jessie, I fear the men of the Thompsons' acquaintance are too self-centered to merit serious consideration. Any handsome features fade upon hearing their conversation. They cannot come to know any woman, for their words seem never to leave the topic of themselves. Never do they inquire of or about a woman. Yet their boasts are lofty indeed! I doubt a single one has ever so much as glanced at the night sky to discover that there is something that stands above them. Their snobbery is an embarrassment.

And with few exceptions the women are without beauty or sense, their accomplishments little. Their conversations succeed in venturing to the far-reaching depths of a mud puddle.

I realize all cannot be philosophers, but have they never taken the time to consider something so full of wonder as the vastness of the oceans and the possibility of an entire undiscovered world beneath, as you often tell me? Have they never contemplated the evidence of intelligence above our own? Their lives revolve around the latest fashion or the worry of a new wrinkle forming on their pampered faces.

No, the qualities they possess should not attract so much as an insect, much less a marriage mate!

Jessica giggled at her sister's candor. It was out of character for Grace to speak in such a way. She always looked for good in every person. Only one thing would explain her harsh words—the people of the Thompsons' society in London must truly be as described. But the Thompsons themselves were agreeable people. Why were they so well-connected with those of such offensive demeanor? Jessica wondered. She returned to the letter.

How is it they manage to secure their man? Yet they do. The one conclusion I reach regarding the matter is that all in their general acquaintance hold that single important possession—money. It is their happiness, their purpose, and the adhesive that binds their society. It is their god. How sad that they will all die wealthy but without ever having known the joy of genuine love.

Jessica could not laugh at this. She realized that money itself did not make a person proud, but the manner in which some elevated themselves because of it. After all, had she and her two sisters not been taught that qualities, not possessions, make the person? Was not her family acquainted with several agreeable wealthy families, as well as poor ones?

The letter continued.

Just today I learned that we will be attending an engagement party in a fortnight. I shudder at the prospect of yet another evening wasted on such frivolous people.

Jessica looked back at the date of the letter. The dance her sister dreaded must already have taken place. She read on.

How I wish you could be here in my stead, Jess. For your beauty and intelligence would topple any of these men from their lofty station.

"That's where you're mistaken," Jessica whispered, looking up at her reflection in the cheval glass across the room. All three Viana girls had inherited their mother's sapphire eyes, but she and her elder sister could not be more different in their other physical traits.

Lofty in height and lean in build, Grace possessed a most unusual shade of hair. Jessica sometimes heard it called strawberry by acquaintances, yet it had equal tones of darker auburn and golden veins throughout that gave it the unusual appearance of shimmering copper. Curls tumbled around her face and down the full length of her back. Practicality demanded that the locks be swept atop her head most of the time, and she submitted by experimenting with a variety of styles. Jessica was always amused to sit on Grace's bed, watching while countless pins disappeared into the heavy locks as they were spun up, woven around, braided, and draped with ribbons and bows. At times she herself would jump to her feet to hold a pin, all the while chatting and laughing with her sister at some of the elaborate styles Grace would invent.

She, on the other hand, was slighter in height and more muscular in build, which could be attributed to the demanding work at the lighthouse. The reflection looking back at her now was almost identical to the portrait of their mother suspended on the wall between two windows in the library downstairs. Her mother's hair, like her own, was the length of Grace's, yet as black, straight, and lustrous as the breast of a raven. Her olive complexion was also reflected in Jessica's own face. The gentle countenance found in the portrait had adorned that wall for the past fifteen years, and Jessica liked to think those pensive blue eyes had overseen her studies. In her opinion, however, the beauty of her elder sister surpassed that of their mother. Recalling her father's words that the portrait fell far short of capturing her true beauty, Jessica accepted that she herself would never be honored with the privilege of making the comparison. She had no memory of her mother.

Her thoughts returned to Grace's letter and her last comment. No, the men of London must be very calloused if they were so unaffected by the charms of the eldest Miss Viana. She started to read again.

A sudden tap on her door startled her.

"Excuse me, Miss."

"Yes, Mrs. Wright?" She looked up at the kind face of the woman who now stood in the doorway.

Mrs. Wright was an industrious woman in her fifties, not much older than Jessica's father. She and her husband had been hired to help tend the home, lighthouse, and Jessica and her sisters. They had been with the family as long as Jessica could remember.

"Two gentlemen just arrived. They're in the parlor."

Visits by friends and admirers had become more frequent as Jessica and her sisters matured, but she was surprised to find Edward Scarborough and his friend, James Gregory, calling so close to the supper hour. Looking first at Mr. Scarborough, who was taller than his friend, she noticed the way his tawny hair waved into curls at the nape of his neck. He turned to her, a warm smile revealing his pleasure in seeing her.

Jessica kept her expression formal. After a brief greeting the three sat down, while Mrs. Wright busied herself in another room.

"I'm afraid Alexandra is off on a ride." She acknowledged the apparent reason for their visit. "It seems she can never get enough of the fresh air. I don't anticipate her return for some time, perhaps even after dark. We're to expect a full moon, you know."

"Oh...well...I'm not disappointed in having the opportunity to be in *your* company, Miss Viana." Edward's gaze dropped, his countenance slipping into one of slight dismay. "And from your sister's perspective," he continued, looking up again, "I suppose that even a conversation with two captivating and handsome young men would not divert her attention from the beauty of the countryside on such a perfect evening."

She realized he was testing his prospects. Mr. Scarborough *seemed* nice enough, but while his family was from the area, she and her sisters had been acquainted with him just a short while. She exercised caution, not willing to surrender to his leadings—unlike her sister, Grace, who promoted his attentions upon their youngest sister.

"Perhaps appearance is sufficient to divert *some* young ladies," she said, "but I fear my sister would be more attracted to qualities such as respectability and an honorable reputation." She tilted her face, meeting Edward's gaze with a penetrating stare while fixing a short smile on her lips.

Now it was Edward's turn to smile. It seemed she had succeeded in giving him the impression she was hoping for—that she was not one so easy to coerce.

"Will your family be attending the Castleton ball next week, Miss Viana?" Mr. Gregory interrupted them.

"Yes. My elder sister is expected home in a few days, and we're all looking forward to the gathering."

At that moment the front door opened. Her father had returned much sooner than she expected. He entered the parlor where she and her guests were seated. Both men stood in greeting, and she noted Edward's expression as he scanned the man of the house from head to toe, his disapproval obvious as he took in the unkempt, loose cotton shirt with its unbuttoned collar. John Viana's filthy trousers with cuffs rolled a few inches above weathered and mud-splattered boots told of his arduous work.

Although his present personal disarray belied it, her father was a poised and handsome man. His outdoor life had exerted little effect on his youthful appearance, despite soft lines fanning from the edges of his eyes. Jessica was fond of the curved crease near each corner of his lips, as they spoke of his inclination to smile and laugh, though at the moment his expression was a serious stare.

She suspected that Mr. Scarborough must have seen only the smudges that covered him as she observed the twitch of Edward's top lip and the crinkling of his brow.

"Father, may I introduce you to Mr. Edward Scarborough and Mr. James Gregory? They've come to call on Alexandra."

"Pleased to make your acquaintance." Edward was first in extending his hand.

"Whoever was it that said the life of a lighthouse keeper is a lonely one?" John asked, accepting the hand. "I believe we've had more visitors than the Mona Lisa these past three years at least." His fists came to rest on his hips. "You oughtn't stay much longer though. It's an hour's ride back to town, and the sun is already setting." He towered above the slim young men.

Jessica tried to conceal her advancing smile. Her father's dismissal of any serious interest on their part amused her.

"You needn't be concerned, Mr. Viana," replied Edward. "We'll have the moonlight guiding our journey." He glanced sideways at Jessica.

"Looks like we'll be having crab for supper, Jessica," her father said, afterward excusing himself and leaving the room.

"Nonetheless, your father's suggestion is well-taken," stated Mr. Scarborough, his gaze lingering upon the empty doorway.

"I'll inform my sister of your visit," she offered, escorting the men to the foyer.

"Well, then." Edward's thumb and forefinger rose to settle upon his chin. His hands were long and slender. "I look forward to continuing our acquaintance at the dance."

Glancing at his hand, Jessica felt the blood rush from her face as she spotted, perched on his smallest finger, a carved gold band with a sparkling square ruby in its center. She caught her breath, unable to conceal her surprise.

Could there be two such rings in existence? She doubted that to be the case. It had to be the same one!

"Very well," she stated, trying to recover. "Good evening, Mr. Scarborough, Mr. Gregory."

No sooner had she closed the door behind them than a loud uproar outside caught her attention. Jessica ran to the sitting room window. The visitors' horses, which had been tied to a post several yards from the house, fought to free themselves. On the ground a large crab was poised atop a rumpled canvas bag that had been placed beneath the animals. The creature must have been as astonished as the horses upon discovering its location when emerging from the bag. With no apparent escape route, it began attacking the legs of the spooked steeds.

The men darted toward them, Edward shouting at the assailant. He skipped and jumped around the crab.

"Stupid vermin!" she heard him call out to the crustacean. "I'll tear you limb from limb!"

The crab pinched the leg of his trousers. He hollered and stumbled over his friend's foot.

"You *idiot*, Gregory! Out of my way!"

Mr. Gregory's horse was first to be loosened, and he pulled the animal to safety. When Mr. Scarborough's horse was then freed, it reared up, whinnying. Even from her distance, Jessica could see the whites of its eyes. It came down almost atop Edward's foot, and the crab had a new hold on his pant leg. He grabbed for his crop and beat the crab away.

"You worthless piece of rubbish!" he said, calling out one more insult before leading his horse away. A safe distance from the crab, Edward held tight the reins until the horse was calm enough to mount.

Before the two reached the forest, Edward's horse tossed its head and bucked once again. Jessica broke out in laughter.

Her father was up to his old tricks. And what better way to uncover the true character of a man!

Chapter Three

"Girls, I have news that will not wait for the return of your sister," John Viana announced as he joined the family for supper.

Jessica was disappointed that her father was not preparing the meal, as he sometimes did for the entire household. On those special occasions he insisted on serving them all, including the Wrights.

But Mrs. Wright was the authority on crab.

Trying not to laugh, Jessica recalled the frantic efforts of Edward Scarborough, who had escaped the last stand of the arthropod that was headed for the pot and the dinner table.

Her father, who looked much more presentable than he had two hours earlier, settled into his chair at the head of the table. Jessica and Alexandra stared at him, but he remained silent, his eyes fixed upon the doorway through which he had just entered.

A smiled teased Jessica's lips despite her effort to keep a straight face. Was it not just like him to heighten their curiosity only to force them to linger in anticipation? She knew him well enough to know that he was awaiting the presentation of the superb meal from which a tantalizing aroma wafted into the dining room.

Looking across the table at her younger sister, she allowed her thoughts to return to the day's events. She had told Alexandra of the visit by Mr. Scarborough and his friend, but not yet about the ring.

She was always amazed at Alexandra's resemblance to their father. Like her sisters, she had their mother's brilliant eyes, yet Alexandra's features, coloring, and sandy hair mirrored the image of John Viana. Jessica's gaze shifted back to her father's strong form and his handsome but modest face.

Left with three little girls when only twenty-nine, he had been determined to raise his young daughters on his own. More than once Jessica had been told of the various boarding schools, nurseries, and nannies whose services he could have employed on his salary as a professor of science at the university in Dublin, but he had decided to tutor his girls himself. Giving up his teaching position that demanded long, exhausting hours, he applied for and secured the job of keeper of Brentwood Lighthouse on England's western coast. He often told them he had been chosen on the basis of his familiarity with the ocean and his knowledge of weather patterns.

One month to the day after Angela Viana's tragic loss at sea, Jessica's family crossed St. George's Channel to her father's homeland. Although he had been in Ireland for nine years, he was not well acquainted with any other families. His work and studies left little spare time, and that which he did have he had chosen to spend hiking, picnicking, fishing, or engaging in other family outings in the Irish countryside. As happy as those times must have been, she and Grace had little recollection of them, and Alexandra, who had been three when they left, had none at all.

The round form of Mrs. Wright appeared in the dining room doorway, a steaming dish in her hands. Jessica left her reverie behind, her attention drawn to the succulent meal about to be served. She giggled as her father's eyes lit up at the sight of the sumptuous deviled crab. He watched the woman spoon plentiful portions onto the plates and then turned his attention once again to his daughters.

"My announcement comes in the form of a letter from an old friend. We attended school together in London when we were young, but have corresponded on only rare occasions over the years." His fork delved into the food before him.

Jessica watched her father's expression as he pulled the fork from his mouth, a broad smile overtaking his clamped lips. His eyes closed, and he lingered on the creamy bite of crab. She and Alexandra laughed aloud to see him in perfect bliss, a matchless moment of pure delight. They followed suit by scooping into their own helpings.

"Nevertheless," John said, returning to present matters before taking another bite, "we have a mutual respect, and I've found time has not deterred our friendship. And his letter brings news that I think you'll find of great interest."

They glanced up from their plates as he produced the letter and began reading aloud.

"Dear John,

"I was taken aback upon receiving your letter. Do you realize it has been almost five years since your last correspondence? And that with no return address! I am delighted to hear of your family's health. I may assure you of the health of the Winterfields as well.

"You have been in my thoughts often over the years, John, in hopes that our friendship would somehow, someday be renewed. Perhaps that time has now come. I am overjoyed to hear you are considering a visit to the London area.

"I would like to invite you and the girls to stay with my family at our home for the duration of your visit. I think you will be pleased with the arrangements. We are near the beach and yet close enough to town that your daughters can enjoy the many activities there.

"I, as usual, am very busy, but my business slows in January. I realize it is not an easy distance, and the travel may prove difficult in England's unpredictable winters. However, I will see to it that you are well provided for along the journey.

"My daughter, Catherine, who is now seventeen years old, is anxious to hear your reply, as I have shared with her much about you and what I know of the girls. As you know, she has only two older brothers who are away most of the time now, and she is very desirous of having in the house the company of other ladies her age. Please do not disappoint her.

"Awaiting your reply,
Richard Winterfield"

* * * * *

Jessica wrinkled her brow. "Richard Winterfield? That name sounds familiar."

Giving her a look of surprise that bordered on disbelief, her father spoke in a voice so low that she strained to hear his words. "I can't believe you remember. Why, you must have been no more than four years old the last time you saw Richard. You, Grace, and I visited his warehouse in London while I was there on business just a few weeks before we lost your mother."

Jessica shrugged.

"Oh, Papa, can we go?" Alexandra's excitement spilled over into her voice.

Her father's soft, deep laugh warmed Jessica's heart. But did she see a shadow cross his eyes? Perhaps not, for when she looked again, the familiar twinkle was there.

"Your old papa has managed to save enough to take the family to Kent in January."

"You're the most wonderful father in all the world!" Alexandra exclaimed.

Both girls sprang from their seats to cover his face with kisses.

"Don't think for one moment that I had just my daughters in mind when I arranged the journey. I was scheming that were I to find suitable grooms for all of you among my old acquaintances in London, I would be free to resume my vocation where I left it fifteen years ago in Dublin."

Jessica settled back into her chair with an unceasing smile. "Father," she challenged, "I'm afraid that while working to secure the futures of your daughters, you have shattered your own."

Her father raised inquisitive eyebrows at her.

"You see," she explained, "in setting the example of what a man should be, you have set yourself upon a pedestal far above the reach of any other man. I find myself convinced there shall never be another so modest and genteel as you. And I will not consent to marry someone even a trifle below your standard. Therefore, you and I at least are doomed to stay put and be lighthouse keepers forever, only dreaming of far away places and the adventures we'll never experience but in the reaches of our imaginations."

The room fell silent. She went back to eating the buttery crab, her father and sister staring at her.

"Well, we *may* find that such a gentleman *does* exist," Alexandra insisted. "And perhaps we may all be surprised to find that man already among our acquaintances."

"Mr. Wright doesn't count, Alex," Jessica teased, reaching for her glass. "He's already married."

"Ha ha." Alexandra gave her a scornful look. "Perhaps the man in question may just turn out to be none other than Mr. Edward Scarborough."

Jessica's hand slipped. Rather than her fingers settling around the glass, she fumbled and it fell to its side with a loud clink. She watched her milk splash across the table.

Jessica bounced with excitement as the coach carrying her older sister and the Thompsons pulled into the depot. She glanced at Alexandra and saw that she, too, was flushed with anticipation. As Grace stepped from the carriage, her father embraced her, placing a gentle kiss on her forehead. Seeing the relief in his eyes, Jessica realized how pleased he was to have her back home. Without a word he released her to her sisters and moved to assist Mrs. Thompson with the parcels in her arms.

Later that evening, after Jessica and her sisters had said their good nights to their father and the Wrights, they gathered in the candlelight of Grace's bedchamber.

"Oh, the sight of Kent! Jessica, even your spirit of adventure could never be filled there, not if you were to live there an eternity! The beauty is boundless. It takes your breath away." Grace twirled about the room, arms outstretched, her full-length nightgown swirling about her legs.

"You sound like Alex, our hopeless romantic." Jessica giggled and tossed a pillow at her.

Alexandra sat cross-legged on Grace's bed, her chin resting on her palm. She gazed upon her oldest sister and sighed.

"How is it that Father ever left there?" Grace wondered aloud, ignoring her sister's remark. "Perhaps a better question is, how can I ever repay the Thompsons for their generosity in introducing me to the area? They *are* the most pleasant of people. How fortunate *you* are, Jess, to be accompanying them to France next spring!"

Jessica had almost forgotten about her plans, *her* special trip with the Thompsons. It seemed such an age away; it might as well be ten years off.

"And how fortunate that we'll all be going to London in January, right into Kent itself!" exclaimed Grace. "I cannot wait for you to see it. Even though it will be less beautiful in the winter, I know you'll both be thrilled."

They talked on and on of Grace's experiences—the teas, parties, picnics, sailing, shopping, museums, operas, and swimming in the sea.

"And with the exception of the society I mentioned in my letter to you, Jess, the people were pleasant and caring. I was greeted with open arms on most every occasion and basked in the attention with which I was showered at each new acquaintance. But it was in London at one particular party that I met a most intriguing young man."

"Oh, I hope you had *me* in mind at that particular moment." Alexandra's eyes lit up.

"Alex, you know how attentive I am for my sisters." Grace cast a smart glance at Jessica. "Yes, even for you, Jess, despite your objections."

"I'm not opposed to marriage, Grace. You know that. There's just a certain resentment I have toward the unspoken rule that a woman is only as important as the man she marries. Why can one not earn respect on her own merits?"

"Yes, I know." Grace smiled as she spun around again and swept her arm out over the room. "You're determined to explore the world! To seek excitement on a quest of discovery and adventure." She turned back to her sisters, the gaze of her indigo eyes settling upon Jessica. "But what will you find out there? What are you in search of? Will you unearth some yet undiscovered happiness that you'll be able to bottle up and bring home?" Pity settled into her expression. "Alex may be our hopeless romantic, but you, Jess, are our insatiable adventurer. Exciting as it is to travel—and, yes, I enjoyed myself more than I can express—you will never be satisfied with that kind of life. Settle for the thing that can bring *tangible* happiness, something *I* can help you obtain—a man!"

All three broke into laughter, and the pillow fight began in earnest.

"Finish telling us about the special man you met, Grace!" Alexandra begged, out of breath. The pillows ceased to fly.

"I must admit that my sisters were the furthest thing from my mind as I danced with him, for he captured *my* affections. His name is Stephen Sutton. He had a kind, quiet manner and showed none of the haughty characteristics of the others in attendance. We met after he spilled punch down my back. He offered such profuse apologies. Any other man I could have suspected of purposeful intent, but not Mr. Sutton. His manners were far from flirtatious, almost innocent. He seemed a bit uncomfortable in that social setting. We spoke but for a little while and danced just one piece together. After that, he disappeared. I saw no more of him. However, I still think of him, even now almost a full month and many dozen young men later." Grace looked bewildered. "Now that I'm recalling the events in London, there *was* another man at a large gathering who caught my attention, but in a much less favorable way. He was about Father's age, and I caught him staring at me several times throughout the evening, although he never approached me."

"Perhaps he was attracted to you, Grace. Your beauty captures the attention of men for miles around, regardless of age," Jessica reminded her.

"No, Jessie, it wasn't *that* kind of look. I don't know its kind; it was…different. But I soon forgot about him, until now, that is."

"Grace, we also had an odd experience during your absence," Jessica said. "Tell her about the young stranger, Alex."

"It was just a couple of weeks ago that I'd been out riding as I like to do in the evenings. When I was returning to the house at sunset, I rounded a corner and found a saddled, but riderless horse standing near the edge of the forest. I rode closer, and just beyond, in the underbrush, a young man was lying unconscious. In a mad dash I rode home to retrieve Jessie. We took the carriage along and brought him and his horse back here. By that time it was nearly dark. I rowed out to Old Stormy to notify Father, and he instructed us to keep the stranger for the night and ask Mr. Wright to evaluate his condition since he himself would not be home until morning."

"The man regained consciousness after Mr. Wright helped us get him on the divan in the parlor," Jessica interrupted. "He managed to eat a bit and said the last thing he remembered was his horse being spooked by a snake in the road, then bucking and darting into the woods. He reported trying without success to control the horse and then striking his head quite hard on a branch. He complained of a severe headache, but thanked us for our hospitality before dozing off again."

"Next morning he was gone!" Alexandra said. "Left in his place was only a note." She looked at Jessica, who left the room, reappearing a moment later with a letter in hand. It was written on their father's stationary. Grace read the letter aloud.

"Thank you again for the kindness and warm meal. It seems I am missing some personal objects, including an heirloom of great sentimental value, which was on a chain around my neck. It is a heavy gold ring with etchings of vines on either side of a modest squared ruby. A poem is inscribed along the inside. Perhaps it took to flight upon my striking the tree. I will search the roadside on my way. If you should locate it, I trust you will return it to the following address.

"I can't make out the signature." Grace stared at the note.

"Neither could we," said Jessica.

"So he's from London." Grace scanned the address at the foot of the page. "And this is all? No plans of returning to inquire whether it has been recovered?" She turned the letter over. "This must be a sketch of the heirloom."

"Yes, his penmanship may be a bit untidy, but the illustration is clear."

"Did you show this to Father?" inquired Grace.

"We searched the road ourselves and didn't find the ring, so we saw no need to trouble him," Jessica replied. "We reasoned that the young man must have found it himself."

Grace nodded, voicing the same thought Jessica had come to wonder. "How strange."

Rather than mention that a ring identical to the drawing had appeared on the hand of Edward Scarborough, Jessica had decided to unearth more information from Edward himself at the upcoming Castleton dance.

John Viana completed his work at Old Stormy under a clear night sky. Light from the moon flooded through the window of the store room as he dropped the four-gallon bucket beside the oil barrels stacked against the crescent wall. It fell to its side, a drop of clear oil on its spout reflecting a ray from the moon.

After easing himself onto his chair, he lit one of the lanterns, rolled its wick higher, and pulled Richard's letter from his pocket. While rubbing his tired arms, he again read his friend's words, "...in hopes that our friendship would somehow, someday be renewed..."

All those years, Richard had never understood, had never even known the reason his closest friend chose to leave him behind, to leave all of his society.

In more than two decades, he had returned to see Richard for just one brief visit, had corresponded just three times, and had not until now allowed him to know his location. Yet, how willing Richard was to renew their friendship. How eager he sounded to see John again.

"You've proved yourself a better friend than I," he mumbled.

But *how* could John have explained? Richard was the son of a very influential man and would be absorbed into society after their university days. He doubted Richard would have believed the tremendous web of corruption he had stumbled upon, and if he *had* believed John's accusations, what could Richard have done? Leave, as *he* had? No, Richard's family was uninvolved, and John was afraid to mention it for fear of entangling him.

How John had missed him over the years! But that was the price he had paid to begin a new life. Even his dear Angela knew little of the deplorable incident and less of her husband's old friend. And when the sea had robbed him of her presence and her love, it had swallowed her scant knowledge of his past.

Now considering the invitation in his hand and the response he would send the following day, John winced. "This may be the greatest regret of my life," he said to the air.

Did he really believe he could avoid recognition in London? How would his former associates react to his reappearance after so many years? Perhaps the foremost question didn't even involve him—was it really wise to take his *daughters* there?

Yet the decision had been made. To second guess himself at this point would be futile. Grace, Jessica, and Alexandra had the right to their own heritage and the responsibility to choose their own futures.

Slipping the letter into his pocket, he groaned as he stood, pressing his fingers against the lower portion of his arching back. He grabbed the handle of the lantern, a yawn seeping from his lungs. Before leaving the store room, he scanned the stacks of barrels that had been delivered by ship earlier that morning and lifted by winch through the outside door into the room halfway up the tower. And still the oil had to be carried in buckets as needed to the crown.

Drawing his watch from his pocket, he found it to be midnight, almost time to crank the weight heavenward. The process would be repeated at four, just before daybreak.

He stopped and stared at the never-ending staircase that kept the worker on duty climbing up or down to complete every necessary task. Dozens of trips were made in a single shift—trimming the wicks, inspecting and oiling the cogs, filling the fuel, studying the activities of both sea and sky, winding the clockwork.

Passing through the engine room and kitchen on his journey upward, he soon reached the bedchamber. The light swept across a small cot, trunks loaded with blankets, and cans of water—in the case of being stranded by a storm. An old clock ticked away the hours upon a crude table beside the bed. Its alarm would arouse him every two hours, reminding him of his enduring commitment as a keeper of the light. He readied the little cot for a long night.

Two more flights upward brought him to the service room just below the mammoth lantern. Concave cupboards brimming with replacement wicks and tools materialized in the lamplight, along with folded piles of clean polishing rags. Crates filled with bottles of white wine were stacked along the wall beneath one rectangular window. The drink proved a superior cleaner for the immense lens, and so it was that John's small family consumed large quantities without so much as a drop passing the lips of a single one of them.

He crossed the small, round room and continued his climb upward to the cramped chamber housing the cogs and clockwork. One link after another of the thick iron chain clinked in place, grasped by the teeth of the gears in a slow, continual revolution. Winding the great weight upward was easy after the first full rotation of the handled crank as the network of oiled cogs and gears groaned into reverse.

Ten additional stairs up, John stepped inside the glass encasement housing the brilliant lens. A massive, complex system of stacked glass prisms and louvers, it rotated like an immense eye. Its circular journey conducted a continuous inspection of the sea.

Already a smoky film was forming on the glass louvers encasing the burners and wicks. Polishing would be required again by morning.

Outside the glass room and down a few steps, he stood at the railing, a collar around the neck of the tower. The white light passed above his head. Its penetrating beam reached a distance of twenty nautical miles over the heaving sea. He felt both proud and humbled to know that his lighthouse served as a warning to weary sailors, its red and white pattern telling of the dangerous rocks lurking beneath the waves.

Gazing at the reflections of sparkling stars dancing and bobbing on the rolling sea, John allowed his thoughts to drift to his daughters. Most mornings they rose before dawn to labor in the heat of the summer sun or in the chill of the winter wind. The days were long, their clothing filthy, and their muscles aching by the time of the dinner bell, which often rang long after dark. The responsibilities of the women far exceeded those on Old Stormy's island. They also tended to the housework and cooking, as well as the cows, pigs, chickens, and horses, and, in the summer season, the gardens. Yet his daughters never complained.

He threw his head back and let the salty sea breezes toss his hair. Absorbed in the vast creation below, he no longer felt the weight of duty, but appreciation for such an inspiring privilege. How often he had heard his girls voice similar gratitude.

Pride filled his heart. Not the pride he had left in London with the lawmakers, the influential businessmen, or the landed gentry. His pride was of a different sort. Because of the life he had created, never would he cringe to see his daughters scoff at a servant or ridicule those of simple station. Humble and modest, they were noble in his eyes. And for *this* he was proud.

John closed his eyes. A sigh the depth of the ocean forced its way from his chest.

To insist on their continued service at the lighthouse was unrealistic and unfair. Now they alone would have to choose the paths their lives would take.

Perhaps one of them would stay to be the next to raise her family here, where life was difficult, yet happy and rewarding.

But buried in their lineage lay a different opportunity. He had known from the beginning that when the time was right, he would have no alternative but to make it known to them.

That time had now arrived.

Chapter Four

After breakfast and chores, Jessica and Alexandra strolled toward Bristlecone, the village that the family frequented for supplies. She and her sisters always entertained the hope of meeting up with a friend for an informal visit. The large town of Penzance, where they traveled far less often, was an hour's ride to the south.

As much as Jessica enjoyed the walk, she could not concentrate on the beauty of her surroundings. Her thoughts kept returning to the previous night's discussion with Grace regarding the incident of the mysterious young man they had found on the road.

"Perhaps he's not from London at all," Alexandra suggested after Jessica had again recounted the story. "After all, the heirloom could indicate he comes from a family of nobility. And aren't all princes handsome, as he was?"

"Oh, Alex, if only *my* thoughts could be so innocent, so unassuming. But I can't ignore my suspicions."

"What do you mean, Jessie?" Alexandra's carefree steps came to an abrupt halt.

"The ring he described must belong to a royal family, I agree, but he didn't fit the part. His modest dress and kind mannerisms, although very gentleman-like, were not eloquent by any means. Also, his atrocious penmanship gives no hint of royal tutoring! Don't you wonder why a prince would not be *wearing the ring*? But, as stated in his letter, he had it on a chain around his neck. Were he a nobleman, would he not have worn it on his hand? I know we've been taught all our lives not to judge a man based on appearance alone, but I do not believe he is the owner of that heirloom. And yet, that point isn't my greatest concern." She squinted in a way that made her sister step back. "What if, upon returning to the scene of his accident, he found the ring was *not* there? Might he now suspect *us* of robbing him while he was unconscious?"

Alexandra gasped.

Behind double doors announcing *William Sutton, Barrister* in gold lettering, the man himself sat at his massive walnut desk. As the shadows of sunset stretched over London, the barrister stared at a young man facing him.

"I'm telling you, Father," the younger man said, "I examined all the public records from Newquay to Penzance, and all the way to Land's End. There is no registration of a John Everett anywhere in the area. I even went offshore to the Isles of Scilly. Nothing. I'm sorry."

"And somehow you have managed to lose the only real piece of evidence we had that would have drawn him forward! How will you ever reach the heights of a barrister when such a simple task has conquered you?" William shook his head. "I should have gone myself."

His son's expression told him his words had stung.

"Did you ever think of approaching the lady and inquiring whether she even belongs to the Everett family?" Stephen defended himself by asking.

"I had no need to approach her!" William lashed back in a slow, angry tone. "That woman was John Everett's daughter. There was no mistaking it, Stephen."

"Father," he chided in a soothing voice, "you've not seen her since she was *seven years old.*"

William rose to walk to the window, his back to his son, and stared at the radiance of a gilded sky. "Stephen," he replied, his anger subsiding, "as a barrister, you must learn the art of observation. Have you never noted the unique brilliance of a burnished copper kettle? It glows with a light all its own."

From the corner of one eye he saw his son lean forward at his hushed tone.

"Every now and again you meet someone with an unmistakable characteristic," William continued. "Never before have I met another with hair that unusual tone except for that seven-year-old girl...until I saw her again."

"With all due respect, Father, this is proving to be no more than a mere coincidence. There are other women with the color of hair you describe. Even I, myself, am acquainted with one."

Chapter Five

John stood in the library. He listened to muffled voices upstairs and the hurried footsteps of Mrs. Wright while she scurried from room to room, assisting the girls with their gowns, their hair, and whatever other particulars women fussed over when preparing for an important event.

He would be joining them at the evening's affair. Pacing the library rug, he checked his pocket watch again. One full minute had passed since his last inspection. He tugged at a thread in the seam of his jacket, twisting it into a large knot and stuffing it into his pocket.

Stopping before the portrait of Angela, he studied her face. Neither fifteen years of raising their daughters alone nor long, laborious hours of work had extinguished the burning torch he carried in his heart for her. At times he could almost feel her silky hair in his fingers and smell the soft scent of the roses from their gardens where she spent much of her time, a scent that had always seemed to linger on her creamy skin. The eyes in the portrait seemed to come alive, and he thought he could see her rosy lips ease into that familiar smile as she returned his adoring look.

At the sound of a soft rustling, he turned to find Grace, Jessica, and Alexandra standing in a row, their grown-up forms catching him by surprise. All had donned modest muslin gowns in fetching, ladylike styles. The simple but elegant dresses, he imagined, would pale beside those in deep, rich tones of satin. But no one at the dance would match their loveliness.

"Here stands the most envied man in the whole of England," he said with a smile, finding it difficult to believe that

38

the three beauties before him had only yesterday been his little girls.

"And I have never seen you more handsome than you are this very moment, Father," Grace said.

He kissed the three.

The horses pulled the rickety carriage as the ladies waved good night to the Wrights. Soon the road turned toward Penzance.

"What a dreamy setting!" exclaimed Alexandra when the carriage neared the Castleton property. The lodge engulfed a high hill overlooking the city to the north and the large bay to the east. Penzance, less forested than the locality of Brentwood, offered magnificent ocean views with a beauty all its own.

The arriving guests were greeted by the squire and his wife and then ushered into the gardens behind the immense house. Upon rounding the corner, Jessica stopped short. The gardens coming into view took her breath away with their winding brick pathways and high mounded beds of begonias, geraniums, and petunias in full, radiant bloom. She and her sisters stepped onto the footpath and wandered under trellises and archways all but hidden beneath tangles of lush vines. All paths led to a large flagstone courtyard. Dressed tables dotted the area around a small orchestra. A grand gazebo on the far end caught Jessica's attention.

Drawn to the structure, she could not keep her fingers from wandering over the intricate ironwork of the encircling banister, around which vines of ivy twisted themselves, almost covering one entire side. A dainty gate kept the gathering guests from entering the covered space.

As her sisters hastened across the courtyard to visit friends, Jessica studied the circular roof of the structure. It was garnished with a delicate iron parapet. Under its ceiling were tables topped with white linen, many adorned with a large arrangement of summer's grandest gladioluses, lilies, and roses. The center tables were laden with silver domed platters. Her stomach gurgled at the thought of the delicacies that must be waiting underneath.

Wandering behind the structure, she looked down a rocky hillside that dropped into the water. The silhouette of St. Michael's Mount—the castle built on the island in the bay—faded with the daylight.

"Jessie!"

"Claire!" She embraced her friend. "How good to see you!"

"Grace and Alex told me they left you here."

"Listen, Claire." She smiled. "Isn't it the most intriguing sound?"

Claire looked toward the spot where the musicians were preparing for the evening. "You mean the instruments being tuned? Jessie, do you realize there are two full orchestras here—one indoors and the other out? If you think they sound intriguing now, just wait."

"That's not what I meant, silly. The sea!" She turned to gaze over the hillside once again. "That constant call speaks to you if you listen. Can you hear it saying 'Cross me if you dare'? It's so inviting, yet so...unpredictable." Scanning the endless waters that were now rusty from the setting sun, she crossed her arms. "She's more calm than usual tonight."

Claire laughed. "Will you never tire of the sea?" She reached for Jessica's hand. "Come with me. I heard Mr. Robertson's here!"

Claire could always put her back on solid ground.

"Don't you think him a bit dull? He has yet to display any sense of adventure from what I've seen."

"You just don't know him. Give him a chance, Jessie." She pulled her toward the gathering crowd.

The setting sun transformed the clouds into pink cotton tufts that filled the horizon and faded upward into the coming night. A number of servants made their way around the yard, lighting the standing lamps and lanterns, while others circled through the crowd with trays of refreshments.

Conversation and laughter filled the air as friends and acquaintances congregated in groups. Soon the gazebo was opened. Partygoers partook of the casual meal, grazing on the vast buffet of meats, seafood, cheeses, succulent fruits, freshly baked loaves, fine wines, and delicate pastries.

During the course of the meal, the small orchestra graced the guests with a minuet. The courtyard, bathed in subtle fragrances from the gardens, made a romantic setting under a canopy of stars.

Within the hour, before cool breezes off the sea could chill the guests, three double French doors leading to the ballroom inside the house opened, and the second, larger orchestra began playing a new Strauss waltz, "The Blue Danube."

Jessica noticed Alexandra conversing often with Edward Scarborough and on occasion with other young gentlemen. Of course, the interaction seem to originate with the assistance and coercion of their older sister. Grace appeared well-pleased over the developing friendship between the two. Jessica, distant toward all young men until she could uncover their true character, questioned the motives of Edward Scarborough.

When the next dance began, Jessica watched from a distance while her younger sister accepted the hand of Mr. Scarborough. Though her ears burned to eavesdrop, she could only hope that Alexandra would remember her earlier caution about giving in to the leading of a flirtatious man—the type of man she already knew Edward to be.

The two engaged in animated conversation and appeared to enjoy each other's company. Jessica breathed a sigh of relief when both later sought out different dance partners. Grace, too, seemed to be enjoying herself, and Jessica even obliged the pleasant but dull Mr. Robertson with a dance.

John remained in the company of the men of his acquaintance, talking and laughing with hearty pleasure, since, for him, socializing was an infrequent event. He seldom danced, even though the soothing music beckoned him. Tonight's only exceptions came when he asked for the hand of each of his daughters. His first dance, though later in the evening, was with Grace.

"I see you've been giving much attention to your sisters' companions," he stated, one eyebrow raised in question. "I'm not concerned as much about Jessica as with Alexandra, for smooth words and a handsome face do not sway Jessica."

"Yes, Father, but you're well aware that a woman may have just two or three seasons in which to find a suitable mate, or risk remaining single forever, destined to a life of servitude to other relatives. I intend to assist my sisters to matrimony as soon as possible, without risking the importance of character and intelligence, you may rest assured."

"Might I remind you, Daughter, that be one a wife or a servant, it is not *what* one is but *who* one is that is of greatest importance. There is many a miserable wife who wishes she had been more selective in her decision. A young man of quality will likewise be as cautious. Now I command you tend to your own affairs and leave your sisters to theirs."

"Of course, Father. Now, as for you, I've seen many attractive ladies glancing *your* way," she teased.

John made no comment as he whirled her through the maze of dancing couples. When the music ended, he grinned and pointed his finger at her. "I'm watching you, young lady."

Jessica's father winked at her when she saw him leave the dance floor. She watched him pass a heavyset matron who was stuffed into a dress so snug that Jessica wondered how the woman was able to move. The stitches of her gown appeared to quiver from the strain. One deep breath, she felt sure, and the battle would be lost. The woman, an affluent member of society, did not even acknowledge the Vianas. When John passed her, Jessica watched her lift her chin, turn her head aside, and shuffle away, the identical response Jessica herself had received earlier. Disgusted, she turned to find Alexandra.

Seconds later, the party was interrupted by a horrific scream. Jessica spun around, ready to be of assistance. The first person she saw was her father, who, rather than respond to the scream, kept walking as though deaf to the commotion.

Making her way through the crowd that had gathered, she discovered the uppity woman panting, eyes wide with fright, one hand over her heart. "It was...it was...huge! I saw it," she shrieked. "Black and hairy! Get it off of me!"

The matron turned in circles, twisting her body and peering over one shoulder, then the other. Astounded that such a sizeable woman could contort herself in that manner, Jessica watched in amazement.

A moment later a large, shadowy form dropped to the floor at the feet of the crowd.

Jessica gasped, her palm rising to her lips.

A man who saw it stooped and caught the offending beast. Standing, he lifted his clenched fist. Others leaned close to get a glimpse of the hairy attacker. He raised his thumb, cautiously peering into his hand.

He began laughing without restraint. "Here's your spider." Upon his palm sat a large knot of black thread.

Laughter ranging from nervous titters to outright roars rippled through the crowd.

"Oh, dear!" the woman huffed, inspecting her gown. "It seems I've pulled a stitch in all the excitement." She excused herself and, with one hand grasping the side of her dress, made a hasty exit.

Jessica fought the urge to laugh. Beyond the people that gathered, she spied her father, a smirk upon his face, conversing with an acquaintance. Upon meeting her gaze, he turned away.

Jessica had forgotten the objective of uncovering additional information from Mr. Scarborough, when her conversation with Claire was interrupted by the man himself.

"Pardon me." He bowed his head. "Are you engaged for the next dance, Miss Viana?"

"I am not."

"Would you oblige me?"

"Yes, thank you."

He bowed again and stepped away from the pair as the present song neared its end.

"He's been watching you for some time, Jessie," Claire whispered.

"That's because he's afraid of me." Her voice was low as she leaned toward her friend.

Claire's brow crinkled in response.

"He's afraid I just may come between him and my sister."

The music ended, and Jessica turned to find her partner.

Two rows of couples faced each other. Edward kept his gaze locked on hers. She reciprocated, refusing to be intimidated.

"I was happy to further my acquaintance with you last week, Miss Viana." He spoke first as they locked hands. The music began.

"And my intrigue increases the more I learn of *you*, Mr. Scarborough." Two short steps spun them in a half circle.

"Is that so?"

"For instance, I might like to inquire about the magnificent ring on your finger."

In this case the direct approach was fitting, she thought. He must have observed her response to discovering the ruby ring on his finger the previous week, for she had been less than discreet when caught by such surprise. And he had the audacity to wear it tonight, as well, a fact that must have escaped her younger sister's notice.

He extended his right hand, which she took with her right, and they swung in the opposite direction.

"For even from this distance," she continued, "it's quite obvious that it's an antique of great value. Might I be so bold as to suggest it's no doubt in excess of *your* family's income?"

Although well-situated, Edward's family was far from affluent, and much farther still from nobility. How could he contradict such a fact?

Once again, grasping both hands, they took a half step back, then forward, meeting toe-to-toe. He towered a few inches above her. She looked up into his eyes, now so close to hers.

"And might I inquire from you whether you are always so quick to invent such judgments against your acquaintances? And if so, how is it you have *any* allies?"

Upon noting his accusing glare, she answered it with a warm smile rather than acknowledge his attempt to turn the conversation. She dropped one of his hands to take that of the lady beside her. The gentlemen mimicked the dance step, and the four moved in a circle together, as did other foursomes about the dance floor.

"The ring is an antique, as you supposed." His voice became smooth and conciliatory. "It's a family heirloom that has been in my father's possession for many years, passed to him from his mother at her death a decade ago. Her father was a wealthy man, though she had not the good fortune to inherit the estate."

Jessica turned to the gentleman beside Edward and took his right hand. Heat flushed her face as she struggled not to challenge Edward's obvious deception. He took the hand of the lady beside her. The couples turned in a circle once again.

"And your family—are they all from this area?" she asked.

"All but one uncle, yes."

The couples switched hands to link their lefts. The circle reversed direction.

"I see," she said, not looking at him, but at the other man. "Well, it's an extraordinary piece. Perhaps I will have the opportunity sometime to admire it upon closer inspection."

"I can think of no better time than the present," he offered in a confident tone.

She smiled when his response was just what she had anticipated. He seemed every bit a willing recipient of admiration.

They dropped the hands of the others. Taking her elbow, Edward led her from the floor. He twisted the ring from his little finger with difficulty and handed it to her. The band was heavy and wide. Its ruby was clear, the engravings ornate and defined, as though it had been well cared for. Inscribed on the inside, though in minuscule letters, were the legible words: *Set me as a seal upon thine heart; for love is strong as death.*

"You may be wondering about the inscription," he suggested.

She nodded.

"It's from a poem written by my great-grandfather."

Wrong again, Mr. Scarborough, she thought, *unless your great-grandfather was a king from ancient times.* She recognized the verse from Alexandra's favorite Bible book, *Solomon's Song.*

"See the abundance one can learn about another from something as simple as a piece of jewelry?" he boasted.

"Indeed, Mr. Scarborough. Sometimes more than one ever anticipated," she said. "It's beautiful. I'm sure you'll give it the careful attention it deserves." She finished her thought to herself rather than verbalize it...*until it can be restored to its rightful owner.*

She returned the ring and excused herself. Stepping behind a potted bush, she peered back around it to watch him make his way over to converse with Mr. Gregory. After they walked out the French doors, she saw them disappear around the corner, then sought both her sisters. It was time to notify them of Mr. Scarborough's deceptive character.

Locating Grace nearby, Jessica apologized for interrupting her conversation and led her away by the hand. "We must find Alexandra at once," she urged at her sister's reluctance.

When they found her near the edge of the dance floor, Jessica pulled her aside, and the three retreated to a quiet corner. She relayed seeing the ring on Edward's finger when he had called at their home the previous week and her conversation just moments before. Reminding them of the detailed description of the ring left by the injured stranger, she added her suspicions of Edward's being a thief.

"But he's the son of a respectable man," Alexandra argued.

"He and Mr. Gregory just made a quick exit around the side of the house," Jessica challenged. "Shall we see whether I'm right?"

They hastened to follow the men. The music and sounds of the party faded, and they found themselves in near darkness, save for a few street lamps standing at some distance. The property in front was crowded with empty carriages and coachmen in small groups. Jessica recognized the two men standing away from the others, under a lamp, Edward speaking in a loud voice.

Jessica led them as they crept in for closer inspection, secure under the cover of darkness. Her eyes adjusted to the surroundings.

"I'd never seen him before in my life," Edward was saying. "He was not from around this area." He curled his right hand into a fist. "One quick blow to the cheek and the man was out flat," he bragged, mimicking a punch in front of his friend's face.

The two laughed.

"And that was when you saw the ring?"

"Yes. I thought, 'this is what you deserve, picking a quarrel with me.' I considered the ring a reward for a great accomplishment. I have the chain, also." Edward stroked his right fist against his lapel as though polishing it for the next brawl. "Handsome prize is it not?" He held out his hand.

The sisters slipped away, then dashed back into the ballroom.

"How could a person be so deceitful?" Alexandra asked. "He didn't strike that man! There was a mark across his forehead from a blunt blow, but no injuries to his cheek. Remember, Jessie?"

Jessica nodded.

"It was just as you suspected," she continued, frowning. "Mr. Scarborough happened upon that man at a most opportune time and robbed him instead of helping him! And to think I listened to him as he charmed me during the dance!"

"What did he say to you, Alex?" Jessica asked.

"He complimented my radiant eyes. I told him they were a gift from my Irish mother."

Jessica groaned. "Flattery is his most successful tactic, I'm sure. I hope you both now see that Mr. Scarborough has proven himself unfit for our association."

"Yes," Grace agreed. "We'll have nothing to do with his likes. I feel we should be content to put this whole incident from our minds." After a moment, she added, "But what about the man who lost the ring? Do you think we should notify him?"

"What if he's not the true owner either?" Jessica argued. "Perhaps he, too, stole it. Sentimental as it may be to the real owner, whoever that is, he will just have to grieve its loss. I'm convinced there's much more to this story than we know, but this is no business of ours. We know not whether there may be some risk to our family were Mr. Scarborough to discover our knowledge of it."

"He's an opportunistic thief, Jessie," Grace countered. "Let's not make him a savage."

"And now he's a liar, as well!" Jessica responded. "Since we don't know the extent to which he may act to protect that ring and himself, I must demand we detach ourselves from the situation."

"Should we not at least tell Father?" Alexandra asked.

"There's no point in that," Grace said. "I agree with Jessie. This isn't our business. I suggest we let it go and enjoy what remains of the evening."

Though disturbed that justice would not come upon the scoundrel, Jessica breathed a sigh of relief that they were all now aware of his true nature. She was most relieved that her younger sister would not continue her attention toward him.

Would Grace now use greater discretion in seeking marriage mates for her sisters?

Chapter Six

The social season gave way to the winds of winter. One chilly November morning, Jessica stirred awake, opening her eyes to icy artwork on her window pane. A gray blur of thick fog obscured her view beyond the lacy frost. Her body begged to stay beneath the feather comforter, her cocoon of warmth and protection; and her mind anticipated with no great eagerness that first step onto the cold floorboards.

She rolled away from the window and closed her eyes again, memories of the previous night flitting about in her mind. Twilight had brought their first winter storm. And storms at Brentwood Lighthouse were as unbearable as they were unpredictable, frigid gales whipping waves high around the pillar. She had just picked at her supper, her concern for Mr. Wright, who would be on duty until midnight, taking a toll on her usual healthy appetite.

Later, they sat around the warming hearth while outside the storm rattled the windows. Her father related stories of fishermen and sailors whose lives had been spared because of the beacon. He told of the years before the lighthouse was built, when dozens of ships had crashed on the rocks, becoming gigantic coffins that doomed entire crews to watery graves.

The stories had sent Jessica into a shivering fright. Images of the roaring sea engulfing the ship that carried her mother had long ago burned themselves into her mind. She had watched the eyes of her sisters, wide and intent on their father's face while he talked on, but her mind took *her* to tales of daring rescues from neighboring lighthouse keepers that had reached them from time to time.

Brentwood had had one such rescue before her family had taken over its keep. She was grateful that none had been required since.

Although the possibility of a rescue always loomed, and indeed was *expected* of those in her vocation, she wondered whether she would answer the call. The ocean had beckoned her to its shores for as long as she could remember. Fascinated though she was by its song, she ignored the summons, never venturing farther than Old Stormy. She refused to accompany her father on the fishing boat, which he would sail miles beyond the lighthouse island.

Jessica often prayed there would never be among them any Grace Darlings, whose fame because of her single rescue had spanned three decades. Perhaps the one commonality between the two families, besides the fact that the Darlings had also been keepers of the light on England's rocky coast, was the name of their daughters. Jessica was happy to leave it at that and to remain an anonymous keeper of the little known Brentwood Lighthouse.

Her father's stories had come to an end near midnight, along with their peculiar mix of allure and terror, and, minutes later, from her bedchamber window she had spotted a hazy red flash and waited in anticipation for the white that followed. Below, in a circle of yellow light from his lantern, she could barely make out her father's form as he fought the driving rain on his way to relieve Mr. Wright.

Recollection that her father had passed the night at the lighthouse now moved her to leap from bed and dress to start the day.

She was surprised to find her sisters already seated at the small dining table, consuming what was left of their breakfast.

"Good heavens, Jessie, it's after seven!" Grace exclaimed after swallowing a sip of tea.

Mrs. Wright shoved a cutting board spread with slices of cold ham before Jessica.

"Just a biscuit," she responded, grabbing one from a basket on the table and rushing toward the front door.

"Don't forget your French book!" she heard Alexandra call out as she grasped the biscuit between her teeth while shoving her arms into her coat sleeves. "You said you would practice with me today!"

"*Oui*, Alex, *merci! Je reviendrai cet après-midi, promis!*" she called back, promising to return in the afternoon and then snatching the book from a table in the parlor.

"And practice that flute while you're out there!" she heard Mrs. Wright holler before the door slammed shut behind her.

Tucking the book beneath her arm, pulling the woolen hood over her head, and clutching it so the wind could not snatch it, she trotted along the pathway and ducked into the forest. The morning at Old Stormy would be a cold one. But at least inside the tower she would be able to escape the wind, which her sisters would not, trekking between the shed, barn, and pens, feeding the horses and pigs.

Jessica's favorite spot to sit and read during the quiet winter watches at Old Stormy was the glass room enclosing the circulating lens. Around ten, to the clinking and groaning of the chain-work, she padded a rickety chair with a blanket from the store room and wrapped herself in another one. Snuggling down, she opened a letter from Claire, who urged a visit to Penzance. It seemed such an age since the summer ball, when they had last visited. During winter months, handwritten correspondence suited the secluded lifestyle to which Jessica had grown accustomed. More than anything, she enjoyed the news an occasional letter would bring.

Following the ball, Alexandra had received two letters from Edward Scarborough, who seemed very eager to pursue a relationship. Of course, the letters were ignored. She hoped Edward had realized that Alexandra would not gratify him with an answer.

Claire's letter brought a report of that man himself. Relief poured over her as she read her friend's words.

I knew you would be interested to learn that old Mr. Scarborough has arranged for his son, Edward, to take a position with his uncle's business in Plymouth. Rumor has it he will be leaving before week's end.

Jessica rejoiced, not so much for her sister as for their friends in Penzance.

In the candlelight of his bedchamber, the young man packed a trunk for the journey eastward.

"Edward!" his father called from downstairs. "Hurry yourself!"

Edward Scarborough growled under his breath.

Leafing through the papers in his bureau drawer, he happened upon a folded document, still sealed with a burgundy wax imprint of the letter 'E.' It was not addressed. He smiled to himself, recalling the encounter he had had with the unfortunate wretch he had stumbled upon alongside the road near Bristlecone.

Concern for the stranger's welfare had at first crossed his mind, but he was soon distracted by a thin gold braid draped across the man's chest. Lifting it up, he had been astonished to find himself staring at a sparkling ruby set in an ornate gold ring. After gazing about to assure that he was alone, he eased the chain over the unconscious man's head. In haste, he searched through all the man's pockets, transferring every item he found to his own jacket.

Within seconds, he had heisted several gold coins, the ring, and this document, which had gone forgotten until this very moment. He now turned it in his hand in the faint light.

"Edward! Now!" his father called in an insistent voice.

He looked toward the hallway and then back at the document. Perhaps someday he would examine its contents. He tossed it, unopened, into his trunk and slammed the lid.

The year's end came and went, and before long John Viana's house buzzed with excitement as his family packed for the long journey to London. The Lighthouse Committee had made arrangements to assist the Wrights for the whole of January.

London temperatures would be chilly, but he thought they might go unnoticed by his daughters, whose minds would be focused on the activities of the city.

Apprehension filled his heart when he considered returning to the town of his childhood. Although fond memories did exist, unpleasant ones predominated when he recalled the life where social standing defined the value of one's existence. Indeed, it determined one's importance and purpose in life. As a child, he had learned with proficiency the role of the condescending son of an influential family. But maturity had brought a different attitude, and he came to despise the charade, the contempt, the egotism. The final break had occurred at age twenty, when he stumbled upon the sudden and shocking episode that drove him from his heritage. He shuddered even now at the recollection.

Exchanging his family's social and political machinations for school at Cambridge had saved him. Before society's influence could seal his destiny, he had walked away from the self-indulgent life of his peers. Instead, he began exploring various avenues of education. To his delight, his studies, and later his work and marriage in Ireland, introduced him to a simpler life of extraordinary value that had brought him greater riches than he had ever anticipated. But along with it had come the wrath of his mother. After some consideration, he had deemed it a fair trade for his new understanding of bond, trust, and security, which were no longer associated with money.

His wealth had come not from the standards of his family or society, but from the excelling value of real love. How sad that his parents had never allowed themselves to experience it.

It was that same love he had attempted to impress upon his daughters, that integrity for which he had taught them to strive, to settle for nothing less.

And now they were bound for London, a place as no other that would put their morals under fiery test.

The journey eastward was three hundred arduous miles in sleet and wind. At sunset the train arrived at the London station. Tired from the journey, John and his family were greeted by a coachman who chauffeured them in an elegant carriage to an inn where Richard Winterfield had arranged rooms for the night.

"I'll be taking you on to the Winterfield Estate in the morning," explained the coachman.

Their accommodations on the second floor overlooked a cobblestone courtyard. His family, welcoming the generosity, was pleased with the warm and comfortable rooms. A simple meal of potato soup served with crusty bread and smoked herring awaited them.

The following morning found his family refreshed and excited as they boarded the plush carriage. John smiled to watch his youngest daughter's finger follow the taut folds in the black leather of the seat, dipping where they were pressed down by large brass buttons to create a diamond pattern. Even the ceiling overhead flaunted the leather and brass cushioning. He laughed to himself, imagining the head of an aristocrat bumping against the pillowy ceiling when the carriage hit an unexpected hole in the road.

Along the way his daughters chattered with excitement about the adventures awaiting them.

"Mr. Winterfield must be very wealthy, Father," stated Grace. "How did you ever become acquainted with him?"

"We grew up together."

He had told his daughters little about his past and even less about his mother, their grandmother. His father had died while he was away at University, and after that his mother wanted little to do with him. And he could not tell them anything of substance about his wife's family, for he had known almost nothing about Angela's parents. On just one occasion—after Grace's birth—had he met his mother-in-law.

"Mr. Winterfield must also be a very *kind* man, or you would have had nothing to do with him," remarked Alexandra. "And, oh, I cannot wait to meet *Miss* Winterfield!"

The countryside was just as he had remembered—green, rolling hills with the occasional rooftop or stone chimney peering out. Perhaps the view was even more magnificent in the winter, he pondered, viewing the chimneys' curling smoke rising to blend with the mist shrouding the hillsides. He chuckled at his daughters' expressions as they stared in awe, unable to pull their faces from the glass.

Before long the carriage rounded a corner and passed two brick pillars on either side of the road, the tops of each displaying a large carving of the letter 'W.' John had never before seen his friend's home that was built sometime after Richard had married, but his curiosity mounted as they continued their drive for at least three more miles amidst grounds of thick woodlands. Mossy vines draped the tree branches like shawls, and mist crept along the carpeted floor of the forest.

"How could any land be more beautiful than what we saw around London?" asked Jessica. "And yet there's more splendor with every step! I think this must be the Garden of Eden itself!"

Even John had to admit being overtaken by wonder and awe at their surroundings. When they reached a clearing, the carriage stopped just long enough for the lips of his daughters to drop open, eyes widening as the house came into full view. They all rushed to one side of the carriage.

"Oh, my word." The expression escaped Grace's lips before her breath stopped.

John's own eyebrows arched high as he studied the castle-like structure coming into view, a stone monument amidst the vast gardens and woodlands.

"Thirty windows!" Alexandra exclaimed, pointing at the count of each one. "And that's just in the *front*! And *six* chimneys."

The carriage resumed its approach toward the hall along a straight road bordered by a wide, sweeping lawn.

As they pulled to a halt in front of the house, several servants exited the arched, mahogany front doors. Stepping from the carriage behind his daughters, John looked up. The entrance tower reached a full four stories, its steep roof looming an additional story above a house with rooflines of varying pitches and heights. On the left it boasted a wide four-story stair tower and on the right, a large, single-story solarium. The entire stone house was trimmed with ornate copper parapets and sharp spires that had weathered into dusty green.

His daughters' expressions told of their astonishment. All stood in silence, their necks craning to gaze straight up at the structure that dwarfed them.

"Oh, my," Jessica whispered.

"Magnificent, is it not?" her father replied. "An outstanding example of the French Renaissance style."

His daughters all looked at him, then returned their full attention to the massive house in front of them until they were led across the broad, uncovered stone porch, where several ceramic planters sat empty, silently awaiting the spring. John could imagine them running over with colorful flowers. Upon entering the mansion, they were escorted up two wide steps of onyx into a receiving hall, their footsteps echoing around them. The girls stared in astonishment, turning about, looking around and up, mouths gaping wider with every turn.

First to meet them in the hall was the iron figure of a life-sized knight perched on his mighty stallion and suited for battle. The statue soared above them from atop a great marble block. With a rumpled brow, the knight stared over their heads as though viewing an opposing army on a distant hillside. *Humble greeting*, Jessica thought, gazing up at its stern face and lance poised in one arm, its helmet underneath the other.

She moved to the warrior's right, where the entrance hall opened up into the grand solarium, sunken several steps down. Large stone archways surrounded the room, leading off into several corridors and chambers. The front wall was a full-story of arching windows, and an angular glass roof topped it. The little sunlight that was able to seep through the clouds above illuminated a floor of immense white marble tiles scattered with ficus, ferns, and tall palm trees, no doubt imported from some exotic land. Intricate bamboo lounges, chairs, and tables enhanced the flavor of the unexpected tropical paradise.

High above, from heavy iron chains, dangled several enormous wrought-iron lanterns encircling the entire room. Jessica's gaze roved to the center of the garden where the bowl of a large fountain held a marble statue of a small child underneath a cumbersome umbrella. The fountain loomed over a crescent table on one side, which was being dressed by still more servants.

As Jessica absorbed views even more exquisite than the grounds outside, she was startled by the echo of approaching footsteps and a loud voice coming from the opposite end of the entrance hall.

"Could that be my oldest and dearest friend?" A handsome man appeared, walking swiftly toward the guests. He was tall and stout with dark hair beginning to gray at the temples. John hastened toward him, and the two met in a firm embrace.

"Richard Winterfield!" exclaimed Jessica's father. "It has been far too long!"

"John, the pleasure is all mine, I assure you," he said, pushing her father an arm's length, eyeing him head to toe. "My mind is put at ease after fifteen long years. Now I can see for myself that you are in good health. You haven't changed, my friend. I trust your journey was safe and your room at the inn comfortable?"

"I can't thank you enough for the hospitable arrangements," John answered. "It was much more than I ever expected." He stood a couple inches above his old friend. "Allow me to introduce my daughters, Grace, Jessica, and Alexandra."

Now standing in a row before him, they each curtsied in turn.

"My goodness!" Richard's gaze came to rest upon Grace and Jessica. "Is it possible these young ladies before me are the same tiny children I last saw peering from behind their father?" He spoke to Grace. "You probably don't remember me."

"But I do," Grace insisted.

"Yes," John interjected. "You were seven when you last were here."

"Was *I* here?" Alexandra asked.

"No, you stayed with your mother in Ireland. You were just three years old."

"Who gives children permission to undergo such transformations?" Richard asked, his smile speaking his approval.

"Though I've never met *your* daughter," Jessica's father responded, "I'm sure to find her in much the same condition."

"Indeed you will. Please forgive her absence and that of my wife. In all the excitement of your arrival, it seems some little matter was overlooked. Catherine insisted on perfecting each detail, so the two drove into town earlier and will return soon. In the meantime allow me to welcome you to our home by showing you to your rooms."

This is a home? Jessica looked around at the high ceilings and supporting three-way arches leading to countless rooms and hallways within the almost endless expanse of the mansion. *I would call it a cathedral!* she thought, not daring to voice her opinion.

They were escorted to the grand staircase tower. Taking hold of the black iron banister spiraling upward, she glanced at three landings high above and was reminded of the winding stairs leading to the crown of her lighthouse, though much narrower than this elegant column.

Burdened with luggage, servants followed behind as Richard led them upstairs.

On the second floor landing, statues of bronze and granite seemed to mock their modest traveling attire as they passed.

"I consulted several dozen architects, designers, and sculptors in planning the house." Richard explained its history, which had been six years in the making. "Over a thousand workers were employed in its construction. Railroad lines were laid right up to the site for the transporting of enormous amounts of timber, rock, and marble."

One by one, Jessica and her sisters stepped into their separate bedchambers, gazing about at rooms that seemed larger than their entire Brentwood home! Each bedchamber, though unique, was furnished with beds canopied with exquisite fabrics, one of a heavy tapestry and the other two with sheers matching those draping wide balcony doors in each room. The wood bed frames were painted with bows and dainty garlands in soft pastels.

Jessica, speechless in awe over the lavish furnishings, stared at her reflection in one of the gold-framed mirrors. Marble-topped, bowed chests of drawers; elegant dressing tables with sleek, curved legs; voluminous arrangements of dried flowers; and heavy mahogany wardrobes graced the room that would be hers during their stay.

She wondered how she would be able to find comfort amidst such extravagance. Why could she not share a room with her sisters?

After the others moved into the hallway, Grace pointed out to Jessica that the lavender on the walls in her room was in reality a lining of silk. Jessica's fingers glided over its buttery surface. She raised her eyebrows at her sister, then followed the others.

Delectable aromas of the evening meal being prepared in the basement kitchen of the house wafted into the hallways. The smells began to entice Jessica's stomach, which responded in soft rumbling.

A servant appeared, explaining that Mrs. and Miss Winterfield had just returned home. The party hastened down the main staircase and exited by way of the front entry. They crossed a cobblestone drive toward a cheerful flagstone courtyard beyond the north wing of the house, where they found the two women entering the courtyard from the other side near the carriage house. Large shopping bags swung from the arms of each. The two parties met in the center.

"I'm pleased to at last make your acquaintance, Mr. Viana," stated Olivia Winterfield, though she did not extend her gloved hand to him. The feathered brim of her hat shadowed her eyes, and her painted lips offered no smile.

"Likewise," he replied, bowing his head in his usual gracious manner.

Jessica watched as Olivia raised one eyebrow, remaining silent while she and Catherine were introduced to her and her sisters. The woman's face remained tilted upward as her eyes shifted down to gaze upon them.

She turned back to Jessica's father. "I'm sure you're all tired from the journey. The accommodations on the train must have been dreadful. I'm tolerant of most conditions, but to travel so far in anything less than first class would be unbearable in my opinion."

"Rest assured, we're all fine. Thank you for your concern," John replied.

Concern! Jessica thought. He had just thanked her for insulting them! *And as for toleration, we shall certainly see if she can endure an entire month.* Jessica prepared herself to impose as little as possible upon their gracious hostess.

"Oh, Father," Catherine said turning to Richard, "tell me you didn't show them the house yet."

"Only their bedchambers, dear."

"Good!" Catherine said, looking first at Grace and then the others. "I want to show you my favorite room. I think it will be a favorite of yours as well."

Jessica liked Catherine already. Her face glowed with the same innocent smile as that of her own younger sister.

Catherine took Alexandra by the hand and led the group back to the house.

Once inside, Olivia excused herself, explaining she had some task to attend to. As the woman left their company, Jessica took note that she never looked back before disappearing down a long hallway.

Catherine led the group into a room adjoining the large entrance hall opposite the solarium.

"This is the tapestry gallery," explained Richard, "which doubles as a ballroom when the mood strikes Olivia. It's an easy task to remove the furnishings and rugs, and a modest orchestra settles quite well into that corner." He pointed to the far end of the room.

Jessica could imagine guests by the hundreds converging on their hosts. She gazed up at a tall limestone fireplace flush to one wall and between tall tapestries woven into scenes blooming with color. A mural of hunters atop their ambitious steeds amidst a forest decorated the soaring fireplace hood. The room, longer than it was wide, offered a number of comfortable-looking leather chairs. Hooked rugs covered most of the polished wood floor. Small round tables with tapered legs sat in various locations, some topped by tasseled cloths, others by candelabras or wildlife carvings, inviting Jessica to settle into an evening of reading.

"And this is your favorite room?" asked Alexandra of Catherine. "It's quite nice."

"Oh, no!" came the reply. "This is just the way there." Catherine beckoned to the guests and walked through the long gallery. At its end was an insignificant doorway. The party followed her through. As they stepped across the threshold, Jessica drew a deep breath upon discovering the magnificent sight.

The chamber's two-story walls were lined with shelves that brimmed with books by the thousands.

"We're the privileged owners of over twenty thousand books," reported Richard. "Some date back to the sixteenth century. Several languages are represented, as well."

"Do you speak them all?" Jessica asked of Catherine.

"Just three." Catherine blushed. "But I *am* an avid reader."

The party fanned outward, each stepping in a different direction. Jessica scanned the room. A winding staircase in one corner led to a second-story balcony framing the entire room. Small candelabras sat at intervals along the perimeter of the carved brass railing.

A mural overhead caught her attention. She stared two stories above, where a painting of a stormy coastline engulfed the entire ceiling. Once again she was reminded of the lighthouse and home.

"We wanted a sense of the outdoors while in this room," Richard stated as he walked up beside Jessica.

"Well, you have succeeded," she said in return.

"Look at this," Catherine said, stepping to the black marble fireplace in the center of one wall.

Jessica was drawn to the heavy walnut mantle that was matched by a tall ornate frame above, encasing another tapestry. She watched Catherine step around the large fireplace and grasp a knob in the woodwork. Jessica and her sisters gasped as a passageway and staircase appeared behind a hidden door.

"It leads to the second floor guest bedrooms," explained Catherine.

John turned to his friend. "Richard, I knew someday you would be a successful businessman, but I could never have imagined to this extent!"

"Our import business started small, as you know from our last meeting together," Richard explained, strolling toward the other end of the library. "When Olivia and I married, we never guessed how much joy and satisfaction would be derived from exploring other cultures. The handiwork and creativity of man left us dumbfounded. After bringing a few of Olivia's favorites back to England, which we found to be much admired by our friends, we realized the business potential of importing unique pieces. The demand increased at once. Before we knew it, there was no turning back. Britons could explore the continents and cultures without ever leaving the comfort of their homeland. Shipments of items by dozens became shipments by hundreds. Soon after I last saw you, John, Winterfield Imports expanded, and now we employ buyers in many countries on the mainland and even in parts of Africa, as well as India." He stopped before five portraits. "The construction of Winterfield Manor became a necessity, as Olivia collected her most treasured pieces. Since then, she has also begun importing and collecting rare plants during our travels, adding to the ambiance now found throughout our home. Winterfield Manor has become a museum of sorts, I suppose.

"This is our son, Roman," he said, lifting his palm to one of the portraits. "He oversees the purchasing in much of the mainland market. He's now in Frankfurt and will be traveling into Italy and back up through Austria in the spring, where Olivia will be meeting him. From there he'll venture into Hungary and Romania, and by year's end will be in the Greek islands."

Jessica stood beside her father and studied the portrait. It depicted a stern face, tilted a bit to one side, the chin raised. His dark features were handsome, and she wondered about the man behind them.

"Our other son, Andrew, is his younger twin. He and Roman are twenty-six now," Richard said, stepping to the next portrait. "Andrew captains one of our ships that sails the English Channel, along the French coast into the Bay of Biscay, and at times even down around the tip of Spain and into the Mediterranean, although of late he has been staying much closer to home. Political factions, storms, and reports of disease can at times prove obstacles, however cautious we attempt to be. We're very careful with our fleet and, overall, manage to avoid harm's way, having yet to experience a single shipwreck or loss of even one life on land *or* sea."

He moved away from the portraits and was followed by the others. Only Jessica remained before them, lingering to study the faces of the two sons.

"We started the building of Winterfield Hall soon after I last saw you, John, fifteen years ago," Richard continued.

"It's magnificent beyond description, Richard," he stated.

Several minutes later, Jessica's attention upon the portrait was interrupted when Alexandra called to her.

On the wall opposite the fireplace, three sets of double doors opened up to a large, well-protected balcony above the walkout basement, which is where Jessica found Alexandra overlooking acres of the wooded hillsides. In the distance were scattered several buildings.

"Look, Jessie! As far as the eye can see is Winterfield property. Is this not a feast for the eyes?" She pointed to the right. "Catherine said that group of buildings is a winery."

"Why, of course," Jessica said. "You can see the rows of the vines."

"Mr. Winterfield has approved of my taking one of the horses out after supper. Isn't this countryside just...*divine*?" Alexandra raved.

The tour of the main floor of the mansion continued, leading the party through other magnificent rooms. There was a quaint breakfast room, a salon with a draping brocade ceiling woven of wool, the music room with its grand piano.

Each was filled with the finest materials from Europe and the eastern world—topiaries, oriental screens, candles, embroidered upholstery, fine metals, gilded lamps, Persian rugs, ceramics, rich mahogany, walnut, oak, leather, silk, and wool—more items than Jessica could ever dream of, even with *her* adventurous imagination.

They returned to the entrance hall, where the tour had begun.

Jessica was happy to learn that the fuss being made over the dining table in the solarium was for the purpose of entertaining her family that very evening.

"There's more," Richard explained, "but perhaps we should break for supper before continuing."

The meal, served amidst the sweet-smelling plants of the solarium, began with a tasty potato soup. Turnips and carrots complemented the succulent lamb roast. Not to be forgotten was the warm white bread, of course served with whipped butter.

Amazed, Jessica watched an endless array of servants bustling around the room, up and down the corner steps, back and forth through the hallways, fulfilling every desire and demand of their mistress.

The conversation was casual and merry as the two old friends became reacquainted. Even Mrs. Winterfield appeared less guarded. Most of her conversation centered around her children, the eldest of whom she seemed to favor.

"How I would have enjoyed having three daughters, as you have been so blessed, John," she said in a tone that, to Jessica's relief, at least *sounded* sincere. "Indeed, I prayed for a girl both times. I believed my prayers to have gone unanswered when I gave birth to twin sons, and it was not until they were grown that I realized my expectations and wishes had been far exceeded in the men we had raised. The younger of the two, I admit, is a bit difficult to understand at times, but, nevertheless, I'm grateful and believe my prayers have been answered in an unexpected way."

"Little did she know," Richard laughed, "it was *my* prayers that had been answered, as I had asked for strapping sons to help run our business."

"Of course, I was blessed when our dear Catherine came along," Olivia interjected, "though the nine-year wait seemed an unbearable duration." She proceeded to brag on and on about the older of the twins, Roman—his unique charm and great intelligence. "Oh, he is a shrewd businessman," she said, smiling. "He can talk a barnacle right off the hull of a ship, and off he is to the next venture."

Catherine was seated between Jessica and Alexandra. As the adults conversed, Jessica turned to Catherine. "What fine older brothers you have, Catherine. It would seem that Roman, in particular, is a man of many fine qualities."

"Indeed, I looked up to Roman from the time I was very small," Catherine answered, "but I found I was far beneath his notice. It was Andrew who took a *true* interest in me. It was he who taught me how to ride and who taught me archery. He used to take me sailing, just the two of us." The fondness in Catherine's eyes saddened. "But as he grew older, his love for the sea won out, and I became more involved in my studies. I rarely see him now. Every few months he returns for a short time. Andrew is a very patient and kind man, and I miss him very much at times. Roman is charming, as mother claims. Oh, and very handsome! Both my brothers are. They are not identical, but their good looks are well matched."

Jessica appreciated the young woman's warm affection and wondered what it must be like to have brothers.

"Mother," Catherine raised her voice across the table, "remember the time when you and father returned one evening to find Andrew's horse wandering about inside the house, nibbling on your African Violets?" Catherine giggled.

"Oh, yes," Olivia chuckled, throwing one hand into a casual wave.

Catherine looked back at Jessica, as Olivia continued talking with the men. "Andrew was chastised for what appeared to be his doing. I felt sorry for him. He took the discipline without complaint, knowing he could not prove himself. That was before we had many servants at the stables. Although Andrew insisted he was innocent, my parents believed that he would have been the one to have left the stable door ajar since Roman didn't take much interest in the horses. It was weeks later that Roman confessed to the crime, playing it off as a great joke. He never received his due punishment.

"Andrew was never one to bring much attention to himself, although he is very humorous in his own way. Perhaps that is the reason Mother gravitates more toward Roman. Even as a youth, he always commandeered the situation and demanded so much of my parents' attention.

"Please do not misunderstand my meaning. Both my brothers are good men, and I love them both."

Jessica listened with rapt attention as Catherine talked on about her brothers.

The remainder of the meal passed without event and ended with sweet rice pudding. After consuming his generous portion, Richard wiped his napkin across his mouth.

"Allow me to show you the banquet hall," he announced, rising from the table.

This time Olivia accompanied the party as they ascended the steps from the sunken garden room. Crossing a wide hallway, they entered another enormous room—the largest in the mansion, Richard reported.

Jessica stared up at a vaulted ceiling arching two full stories above their heads, ribbed with dark, barreled rafters, as though the skeleton of a mighty ship had been turned on its belly and suspended high above them. On the outside wall domed windows began midway up the first story and stretched up between the rafters, flooding the hall with the diffused amber light of sunset.

Two immense circular candelabras, containing dozens of candles, adorned the massive hall. A long oak table, the centerpiece of the room, was dressed with a linen runner and vast floral arrangement. She counted thirty mahogany chairs upholstered in deep green velvet. Three of the walls boasted more huge tapestries. The final wall in its entirety was a great, carved marble fireplace and chimney, consisting of three separate fire nooks. The enormous mantelpiece was sculpted with near-to-life-sized figures of men, horses, and carriages in a long parade. It was supported on either side by wide marble columns. Jessica could not help but wonder about the purpose of such extravagance.

"This room must have been built for a king," she said.

"A king, indeed!" answered Catherine, taking the arm of her father. "King Richard."

Everyone laughed.

"Catherine," said Olivia, "why not take the girls to the music room?"

"While I show John my billiard tables," interrupted Richard.

The party split, the women exiting the banquet hall doorway through which they had entered, and the men through a small, obscure door in the far corner of the grand dining hall.

John stepped into what Richard described as his own favorite room and looked upon walls of oak paneling graced with the hunting trophies of the house's master, among them several large geese and pheasants. In the center of the room were the bulky rectangles of two mahogany billiard tables.

The glow of a crackling fire in the large fireplace on the far wall settled upon a bearskin rug lying before it. Above them was perched an ornamental ceiling, and below, carpets of crimson and gold.

"John, I can't tell you how much your visit means to me," Richard said, stepping over to a rack of cue sticks. Handing one to John, he reached for another.

John examined the stick. Its center was inlaid with ivory banded by gold. "I'm sorry, Richard, for disappearing so many years ago without revealing to you my whereabouts. At the time I felt it would be in your best interest, as I hoped to avoid involving you in my family's affairs."

"I must admit I didn't understand, and I grieved the loss of my friend," Richard said without looking at John, "but elected to let the matter go, trusting you had a better comprehension of the situation than did I. No apologies are necessary." Richard set up the billiard table for a game. "I saw William Sutton last year."

"William Sutton," John repeated. "Why, I haven't thought about Will for years. William Sutton," he repeated once more, nodding his head. "That man had the mind of a thousand brilliant men. He almost found himself expelled from University on many occasions, you know. You were not in our Latin group, Richard. He used to anger our professor to the point of exhaustion. He would answer in sentences part Latin and part Greek, and would speak at such speed that it would throw our poor professor, who was such a proper and slow speaker, into horrible confusion. He grew so frustrated with Will." Both men enjoyed a hearty laugh at John's memory. "And anatomy!" John continued. "He was in constant disputes with his tutor."

"Yes, I recall one debate about the eating habits of the European harvest mouse."

"By the end of it," John added, "Will had him convinced that the little rodent, who seemed so harmless, was a seething carnivore!"

The two laughed until their eyes ran with tears.

"Soon after that he began studying law." Shaking his head, John laughed more. "Will Sutton. He must be London's most successful barrister by now. I can only imagine the trouble he brings to the courtroom, no doubt under a very serious guise."

"I'll let you break, since you're my guest," Richard offered, holding a hand toward the triangle of colorful balls. "You were not without wit yourself, my friend," he added as John stepped up to the table. "I seem to recall a certain lecture room, which later became the laboratory. I remember it had a curtain dividing it from the storage room."

The cue ball cracked into the triangle of poised balls, sending them scattering.

"One day just before lecture began," Richard continued, "a certain student disappeared." He stepped up to examine the balls. "Before long, the laboratory skeleton was standing before the curtain spouting Shakespeare to the entire assembly, one bony arm extended by a puppeteer behind the curtain, its jaw in motion to the voice of Juliet's 'Romeo, Romeo, wherefore art thou, Romeo?'"

Again the men laughed, after which Richard took a shot at the number six ball, missing the pocket.

"Any wit I possessed," John answered, "I learned from Will. Indeed, wherefore art *thou*, William Sutton?" He leaned over for the next shot. "How is he?"

"He called on me last year at my office." Richard's face turned serious. "Soon after the death of your mother, John."

John's smile disappeared. He looked up. "Oh. I hadn't heard."

"I'm so sorry...I felt certain you knew by now. Will was seeking your address. 'A pressing family matter,' he told me. I assumed it was regarding the estate. I told him I hadn't heard from you in several years, but that you had been doing well at the time. And I added that I had no return address from your last correspondence."

"Now I know I made the right decision in not revealing it to you," he said.

"John, the girls could use the money."

John turned away. Silence filled the air. He looked around the plush room, drawing a heavy sigh as Richard awaited a reply. "As you know," he said after a moment, "my father was an excellent man. He had integrity and strength, kindness, and fairness. Because of his example I bore the Everett name with pride."

"And you were crushed upon hearing the news of his death when we were away at University. I remember that day, John. We were twenty years old."

"You were twenty," he said turning back. "I was nineteen, and yes, I was crushed." He sighed. "And you knew my mother."

"As much as one can come to know a hard, cold stone." Sorrow resounded in his voice.

"There I was," John replied, "the only son, the only child, of a long line of lawmakers, but I was interested only in studying the sciences. Mother disapproved. It was all she could do to support my schooling. When I accepted my degree in mathematics, I received no graduation acknowledgment, not even her presence at the ceremony.

"From that time onward, my mother viewed me as someone diseased—loathsome and detestable. So I left behind my former associates and chose Ireland as my residence, a nation struggling in the throes of that horrid famine, a social stigma to the wealthy English."

"And that's where you married," Richard added.

"Dublin was where I met her—a beautiful, vibrant, and invigorating woman." John's face dropped as he paced the room. "I fell in love with Angela. We were married in a private ceremony at the courthouse. I wrote to my mother, begging her for the opportunity to meet my wonderful new wife. Perhaps I should have omitted from my description the fact that she was not only Irish, but half Spanish, yet she would know by her name. The response I received was pure abhorrence. 'How could I tarnish the Everett name—a name that had represented a strong pillar of political influence in England and almost stood for Parliament itself? How could I bring reproach upon the family by allying myself with a common Spaniard? How could the Everett fortune be bestowed upon on one so undeserving? Such filth and shame I had brought upon my family name,' her letter said. In her eyes, Angela was my casket and Ireland, my burial plot."

"Angela's mother was Irish, correct?" Richard queried.

"As red-haired and blue-eyed as Grace." John smiled. "And her father, Spanish. Angela inherited her father's skin and hair tone, but her mother's eyes, which were passed on to each of the girls. I met her mother once, just after Grace was born. She traveled from Spain to assist Angela with the new baby for a short while. She died before Grace was four, when Angela was expecting Jessica.

"I wrote my mother after Grace's birth, announcing the arrival of her first grandchild. In response I received a telegram from her attorney, who was *not* William Sutton, notifying me of the removal of my name from her will." He looked up at his friend. "Her only son, Richard! And all for what? For finding true love and decency? For wanting a good life for myself and my family? The tiny child I held in my arms became the final nail in my casket. I was once and for all *dead* in my mother's eyes." He drew a deep breath and continued. "I had no reason to inform her of the birth of her other two granddaughters. I'm certain she went to her grave unaware of their existence. I can't imagine the reason Will Sutton would be seeking me on behalf of my family. It couldn't be in regard to my mother's estate. I'm sure, Richard, she would not have left us so much as a shilling."

"How much do the girls know of her, John, of your birth-right?"

"I can't bring myself to tell them of the disdain their own grandmother had for them, so I've told them very little."

Silence permeated the room.

"There are not many decisions in my life that I regret, Richard, but one has haunted me for years—the day I allowed my precious wife to board that ship to Spain. Her father had died. Her sister requested her presence, as his estate had to be allocated." John's eyes became misty when he recalled the sweetness of her last words. "I waved good-bye from the dock, with two little girls by my side and one in my arms, not realizing it would be my final farewell to the one I cherished more than life itself.

"The news of the shipwreck off the Spanish coast reached Ireland several days later. There were only a handful of survivors, and her name was listed among the deceased." John closed his eyes. Determined to maintain composure, he lifted his head high. "I desired sympathy from no one, most of all my mother. And yet it was almost unbearable to think I would *not* secure her pity. I know she heard of the tragedy. I sent her a telegram myself.

"One month later, on a crisp June morning, my young daughters and I left Ireland as Everetts, and arrived in England as Vianas—my wife's maiden name. Never again would I be connected with my remaining relatives. We've retained the name Viana ever since."

"John, why did you bring the girls here, feeling the way you do about this society?"

"The youngest is almost grown now. It would be wrong to keep them from their true heritage any longer. I raised them with the good principles and education I received, but apart from the snobbery. It's time to introduce them to this society and let them make their own decision as to where they'll reside, what kind of life they'll pursue for themselves. I'll also take them to Ireland and to Spain. The choice is theirs, not mine. I'll offer no opinion and will be proud of the decision of each one, no matter what it may be."

"Your daughters are unaware of the priceless treasure they have in their father," Richard said.

"Yes," John smiled, "so priceless, in fact, that one day I'm sure to be replaced by *three* men, and will be forced to call each one 'son.' How I dread that day. In that, you can be *sure* they'll hear my opinion. Now let us return to our game so I can demonstrate that even the lapse of fifteen years hasn't robbed me of my skill at billiards."

Chapter Seven

Later, after the two families had bade one another a good night, John gathered his daughters into Grace's bedchamber.

"I owe an apology to each of you."

His daughters sat on Grace's bed as he paced before them. They exchanged perplexed looks.

"I concealed the true reason I decided to bring you here."

"It was your desire to have a nice family holiday, Papa," Alexandra piped up.

John smiled at his youngest daughter. She was yet so innocent, so youthful.

"Yes, but there's more, Alexandra." He looked at the trio and asked, "Have you never wondered why I, an Englishman, would bear a *Spanish* surname?"

Alexandra shook her head. Jessica looked down. She appeared embarrassed. He realized the thought had never crossed her mind.

"It's because we changed our name, Father," Grace said.

Her sisters looked at her with surprise.

"You told us after we arrived in England we would no longer be called by your family name," Grace continued, "but instead would be called by our mother's name."

"That's correct."

"What was our name, Father?" Jessica asked.

"It was Everett. Jessica, Alexandra, you were too young to remember that conversation. Grace, for what reason do you recall I made that decision?"

"I have believed ever since, Father, it was in memory of our mother."

John smiled and looked down.

"That's not the reason, is it?" Jessica asked.

"No...that wasn't the reason." He began to pace again as he explained. "Your father belonged to a very prominent family here in London. It was expected I would follow *my* father's footsteps in politics. As you know, he died when I was a young man. But I had no interest in that vocation. My mother was very displeased and so renounced me after I'd moved to Ireland and married your mother. Many of the people in this society, including my remaining relatives, were also disappointed by my decision. They were a prejudiced people then. I know not how they are at this time. I brought you here because I feel you need to learn of your heritage."

"Will we meet our grandmother?" his youngest queried.

"No, Alexandra. I discovered this very evening that your grandmother died last year."

"Why then is it, Father, you feel the need to tell us these things after so many years?" Jessica asked.

"I'm certain you'll never have the social standing here that I had. You'll always belong to a poor family. But staying in the Winterfield's home and mingling among their class, I wanted you to experience the life from which your father descended, but turned his back on. You may decide to settle here, to marry here."

"Father, we would never leave you!" Jessica argued.

"You will always be my daughters, no matter where you choose to live. But while you are here, know that there are some in this society who will remember me. They'll recognize me." He crouched down before them. "I'm afraid there may be some who will mistreat you because of me. Don't be intimidated by the prejudice of others, and don't be prejudiced toward them yourself, regardless of their treatment of you. Stand tall, proud of the person you are—women of honor and respectability, whether a Viana *or* an Everett." He smiled and then stood. Leaning over, he kissed the cheek of his eldest daughter and took the hands of the other two.

"I have just one question," Alexandra said, but looked almost afraid to ask.

"It's all right," he reassured her. "You know you can ask me anything."

"Father...," she hesitated, "...did you live in a mansion like this as a child?"

"Alex!" Grace scolded. "That's none of our business." However, she turned to her father. "But did you?" A broad smile formed on her lips, her eyes expanding until her family was moved to laughter.

"No," he said, patting Alexandra's cheek. "Not at all like this." He coaxed his younger daughters to the door. "It was much grander."

The three girls squealed at the response.

"But!" he called out above their excitement. "I abandoned it all for something of even greater worth. Your mother and you were far more valuable in my eyes. Now off to bed!"

Jessica lay awake in the darkness, her father's words playing over and over in her mind. She could not envision his living in such a place. And did he really expect they would settle here, *marry* here?

Marriage. It was such a daunting word, such a daunting prospect. What did it truly mean? What was it all about? It must be more than mere mutual attraction, much more, yet that's all people ever talked of. 'The handsome prince and his beautiful princess,' 'Jessica, I think he likes you,' Claire would say of Mr. Robertson. How could he like her if he knew nothing about her? It was because of his attraction to her, as it was between so many others. No, that couldn't be a proper start. There had to be like qualities. There had to be *adventure*!

Often, she tried to imagine her father married to the woman in the portrait in their home. What were they like together? He must have respected her. In fact, he treasured her more than all the riches of London...why, just tonight he had said so himself.

Would she, Jessica, someday be cherished by a man? She thought of some of the married couples she knew, and her darkest fear enveloped her like the shadows of night. How could something as strong as true love diminish to mere toleration?

When did the pleasure of growing together give way to monotony? Once impatient for each other's company, some couples she knew were now eager for time apart. And the undignified way some women spoke of their husbands! Would this have happened to her parents?

Never would she allow it to happen to her! But how could it be avoided? Perhaps the deterioration of the relationship was so subtle that neither even noticed. That's why she preferred adventure instead. To travel and explore the world would never become mundane, despite what Grace said. No, she could reassure her father that she would *not* settle in London. Perhaps she would not *settle* anywhere...ever!

The house had fallen silent except for the low chimes from the grandfather clock in the hallway outside Jessica's room, announcing the arrival of midnight.

She lit the bedside candle and crept out into the hallway. Locating a small door close by, she opened it and entered a dark stairwell. Her echoing footsteps sent shivers up her spine, but in moments she stepped through the secret door into the library.

Lighting a few lamps in the room, she sat on the edge of a chair and stared at shelves upon shelves of volumes. Speak of adventure! She wanted to read one, but where to start? How could one choose a single grain from the sands of these literary seas?

She was reminded of an ancient proverb, "Of making many books there is no end, and much study is a weariness of the flesh." Yes, here she was surrounded by centuries of philosophy and wisdom; yet where in the entire collection was the formula for the end to war, or the antidote for aging, or the remedy for poverty? She was convinced that the answers did not lie in the realm of human thinking.

But what better way to explore faraway lands!

Jessica's attention was drawn to a large globe of the earth on a brass stand beside a burly desk. She stepped over and spun it with her eyes closed. Pressing her finger on a spot, she brought it to a stop. When her eyes opened, her finger rested on Morocco.

"Maybe someday...," she whispered.

The family portraits she had seen earlier in the day caught her eye. She passed over the faces of Mr. and Mrs. Winterfield and Roman, but allowed her gaze to settle upon the likeness of Andrew. She studied his features, recalling the fine accounts his sister had relayed during dinner. Similar in appearance to that of his twin, though somehow different, Andrew's portrait depicted a man of a more gentle nature. The solid black eyes betrayed a sense of self-confidence rather than the arrogance in his brother's eyes; the well-shaped, firm lips no doubt uttered only truth. His hands appeared strong, resting one over the other atop one leg, and revealed a man dedicated to hard work. She felt a sense of admiration, knowing full well she herself would never have the opportunity to compare his true character with the one sketched by his biased younger sister, although no doubt done so in innocence.

Looking back to the desk, she noticed a set of books. The hard leather covers bore no titles, no authors' names. Reaching for the first one, her fingers skimmed over the worn leather cover. Opening it, she was startled to read the words neatly scrolled inside:

Daily Log
The Emerald
Capt. A. Winterfield

Dated two years prior, it listed the names of the attending crew members. Browsing through its pages, she found that it covered the daily events on the ship for the period from spring to fall.

Reading some of the entries, it was as though she were reading a stranger's diary. Consumed by guilt, she abruptly closed the book, but then looked over at the other two books on the desktop. Here they sat, in the library, on public display for any guest to see, she reasoned.

Curiosity prevailed.

She sank into a soft overstuffed chair and opened the book near its middle. How strange to read Andrew Winterfield's own handwriting! It was as though he were addressing *her*. The penmanship was elegant, though hurried at times, and the style, casual.

17 July, 1870, 3.00 p.m.

Third day in port now, and the men are getting restless. Yet I stand firm. They will not leave the ship until word comes to clear us to load the cargo. The men know cholera can prove fatal. There may be one case, may be a thousand. Yet, even a report of this nature cannot keep an impatient pack at bay for long.

If no word by dawn, will cast off and return next month for this load. Next port home, two days away. At least work on a moving ship will keep them busy, unlike this idle time of nothing more than poker and solitaire. The heat is stifling. Feels as though we are suffocating.

The next entry followed almost two days later:

19 July, 1870, 2.00 a.m.

Cholera outbreak contained. Took a full 14 hours to load cargo. Most of crew left ship at 8.00 p.m. with exception of first mate. Instructed to return by midnight, all are still missing. They will return, tired and sore from the load, sick from the drink. Yet cast off will happen as planned at 6.00 a.m. In Chatham all will be paid and let go. There are many seeking a decent wage. This crew will not sail *The Emerald* again.

She read on with intrigue, learning more about daily life aboard *The Emerald*. Most days seemed uneventful, a tiff here and there between the men, discussions over damaged cargo, lists of inventory, a brief meeting with Roman, export and import tax and customs records. In August they managed to stay ahead of a large storm for several hours, the crew (no doubt a new crew) in awe over large 'water funnels,' as was described by the captain. Jessica read of the sighting of exotic sea creatures, of swimming amidst the Greek Islands, of fishing from the rowboats near the Spanish coastline.

There was even an entry of discovering an additional man on board—a stowaway! He was described as perhaps twenty years of age, of medium build with dark hair, eyes, and complexion, and was clothed in rags. He managed to evade capture by any of the men and disappeared into the darkness of the port in England. The captain had noticed a tattoo marking on his right shoulder, and the entry in the log expressed extensive wonder about the man. Who he was, where he was from, why he was traveling to England. Or was he fleeing from someone, satisfied to reach any port at all? The questions would remain unanswered.

Jessica found herself riding along, a passenger aboard *The Emerald*. She had always had a fascination for the sea and often daydreamed of sailing the open waters. Often she was yanked back by the reality of her mother's disappearance in the unforgiving waters.

The writings revealed Andrew to be a man of strength and uncompromising integrity, one unafraid to contribute to hard work aboard the ship as well as on the docks. He seemed a man of order and precision, who lived by his own rules and yet was not rigid in them. He commanded respect and condoned no misconduct. Penalty was swift and straightforward. The crew no doubt knew what to expect from their then twenty-four-year-old captain. By his own words he worked them hard and paid them well.

Jessica grew drowsy when the writings neared the end of October and decided to continue the secret rendezvous another time.

Returning to her room, she fell asleep before the clock struck two.

The following week, Olivia mentioned a large upcoming ball to which Jessica's family had been invited as guests of the Winterfields.

"They simply must have new gowns, Richard," Olivia informed her husband at dinner. "And how Sophie will relish the opportunity to put her talents to work on those robust manes!"

Although Jessica's father argued against it, their hosts would hear of nothing less, insisting on covering the full expense. A shopping extravaganza was planned, for the ball was now just days away.

The lady of the house seemed all too happy, Jessica thought, to flaunt her high-society acquaintances to her visitors. Or was it the other way around? Olivia voiced her admiration of the beauty in her and her sisters, even calling it 'lofty.' Was Mrs. Winterfield's apparent delight in having them accompany her because of the attention they attracted from her friends? Jessica began to suspect this was the reason for the numerous invitations they had been receiving, noting that most every new greeting included a statement of how lovely the three were, and which comments seemed to boost *Olivia* higher each time.

They were chauffeured to glamorous tearooms, expensive shops, luncheons on the Thames River, and tours of luxurious homes, pampered at every turn and drowned in attention. Such fuss over their comfort and every need bordered on the ridiculous! Not that any of them minded. Even Jessica appreciated the hospitality, but couldn't quite comprehend which of their qualities merited such attention from this populace. It seemed that what she and her sisters lacked in fashion was ignored in favor of their appearances. They were at times even called 'good,' 'intelligent,' and 'gifted' before ever opening their mouths! What kind of standard was this? Jessica shook her head at such confusing thoughts.

And what of the beauty in Catherine's face? No one seemed to notice the younger sister of the two handsome older brothers. Also, while expressing interest in the physical comforts of her guests, Olivia withheld her affections from them all, even her own daughter. Although taking apparent delight in many things, she expressed no pleasure through a smile or compassionate word. How thankful Jessica was to have been raised in a warm and loving home with her father and the Wrights!

One afternoon, Catherine and Grace strolled through the meadow behind the Winterfield gardens, Catherine's two St. Bernards plodding alongside. Nearby, Jessica and Alexandra trotted on horseback, disappearing into the forest and reappearing several yards ahead of or behind the pedestrians.

The crisp air turned their cheeks and noses a rosy hue. Their breath formed into mist before them, then vanished.

"Every time we walk out here, I am overwhelmed by the vastness of these grounds. You're so fortunate in your heritage," Grace said to her young hostess.

"Thank you, but I often find myself quite alone. I love my horses and my dogs, and on occasion will have a friend over, but my parents focus much attention on the business. How I long for a sister at times."

"How often do your brothers return?"

"Seldom. I'm afraid my mother's good intentions have managed to drive them away. You see, she has chosen a particular young lady for each of them, and reminds them in no uncertain terms of their obligations to both family and community. She hopes they'll both settle down in London or Canterbury." Catherine sighed. "So my brothers stay away, content for now to live as bachelors."

"And how do you find your mother's selections?" Grace inquired. "Would you be happy to have one of them as your sister?"

"Caroline Landly is a pretty lady. However, my admiration for her stops there. She treats most all of her acquaintances with contempt, with the exception of my mother, whom she is eager to please. And she has taken no interest in me. Perhaps she *would* be a good match for my brother, Roman."

"And what of Andrew?"

"He's quite the opposite. My mother will never find his match, no matter her attempts. It seems there's not yet a place for a woman in his life. The majority he knows are spoiled weaklings, as he says, with no sense of individuality. I do feel, however, that he would cherish and care for a wife, were he to find the right woman. But he expects more. Intelligence and strength, coupled with compassion and sincerity, a true companion. Not just a showpiece, with which men in our general acquaintance seem to be satisfied. To find a woman of such character would be difficult, if not impossible."

Grace contemplated Catherine's words and dismissed the idea she had been fostering—that her sister, Jessica, would be the ideal woman. However, a man of such standing would never consider an alliance with a member of their class.

"And perhaps the situation is better left alone," Catherine continued. "Andrew seems to find pleasure in his ship and the unpredictable and wild beauty of his one true love—the sea."

"Then the situation seems quite hopeless," Grace agreed, and her thoughts moved to other eligible men for her sister.

Chapter Eight

Morning brought a clear winter sky along with the frost on the window. Jessica and Alexandra donned layered clothing for a brisk walk among the gardens. Grace preferred to read in her room.

The instructions from Olivia Winterfield had been clear—a light breakfast at nine and off to town right afterward. The men would tour Winterfield Imports warehouse while the women shopped.

All of a sudden, the halls echoed with loud voices. One of them Grace recognized as Olivia's, but the other, that of an unidentified man, boomed through the house, though she could not quite understand the words. Almost as soon as the conversation began, it ended.

Within moments Catherine was at Grace's door.

"Grace, come quick!"

"What is it?"

"My brother has just arrived!"

"Andrew?"

"No, Roman. This is quite unexpected. He was not to return home again until summer, but he is here! You must come meet him."

She could not discern whether Catherine's reaction was one of pleasure or fear, but she herself was in no hurry for the introduction.

As the two descended the main staircase, a very bewildered Olivia met them.

"Where has Roman gone, Mother?"

"Out to the stables. He was anxious for a ride. I told him of the ball and that we will be leaving soon for town in preparation of it. I'm delighted he has agreed to attend. However, I had no opportunity to explain we have guests." She seemed a bit disoriented by the surprise. "Oh, well. No matter. He'll be introduced this evening."

Grace hoped that Roman would not cross paths with Jessica and Alexandra. If met with such an encounter, Jessica, she feared, would not take a fancy to him.

When her sisters returned, Grace was relieved to hear that no such meeting had occurred. She related to Jessica the morning's events and the conversation she had had with Catherine the day before, even confessing her own hopes for Jessica and Andrew.

"Thank you for imagining me alongside such a man," Jessica said with a laugh. "You realize, of course, this family— much less this society—would never tolerate such a union."

Grace nodded, frowning.

The carriage and horses were prepared, and off the small party went, heading toward town.

The ball was just two nights away! They met first with Sophie, who appraised the Viana girls' beautiful tresses and sketched their names into her appointment book.

"Your father will be astonished," Olivia said to Jessica and her sisters on their way back to the mansion after an exhausting day of shopping and planning.

She knew not whether to feel complimented or slighted by the comment. In fact, she suspected the motive for purchasing gowns for all three was for the purpose of flaunting them all the more so.

Feeling more like a pawn than a guest, Jessica was growing more impatient with Olivia's condescension toward others. The manners and morals her father had taught were being tested to the full.

And how grateful she was for his principles, for the introduction to the infamous Roman Winterfield yet lay ahead. Jessica hoped there would be opportunity for a warm bath prior to the dreaded event. Perhaps she would even find the opportunity to prepare some kind words for Catherine's oldest brother.

The men had spent the day touring the gigantic warehouse and offices belonging to Winterfield Imports, which spanned several acres on the wharf in Chatham and employed over a hundred workers. John watched a dozen men unload the freight from one of the Winterfield cargo ships. Trunks, barrels, and crates by the dozens disappeared through the large bay doors.

"Much of the inventory has been pre-purchased," Richard explained, "in particular the furniture. Customers will wait months for a painted chest from Bavaria or a carved mirror from Switzerland."

The two men stepped inside, where Richard showed John porcelain from Poland and silk screens from Asia. A full eight hours later they reached the conclusion of their excursion in a small room filled with fabrics and clothing from places as far away as India.

"John, do you remember your last words to me the day we graduated from school and parted ways?"

John struggled to recall that day so many years ago before shaking his head.

"I asked if you had any parting words of wisdom for me," Richard said. "Not knowing at the time the direction either of our roads would lead us, you replied, 'Be not the holder of many possessions, lest you find your possessions holding you.'" Richard pulled a small trinket from a crate sitting beside him. "I didn't heed your advice, my friend, and I've experienced the truth of that statement many times over. I find myself enslaved to this business. Where did such a young man obtain so much wisdom?"

"I saw the effect the pursuit of riches had on my family," John replied. "The root of oppression and poverty, greed sparks many of the battles fought and has blinded countless intelligent minds. It turns brother against brother and stands as a mountain, hindering solutions to the world's problems. It's the foundation of every evil thing, Richard. It cost me the love and respect of my own mother when I chose a different path."

He cocked his head to one side. "I'd forgotten what I said that day. I'm impressed you remembered."

"Yes, well, perhaps someday I'll have the courage to apply it as you have."

"You have money, Richard, but greed has no hold on you."

Richard looked away.

The reprieve Jessica hoped for did not happen, for she and her party ran head-on into Roman Winterfield as they entered the house. Olivia made a quick introduction, but without a word to Jessica or her sisters, or even his own sister, Roman turned to his mother.

"I'd like a word with you in private."

The two entered the nearby tapestry gallery. Jessica looked at her sisters, irritation swelling in her heart. Never had they met with such incivility. Catherine, however, did not seem to be to be surprised.

"Mother, I am here but a few days." Roman made no attempt to quiet his voice. "Can't they be put up elsewhere? How can I be expected to relax with *four* ladies underfoot? My sister alone is enough—but *four*?"

"Roman...darling...these are your father's guests," his mother pleaded with him in a tone that sickened Jessica. "Might I remind you, dear, that it was *your* visit that came as a surprise? We'd planned for them since fall. You needn't keep company with them. I'll do everything I can to keep them out of your way."

Roman persisted in the argument, but Jessica moved toward the stairway, lest she be tempted to interrupt and speak her mind.

"I see no reason to eavesdrop on this *private* conversation," she announced. Retreating to her room, she leaned against the closed door and mumbled, "He didn't even acknowledge his own sister. Well, perhaps *he* will keep out of *our* way."

The hot bath Jessica desired soothed her irritation, but all for naught when she learned that Roman would join them for dinner.

Making the best of the situation, she determined to appreciate the hospitality she had enjoyed thus far.

"Conquer evil with good," she repeated while taking one last look in the mirror before descending the staircase.

To her surprise, the table was set, but not in the solarium as had been the custom since the arrival of her family. It was apparent the presence of the eldest son had prompted Mrs. Winterfield to serve the meal in the main dining hall. Jessica clenched her teeth at such obvious partiality. He was a spoiled and selfish child, and it was all his mother's doing.

Jessica forced a smile as she entered the gargantuan hall, the last of the ladies to arrive. *Eight people seated at a table built for thirty. How ridiculous!*

The middle fireplace blazed, warming the entire room. Exquisite china, crystal, silver, and a huge arrangement of dried flowers flanked on either side by silver candlesticks overpowered one end of the table. Jessica wondered how her father would react to such a showy display.

He and Mr. Winterfield joined the party in short order, just returning from the warehouse. Her father cast a puzzled glance around the room, as she had suspected he would.

Roman made a grand entrance after all were seated, his usual custom in the pursuit of self-glorification, she assumed. Roman's father must have been told of his son's surprise visit. The two greeted each other, but Jessica detected no particular intimacy between them.

Trying to be discreet, she studied the newcomer. His features were chiseled and his chest and shoulders, broad. His thick mahogany hair complimented his dark eyes. She watched him put on an artificial smile as he approached her father.

"Mr. Viana, I've heard much about you over the years. How pleased I am to at last make your acquaintance. You're very welcome in our home."

Our home? Jessica thought. She was certain *he* had not contributed so much as a shilling to its preservation.

Grace looked her sister's way, but Jessica kept her gaze focused on Roman to see whether he would address his sister or any woman in the room. The conversation continued between the men.

"I remember you as a child," her father said.

Grace leaned over and whispered, "He's just like the men I encountered in London last summer."

Jessica recalled the words of her sister's letter, and his handsome features faded as a brilliant sunset giving way to the pitch of darkness. Roman Winterfield's good looks masked a cold and selfish heart.

"I was treated to a tour of your spectacular warehouse today, Roman," her father continued. "I'm very impressed with the business. Winterfield Imports has grown a hundredfold since I was last in town. I understand much of its success is owed to you, as the primary buyer for the company."

Oh, just the words a man of his nature needs to hear. Jessica rolled her eyes toward Grace.

Catherine and Alexandra, lost in a conversation of their own, paid no heed to the others.

"I can't take *all* the credit of such a generous assessment," Roman responded.

How humble! Jessica fought the sarcastic comment that rose in her throat.

"After all," he continued, "a fraction of praise belongs to my mother, who from time to time assists in the buying process, though she still has much to learn."

Egotistical, presumptuous, conceited snob! What does he have that was not handed him on a silver platter? Jessica battled to control her thoughts, but to no avail. They crashed through her head like the waves of an angry sea, fighting to break loose.

She focused on her father. His eyebrows furrowed as he glanced at Richard, who ignored the comment. It was obvious Roman's parents were accustomed to his arrogant behavior.

Jessica fumed as he failed to acknowledge any woman at the table besides his mother. Even more, he owed them an apology for his earlier disgraceful manners—in particular, his own sister! Forced by proper manners to tolerate him, she attempted a diversion, turning her attention to the delicious courses arriving from the kitchen in a steady stream. As the meal wore on, she tried to converse with Catherine and her sisters, but his booming words dominated the hall.

"And the man's servant—imagining he was speaking proper English—suggested I take the thoroughfare," he was saying, as though enjoying the echo of his own voice. He laughed and spooned more potatoes into his mouth. "Can you believe? A *servant*!" he said and swallowed the food. "As though *I* would get lost."

"I'm certain he was just trying to be of assistance," Jessica's father said, which made her smile.

"I assured him I knew *my* way around Germany better than he knew *his* way around the English dictionary," Roman continued. "And what's more absurd," he said, laughing, "is the fact he didn't even understand my meaning!"

His mother laughed with him.

Jessica's father turned away from the belligerent man. "Richard, tell me," he began. It was obvious by the gesture he was imploring him for a private conversation.

"Father," Roman interrupted, "wasn't I right? The music boxes I sent from Frankfurt were magnificent, weren't they? I told you you'd have no trouble selling them for five times the purchase price. Tell me, what price did they fetch?"

"Indeed, you were right, Roman," his father said. "They sold for three hundred pounds apiece."

"Outstanding!" Roman boasted. "Never underestimate me, Father."

"Dear," Olivia said, reaching over to touch Roman's cheek, "I can't quite determine the reason for your shrewdness. You didn't learn it from either of your parents."

"It's a gift from God, Mother." His tone dismissed her while he shooed her hand from him and turned his attention back to his plate.

While the final course was being consumed, Olivia brought up the subject of Caroline Landly.

"I saw her in town this morning, Roman. She seemed very pleased to discover you're home, and was delighted to hear you'll be at the ball night after tomorrow."

"Mother." Roman sighed and rolled his eyes. He set his silverware on his plate, glaring at Olivia. "I feel it's time we settle this matter that seems to be ongoing between you and Miss Landly. I exclude myself because I'm not a party to this scheme. Caroline Landly is *not* my type, and I venture to say that in the field of romance, you would do me a better service in not serving me at all."

Jessica was relieved when Olivia drew back, at last showing surprise at the manner of her son's address, but it was Jessica herself who spoke up.

"And just what *is* your type, Mr. Winterfield?" Her words were clear and loud, and all in the room stared in amazement at her, for, to this point, she had not spoken so much as a word aloud. "Perhaps a woman of virtue and justice, kindness and charity? A woman of moral excellence, Mr. Winterfield?"

Roman cast an amused look in her direction. "And perhaps the woman of your description is...*you*, Miss Viana?"

"Oh, no." A half laugh skipped from her chest. "I was thinking more along the lines of...Florence Nightingale."

The whole room burst into laughter, except Roman, who appeared a bit annoyed by her mockery.

The servants had just brought the dessert.

Before Roman had a chance to respond, Jessica stood up from the table and circled around her chair.

"No, that's not the woman of your choice, is it, Mr. Winterfield?" She strolled to the end of the dining table where his father was seated. "No, the woman I imagine you with will be stately and fashionable, charming and self-confident. A woman of position, perhaps a bit of a tease, demanding yet alluring. Oh, yes, a true beauty on your arm for all to see."

Roman puffed up a bit more with every word. Jessica watched him relish the vision.

"Together you will be admired by one and all," she continued. "Others will talk of your superiority. 'The perfect couple,' they will say." She rounded the table, taking a position beside the man and glaring down at him. "But take heed, Mr. Winterfield. You may die a wealthy man with your trophy by your side, but, to quote a well-respected woman of my acquaintance, 'your life will be void of any real happiness, and you will *never* know the joy of genuine love.' What a misfortune *that* will be, Mr. Winterfield."

She turned on her heel and strode out of the room. Just over the threshold she passed a servant entering the dining hall.

"Thank you for a wonderful meal," she stated in a sweet voice to the servant, loud enough for all to hear.

She was pleased when Grace found her in her room after the exchange at the dinner table.

"Yes!" her sister said. "I knew you would be the one to bring them down, Jessie."

"I don't know that I want to 'bring anyone down,' Grace. But he's such an ogre, and *someone* should canvas his flaws. It seems apparent no one in his society has ever stood up to him, including his parents, so it may as well have been me—someone he can forget with ease. I *am* concerned about Father, however. I'm afraid I made a fool of him, and for that I deserve to be chastised."

"Oh, I don't think so, Jess," Grace responded with a smile. "You should have seen the smirk on, not only *his* face, but on Mr. Winterfield's."

"Really?"

"They resumed eating their dessert as though nothing at all had happened. Roman and Mrs. Winterfield sat speechless for the first time since the meal started, just staring at each other."

They burst into laughter and could not stop for several minutes.

Jessica saw nothing of Roman the following day and, finding no reason to subject herself to his tedious company for another meal, requested that her dinner be served in her room that evening.

Chapter Nine

The day of the ball came much too soon for Jessica's liking.

She kept to her room, engrossed in a book she had selected from the library. For several preceding nights, she had sneaked down to follow the adventures of *The Emerald*. However, this day she chose a different subject for reading, feeling a certain disdain for the Winterfield family in general and what they represented. She liked Catherine well enough, but was sure the fine report given about her brother, Andrew, grew out of a younger sister's adoring heart and was colored to fit her own perspective. After all, no man could be raised in such an environment and remain unaffected. No, he must be just like Roman; therefore, what was the point any longer in taking part in his adventures, exciting as they sounded?

She tried to concentrate on the book, but then tossed it aside, admitting it didn't begin to approach the thrill of the captain's journals.

Grace and Alexandra strolled around the gardens. Though the morning air was chilly, the sun warmed their cheeks.

"Grace, do you suppose this ball will be similar to those you attended in London last summer?"

"No doubt, although I have a sense it will be much larger."

"Do you entertain the hope of meeting up with Mr. Sutton again?" Alexandra teased.

"I must admit, I've pictured his face in my mind a thousand times since then." Grace was grateful for the crisp morning and hoped Alexandra would interpret the blush in her face as a natural response to the cold air. "Ever since our arrival, I catch myself looking for him when in town. Though I'm grateful for our recent outings to Canterbury, I doubt he spends much time there. I have to admit I'm excited to be going back to London!"

"Will the ball take place there?"

"Yes." She paused, reflecting on her growing anticipation. "This gathering will be one of high society, Alex. Our speech and conduct must be exemplary. We don't wish to be an embarrassment to the Winterfields after all they've done for us."

"Oh, dear! What if I don't know *how* to act?"

"From my experience here last summer, I doubt that after meeting the majority you'll even be concerned to gain their approval. Regardless, I found the manners father has taught us rendered me well-prepared to mingle with the elite. Don't worry, little sister. We'll fit in just fine, and we'll be careful to stick close together."

"Oh, good." Alex sighed.

By late afternoon the manor bustled as the families prepared for the evening. Mrs. Winterfield trailed her female servants from room to room, barking commands. Jessica felt sorry for them, though they seemed quite adapted to their mistress' officious attitude.

Sophie and staff arrived near five o'clock and began their work. Curling, twisting, and pinning Jessica's hair, they fashioned it into a masterpiece replete with ribbons, then highlighted her sisters' hairdos with tiny flowers. Mrs. Winterfield was fitted with a delicate pearl tiara.

John paced his bedchamber, his anxiety reaching new heights, try as he might to overcome it. Thus far, he had managed to avoid any encounters with old acquaintances and relatives, but he expected this night would prove different.

It being more than twenty-four years since his last meeting with any from London's elite, he prepared himself for significant changes in its society. However, as he peered into the full-length mirror, he wondered if *he* had changed much. Was he now unrecognizable? Had he been forgotten by this time? No. The recent death of his mother had no doubt reminded many of his existence. He could envision them all wondering who, if not her estranged son, would inherit the vast estate. Yes, they would recognize him, and the fortune hunters were sure to come out of the woodwork.

On the other side of the mansion, Richard Winterfield studied the face staring back at him in his mirror. He cocked his head to one side, hoping the different angle would lighten the shadow between his eyebrows. But it was no use. The source of his anxiety lay close to home. His wife had known all along most everything *he* had about John's life—and that he was the sole heir to a vast fortune he had walked away from years before. She now was also privy to his name change and his chosen profession as the simple keeper of a lighthouse. What she did *not* know were the reasons behind it. Thus far, Olivia had managed to show respect for the man, but in private she had expressed disdain for what she called his 'unreasonable choices.' And he could only assume that Olivia had made known all John's dealings—as well as his presence—to her numerous friends.

They would be expecting his attendance at this evening's affair. Most would respond with scorn, something his friend could tolerate, even welcome. It was the others, those who would greet his family with enthusiasm, Richard feared. He knew them too well. To form an alliance with one of the daughters would thrust any young man into a potential position of prominence and wealth.

He also feared the response of any fellow Parliament members in attendance. His membership in the House of Commons had spanned several years. Had John stayed in London, *his* seat would have been with the House of Lords. His peers might question Richard's motive in connecting himself with a renegade. Both of their evictions from the gathering loomed as a possibility.

94

Yes, there was much to be anxious about, but Richard would do what he could to protect his guests.

The final touch for the women was a mist of the finest perfumes, which Jessica and her sisters had never experienced. The fragrance drifting about the room made her think of the gardens she had strolled through at the party last summer in Penzance.

At the end of the preening session, five exquisite ladies emerged, met by the two pacing men in the entrance hall. Servants assisted the ladies with satin capes, draping hoods over their delicate coiffures.

"Roman went ahead in his own carriage," announced Richard.

Jessica breathed a sigh of relief and hoped the gathering would be large enough to avoid him.

"Now I know how Cinderella must have felt as she pulled up to the ball," Alexandra whispered to Jessica, who understood just how she felt.

She wanted to rip the long, white gloves from her arms, but was distracted as the carriage, after bumping over a rough road for more than an hour, rolled onto a gravel drive. They entered tailored grounds decorated with topiaries and small dry pools with accompanying fountains, all in hibernation for the winter and illuminated by bright lamps. Marble statues alternated with the lamps along the road on both sides.

The coach paused in a long line of carriages, and Jessica watched guests disembarking to ascend wide marble steps to the entrance of a well-lit, immense mansion that paled Winterfield Manor.

"I think it's a palace!" she whispered to her younger sister.

As they entered, they were introduced to their host and hostess, a Lady and Lord. Ushered to a podium, they were next handed an itinerary of the evening's events, including each dance and seating assignments for the meal.

Jessica noted her name scripted in gold elegance across the top of the card. A small pencil was attached, which she pondered for a moment before noticing the names of gentlemen sketched beside several of the dances.

"Grace," she whispered, "your card."

Grace, already reviewing her own card, whispered, "When in Rome…"

Jessica nodded, complying with the arrangements, but after being escorted to the dining room filled with dressed tables, was disappointed to find that she and her family members would not be seated together. She would be seated beside Mrs. Winterfield, but was relieved for Alexandra, who was assigned with their father. Likewise, Grace would be with Catherine and Mr. Winterfield. Each table was large and, though now empty, was set for perhaps a dozen.

Jessica's father pulled her and her sisters aside.

"Although marriages are no longer arranged in this society," he explained, "it's customary for parents to see to it that their older children mingle with other young adults of select families. They hope marriage alliances will take place in the natural course of events, under the strictest of supervision, you understand."

Jessica almost objected, but thought better of it.

"I'll be keeping a close eye on all of you," her father added, "though I trust the intelligence and maturity each of you possesses. I am confident in your ability to defend yourselves." He reached for their itinerary cards and sketched his own name on each for a dance.

While reviewing Jessica's card, he smirked before handing it back to her. She wondered about the amusement in his expression.

Leaving the empty dining hall, they followed the hum of a gathering crowd in an adjoining room.

Jessica marveled as she stepped into an enormous ballroom constructed of white marble. Six columns stood at attention, three along either side supporting a balcony that framed the room high above. The columns bulged at their centers, as though struggling to sustain the great weight. A curved marble staircase was concealed on one side beneath the balcony, and Jessica felt the urge to climb it and explore the story above. Her hand covered her gaping lips when three enormous crystal chandeliers dangling from the high ceiling caught her attention. They cast a spray of starry light on the polished dance floor. Even in her new lace-up shoes, she felt unworthy to stand upon the marble floor.

While the guests mingled, Jessica wandered to the far end, where she peered out the glass of one of six sets of high double doors. Outside she discovered a large veranda set with stone and marble benches and potted evergreens. She made out a heavy stone stairway that led to shadowy gardens below.

The guests began taking their seats for the meal as more continued to arrive. The flow into the room seemed endless.

Jessica seated herself beside Olivia Winterfield.

"Please pardon my asking," Jessica said in her most pleasant tone, "but would you identify the gentlemen on my program?"

She read some of the names to Olivia, who pointed them out to her as she located them, giving her a little description of each one and a brief history of his family.

"How I'll relish in making the introductions," Olivia said, rubbing her palms together. Jessica felt uneasy for Olivia's young prey. "Not a single one agreed without a fierce argument to dance with you."

"You mean *you* arranged these partners?"

"Of course! Through the coercing and insistence of their mothers. Just wait until they cast their eyes on you! They'll be sorry they agreed to only one dance. And when they beg for another, I'll put them down in no gentle manner!"

Jessica did not appreciate playing the bait in Mrs. Winterfield's sport. Just when she was about to object, she was distracted to find, farther down on her card, the name of Roman Winterfield! Though elegant, the handwriting was different than the rest of the flowery penmanship. He had, it seemed, sketched in his own name before she arrived!

Why would he do such a thing? she could not help but wonder. Out of sheer curiosity she decided she would oblige him, but did not mention his name to his mother.

Now she understood her father's humorous reaction after reviewing her card. She smiled to herself. It seemed the eldest Winterfield son had not had enough of her reproof.

Over an hour later all the guests had been seated. There must have been upwards of five hundred!

The Lord, their host whose name Jessica had forgotten, stood up in the front of the room, and all fell silent. He announced that the occasion had been arranged for the debut of his daughter, who also stood but remained silent. The room thundered with applause.

The meal was served in several courses. Drink flowed freely; conversations were warm and light. Jessica glanced at her sisters often for reassurance.

Throughout much of the meal, her father was in deep conversation with Alexandra, and she could imagine his topic of choice—that of advising her on matters of friendships and marriage. Doubtless, he was drawing out Alexandra's opinions and viewpoints as he had done many times over the years with all his daughters. Her sister was engrossed in the conversation. Jessica, after glimpsing the stoic Olivia Winterfield, who was also busy in conversation, longed to be at the table beside them. She smiled at the thought of the love her father showed them and the individual time he had spent with her and her sisters from the time they were small.

And she had never seen him look more handsome. Already she noticed that he had captured the attention of more than one lady, some in small groups whispering amongst themselves and looking his way, even pointing. But he seemed oblivious, focusing instead on the more important matter of his daughter.

Grace recognized many faces from her previous visit to Kent, and was quick to note that the topics of conversation had not changed, still dominated by fashion, wealth, and gossip.

It seemed she had missed nothing of importance in the six months that had passed. Unable to picture herself among this society for long, she tried to be warm and cordial. She could talk of fashion as well as the next and was quite content with idle subjects for one evening.

The young men at her table seemed more attentive to her than during her last visit. They vied for her conversation, ready and willing to share their fine qualities with her, and some even asked for her hand in a dance. Her card began filling up. Even with all the attention she was receiving, she kept searching the room for any sign of the handsome Stephen Sutton.

At one point during the meal, she overheard a conversation between two ladies at her table. Though she tried not to eavesdrop, the topic caught her attention.

"Did you notice that Roman Winterfield is here?"

"Yes!" the other replied, keeping her voice low. "He's an absolute *dream*!"

The two giggled.

"And the best news of all—he's still unmarried!"

"Fancy the one fortunate enough to run her fingers through *his* locks."

"Never mind that," her friend retorted. "Fancy the one fortunate enough to run her fingers through his *fortune*!" They both tittered at the prospect.

"Quiet!" one of them whispered. "His sister may hear you."

On Grace's other side, Catherine, engrossed in a conversation of her own, appeared to be unaware of the two young ladies.

"Who do you think he'll dance with?" the first young lady posed.

"Caroline Landly, I'm sure," the other sighed.

"What would you do if he asked *you*?"

"I'd faint straight away!"

Poor things, Grace thought. Both girls were very plain, and neither had the slightest chance of landing even a glance from the self-absorbed Winterfield son.

"Look at him," one said.

Grace's gaze moved to the arrogant man. He sat several tables away in private conversation with another male guest, his arms locked across his broad chest. She wondered if he ever smiled, besides when mocking someone.

"Look at those eyes," the other said, her chin dropping into her palm as her elbow settled upon the table. "A woman could just *dive* into them. And such a firm chin and straight nose."

"I like his eyebrows," the other replied. "They're so fine. He's simply perfect, an ideal man."

Grace wondered about their definition of 'perfect.' Would he 'perfectly' put up with the imperfections in either of them, or any other woman? She pitied the woman who danced with him, much less *married* him.

But on and on they talked. "And don't even let me *start* on his lips!"

"Quick!" the other said. "Turn away now before your desires get the best of you!"

They laughed harder. All Grace could do was roll her eyes in disgust.

Jessica fell into conversation with a lady seated on her other side. She was perhaps ten years Jessica's senior and said she had been married almost that long.

"Oh, but life with Ted has been one adventure after another," the woman rambled. "After the birth of our first daughter, do you know what he did?"

Jessica shook her head.

"Well, after the tedious process of interviewing governesses—if one isn't of good enough fortune to have a recommendation, then one must turn to the public." The young woman shoved a bite of ham into her mouth. "And I'm sure you would agree that the best the lower classes produce aren't suitable for the care of a *pig*!"

I beg your pardon. I care very well for my pigs and would prefer them any day to your little darlings. Jessica sat, unaffected. This woman was not worth the energy it would take to be offended.

"Anyway," the woman continued, "he arranged for a trip, and guess where?"

"I couldn't imagine," Jessica said, unable to envision another hour with her, much less an entire holiday!

"The Riviera, that's where. Isn't that just dreamy?"

"Mmm..." she responded in a flat tone.

Try as she might, Jessica could not turn the conversation from the woman's life. She had to force herself to listen to the details of a luxurious home and gardens. The absurdity of it all ran through her mind. *Just who was it that built the home and carved the statues that decorate it? What does she do besides live in it? And who tends those beautiful gardens? To whom should the credit belong?*

The woman had not asked a single question of Jessica after obtaining her name. She began to understand Grace's frustration with this society. Never would she impress this league, nor did she foster any desire to do so.

Mrs. Winterfield remained preoccupied with others at the table, laughing and chatting. Jessica felt considerable gratitude when the numerous courses ended and they were invited to enter the ballroom.

Her family and the Winterfields reconvened as the large orchestra played warm-up ballads. The first dance started at nine o'clock.

Counting her present blessings, Jessica was grateful that their father had taught them all the dances they would need for tonight's program. And she breathed a sigh of relief when she realized neither she nor her sisters were engaged for the first dance.

Olivia Winterfield instructed her daughter to introduce Grace to each of her prospective dance partners, while she paraded off with Jessica, ready to put her on display.

Jessica put one gloved hand over her eyes in embarrassment as she was pulled along by her hostess. What sport Olivia was about to make of her.

Mrs. Winterfield's desires were well satisfied with the introduction to the first dance partner. Jessica watched with astonishment as he struggled to contain himself, but there was no mistaking the bulging of his eyes and the stuttering in his voice. Just as Olivia had predicted, he begged for another dance, and, as planned, she brushed him aside, leading Jessica to the next victim on the list.

"Oh, this *will* be an amusing evening," Olivia said under her breath. "I only wish I could introduce your other two sisters."

Jessica was not quite sure what to think of the whole escapade. She didn't care that any of these men were being made into a mockery, but despised being a party to the scheme. Repeating her sister's words in her mind about 'when in Rome,' she trailed along, convincing herself it was only one evening that would soon be over.

As the night progressed, Jessica found at least the music inspirational. She delighted to have her sisters nearby while dancing and wondered if she herself looked as elegant. She would have enjoyed the dancing more had her partners remained silent. They were handsome, as Grace had reported last summer, but their conversation was even more mundane than the woman with whom she had dined. In similar manner, they talked of nothing but themselves in never-ending boasts and constant comparisons against their friends, who somehow always came up lacking. How relieved she was when her father's name came up on her card!

"When will this night be over?" she whispered to him.

He laughed.

"How did you put up with this when you were young?" she wanted to know, certain he was aware of the spectacles she and her sisters had become.

"I knew no different. What I've seen tonight is what I expected."

While John talked with Jessica after the dance, he heard the stern voice of an older man behind him.

"Mr. Everett."

He had not been called by that name for years and was caught a bit off guard. He turned to find a stout gray-haired man, whom he recognized as one of his father's old associates and a Member of Parliament, Paul Eastman. Two other gentlemen stood by his side. It had been more than thirty years since he had last seen Mr. Eastman.

John concealed his recognition of him.

"Or should I say *Lord* Everett?" the man continued. "How surprised I am to find you among my associates this evening." He did not offer his hand.

John gave no reply.

"And what, may I ask, *Sir*, has aroused your interest in this society after your abandoning us so many years ago? Perhaps the passing of time has caused you to reconsider your view of us. Or could it be something as simple as your father's estate that has induced your return?"

"I beg your pardon," John replied. "It's not my intention to show *any* interest in this society. Though not obliged to answer your questions, with few exceptions my view of you and your people has not changed. Furthermore, your attention to my parents' estate, by most standards, would seem somewhat intrusive. My mother's barristers no doubt handled her assets *however* she wished them distributed. Now if you will excuse me…" John took his daughter by the hand and escorted her from the scene.

"Father," she whispered, "what did that man mean by calling you *Lord*?"

"At this moment, nothing at all."

Later, while refreshing themselves at the punch bowl, Grace and Catherine talked of their dance partners. The unexpected voice of a young man came from behind Grace, startling her even more when its owner touched her elbow. She turned to find he was none other than Stephen Sutton! Astonished, this time it was *she* who spilled her punch down the front of *him*.

"Oh, I'm so sorry!" she gasped, scrambling to find a cloth.

"I suppose I deserve it after shocking you with a cold shower of punch last summer."

She handed him a napkin and attempted to help him with another.

"Perhaps we should stop meeting at the punch bowl," he said, wiping his black jacket.

"Well, at least our form of greeting is unique."

After being introduced, Catherine excused herself.

"I apologize for disappearing without saying good-bye at the dance last summer," he said. "I'm delighted to find you here this evening. Are you engaged for the next dance?"

"No, I'm not." She handed him her card.

Perusing the long list of names, he groaned, then smiled. "It seems the next dance is one of the few free, so would you do me the honor?" Bowing, he held out his hand. As he led her to the floor, she gave her arm a light pinch, ecstatic to find she was not dreaming.

The music began, and the room around her seemed to disappear as she became lost in his eyes. Even the sound of the orchestra faded away. Her single awareness was the touch of her hand in his.

John Viana was making his way through the crowd when a middle-aged woman stepped into his path.

"Excuse me," she said. "My friends and I were just noticing what a striking resemblance you have to an old acquaintance of ours, the late Margaret Everett. In fact, one of them remarked that, had she not known better, she would've mistaken you for Margaret's son, John."

"Well, Mrs...?"

"Dover. Charlene Dover."

"Mrs. Dover, I'll take that as a compliment. I've heard John Everett is a dashing fellow. Please give my regards to your friends. If you'll excuse me..." he smiled and sidestepped past her.

Jessica had forgotten all about Roman Winterfield until she again read his name on her card, which gave her heart a little jump. The time for her to accompany him to the dance floor arrived in all its splendor. She had spied him earlier in the evening surrounded by women, of course dominating the conversation. One young lady in particular seemed in complete awe of him, and Jessica assumed her to be Miss Landly. He had glanced Jessica's way as she passed, his gaze following her as he fell silent. She could not quite discern the look in his eyes, whether it was disdain or simple hatred. She had smiled in a mocking sort of way and moved on.

The gaze of several young men fell upon her as Roman approached and bowed. In silence, she took his hand, refusing to look at him.

Facing him on the dance floor, she awaited the start of the music, focusing her attention on anything but her partner—the other couples, the orchestra, the room of marble around them. She scanned the gathering for any familiar face when she noticed her father. Then she smiled. He winked and smirked again. Holding his glass up to her, he turned away.

She felt Roman's eyes fixed upon her. Keeping her posture upright, she continued her inspection of the crowd, observing Grace talking with a gentleman whose back was toward the dance floor and Alexandra with a handsome, but no doubt empty, young man. The music started, and the dance began.

She remained silent until Roman spoke, which she knew was inevitable. He would not have etched his name on her card had he nothing to say to her. That their eyes should meet was a requirement of the dance. She complied, even offering a polite smile.

His first words surprised her. "You look striking this evening." To her amazement his soft voice complemented the music. He took her right hand in his, and they turned in a half circle.

"Thank you." It would have been proper to return the compliment, but his mild tone did not excuse his past behavior.

"However, don't think I reserved this dance for the purpose of praising you, Miss Viana." His tone sharpened to match his expression.

"That thought had not crossed my mind," she retorted in a similar tone, "so I must admit you have piqued my curiosity, Mr. Winterfield."

"My purpose is the intention of setting matters straight between us, since we'll be sharing the same household for at least the next two weeks."

Will he be staying that long? Perhaps she could coax her father into renting accommodations elsewhere for the rest of their visit.

"I'm offering you a friendly warning," he continued. "I'm not a man to be mocked and will not tolerate ridicule by subordinates like you, such as was heaped upon me two nights ago."

"I'd rather hoped, Mr. Winterfield, that you would have considered the words I 'heaped' upon you. They were intended as a warning to you for the consequences that a man such as yourself may well face one day." Once the words were out, she wondered whether she should have unleashed the anger that now blazed in his eyes.

"Your behavior toward men of class and respectability is offensive, Madame."

"My father is such a man, and *he* takes no offense to my behavior. Therefore, I must conclude that it is only arrogant men who allow themselves to *be* offended."

They turned in opposite directions, following the rhythm of the music, and glided around and behind the dancers beside them. Then they faced each other once again.

"Is your father *really* such a man?" The anger in his face gave way to vengeance. "Is a man who has concealed his true identity from his own daughters considered respectable? What of a man who has hidden himself from his own family and society?" They linked hands and turned. "Is a man who has withheld a fortune from his daughters a man of class? Your father is a coward, a liar, and a cheat! His entire life is one of deceit. It's no wonder he has produced such a disrespectful and inconsiderate brood as you and your sisters."

"My father…" They dropped hands, turned in a circle, and faced one another again. "…is a hard-working man of integrity," she replied in a sharp, yet low tone so as not to draw attention. "He would never slander another person, even a bitter enemy if he had one, as you have just done to him, Sir! It's obvious you know nothing about my family and even less of decency and goodness." She refused to take his hand again. "I see no reason to continue this pointless exchange, Mr. Winterfield. Please be assured that I will not be in your way. Between the expanse of your father's house and its grounds, we need not cross paths again." She whipped around without excusing herself and left him on the dance floor. "Evil man!" she muttered to herself, making her way through the crowd.

How could anyone hurl such accusations against her father—a man who, to her knowledge, had not a single adversary, with the possible exception of this egotistical society? To be disgraced in such a way by his former community, and the son of his very good friend—what a disappointment! After this evening's events, she no longer wondered why her father had left these people. She could not wait to leave them herself.

Her anger grew hotter still for allowing herself to be drawn into such a conflict. Recalling her similar encounter with Edward Scarborough, she could not have imagined one day being grateful for that unpleasant experience. Yet it had prepared her well for the more formidable Roman Winterfield.

In need of some cool air, she headed toward the veranda doors and slipped outside. With a jolt she met the chill of the night as the door closed behind her. The sounds of the party were muffled as she took a few steps toward the banister.

Without warning, a deep voice from the shadows to one side startled her.

"Have you tired so soon of the dance?"

"Oh!" She reeled around, but saw only a dark figure sitting on a stone bench just out of the light's reach. "I'm sorry. I didn't intend to invade your privacy, Sir. Please excuse me."

She turned to retreat back inside.

"And how do you find the society here?" he asked, jumping to his feet and stepping toward her.

"Well…," she said, turning back. Failing to think of even one complimentary word and still angry, she stated, "I don't wish to injure the feelings of any person, but since you asked, I'm obliged to say that this is the most presumptuous, self-centered, and snobbish group with which I've ever been associated, and my parting cannot arrive soon enough." What did it matter now who she offended? For the second time she excused herself, having no intention of entangling herself in an argument with another of their society.

But once again he would not allow it.

"Why is it you think you find *me* out here, concealed in the shadows?" he asked, after laughing out loud.

Her eyes were beginning to adjust to the darkness, but still she could not make out his facial features.

"My mother is doubtless seeking me at this very moment," he continued. "She's been harboring a vicious plot of promoting a romance between me and a certain young lady."

"I understand that's a common practice among your people," she replied, "perhaps one which has its advantages as well as its disadvantages."

"Yes, well, in this case the disadvantages prevail, but, it seems, in my eyes only. All other parties are in agreement."

"Might I ask what protests you have against the lady?"

"No doubt the very ones that drove you out into this night air." In the shadows she thought she saw a smile form on his lips. "Why is it you didn't finish the dance with Roman Winterfield? Perhaps you're unaware of his notoriety among his contemporaries. To them, he's a man of mystery and intrigue, one whom no woman feels worthy to approach." He stood and began walking away from the doors, holding out one arm for her to join him. "He's untouchable in the eyes of the ladies and, because of his powerful personality, is intimidating to many of the men. To be invited to dance with such a renowned man is an honor indeed. Yet, you seemed in agony on the floor with him."

"The women of your society may keep Roman Winterfield," she replied. "I pity the one who aligns herself with such a man. Indeed, he himself is to be pitied. Admiration for the qualities of another is noble, but this worship of a man who is without compassion, principles, or conscience is pure idolatry. It sickens me." Her eyes dropped in sudden shame. Never before had she been so forward with a complete stranger. To criticize his society was uncivil. Her tone softened. "I've been taught from infancy to value the feelings of others and never to be hasty in forming adverse opinions of them. And so I apologize that my words have expressed inconsideration of your people in general."

She was getting quite chilled. However, since feeling more comfortable with this man than with the group inside, she decided to stay with him a bit longer. She was surprised when he removed his coat and placed it over her shoulders.

"It sounds as though you were also taught the value of honesty, and your sentiments are an expression of your sincere observations. No offense is taken." He placed his hands behind his back as they continued their stroll across the veranda. "Your parents must be admirable people."

"I lost my mother when I was a child. I don't remember much about her."

"Were you raised with a governess?"

Her answer lodged in her throat. A truthful response would disclose the fact that her family belonged, not to the elite, but instead to the common working-class. Such would no doubt end their conversation. But were that to be the case, so be it.

"No," she said in a firm tone. "My father raised and taught us himself with the help of a married couple who live with us." There it was. Working-class families often joined together in one residence to assist in the raising of children.

"Then I praise your father for the fine principles he has instilled in his children. It's indeed a rare occasion to find a woman who can speak out with honesty about the transgressions of society. I admire such a quality."

She was caught by such surprise she did not know how to respond!

"Well, then, I'm afraid you must have many opposers," she managed to say. "I, too, have seemed to collect a fair share in this community."

"That's another reason you find me out here this evening. Although not as bold in expression as you seem to be, I've not conformed well to society's demands, and so at times find myself a bit of an outcast. Oh, but my mother does keep up her endeavors on my behalf. I credit her for her attempts."

Their conversation continued for some time. "Oh, goodness!" she exclaimed. "It must be getting late. My father will be searching for me." Excusing herself, she returned his jacket and rushed back to the dance hall entrance.

They would not be meeting again, as she would be leaving the area soon with no intention of returning and, as such, saw no need of asking his name. She would remember him as the only decent acquaintance she had made at the ball. In silence, she thanked him for softening an otherwise unbearable evening.

Just after Jessica closed the veranda doors behind her, Olivia Winterfield whisked past her without even a hint of recognition, a young lady in tow. Jessica spun around and watched as Olivia flung open a door to the veranda and called into the darkness outside.

"Andrew, I know you're out there! Come in here at once!" After pausing for a moment and receiving no response, she closed the door and stomped away with the young lady, continuing her search.

Jessica stared in amazement. The young man with whom she had conversed for almost an hour was Andrew Winterfield—the very one whose portrait she had admired, whose logs she had read with wonderment, the one whose virtues had been extolled by his sister! How had *he* been at the ball? She recalled his mother's mentioning that he was across the Channel and would be there for some time. Yet here he was!

As a guest in his house she would doubtless be seeing him again now.

Unable to wipe the smile from her face, she pranced over to where her father and sisters had gathered, but said not a word of her interlude with Andrew Winterfield.

Chapter Ten

The large clock in the second-floor hallway announced the arrival of the one o'clock hour. Jessica flitted about her bedchamber as she undressed, knowing it would be some time before she would be able to sleep.

Donning her cotton nightgown, she sneaked down the hallway to Grace's room and slipped in.

"Oh, Jessie, this evening had a most wonderful outcome!" Grace whispered, excitement lighting her face.

"We saw so little of each other among all those people. Tell me about it!"

"Most of the night, I noted many familiar faces from my visit last summer, faces that I would have been content to forget." Grace paced about the room, pulling a brush through her flowing hair. "I made the most of it, however, and enjoyed the dancing. But about eleven I met up with the man I told you about last summer!"

"Stephen Sutton?" Jessica giggled with excitement.

"I looked for you everywhere so you could meet him for yourself, but couldn't locate you *or* Alex. At any rate, we enjoyed a few dances together. I thought I would faint, Jessie! It seemed like a dream. He's the same as I remember—very polite, a bit shy, a perfect gentleman—and even more handsome. I was engaged for several dances, but he waited for me! We talked for a bit after that in a quiet corner, and then he said he had to go. He'll be leaving on business early in the morning and will be gone for several weeks. As sorry as I was to say good-bye to him, I was so elated to see him at all!"

"Then you'll not be seeing him again before we leave Kent? Too bad." She tried to think of a way Grace and Stephen could meet again. "Perhaps you could stay on here as Catherine's companion."

"I wouldn't dream of imposing on the Winterfields. Besides, I've not been invited."

"I suppose you're right."

"I gave Mr. Sutton our address at the post office in Bristlecone and told him he could write to me there."

"Then I'll not be surprised to find a letter waiting for you upon our return."

The two laughed together.

"Oh, I hope so! Now tell me of your evening, Jessie."

"Not much to speak of." Rather than relate her meeting with Andrew, she would wait to perceive his reaction to her when he discovered she was a guest in his home. This was quite a different setting, and she could very well find his personality contrary to the one he had presented at the ball. Depending upon his actions, there might be no need to tell anyone of their meeting. "Except, of course, I had the pleasure of dancing with Roman Winterfield." Jessica smiled, hoping her sarcasm showed in her expression.

"*You* danced with Roman Winterfield?" Grace's eyes widened, disbelief shadowing her face. "Jessie, you should've heard how the ladies raved on and on about him. They reveled in the fact that he was there and were even more excited to learn he was still single. How was it that *you* danced with such a revered man?"

"He etched his name on my card," she replied. "See for yourself." She handed the card to her sister and sat on the edge of Grace's bed.

Grace examined the handwriting. "Well, it's no surprise to me that he wished the hand of the loveliest lady in the entire assembly. Perhaps it was so he could arouse a bit of jealousy in the others. Your being a stranger would certainly have added to the intrigue."

"I assure you, Grace, that was *not* his intention. He did compliment me on my appearance, but at once stated his true purpose was to grant me a 'friendly warning,' as he called it, that behavior such as mine would not be tolerated."

"No doubt referring to the counsel you bestowed upon him the other night, which *I* thought was warranted."

"When I informed him that Father gave me no reproof, he went on to accuse him of some dreadful things. He said our father has done us great injustice by deceiving us about his and, therefore, *our* true identities. He added that, by withholding from us family connections, Father had cheated us out of a large fortune. Grace, what would be the motive for such an attack on a man he doesn't know? And what is he talking about? It makes no sense."

Grace lowered herself to sit beside Jessica. "As for the fortune, I'm certain our grandmother's estate was dispersed long ago, and as regards our true identities, I imagine that the senior Mr. Winterfield knows about our history and has passed some of that information on to his family. Roman no doubt came to conclusions of his own. However, that doesn't excuse his behavior and attitude toward you *or* Father. I'm sorry you had to be subjected to his abuse."

"I care not what Roman Winterfield thinks of our family." Her arms crossed her chest as she looked away. "He doesn't deserve to know the truth. However, an unrelated incident has left me a bit baffled. I was with Father when one of his former associates approached us. In a scornful voice, he called Father *Lord* Everett!"

"What did he mean by that?" Grace gasped.

"When I asked Father that very question, he said it didn't matter. Who *are* we, Grace?" She stood and paced to the dressing table, pulling the pins from her hair. She turned back to her sister and sighed. "Tell me about Alex and Catherine. Did they enjoy themselves?"

"One young man in particular seemed to pay attention to Catherine," Grace said. "He was handsome. They would make a nice couple. His name was Gregory Westcliffe, I believe."

"I think she would be wise to turn and run as fast as possible from London. It seems any *real* gentlemen have already done the same," Jessica said, then laughed with her sister.

"Good night, Grace. I won't wish you pleasant dreams, however, since thoughts of Mr. Sutton are certain to forbid you getting any sleep."

They laughed again before she tiptoed back to her own room.

As she snuggled under the down quilt, her thoughts remained on her father and what dreadful things he must have suffered during his lifetime. He had been a loving and attentive parent, and she would allow no slanderous report to dissuade her loyalty to him, regardless of how the situation appeared to outsiders.

Her thoughts then drifted to her conversation with Andrew Winterfield. He was somewhere in that very house, unaware of her presence. What a surprise awaited him!

She thought of what his life must be like and drifted off, dreaming of sailing the oceans and of the storms at sea he had described in his writings.

Jessica rose with the sun, but remained in her room, recalling her words to Roman about keeping herself out of his way. But how was she to see Andrew were she not to breakfast with the family?

A hurried knock on her door answered her question. It was Catherine.

"Jessica, did you hear the news? My brother Andrew was at the ball last evening, though I never saw him. Mother said he arrived without notice just after the dancing began."

"Your brothers seem to enjoy surprising your parents."

"It does seem that way, doesn't it? Andrew told Mother his plans had changed, and he was in London just for the night. He came to the dance to see us, but disappeared when Mother began her escapades with Miss Berkshire. I didn't even get to see him." Catherine sounded very distressed.

Jessica sympathized. "How disappointed you must be!"

"Mother sounds very angry with Andrew for his disappearance last night," Catherine continued. "She didn't meet up with him again until early this morning when my brothers informed her that both of them were leaving for France. Roman made a sudden decision to join Andrew on the ship, and they're now gone. Mother may not see Roman again until she joins him in Austria in April, and we don't know when Andrew will return. I'm just so hurt my brother didn't wish to see me."

"I'm sure, Catherine, he would have seen you had circumstances been different." Jessica recalled that he had spoken to her about a younger sister he adored, but his business kept him away much of the time.

After Catherine left the room, Jessica tried to sort out her thoughts. Thrilled that Roman had decided to depart earlier than expected, she wondered whether she had had an impact on his decision. But her heart sank to think she would not be seeing Andrew again. Yet, she supposed, it was for the best. She had had no expectation of ever meeting him anyway. She would just have to leave it at that.

However, during the week that followed, Jessica spent much time in the family library, again surrendering to her thirst for adventures aboard *The Emerald*. The captain's writings etched themselves into her heart, as though letters written to her alone.

The remainder of January slipped away, and the last few days were spent at the Winterfield's beach front property near Ramsgate, where it was cold and overcast. Jessica, bundled in warm clothing, strolled with the dogs or rode the horses along the beach with the other girls.

She often found herself gazing into the mist of the Channel, her mind entranced by memories of Andrew whenever she caught sight of a ship. But yielding to reason, she dismissed her meandering thoughts of the second Winterfield son.

At night, fog rolled in from the Channel to hide the landscape. Even the glow of the full moon could not penetrate the soupy haze. The four girls shared two bedrooms and slept under the warmth of thick feather-filled quilts with the windows cracked open. The distant sound of foghorns and bells on the buoys comforted Jessica, reminding her that the time had arrived for her family to return home.

The journey west would be long and difficult. John's small family huddled under warm blankets in the carriage that took them to London's train station. Soft rain pattered the windows. He listened as his daughters talked of the adventures they had experienced.

They were returning home with many new things—trinkets and souvenirs they had picked up in the numerous shops; gifts from Catherine and Olivia; new clothes, shoes, and jewelry; a bottle of the perfume each had worn to the ball; and, of course, their glamorous gowns, packed with the utmost care in new trunks, also bestowed by the Winterfields.

"Father," Jessica said, "although we may seem consumed with all these material goods, most precious to me are the memories of the grandest holiday we've ever had. I can only speak for myself, but the things I'm taking home will only serve to spark my remembrance. Thank you." She leaned over to kiss his cheek.

"And despite the snobbery of Olivia Winterfield and her many connections," Grace added, "as was true last summer, there were plenty of good-natured souls around every corner of our ventures."

"I've missed the Wrights," Alexandra added.

They all agreed.

Yes, John was sure they would talk of their journey for years to come. As they discussed all the events, he listened with keen interest to their expressions, seeking to discern the general impression of each and knowing it would take some time for their thoughts to settle.

The carriage kept pace through the biting rain. John nestled beneath the blanket, and as he began drifting into a sleep while listening to the rain on the roof and the gentle clinking of the harnesses, he realized his little family had reached a turning point. His girls would soon move on and establish their own lives, and the lighthouse would have served its purpose. He would be free to move on as well, but where would his path lead him?

Chapter Eleven

In preparation for Jessica's upcoming trip to France, the entire Viana household converted to speaking French, each member offering a friendly word with every meeting. Mrs. Wright prepared delicious pork medallions in creamy sauce, chicken and basil with cabbage, delicate pastries, and chocolate mousse.

"Very pleased to make your acquaintance," Alexandra said one day to Jessica in French after a near collision with her while rounding a corner.

"The pleasure is all mine," came the French reply, followed by a curtsy. "Could you please direct me to the most handsome gentleman in your town?" Jessica giggled.

"Oh, I would be happy to, Mademoiselle. He's perfect for you, your match in every way," Alexandra said, kissing her fingertips. "His name is Roman Winterfield." The words barely escaped in French before the two burst out laughing so hard they had to hold their bellies. Alexandra continued the charade, still laughing. "Oh, what a fine pair you'll be, and what beautiful children you'll produce."

"Indeed, they'll be just like their father—rude and offensive to all they meet," Jessica joked. "The little ogres of the neighborhood, they'll be called. How proud their father will be."

They chuckled and smirked when their own father entered the room. "It appears that *I* have produced the little ogres," he said in perfect French under his breath as he passed them.

"Jessie, I think you'll do just fine in France," her sister said in English before bursting out in more laughter.

"Except for the homesickness I'm sure to suffer."

"Six weeks is a long time. But here's your chance for adventure, Jessie. Three weeks in Paris and three weeks in Nice! You'll have no time to miss us."

"Oh, Alex," Jessica said, glancing around the corner before continuing, "do you think I should be leaving Grace, feeling the way she does? I'm so disappointed Mr. Sutton hasn't written."

"It's as you reminded her…the man said he has a very hectic business schedule. Don't despair. After all, he waited for her during all those dances! I'm certain she'll be hearing from him the minute he has time to write. She'll be just fine, you wait and see."

Jessica was not so sure.

A damp chill permeated the March night in Plymouth, the usual midnight fog shrouding the empty streets. One lonely soul made his way from the pub back to his second-story flat, wandering in darkness between the dim street lamps and muttering to himself.

Edward Scarborough stumbled up the stairs and into his tiny flat. He lit an oil lamp, and a small, untidy room appeared. The furnished quarters had been provided by his uncle, as had his employment at the print shop since last fall.

He sat down hard on the desk chair and glanced into the mirror that hung on the plain wall above it, his thoughts fuzzy, the music from the pub still ringing in his ears. A pitiable and wretched face stared back at him. Looking down, he turned his hands over and back, the ink stains that covered his fingers and seeped into the crevices of his knuckles and around his fingernails holding his gaze.

"Six days a week!" He threw one floppy arm into the air. "Fourteen hours a day. And all for what? A measly two pounds per fortnight!" He stood, weaving, then fell back onto the chair. "Oh, Eddie-boy, you sure know how to live it up!" His head dropped as his fingers ran through his hair.

The one day out of seven he did not work was spent in prolonged slumber. Tomorrow would be that day.

Although Plymouth was a city rich in history and culture, he viewed it as a living tomb, draining the life from him. He had come to loathe his drab existence.

Pulling an inkwell toward him, he picked up a pen and opened a drawer to withdraw a piece of stationary. He would write to his father and request the opportunity to accept his offer of schooling, and the drink had provided the courage he needed. For two years he had resisted his father's wishes, more interested in play than education. The preceding summer, his father had given him the choice between school and work at the printery. When he chose the latter, he didn't understand the difficulty of the work involved, and as he examined his uncle—a middle-aged man, ragged and worn and almost deaf from working the machines for so long—he realized the folly of his choice.

As he reached for a sheet, another item caught his attention. Underneath the box of stationary was the unopened document he had heisted from the man alongside the road the previous summer. It had been thrown in the drawer along with some other papers several months before.

"Good for nothin' but kindlin'," he muttered. Rising from his chair, he steadied himself. Then he stepped across the room to the cold hearth.

A chill seeped through his overcoat. He shivered, rubbing his arms. He lost his balance as he leaned over for some firewood and stumbled onto his knees. Grabbing two small logs from the dwindling stack, he tossed them onto the grate.

Prior to rolling the document to light one end, he peeled off the wax seal. The top portion of the papers unfolded, and his eyes were drawn to three words—*My Dear Son*.

"Well, well, well, what have we here?"

Pressing his back and one palm against the wall, he eased his body upward before unfolding the letter. Three pages long, it was written in a shaky hand and dated some two years prior. He squinted to read it.

My Dear Son,

If you have come so far as to read the first sentence of this letter, I only ask that you do not discard it. The information contained herein is of a crucial matter.

It has been many years, and not a day passes that a thought of you does not enter my mind. I have often thought of what you used to be, who you used to be. You had so much at your disposal. The stars of the heavens would have bowed in subjection to you. Your father, having been an Earl, left to you his title, along with his fortune and property. The whole of England would have been your footstool. Under your direction, this society would have improved. With your concern for the poor, you would have profited the entire country.

This is the reason, my son, that when you have entered my mind these past years, a seething hatred has accompanied my memories of you, an unforgiving and irreconcilable anger. Instead of choosing the course laid out for you—handed you—you turned your back, not just on your community, but on your family, your father's good name, and your very heritage. Choosing not to bestow your talents and efforts on your homeland, you instead sacrificed them to an unappreciative people, a people who no doubt squandered your intelligence. Although an extension of this great Kingdom, Ireland has brought much shame upon it. The Irish are a disdainful people and care not to improve themselves, giving ill regard to the restoration of their land. How despicable that, instead of leading your people, you chose to follow theirs.

This disgrace was exceeded, however, when I heard the news of your chosen bride, whose heritage was not only Irish, but equal in Spanish descent! A marriage for you would have been acceptable had you allowed your family to arrange for a suitable match. But to enter without the Everett blessing into such a union with a commoner and pollute your posterity was unjustifiable. Your fine family name was then dishonored.

Yet the wound gouged deeper still; it cut to the very heart and soul of the one who bore you, for you ripped from me the one and only child I ever birthed.

I am writing you these things because now you are older and wiser, and perhaps can grasp the understanding of a blow such as the one you inflicted upon me.

That is how I felt for years, John, at the mention of your name. It sickened me to my very inward parts.

However, now, Son, I no longer feel that way. No, now I have been dealt a blow of a much different nature. I am ill with an affliction that will end my life very soon. Over the past several months I have been faced with matters and emotions that I did not recognize before, which have caused me to reevaluate my entire life course.

What I have discovered may well surprise you. I have found that it is I, John, who has become wiser, for I have come to understand you. I now see that my life has been one of narrow-minded prejudice, arrogance, and condescension toward others. Today I detest the woman I have been. My vile conduct and thoughtless treatment of others is inexcusable. I suffered from the most shameful type of pride—that I could better other people, when instead I should have allowed others, in particular my own son, to better me. In pressuring you to become your father's replacement, I succeeded in driving you away from your people and from me. I accept full responsibility for your decision to leave.

I realize this letter may never reach you, in which case my life in most of its entirety will have passed in vanity. However, it is with the smallest sliver of hope that I am writing to you.

There are two missions I hope to accomplish through its employment. First, it is my fervent wish to gain your full and unrelenting forgiveness for the disappointment I became to you. Second, and most important, I would like to restore to you the most valued treasure you have ever had in your life.

As evidence of this priceless possession I present the enclosed keepsake. Please contact my barrister and your friend, William Sutton. I am in dire hopes that I am not too late. Please know I love you, my son, and feel deep and earnest sorrow for the pain I have caused in your life.

Your Mother,
Margaret Everett

At the bottom of the last page was a London address of barrister William Sutton.

Edward's hand dropped. He was perplexed by the disclosures and what it could all mean. However, the hour was late and his faculties blurred by drink. The note to his father would wait for another day. He left the letter on the desk, stumbled into bed, and faded into a heavy sleep.

The following day he sat down at his desk and read the letter again. Although nursing a headache, at least he was now cognizant. He pulled a small box toward him, which contained various trinkets. Fumbling through them, he pulled out the ruby ring, twirled it in his fingers, and wondered what significance it lent to the puzzle.

During the weeks that followed, Edward pondered the message in the letter, reading it again and again. An obvious fortune awaited the owner of the ring. Margaret Everett was a familiar name. He recalled his father reading aloud from a newspaper article about her death some time back, and about her estranged son who had disappeared years before. But who *was* this man? The messenger carrying the letter and the ring had no doubt been in search of him and may even have narrowed down his whereabouts to the Land's End area. Edward was quite certain the son had not yet been located, for news of the estranged Earl's return would be quick to spread. This man must have no desire to be discovered. Something valuable, indeed, would be required to tempt him out of hiding. The letter revealed very little about him. His given name had been disclosed, but Edward could think of at least five men named John or Jonathan in his locality. However, none were former residents of Ireland, and all had married *English* women.

As a thought occurred to him, a grin traversed his face. *Of course! The odd man who tends Brentwood Lighthouse!* The eldest daughter was of obvious Irish heritage, and he recalled the youngest daughter mentioning that her mother was part Irish. Also, the family carried a Spanish surname, though he could not account for the reason, since the man was English. Although unable to fit *all* the pieces together, he had no doubt that John Viana was, indeed, John Everett.

He also felt quite certain that he, Edward Scarborough, was the only one from Cornwall County, besides John Everett himself, who possessed the knowledge of his secret.

Chapter Twelve

The early spring had been more harsh than usual, and frequent storms battered the rocky coastline. While the air grew warmer with every passing day—and none welcomed the gradual changes more than Jessica and her family—nights remained difficult. Jessica's fingers often grew numb, even inside the lighthouse tower, as she carried the load of fuel to the top of the column, pouring it into the thirsty well. Just as it did during winter months, the cold slowed the progress of all the work at the island.

One stormy March night, while Alexandra and her father were on duty, she burst into the house, calling for Mr. Wright in near hysteria.

"A ship!" she cried as he tried to calm her. "A wreck...out on the rocks...a few miles out! Grace, Jessie! The boat, Mr. Wright! Father said to send you three with the fishing boat while Mrs. Wright and I prepare food and bedding for a dozen men!"

Grace jumped to her feet in an instant. Within seconds she had one arm in her oilskin coat while Mr. Wright moved at a pace quick for his aged frame.

Jessica froze.

"Jessie, *quick*!" Alexandra exclaimed.

But her feet refused to budge. It was as though her shoes were nailed to the floor. She could do nothing but pant, her heart racing. Pressing her fist against her breastbone, she said in a shaky voice, "Go with Grace, Alex."

"But Father said—"

"Go! Now! I'll help Mrs. Wright."

124

With the other two already gone, Alexandra stared but a moment at her before racing out the front doorway. She left the door open in her haste.

Two hours later, the sitting room appeared more of a soldiers' camp than a civilized home. Soaked clothing was strewn about the room. Ten dazed and shivering strangers, wrapped in wool blankets, sipped hot coffee or paced the room or sat in quiet shock.

Jessica dashed from room to room, assisting her sister with a hot bath or attending to other needs of the men. She stopped now and then to listen to an account of the shipwreck or of family at home. She had not noticed the absence of her father until Mrs. Wright whispered in her ear.

"You asked for me, Father?"

She found him sitting behind the desk in his study, but could not look into his eyes. Her head hung as the door clicked closed behind her.

It seemed a lifetime before he spoke. When she lifted her eyes, she saw his face was turned away, as though he could not look upon her.

"Two of those men almost lost their lives out there. Why didn't you come?"

"I'm sorry, Father."

"Apologies are useless in this situation, Jessica!" His fist pounded the desk. To hear anger in his voice was rare, and this was the first time to her recollection that she had ever been the object of his outright fury. "I asked for you. *Why didn't you come?*"

"I sent Alex in my place."

In an instant he was on his feet. "You know you're stronger than your sisters!"

"No, Father! I'm not strong! I couldn't move! I couldn't go!"

"You keep a lighthouse, Jessica! Lives are in your hands. What would you have done had you been here alone? *Let them drown?*"

"No! I don't know!" A tear slipped over her cheek. "I don't know…"

"Others depend on you to answer that call. This suffocating fear of yours will no longer be tolerated. You've risked the lives of others …and have brought me great disappointment."

She could bear his anger better than the calm that now overtook his voice. He sounded as though he had lost feeling of every sort for her. Unable to listen to another word, she fled from the study and up the staircase to her room. Closing the door behind her, she fell onto her bed, her chest heaving with sobs.

A few minutes later, she heard a soft knock, followed by a footstep on the floorboard inside her room.

"You're going out on the fishing boat with me tomorrow, regardless of the weather."

She twisted around. "No, Father!" What had come over her? Never in her life had she challenged him. She cherished him and had always obeyed.

"I've done you no favors in ignoring this matter. You *will* come with me. And you will do so every day until this passes."

"*Please* don't force me!"

His back was to her. "It's my responsibility. I'll shirk it no longer."

He stepped over the threshold and was gone.

After hearing the click of the doorknob, she was deluged with sobs, almost unable to breathe. All she could think of was her mother and the fear she must have experienced as the cold sea engulfed her so many years ago. She envisioned her desperate struggle, calling for aid as countless others around her succumbed, all helpless to escape their fate.

Had she been knocked unconscious by some debris, never knowing the terror of taking her last breath? Or did she tread water for a time before submitting to exhaustion and relinquishing the fight? What had filled her mind as water filled her lungs and she watched the sea's surface rise above her sinking body?

How could something as wondrous as the sea, so often tranquil and beckoning, be so violent, so unforgiving?

Jessica buried her face in her arm, the bedding soaked from her tears. What was wrong with her? Why were her sisters not given to such fear?

She fell into a fitful sleep, horrific visions filling her dreams. But rather than her mother, it was she herself fighting the onslaught of vicious waves.

As spring blossomed forth, Jessica often accompanied her younger sister on rides through the countryside. They frequented meadows carpeted with flowers, trickling streams, and roads favored for their spectacular views.

When the time arrived for her to pack for the journey to France, she was grateful to the Winterfields for the spacious chest they had purchased for her in London. The journey would be long—down to Portsmouth, across the Channel to Le Havre, then on to Paris. She found sleep impossible the night prior to her departure.

The morning was a jumble of emotions—tears from Alexandra and elation from Grace. She herself struggled with the part of her that didn't want to leave her family.

But it was her father's response that brought her own tears forth. As she wrapped her arms around his neck and kissed his cheek, rough with stubble, he enfolded her in a long embrace. Squeezing her eyes tight, she recalled the time when she was no taller than his chest. His large hand would engulf her head, pulling her against him. She wished she could recall the last time. When was it she had reached his shoulder, and then his ear?

"I'm so proud of you." His deep voice pulled her back to the moment.

"Thank you, Father," she answered, pulling away to look at his face. His eyes told her he knew she was thanking him most of all for escorting her out on the fishing boat. They had sailed—not far enough to lose sight of the lighthouse—several times in varying weather. Conquering the ocean swells had not cured her of her fear. No, he told her it would always be with her; but he helped her prove to herself that she was stronger than the fear.

"Let it live," he had said then. "It'll keep you humble. But *you* are the captain of your life. Never let *it* command you."

Smiling and waving as the carriage pulled away, she called out a promise to write as often as possible.

The late-April air was cool, but the skies were a deep blue and the sun warm on her face. Soon the carriage arrived at the depot in Penzance, where she joined the Thompsons. They reached Portsmouth within a few hours by train.

Jessica had not been on a large passenger ship since she was four years old, when her family set sail to England. Of that journey she recalled little. During the few jaunts she had taken out on the fishing boat with her father, the land never left her sight. Her nerves were eased by the fact that she would not be sailing on the open ocean, and the trip across the Channel would be brief, quite unlike her mother's, which was four times the distance and in dangerous waters.

The port bustled with people, crowds passing, masses moving here and there, and ships and boats casting and docking.

As they hurried along the dock, Jessica looked up and saw in the distance what looked more like a building than a ship. It reached far above the warehouses on the wharf. Large white letters spelled the name of the passenger liner, *Napoleon*. Tall cranes transferred luggage and supplies onto its deck, where men hauled it below at a feverish pace. While waiting to board the ship, she fought and prevailed against the visions that had haunted her for most of her life.

Jessica and the Thompsons soon found themselves high up on the top deck, waving to the figures below as the ship pulled away. Although not knowing a single person on the dock, Jessica was caught up in the spirit of the people around her who called out good-byes to loved ones, some crying, others laughing, hats and handkerchiefs flapping from the hands of many.

Before long Jessica strolled the decks with Mrs. Thompson, the breeze in their faces, talking of the sights they would see, the museums they would visit, and the people they would encounter. Jessica brought the fashions she had acquired in London, excited to once again wear her evening gown.

Mrs. Thompson, a frequent traveler, described outdoor markets and cafes, little bands and solo violinists on cobblestone street corners playing ballads to passersby. Lush parks where lovers strolled at sunset, fine dining, exquisite shopping, carriage tours of the city, large manors, and country vineyards would be among the many points of interest they would enjoy.

Jessica tried to imagine herself in Paris, the city of romance. She could not picture herself involved in a rendezvous with a handsome Frenchman. But Grace had been quick to point out that romance often occurred at the most unexpected places and times. Jessica smiled, recalling her sister's words. It was Grace who should be visiting Paris, she thought.

But perhaps not, for just prior to Jessica's departure, Grace had received a letter from Stephen Sutton, who apologized for not writing sooner and explained he had been involved in a grueling course of study. He assured her it was now over, and he would be able to write more often. No, Grace would not fully enjoy the travels with her mind so preoccupied with thoughts of the Englishman. Jessica would not feel bad to be going instead.

Time sped by as they enjoyed the cool salty breezes. Jessica heaved more than one sigh of relief when the often rough waters of the English Channel remained placid. She even relaxed enough to be amused by the gulls that soared over the liner to nip from the air the cubes of bread tossed by the passengers on deck.

As the sun set, she tightened the ribbons on her bonnet. Although most of the passengers retreated into the dining hall, she stayed behind to watch purples and pinks overtake the broad sky. Perhaps sailing the ocean was not so bad when it offered such magnificent views.

The sea breezes reminded her of being atop Old Stormy. Already, she felt homesick. How she wished her sisters could have come along to share her experiences!

She joined the Thompsons in the dining hall after the cool air caused goose bumps to skitter across her arms. They finished their food just before a purser announced that the ship would be docking. Her hosts had arranged for an overnight stay in Le Havre, and it was well past midnight when, weary from travel, she fell into bed. She still could not believe they were on French soil.

In a half-dazed state, as the dusty light of morning entered her room, Jessica heard the voices of two servants in the hallway. At first she did not comprehend the words. But stirring to fuller awareness, she recognized their French phrases, recalling with suddenness her location.

Soon they were traversing the countryside by train, en route to Paris. They would stay in the home of a friend of the Thompsons, who was away for the summer. Although they would not be visiting the wine country of Bordeaux in the southwest, Jessica spied a vineyard or two along the way. No doubt she would have the opportunity to sample the produce from the famous southwestern wineries.

A cobbled drive brought them to the front door of an ivy covered stone chateau. Jessica stepped from the carriage and approached the porch. Large shade trees sent speckles of sunlight dancing over its floorboards when the breeze fluttered their leaves.

The cozy house sat on the edge of a small town near the outskirts of Paris. The bed in Jessica's room was covered with embroidered pillows. She fell backward, sinking into the feather-filled quilt, gazing up at a white linen canopy. Forcing herself up to wander out two French doors before unpacking, she stepped onto a half-circle stone patio shaded by thick forest and encircled by a short stone wall. Her eyes closed, she took a deep breath, smelling a faint aroma of pine.

Trying to absorb it all without missing any detail, she spun around, her arms trailing through the air. She overflowed with excitement over the upcoming events. They were to dine in the village that evening, and their adventures would begin the following morning. First, they would tour the massive palace of Versailles and its grounds. Other delightful activities would highlight the weeks that followed.

Jessica returned inside her bedchamber and struggled to pull one large trunk atop her bed. It brought back memories of her trip to Kent. She must have been the most fortunate girl in all the world to have embarked on such fabulous journeys!

After her garments had been folded and placed in the drawers of the bureau, or hung on hooks in the wardrobe, she stretched her arms overhead. There was still time for a brief stroll in the forest.

Mid-May found the remaining Viana family busy caring for Old Stormy. Unrelenting winter storms and wind forced needed repairs, and a thorough cleaning of Brentwood House had begun. The gardens required tilling in preparation for spring planting. The work was more difficult with the absence of one.

Grace thought often of her sister and what a glorious three weeks these must have been thus far. She walked out to the railing of the lighthouse crown overlooking the sea. Eager for an intermission from her work, she pulled her sister's letter from her dress pocket.

My Dear Family,

Paris is much more than I had ever imagined! If I could only find the words to describe its splendor. Our activities have not stopped since our arrival. Even now I am sitting outside the Louvre, awaiting Mr. and Mrs. Thompson to complete their tour. (I brought some stationary along today in hopes of taking a short break to write.) The air is warm and pleasant today.

Oh, the sights to see! We have toured the Palace, museums, and castles, much of the countryside, parks, and marketplaces. Oh, and the two small islands on the Seine in the center of the city—remember reading about them?

If you could only see the sculptures, paintings, glasswork, and architecture! And the food—*magnifique*! The bakeries, sidewalk cafes, and wines! It's just too much to describe!

I am disappointed in only one aspect—that of social gatherings. I was hoping for more opportunities to flaunt my beautiful ball gown. However, I will be able to do so at the theater tomorrow.

The people I have met seem very pleasant. The women are glamorous, very stylish. They have soft voices and kind smiles. The men are handsome but perhaps a bit forward. I find their flirtatious demeanor a touch embarrassing. But I must admit I am drawn to the beauty of the language. Even teasing remarks have a melodious tone. It is more difficult than I had imagined, however, speaking and thinking in French every day. That is wearisome, and I speak only English with the Thompsons.

Another unique aspect here is the enchanting music. Soloists on the street corners can be heard now and again as they captivate the people with the whine of the violin or the sweet hum of the accordion. It is, as reputed, a very romantic place.

We have a few more days here, and then off we'll be on the journey to Nice. I promise to write from there. I long to be with you again, and am most hopeful that work at home has not proven too difficult.

Yours, Jessica

"They must be on their way south by now," Grace said aloud, tucking the letter back into her pocket.

Jessica and the Thompsons reached Nice as planned after a scenic, but uneventful journey. The sun felt warm as she strolled with Mrs. Thompson along the boardwalk in the early afternoon.

Upon returning to their villa, Mr. Thompson handed a telegram to Jessica. "It's from your father." His face held a look of concern.

She read it at once, untying the laces of her bonnet with one hand as she held the post in the other.

> All are fine. Pressing matter requires your immediate return. Pack one small case. Have requested Thompsons bring remainder. Arranged your escort to Marseilles, Pier 16. You will port in Chatham. Richard Winterfield to schedule train passage to Bristlecone. Father

Terror struck her. What could it mean? Nothing but the utmost urgency would cause him to interrupt her holiday in this manner!

At once, Mr. Thompson began organizing her trip to Marseilles. His wife did her utmost to calm the distraught Jessica.

Chapter Thirteen

The following day Jessica hugged the Thompsons farewell. She had packed one small trunk and would retrieve her remaining belongings in three weeks from them at their home in Penzance. The cool early morning air sent a quick chill through her body. Or was it the anxiety?

The carriage pulled away, and she was alone. She would have several days in which to dream up every imaginable horror awaiting her at home, not to mention the sleepless nights that would be filled with worry and fear.

If that were not enough, she could not even *think* about the fact that she would be sailing on open waters! Trying to remain calm, she repeated to herself that the ship would no doubt be following the shoreline. But any reassurance, slight as it may have been, vanished upon her recollection of the small cargo ship that had crashed on the rocks only a few miles out from Old Stormy. No, being close to shore was no comfort. Recalling her father's admonition, she knew it was time to prove that she was, indeed, stronger than her fear. Otherwise, she could not survive the next several days.

Focusing her thoughts on the wonderful experiences she had had in Paris, she reviewed the details she would relive with her sisters. She had purchased a beautiful brooch for each and had packed them with tender care in the small trunk that accompanied her.

The telegram had reported her family was fine. But if this were so, what was the pressing emergency that required her immediate presence at home?

Lost in her thoughts, she did not notice the passing of

time. Before long, the carriage pulled to a halt at the wharf in Marseille.

She pressed against the seat, her body stiff. Closing her eyes, she drew in a deep breath and with slow precision let it out. She would be brave, and the journey would go just fine. "I'll be home in no time at all," she whispered to herself. Gratitude for her father's insistence on their outings in the fishing boat washed over her.

Assisted by the coachman, Jessica stepped out of the carriage and stood with her head held high. He climbed atop the coach and struggled to unload the single trunk. After he steadied the trunk upon his shoulder, Jessica followed him down a long ramp to the docks below. She looked with trepidation at the busy pier, where countless men hauled large loads of cargo onto several waiting ships.

Her heart sank. She saw no other passengers.

Reality struck her. She would be spending the next several days on a *cargo ship*! Once again she took a deep breath and stood erect. Her father had made the best arrangements possible for her, she was certain. She, in turn, would complain as little as possible.

The coachman still ahead of her, she walked across the planking of the dock toward a ship at the far end. As they approached the vessel, she stopped and stared in amazement. Written in large white letters on its hull was *The Emerald*.

She stood, recalling once again the writings in the logs she had read while in London, of which she had reminisced now and then during the past several months, along with the one conversation she had had with their author. The deepest impression she had received from the logs was that the captain of *The Emerald* was a competent and trustworthy seaman. Her fears melted away as she proceeded on toward the ship's ramp.

The coachman spoke with a ragged, burly man who appeared to be about her father's age, although life and hard work at sea must have robbed his countenance of any semblance of youth. Time had etched hard lines around his eyes and mouth.

His sharp Irish brogue evoked vague memories of the land of her birth.

"Been expectin' ya, Miss. Name's Harry McGuire."

Jessica smiled at the man.

"Right this way, Miss." He stooped over and lifted Jessica's trunk, hurling it onto one shoulder in a quick swoop.

She bid her coachman good-bye and hurried along behind Mr. McGuire, up the ramp onto the ship. "Are you the First Mate, Mr. McGuire?"

"Nah." He spoke as he walked. "That was Jacob. Ol' Jake abandoned us just this mornin' after a run-in with the captain. Jake said he's livin' by double standards. Ya see, one of the captain's rules has always been 'no women on board,' no matter the reason, and well…here ya are, Miss." He looked back at her from time to time as he walked on. "I heard 'em bickerin'. Captain said wasn't nothin' could be done about it. Said it was orders from his father. He owns the ship, see. So, Ol' Jake said he wouldn't sail with him no longer. Said sittin' in a port unemployed was better'n sailin' with a hypocrite. Me? I think he was just lookin' for any old excuse. Sailin's never been in his blood. So Captain paid him his due wages and that was the last I saw of him. But you needn't worry, Miss. Second Mate Matt Clark is a fine sailin' man, and, well, ya couldn't ask for a tighter ship. She's seen a lot'a years, but *The Emerald* looks and feels brand new. A real gem. Fittin' name, I s'pose." He laughed.

He led her across the deck to the bow of the ship and down a narrow stairwell.

"And Captain Winterfield—well, Miss, ain't no better captain on the seas. He's a good man. Keeps a bit to himself, but I s'pose that's how it is when ya got so much cargo and so many men in yer charge."

"Well, I hope all the men are as friendly as you are, Mr. McGuire."

"Call me Smiley. Ever'body else does. Guess it's b'cause I like almost ever'one I meet. Don't have a single enemy that I know of. Well, here we are, Miss." He opened a small door on the second deck. "Captain said to give ya *his* quarters. He'll be bunkin' with Mr. Clark. Not as fancy as what yer used to, I imagine, but it's comfortable."

The stateroom was tidy and well lit from two round windows on one wall. She took in the room's furnishings. Most were simple—a soft-looking mattress under the windows nestled into a wooden frame attached to the wall by heavy brackets; a large desk beside the door with an inkwell and pen; several books behind a short railing fastened above; and two brass gimbaled candlestick holders affixed to the wall on either side of the desk. A small table rested next to the bed with a candle and small clock sitting atop. On the wall opposite the bed was an ornate mahogany wardrobe with large mirrored doors. She wondered if it had been acquired by one of the Winterfield buyers. Along the length of the wall at the head of the bed was a high shelf brimming with books. Like the ones above the desk, a short wooden railing held them in place.

All the Winterfields must like to read, she thought.

"We'll be castin' off within the hour, Miss, so make yerself comfortable. I'll be bringin' supper to ya in a few hours." He set her trunk beside the wardrobe. "We have one stop t' make on the way. It'll be a few days b'fore we reach Chatham. Just make yerself at home."

Jessica thanked him again for his hospitality before he stepped out and closed the door behind him.

She shook her head, not quite believing that she was aboard Andrew Winterfield's ship and occupying *his cabin*! His reaction upon seeing her would no doubt be one of complete surprise, for she had not introduced herself at their casual outdoor meeting in January. Even if his father told him the name of the unexpected passenger, he would have no reason to suspect it would be her.

Yet, perhaps *she* would be the one to be surprised, for she had not 'seen' him at their meeting. Even after her eyes had acclimated to the darkness, she could not discern his shadowed features. Of course, she had seen his portrait in his father's library, but would the likeness be accurate? Would she recognize him? Perhaps he had forgotten all about her by now.

Oh, the anticipation was maddening!

All at once a horrible thought crossed her mind. What if 'Captain Winterfield' was Roman, not Andrew? What if the two had tired of their positions in the company and had switched stations?

She laughed off the thought at once. After all, had not Mr. McGuire described the captain as a good man? And Roman would *not* treat a man like Smiley McGuire with decency.

Jessica sat on the edge of the bunk and gazed around the small room once again. Her hand covered her mouth as she yawned. The emotional turmoil of the previous twenty-four hours had left her exhausted but sleepless. Without so much as removing her shoes, she fell back onto the down mattress. Rolling to her side, she pulled her feet upon the bunk as well.

A faint manly scent entered her nostrils as she closed her eyes.

Jessica awoke to a light tapping on her door. She opened her eyes to near darkness. Remembering the candle on the stand beside the bed, she reached over to light it.

"One moment," she called out, sharing the flame with the candles on the walls. When she opened the door, the friendly face of Mr. McGuire greeted her.

"Came by earlier, Miss, but got no response. You were out like the lamps. Decided to come back later."

She felt the soft rocking of the ship on the waves. They must have been sailing for some time. Her usual reaction would have been one of panic, but as long as the sea remained calm, so could she.

"What's the hour, Mr. McGuire?" She yawned. "Excuse me."

"Around eight, I think, Miss. I brought ya some eatin's."

She looked down and saw he was holding a small bowl of porridge. Reaching out to touch the bowl, she found it stone cold and withdrew her hand at once.

"Mr. McGuire, would you be so kind as to take a message to your captain for me?" She would put Mr. Winterfield to a small test.

"I will, Miss."

"Please inform him that, as a guest on his ship, I request steamed vegetables and a pot of tea."

"Yes, Miss," he answered, looking down at the floor.

"One other thing, Mr. McGuire. Please inform him that his reputation is one of a man of integrity and decency. How does he expect a hard-working crew to achieve proper nutrition from cold porridge? I insist he feed his crew a decent meal that includes meat and milk."

"Yes, Miss," he muttered. Then he turned and left with the untouched porridge.

Andrew Winterfield sat on an empty crate at the makeshift desk he had set up in Mr. Clark's quarters, taking an account of the cargo that had been loaded in France. Two lamps flooded the cabin with light.

The door cracked open and Smiley McGuire poked his head through. "Excuse me, Captain, Sir."

"By all means. What is it, Mr. McGuire?" Andrew replied, looking back at his work.

"Well…uh, Sir…it's the lady. She…well…she said to give ya a message, Captain." He swallowed and then blurted out, "She prefers vegetables and tea for her meal."

"To what?" Andrew did not look up.

"Sir?"

"She prefers vegetables and tea to what?" he inquired, continuing the examination of the documents before him.

Rather than reply, Mr. McGuire slid a bowl under the captain's eyes.

Andrew stopped his work and stared at the cold, hardening slop before him. Feeling a chuckle well up in his throat, he pursed his lips and managed to suppress it. He gave Mr. McGuire a serious look, his eyebrows raised in question.

"I had nothin' to do with it, Sir," Smiley stated. "Was just followin' orders in takin' it to 'er."

"Whose orders, Mr. McGuire?"

"Cook's."

"Orders come from the captain, Mr. McGuire, not the cook."

"Yes, Sir."

"Take this slop back to Mr. Harrison, and tell him I order freshly steamed vegetables, a few slices of bread, and a warm pot of tea for our guest. Did she have any other requests, Mr. McGuire?"

"Just a message for you, Captain, Sir."

"Oh? And what was that?"

Smiley cleared his throat. "She says a man of integrity like yerself should feed his hard-workin' crew meat and milk, Sir."

Andrew placed the ink pen upon the desk and folded his arms across his chest. "Is that so, Mr. McGuire? And did you explain to the lady that, just this afternoon, you had your fill of stew loaded with vegetables, potatoes, *and meat*?"

"No, Sir."

"I see. Perhaps you should also relate to her how, in one sitting, you devoured nearly an entire loaf of bread yourself. Now it's a fine woman, indeed, who expresses concern for the crew who has been so quick to belittle her, would you not agree, Mr. McGuire?"

Smiley nodded, looking down.

"Now please expedite the order to Mr. Harrison."

Smiley took the bowl from the table, turned, and pulled the door closed behind him.

Captain Winterfield stared at the door for a moment. When sure that Mr. McGuire was out of earshot, he let a low chuckle skip from his throat while he shook his head.

The hour was late by the time Jessica finished her meal. The captain was indeed a man of humility and apparent integrity as well. Not a single question had been posed, nor any objection raised to her demand.

Still wide awake after having slept so well earlier, she walked about the small cabin. Her gaze was drawn to several manuals on the desk. She recognized them as more of the captain's logs and pulled one leather-bound volume down just to read the date inside. It was a recent journal, covering the time from November through March.

Curiosity crept into her mind. Had the captain mentioned anything about his meeting her on the fifteenth of January? She supposed not, reconsidering her question. These journals were not for personal notes, but rather for the purpose of recording the activities aboard the ship. Besides, she could not bring herself to pry into his writings any further. She had invaded his privacy a great deal already.

On the other hand, the journals she had read disclosed the author's feelings about many things, and no doubt this journal would wind up in the Winterfield library with all the others, exposed to any Winterfield guest. Once again, her curiosity got the best of her. She felt sure their meeting would not be mentioned anyway. She turned to the date of the ball. The entry was short.

> 15 January, 1872, 10.00 a.m.
> Casting off from LeHavre. Change in plans. Load larger than expected. Will make a quick run to Chatham, unload, and cast off again by 6.00 a.m. tomorrow.

She heard a knock on the door. Jumping up, she closed the book and returned it to its place.

"Yes?"

"Just checkin' on ya, Miss, before retirin'." It was Smiley.

"I'm just fine, Mr. McGuire. Thank you."

She heard his footsteps and whistling fade as he disappeared.

She returned to the journal.

> 16 January, 1872, 3.00 p.m.

The day after they had met!

> Without any notice Roman joined our journey back to the mainland. Put him up in Mr. Clark's bunk. He has been sleeping all day. Will drop him in southern France, next port.

Find myself feeling a bit out-of-sorts entire day, perhaps due to lack of sleep—have slept few of the last 35 hours. But in reality, I think, due to meeting a beautiful and intriguing woman. Who was she, anyway? Am regretting more and more my neglect in not asking.

That was it! No more was written that day. Jessica bounced with excitement in the chair as she scanned subsequent days for other comments about the mysterious woman. She was disappointed to find nothing more. Turning back to the sixteenth, she read the last three sentences over and over. Could the entry have been written about another woman at the party the previous night? She hoped not!

"This may, indeed, result in an exciting adventure," she said to herself and the book on which she again noted that faint masculine scent. Smiling, she extinguished the candle.

At ten o'clock the following morning, Smiley McGuire once again disrupted Andrew Winterfield. The captain had risen at five to check the equipment and the ship's location. A stiff, warm wind from the south filled the large sails on their masts, driving the ship at a comfortable ten knots. He had returned to his administrative work at six-thirty.

"Excuse me, Captain, Sir."

"Yes, Mr. McGuire? What can I do for you?"

He liked the old chap. They had been sailing together for at least a year now, and he had yet to hear a word of complaint from the sailor. He was a hard worker, and one, Andrew suspected, who would die on the sea an old and poor man, the rope of a sail in his hands, or perhaps an oversized crate balanced on one aged shoulder.

Andrew paid him a bit more than he did the other hands, but still the salary was meager, and who or what did he have to spend it on anyway? The man had no family to Andrew's knowledge, and he never spoke of any dreams he had for himself. He seemed quite content just to work hard on a sailing ship. It was his life. He appeared to be happy as long as he was at sea.

"It's the lady again, Sir." He wrung his white hat in his hands. "Seems she's gone off wanderin' about the ship. Just saw her sneak down the hatch to the hull, and well, Sir, the cargo bay could be a dangerous place, if I may say so, Sir. She could get hurt down there."

"Thank you, Mr. McGuire, but remember she's a passenger, not a prisoner. She's free to explore any part of the ship she chooses. The cargo bay is very safe. All crates are secured, are they not, Mr. McGuire? You checked them yourself."

"Yes, Captain, Sir."

"I believe we only need worry if we see her go overboard."

Smiley smiled, nodded, and excused himself.

After the sailor departed Andrew pondered, *Why is she sneaking around the ship? She knows not whether she could be hurt. The entire crew could be at peril were she to tangle herself in some rope or were her dress to catch on something. This one seems a troublemaker. I may next hear she has climbed her way up to the crow's nest! Why did I ever agree to this fiasco?*

Jessica had made her way to the bottom of the ship and into the hull itself. She had brought along a candle on her expedition and employed its use upon descending the dark, steep stairwell. A few high windows lined the top of the vast, shadowy bay. Streams of dusty light sprayed onto column upon column of crates and trunks stacked in neat rows. They seemed to stand a mile above her head.

The only noises she heard were the loud creaks and groans of the burdened ship as it rocked through the waves. Recoiling at the damp, musty air, she wandered down a main corridor, peering up at the mysterious crates. This all seemed familiar in a strange way, though she could not recall ever being on a cargo ship before.

Standing in the stream of light from one of the windows, contemplating the familiarity of her surroundings, she was startled by a voice from the shadows behind her.

"This is no place for a lady."

She stopped in her footsteps without turning around. Chills climbed up her spine and spanned the length of each limb.

"I apologize, Captain. I was feeling a bit cooped up," she responded, her back still to him.

"How is it that you know I'm the Captain?"

"Because we've met before, Sir." She turned around.

As she came into his full view, he gasped and took a half step backward, deeper into the shadows. "My father's message said only 'the daughter of a friend.' Please tell me...*who is your father*?" His words came to her in a whisper.

"John Viana."

"John Viana?" he repeated. "John Everett! *You're John Everett's daughter*?"

"I am, Sir."

"Then...how nice to meet you...for the *third* time, Miss *Jessica* Everett."

"My father prefers Viana, as do I. What do you mean, the third time? And how do you know my first name? If you know my father, then you would also know that he has *three* daughters."

"Do you mean to tell me you've forgotten our first meeting, Miss Viana? No, it was *not* the night of the fifteenth of January. We met as children. Allow me to refresh your memory. Your father came to Kent on business. You and your older sister were with him. You were but four. I was ten. The three of you met my father at his warehouse office. As they discussed business, I was to supervise you and your sister. At once, you disappeared into the warehouse amidst the columns of crates, playing hide and seek with an all too unwilling playmate. I could not keep up with you, as you were at all times several steps ahead of me. I followed the sound of your laughter and kept calling your name, but you thought it was a great sport. When I did catch up to you, I grabbed you by the hand and escorted you back to your father. Had you climbed into an open crate and become trapped when its lid closed you in, you could have been lost for good. You had no idea of the danger, and scared *me* to no end."

"Then it's no longer a mystery as to the reason this 'warehouse' seems so familiar to me today. As musty and dingy as it is, I'm not afraid to be here, no doubt because my memory was that of being in a pleasant place of laughter and play. What a fine supervisor you made then…as you do this day also."

He remained silent.

"That's not the only coincidence in our meetings, Captain Winterfield. It seems I'm at quite the disadvantage. You see, I don't remember your face as a child, and each time we've since met, although I've been in your full view, you've been hidden in the shadows. So you see, I can't recognize you even if I *had* remembered you."

One step, then two, brought the tall captain into the dusty sunbeams. Jessica looked up at his face. His features were strong yet kind, his lips full, eyes deep-set, jaw square. His dark hair, neat and trimmed and with a slight wave, matched his eyes in color.

"No, Mr. Winterfield, I do not recognize your face." His portrait in the family library did him no justice, for his was the most handsome face she had ever seen.

"Let me introduce you to my ship so you'll be familiar with it the next time you decide to venture out." He smiled and held one hand out ahead of them, while placing the other behind his back. "She's a tea clipper, a smaller version of the typical clipper ships, able to hold much cargo, and yet is lighter and swifter. She's twenty-seven years old and was built in America."

"Is that so?"

"She was a gift from an associate of my father's when he first started the business."

"Your father is a good man. I met him in January," she said as they walked.

"At the dance?"

"Oh, long before the dance." She looked up at him. "We were guests in your home the entire month."

"A guest…in *my* house? Had I only known! I've been curious as to your identity since our meeting at the dance." He stopped and began laughing.

"I fail to appreciate the humor, Captain."

"To put it in a nice way," he said, recovering, "you seem to have made quite an impression on my brother."

"Oh…yes." Why did he have to spoil a pleasant conversation by bringing up the ogre? They began walking again. "Mine was a reaction quite the opposite of what he's accustomed to from other ladies, I'm sure," she said. "I must admit to some curiosity, though. How did he describe me?"

"Let me think…as a belligerent, outspoken, crass brunette. I believe that was his assessment."

"*I* was crass? Quite the contrary, *he* was crass with me from the outset." She paused and then added, "Well, you already know full well my feelings on *that* subject from our conversation on the veranda. I suppose this would be a good topic to abandon before I find myself in trouble."

Her comment brought forth his quick laugh.

Soon the bright sun of the deck warmed their faces. The sea breeze fondled their hair and clothing.

"So, why not a steam engine?" Jessica asked.

"What?" As Andrew looked at her, his brow crinkled.

"Why has your father not replaced his fleet with steam ships? That seems to be the current trend."

She was pleased with the smile he gave her as his head twitched to one side.

"Steam engines," he replied, "although more powerful and faster, make for very heavy vessels, and the engine alone devours a large portion of the hull. Also steam requires a continual supply of fuel, which in turn, requires additional space, additional crew members, and adds even more to the weight of the craft. So the ship is nearly twice the size and affords little additional room for cargo."

"I see." Jessica glanced up at the massive sails. "The tea clipper is compact and swift and is still well-suited for the job. Wise business decision."

Andrew smiled.

The two spent the remainder of the morning together before he excused himself, explaining that the ship required his attention. "I would be honored were you to join me for dinner, Miss Everett—excuse me, Viana," he said before they parted ways.

"Only if you'll be serving porridge."

He laughed. She felt his gaze upon her as she turned and disappeared down the stairwell to the second deck.

The following morning found *The Emerald* docked on the southeastern Spanish tip and the crew busy loading additional cargo. The work completed and the hour still early, the captain gave the crew a two-hour leave, while he stayed aboard and prepared the payroll.

Smiley McGuire poked his head into the captain's cabin. "Gave the lady her breakfast, Captain, Sir."

"Thank you." He counted out several coins for Smiley, then paused and looked up at the sailor. "Mr. McGuire, may I ask you a question?"

"Ask anythin' ya like, Sir."

"Mr. McGuire…Smiley…Just curious. In the year or so you've been on my ship—"

"Eighteen months, Captain," he interrupted.

"Eighteen months…you've purchased for yourself one new pair of shoes and two new shirts. I provide your oilskins, your meals, linens, soap, and razors. You seem to have no fondness for drink or tobacco. You seldom leave the ship, even when I give you permission. Please forgive the intrusion, Mr. McGuire, but what do you do with your income?"

"I send it to my daughter, Sir."

"You have a daughter?" His brows arched at the statement.

"Oh, yes, Sir, and a wife. But I'm afraid, Sir, that though they like to see me money, they don't much like to see *me*."

Andrew sat in silence.

"Ya see," Smiley continued, "I married as a young lad, younger'n you, Captain. Oh, she was a pretty little Irish girl, the finest ya ever set eyes on." A wistful smile crossed his face at the mention of her. "But I found I couldn't stay with 'em. Oh, I tried to see 'em as much as I could, but b'fore long, they adjusted to livin' without me…without any man, I s'pose."

"Why? What happened?"

"Ya see, Sir, just as some get on a ship and b'fore long they get dizzy and start to turn green—you've seen the look, I know ye have—then they get sick. Well, that's how it is when I'm ashore too long." His eyes narrowed. He gave Andrew a stern look. "I've a need to feel the waves beneath me feet, the salty air on me face." His hand balled into a solid fist. "I need that rush ya get when yer outrunnin' a storm." He thrust a burly arm toward Andrew, under side up. "See them blue veins? That's not blood in them veins, Captain." His voice dropped to a whisper now, and he stated with serious eyes, "It's the sea."

Andrew stared in silence at the husky arm.

"Don't let that happen to you, Sir. This ain't no life for a man like yerself. Find a decent lady and settle down. You don't wanna be a prisoner, Captain. You'll be just like me. There'll be no turnin' back." Smiley nodded once at his captain, leaned over, took the coins from his hand, then turned and left the room.

Andrew sat and stared at the empty doorway, then with sadness at the void beyond.

"Too late."

Jessica wandered about the ship after they cast off again in the late morning. She stood at the starboard railing, watching the ocean waves disappear in a mist on the horizon. Filling her ears was the rushing sound of the water as the ship cut its surface and the waves slapped against the hull. Besides the gentle rocking, this was really no different than standing atop Old Stormy. What did she have to fear?

Tilting her face upward, she studied the high white sails. They were taut, but the wind sent ripples across their faces, ending at the edges in little whips. With goose bumps rising on her arms, she retreated to her cabin.

When alone, her thoughts returned to her family. Worry again settled into her mind. Placing one palm against her belly in an attempt to calm the churning that started again, she forced her thoughts in a different direction and instead relived the time she had spent with the captain the previous evening.

The meal had been as tasty as any she had had while in Kent. Even he had expressed surprise at the appetizing courses and commented on it several times throughout the evening.

She had had second thoughts about dining alone with him—whether or not it was proper—and almost requested that they dine with the crew. However, the majority of them did not even glance her way. It seemed they avoided her on purpose. When she did offer a greeting, they would grunt and keep about their work. Rather than taking offense, she understood their anger over her presence and expected nothing more of them.

One exception, of course, was Smiley McGuire, who appeared content to wait on her hand and foot.

So, in the end, she agreed to dine alone with Captain Winterfield, with an occasional interruption by Mr. McGuire as he served the courses and tended to their every need.

Their conversation came with the same ease it had on the veranda at the party in January.

"I've read so much about the sea and stand in awe over its power," she had said during the soup course. "One would think I'd take great pleasure in sailing its waves."

"Why then do I detect apprehension?" he asked.

"I'm sure you're aware of what happened to my mother," she said, trying not to conjure up her lifelong terrifying images.

"Let me tell you about my first experience sailing on open water," he said.

"Was it aboard *The Emerald?*"

"She's the only ship I've ever captained." As Smiley delivered a steaming loaf of bread with butter, Andrew continued, "Up to that point, I'd not ventured beyond the Bay of Biscay. My father didn't much like the idea of my taking his ship into the Mediterranean, but I was confident, reminding him I had an experienced crew backing me. With some reluctance he agreed, and we set sail, hitting the high seas. I knew of the approaching storm, but had faced many storms before. I thought it would be a good test for me; I would prove I was a capable captain."

"How old were you at the time?" she interrupted.

"Twenty-two."

"Say no more of it," she said, putting her hand up and wilting against her chair. What was his father thinking? He seemed such an intelligent man!

"I'm here, aren't I? It has a good ending," he said with an easy smile, "though to this day, I've not experienced a fiercer storm. That sea—this very sea—taunted me and laughed in my face that night. She tossed my ship about as a leaf in the wind. We fought her with our last bit of strength, and the next day how relieved we were to finally catch sight of land, though we were nowhere near our intended destination. We docked in the Canary Islands."

"Good heavens!"

"I learned a lot that night. Looking back, I can't be more grateful for that storm."

"How can you say that?"

"Because I came out of it a good captain. The sea hurled her worst and was unable to defeat me. But through the experience I learned respect. Because of that, I'll never underestimate her power. I'll always know she has the strength to crush me, but never will I allow her the upper hand." Declining a second helping of roast beef from Mr. McGuire, he slid away from the table and stood, holding out one hand to assist Jessica from her chair.

After strolling the upper deck for some time, they paused at the railing, she with her back to the sea, the wind twisting her skirts around her legs. In the moonlight, she watched his dark eyes settle upon the expanse of the black waters.

"She has many faces, this great Atlantic," he had said. "I learn something new with every excursion. And yet there's so much I don't know. So much I long to discover. I've seen but a drop."

Her thoughts brought her back to the present. It was at that moment, with those words, that a sudden realization had flooded her mind. From the time of her reading his journals she had known a strange and yet comforting attraction to this man. From the beginning she had discovered that she shared many of his loves, but it was not until she heard his words, standing there at the railing the previous night, that she understood in a frightening way the sea's hold on him. It was as though he were iron and it were a great magnet, pulling him—irresistible and unrelenting.

She shivered at the recollection.

The following day Jessica spent in solitude. The cool breeze whipped at her skirt and tugged wisps of hair from the bun at the nape of her neck as she stood at the railing of the stern, staring out over the watery expanse. The whole scene pulled her in. Now and again calls from the sailors hard at work on deck pierced through the whir of the wind.

Not wanting to appear that she was attempting to attract the captain's attention, though she had yet to see him, she stepped to a lower deck, away from plain view. After some time, she decided to return to her cabin.

Gathering her skirts in both fists, she trotted up the few steps to the upper deck, keeping her eyes on her feet so as not to trip. At the top of the stairs, she ran headlong into one of the sailors.

"I beg your pardon!" she said. Looking up, she was met with a scowl. He turned away after grunting.

"Two more days," she heard him mumble, not three steps from her, "and we'll be *rid* of ya!"

"Excuse me?" She could not help but challenge him and was surprised when he turned back to her. "I'm sorry if my presence has caused some undue hardship on you." She tried to sound pleasant, even though his comment had prompted the drawing of her sword.

"Hardship?" he hissed. His jaw, covered in stubble, tightened. "Larger-than-expected load, one man short, and rushin' just to get our little passenger home safe and sound...No, no hardship. Don't fret your pretty head over *us*."

He stepped away again, but his tone had been so accusatory that she could not resist a reply.

"What is your name?" she demanded.

He stopped where he was and spun about, casting his hot glare upon her. "Clark. Matthew Clark."

Ah, the new first mate! Somehow she had assumed he would be grateful for her appearance on his ship, since he was sure to receive a pay raise with the new position. She must have been wrong.

"Your assessment of the situation, Mr. Clark, seems one-sided, at best. Tell me just how it is I am responsible for the disappearance of your first mate. From what I hear, the decision to leave was his own. If anyone has the right to be angry, it's your captain, and it seems he's in no such state."

"*My captain*," his lip curled to expose several tarnished and broken teeth, "whose eyes are blinded by the wool you've pulled over 'em! Stay away from me," he said, pointing at her, "and we'll get along just fine."

With that, he stomped away and left her as angry as he was. Wanting to chase after him, tangle his feet in a rope, and hoist him to the top of the mast upside-down, she only growled and slammed her heel on the deck.

Once again, Jessica was invited to dine in the privacy of the captain's presence.

She had put the encounter with his first mate out of her mind long before, content in the knowledge that she would soon be rid of the whole situation!

It was only Andrew she would regret leaving, and maybe Mr. McGuire.

This time, the captain ventured to inquire more about her.

"May I ask why it is I find you aboard my ship?"

"I'm not certain I can answer that, Captain, as I don't quite know myself. My family's in some sort of trouble. Father's telegram wasn't explicit. I was on holiday in Nice when he summoned me home."

"I see. Then I'm certain you're anxious to reach port."

For the briefest of moments, she was anxious only to spend more time with the intriguing captain of *The Emerald*. But her mind turned back to her family's trouble.

"Tell me about your home," he continued when she grew silent. "I understand your family lives in Cornwall, but Father hasn't disclosed much about your father's vocation."

"We're the keepers of a lighthouse."

"Oh?" Instead of reacting with condescension, he seemed intrigued, and she at once recalled their conversation in January on the veranda and how he had responded upon learning of her social status.

"It was a humble upbringing, but one I wouldn't trade for the world," she said. "To stand at the crown overlooking such power is frightening, but my wonder over distant lands has almost prevailed over the apprehension I've managed to harbor these many years."

"Would it be fair to say the ocean is as much a part of you as you are of it?" he asked. "I think you wouldn't be happy apart from it."

She found his comment odd and, while not responding at first, supposed there was some truth to it.

"You may be right," she said after a bit and thought she saw a slight reddening in his face before pulling his gaze away.

"I have to admit my crew has never sailed the western shores of England," he said. "I don't know much about it."

"*None* of you?" She found that strange.

"It sounds ridiculous, does it not?"

"I'm certain your father has other means of obtaining Irish wares," she said after shrugging. "Perhaps there exists no reason to send *The Emerald* west. Your time is better spent at the mainland ports."

"You know, I'm astonished at your business sense."

"Don't be. Any understanding I have is only due to the tedious lessons on economy my father made us endure in our studies. I'd much rather hear about the sea creatures you've encountered. Now there's a subject of which I'll never tire."

It was late when he escorted her back to her quarters.

"Thank you for a pleasant evening," she said. "I appreciate your inviting me at the risk of disapproval from your crew."

"Most of the time I dine alone," he said. "On occasion I join my men, but more often than not, there's paperwork to do. I find it goes faster when coupled with a hot meal and an ale. You've spared me that monotony, and so *I* thank *you*." Before leaving, he said, "Allow me to remind you of one last port we have in the morning. And then we'll be on our way to England."

He bade her good night and disappeared into the darkness.

And now in a few fleeting hours she would be back in her homeland and on her way to Brentwood. It would be a bittersweet departure, for she was anxious for her family, yet when, if ever, would she see him again?

The following day eased into late afternoon, and Jessica had not seen or heard from the captain. Feeling she had distracted him from his work far too much and not desiring a run-in with Mr. Clark, she decided to remain in her cabin for the duration of the trip, using the time to write in her own journal. Now and then she would open his, reading again his thoughts of her.

No longer the 'mysterious woman' of intrigue, for a moment she almost regretted becoming known to him, but then dismissed the thought, thankful to have had the opportunity to be in his company and to confirm his character. Yes, he was just as she had thought while reading of him at his family estate—kind, fascinating, and oh how handsome! Several times during their dinners together, she had forced herself to look away, astounded that he had invited her to dine with him—

astounded with the whole experience. She was on a ship! On the ocean! And in the company of *Andrew Winterfield*!

Later, she watched the sunset from her cabin window, disappointed to have heard nothing from him. Orange rays broke through the overcast skies in shards. In a strange way the image mimicked her feelings. Her elation to be with Andrew was, like the sun, restrained by the gloom of the danger her family was facing.

A soft knock on her door interrupted the silence of her thoughts.

"Here with supper, Miss." Smiley's voice came from the other side of the door.

"Please come in, Mr. McGuire."

She grinned at the man of whom she had grown quite fond.

"Captain wanted me to tell ya he's feelin' a bit under the weather today," he said, setting the tray down. "Has been in his cabin since ten. Won't eat nothin'. Also said a storm's movin' in tonight. We have no choice but to get through it as fast as we can. Said to tell ya it'll be a bit rough tonight, and cold. Said there's a down quilt in the wardrobe ya just might wanna make use of." He opened the wardrobe and pulled it out for her.

"Do you think the captain is all right, Mr. McGuire?"

"Oh, sure. He'll be just fine, Miss. Just complainin' of bein' a bit feverish and some achy muscles is all. We'll be in England by mornin', and he'll be able to rest up a bit b'fore we cast off again. Well, I'll see ya in the mornin', Miss, if ya don't need anything else."

"No. I'll be quite comfortable."

He turned to leave.

"Oh…Mr. McGuire?"

"Yea, Miss?"

"I appreciate your kindness to me. I know the other men are quite put out by my presence and the loss of their first mate. You've made this journey very pleasant, and I thank you."

"Don't mention it, Miss." He closed the door behind him.

The sun was now gone, the colors fading into the grays of night. He had left a tray of meat and cheese, and as she ate, she thought of the immense fear of sailing that had gripped her just days before, and how Andrew had been able to quell that fear. A storm? It was nothing to him, her brave and competent captain.

Twisting her long hair into one thick braid, she tied it with a white sash and climbed into the bed, pulling the quilt up under her chin. She was becoming rather fond of the masculine scent of Andrew Winterfield.

Comforted, she dozed off to the gentle rocking of the ship.

Chapter Fourteen

Jessica awoke in complete darkness, aware at once of the loud howling wind and the pounding of rain against the panes. The violence was so great she feared they might break.

Her fingers fumbling in the darkness, she managed to light the bedside candle. The clock read three. Her pounding heart struggled to keep pace with her whirling mind as she pictured the ship tiny and helpless in an enormous, angry sea. She tried to calm herself by reassuring thoughts of its seaworthiness. Had not the captain soothed her dread, telling her how he had faced countless storms in all their brutality?

Without warning, a loud pounding on the door startled her. Mr. McGuire burst into the cabin.

"Sorry t' frighten ya, Miss, but ya gotta come quick."

"What is it?"

"The captain, Miss. He's doin' bad. Worse 'n worse all night. He's not respondin' t' me anymore. Mr. Clark said to come get ya. Thought maybe ye could help. Here, I brought ya some oilskins."

He helped her pull the protective clothing over her nightwear and grabbed her by the hand, dragging her up to the top deck.

Mr. Clark barked commands above the howling gale. Lightning broke open the sky like a shattering pane of glass. Thunder roared over their heads. Looking up, she saw the sails looming bone-white against the blackness, the edge of one flailing from a gaping tear. She squeezed her eyes closed. Mr. McGuire held her tight, leading her down another stairwell.

They entered a cabin, and Jessica rushed to where Andrew lay on a bunk underneath a small window, eyes closed, his head tossing to and fro. His bare arms and one side of his chest were exposed, the remainder of his body covered by a thin sheet. Jessica sat beside him. His face was clammy to the touch, his hair and sheet wet with perspiration. She pressed her fingers against his throat and detected a faint, almost immeasurable pulse. He mumbled some inaudible words.

"How long has he been this way?" she asked, her glance darting to the sailor, rainwater dripping from her soaked hair.

"Couple hours now. Started with just a few muscle aches, like I told ya this afternoon. Later he started complainin' that his legs and arms were crampin' hard. Since then he's just gone downhill."

"When did he eat or drink last?"

"All I know of is dinner last night with you, Miss."

"Mr. McGuire, that was over *thirty hours ago!*"

He shrugged.

"It could be cholera," she said, looking back at the captain. "I've read much about it but have seen it only once." She paused, then added, "The man died."

She stood to pace, stopping at the tiny window, frantic to recall the suggested remedies. All of a sudden, her eyes widened. Terror gripped her heart. She threw both palms against the wall on either side of the small window. Watching with eyes fixed on a distant sight, she shouted at Mr. McGuire. *"Where are we?"*

"Well...um...Mr. Clark isn't sure. Says we've been blown off course. Lost track several hours ago. He thinks we're now headed toward a harbor of some sort."

"Do you have opium or brandy on board?"

"I can get ye the brandy."

"Please...ask the cook to heat a pot of water with a bit of brandy and two spoons of salt." He turned to leave. "Wait! And several spoons of sugar—for taste. Give as much to the captain as you can, just a little at a time. Hurry, Mr. McGuire!"

Smiley dashed from the cabin.

Jessica leaned over to touch Andrew's pale, cold face. His eyes opened in slits and closed again. She tucked the damp sheet around his shoulders and rushed from the room.

Wrapping the oilskin coat about her body, she took a deep breath, her father's words from the harrowing night of the shipwreck pounding in her head. *You've brought me great disappointment, Jessica.*

She pursed her lips, heading up the stairs and out onto the top deck. The wind slammed her against the stairwell door as it banged closed behind her. The cold, hard rain slapped her cheeks like daggers.

She located Mr. Clark and headed toward him. Fighting to stay upright, she grabbed hold of ropes and railings along the way.

She reached him, and he gripped her arm. "Return to the captain!" he hollered, though his words were almost lost in the howling storm.

"Mr. Clark, turn south! You're in very dangerous waters here!" She struggled to be heard over the wind.

Lightning flashed all around. Jessica pulled her head down into one arm, wrapping the other around a post. To her surprise, she felt little fear, her mind focusing only on the ship's location and the ill captain.

"Return to the captain at once, Madame!" he shouted again.

"Mr. Clark, don't listen to me as a passenger, or as a woman, but as the keeper of *that lighthouse!*" She pointed to the faint light she had seen in the distance from the captain's window, which she had recognized as the unique white, then red pattern of Brentwood Lighthouse. The ship was now headed straight toward it.

He pulled her into a stairwell. Holding both shoulders and glaring into her eyes, he demanded, "What are you saying?"

"You're on England's southwestern coast. If you don't turn south *now*, we will—all of us—perish this very night! These waters are deceiving, hiding rocks that will tear this craft to shreds. *Please* take my word for it. There's no harbor there. Its light is a warning to *stay away!*"

Still grasping her shoulders, he shouted, "Go back to the captain!"

He released her and headed around the corner, bellowing commands to the men as he went. The massive sails began to change direction. She followed, watching him take the wheel from a sailor and force it to the right. The ship groaned into a turn.

She made her way back to Andrew's cabin, stumbling several times. Mr. McGuire had returned with the concoction. He was gripping Andrew's chin with one hand while attempting to pour it into his mouth from a tin cup with the other. Andrew fought the restraint and choked on the liquid. The majority ran onto the bed beneath his head.

Jessica searched the cabin and found two clean rags. She sat down beside Mr. McGuire on the bed and dipped one rag into the pot. As he held Andrew's head, she wrung it over his lips. Liquid trickled into his mouth, and he swallowed. Then she patted his skin with the dry rag. He began to relax.

The wind and rain continued its unrelenting assault on the hapless vessel. Before long Mr. McGuire stood. "Gotta get back to my crew now, Miss. I'll check back with ya when I can."

"Before you go, Mr. McGuire, will you please help me move him to the other bunk? Those sheets are dry." They wrapped the soggy sheet around Andrew's body, and each took an arm over their shoulders. After lowering him into the dry bed, Mr. McGuire removed the wet sheet and covered him with a clean one.

Jessica thanked him as he left the cabin, then administered more water and brandy.

How she longed to see the sparkle in his dark eyes, but he remained as pale as the sheet around him. Realizing the danger he faced, she laid her head down on the bed beside his arm and wept.

The first rays of sun streamed over the horizon and into the cabin. Jessica awoke on a blanket on the floor next to Andrew's bunk. She sat up and climbed to sit near him again.

Dark, broken clouds hung heavy in the morning sky. The storm subsided as rays of sun peeked through here and there. They had survived! The ship was intact! But when had she fallen asleep? *How* had she fallen asleep? By the sliver of the sun at the horizon, she calculated that no more than two hours had passed.

The captain remained in his feverish sleep, his pulse still weak. Jessica forced more water and brandy on him and patted his face with a dry cloth. When she touched his neck, his eyes opened a little. He looked at her for just a moment. His lips moved as he tried to speak, but no sound followed. After he closed his eyes again, a soft rap on the door came, and Smiley McGuire entered. His eyes were red, the cracks in his face even deeper.

"All aboard, 'ceptin' the captain, o' course, are well," he reported. "She's a good ship—tight as a drum. No need to worry when yer aboard *The Emerald*. Best of all, Matt knows our bearin's now. We'll be portin' by dark."

Jessica said nothing of the warning she had given the new first mate.

As the day passed, Andrew seemed to improve a bit, though Jessica feared he remained in grave danger. She continued administering to him as he drifted in and out of consciousness. Exhaustion washed over her, but she left his side only once during the day, to change clothes.

Long after nightfall, the ship docked into the Chatham pier. Jessica stayed with Andrew until someone came for him.

Soon a soft knocking interrupted the silence, and she opened the door to Richard Winterfield. He, too, looked fatigued.

"We were also hit hard by that storm. I've been up all night and day in anticipation of your arrival."

Andrew's uncertain future, as well as her concern over her family, had taken its toll on Jessica's strength. Without a word, she grabbed hold of Richard, buried her face in his chest, and wept. Comforting her, he thanked her for her care of Andrew.

"It will be all right now, Jessica. Mr. McGuire is waiting for you in your cabin. I'll stay here while you gather your things," he said. "A carriage is waiting to take you to the train station. I'll care for Andrew now."

A few moments later, Richard Winterfield emerged from the ship and walked down the ramp to the dock. He carried an unconscious and limp Andrew in his arms. The black sky, dusted with sparkling stars, gave no hint of the fierce storm. Tall lamps brightened the area. Jessica followed behind him and Mr. McGuire, who loaded her trunk onto the carriage. Before boarding, she turned to Mr. McGuire and kissed his cheek in farewell.

"I'll never forget ya," he responded in a firm voice, though she could see mist in his eyes.

She nodded in reciprocation, but had no strength for words.

Stepping to Richard, she gazed into the face of his ill son one last time. A stubbly dark shadow had crossed his jaw line and cheeks. She rested one palm against Andrew's sallow face and, leaning over him, placed a lingering kiss upon his cheek.

The men stood watching as she walked in silence to the carriage. Before it pulled away, she stared at them from the window, tears streaming down her cheeks. Just behind Richard Winterfield in the shadows, Jessica noticed the dark figure of Matthew Clark. He was standing, his chin held high. When their eyes met, he dipped his head and looked up again. No smile appeared on his face, but she understood his gesture to be one of gratitude.

Curling up on the solid wood bench, Jessica fell asleep to the clacking of the train wheels. She reached Cornwall County in the wee hours of the morning.

She was forced awake by the sun on her face. Familiar landmarks began appearing as the train drew closer to her home.

Her stomach rumbled—from hunger or nerves she knew not, but she managed to ignore its prodding.

At the station in Penzance she rented a coach. As it approached her house, the front door flung wide and Grace ran to meet her. Jessica stepped out after it pulled to a stop and they met in an embrace, both weeping.

"Oh, I was so worried, Jess! You sailed right through the terrible storm that struck here, didn't you? I'm relieved you're home!"

All Jessica could do was cry.

While Mrs. Wright drew a hot bath, Grace helped Jessica inside and fixed her some tea. Babbling about the terror of the stormy night and the illness of Andrew Winterfield, Jessica tried to explain her adventure, beginning with the reading of Andrew's journals at his home in the library; then their first meeting at the dance, which up to that point she had revealed to no one; about his finding her in the hull of the ship; their dinners and strolls together along the deck; and the devastation of his sudden illness.

She was weak, exhausted, and confused. Realizing that much of what she was trying to tell her sister was unclear, she at last said, "I think I love him, Grace," and began weeping again.

After the warm bath, Grace helped her to her room and into a cotton nightgown. Tucked into her own bed, Jessica fell fast asleep.

Grace returned near dusk with a tray of soup and tea. Jessica's eyes fluttered open as her sister lit some candles around the room. She managed to sit up, gathering the down quilt around her waist, and sipped the tea. Grace settled onto the bottom of the bed.

"Am I really home?" Jessica asked. "It's all been such a blur. And what day is it?"

"Yes, Jess, you're home, and it's the twenty-fifth of May."

"I believe I'm all right now. Thank you for caring for me." She tasted the soup. "Now tell me—*why* did Father summon me home? Where is he? And where is Alex? Please tell me everything."

"They're both gone, Jessie. It all started about a week ago. Father and Mr. Wright were working on repairs on Old Stormy. Mrs. Wright, Alex, and I were tending to the gardens when a delivery arrived for Father—a parcel. I rowed out to notify him of it. He came back with me, and the two of us went into the library, where I'd left the package. He pulled from it this letter." She drew a folded paper from her pocket and handed it to Jessica.

Upon unfolding the letter, Jessica noted at once that it was no ordinary letter, for it had been written in type, something she had only seen in the society papers.

> Mr. Viana,
>
> I have been thinking how strange life is at times. For instance, when people cross our paths we may wonder what they will mean to us. How can someone affect my life? How can I affect his?
>
> Well, I have discovered something which, I am sure you will agree, is of interest, one which could have a great effect on our lives, both yours and mine, and others as well.
>
> You see, Mr. Viana, I have access to something that belongs to you. That it is of great value I have no doubt. However, I cannot surrender the information without your consent to a certain arrangement, that being the hand of your youngest daughter, Alexandra.
>
> I will meet you the night of the twenty-fifth of May on the bridge in Plymouth at ten o'clock, where we will discuss my terms of this arrangement. I am sure you will have no objections.
>
> As evidence of my knowledge of this information, I enclose a token of proof.
>
> Edward Scarborough

"*Edward Scarborough!*" Jessica exclaimed. "You mean this is all about *him*?" She read the letter again. What could it mean? "What was in the package, Grace? What was the evidence he sent?"

"Well, Father turned it on its side, and out rolled the ruby ring you had described to me last summer—the one he had taken from the stranger! I've never seen Father in such a state of shock, Jess. He backed away from it as though it were a venomous snake. Then he noticed *my* reaction to it, and realized that I, too, had recognized it. He grabbed hold of me. 'What do you know of this ring, Grace?' he asked. I told him of the account you and Alex had relayed to me about the unconscious man and how you later saw the ring on the hand of Mr. Scarborough. Then I remembered the note the injured man had left here. We searched and searched for it, Jessie, but could not locate it anywhere. You didn't destroy it, did you?"

Jessica pulled the quilt down, her bare feet slipping onto the hard floorboards. She crouched to the floor and, reaching underneath her mattress, pulled out a single sheet of paper.

"I put it here, thinking we might need it some day."

"Oh," was Grace's somber reply.

"So, the ring belongs to Father—to his family, to *our* family!"

"I guess so," Grace said. "After that, Father picked up the ring and examined it. I couldn't interpret the look on his face, Jess—disbelief, confusion, anger, grief? He then took the ring and Mr. Scarborough's letter, and locked himself in his study. The remainder of that day and all night, he stayed there, deciding how to handle the situation, I believe. The only response we received when we would knock was that he was fine and not to bother him. Alex and I slept in the library that night in the hopes he would come out.

"At last, in the morning, the door opened. Father looked as though he had been up all night, Jess. He had prepared some telegrams—one to you. Alex would be sent to Kent to stay with the Winterfields, while Father traveled to Plymouth. He instructed me to stay here and await your arrival. Other than that, he would send word in a few days. He and Alex left for Penzance the following morning, where he could send the telegrams before boarding the train. Mr. Scarborough's letter was left on his desk, but the ring is now gone. I assume he took it with him."

"So he went to meet with Edward Scarborough," Jessica said, staring at nothing. "Certainly he wouldn't agree to Alex marrying that man! He must have felt she would be safer with the Winterfields than here," Jessica thought aloud, not knowing what to make of the situation. And Edward's letter was so vague. It made little sense, though it must have been clear to their father.

It *was* clear to her, however, that their father had access to some very valuable possession, perhaps their grandmother's estate, and by marrying into the family, Edward Scarborough would also become an heir to the fortune.

"So the meeting between Father and Mr. Scarborough is to occur tonight," Jessica mumbled. "When will we hear from him again, Grace?"

"In his due time, Jess."

Chapter Fifteen

Stephen Sutton returned to his father's office at the end of an intense day of study.

"Good evening, Son." William Sutton and another man Stephen did not recognize were leaning over a table in the center of the office.

"Hello, Father," Stephen responded and took a quick glance over the shoulders of the two men. A map of England had been spread across the table. Stephen noticed several markers sitting on various points of the map.

Rather than interrupt what sounded like a serious conversation, he headed toward a shelf of books.

"You've made a thorough search of this entire area, correct?" queried Stephen's father.

"That's correct," his associate responded. "I scrutinized every public record and even spoke with many of the locals. There's no evidence of a John Everett in that entire county."

"You've not given up on that case yet, Father?" Stephen spoke up from the corner of the room, intent on browsing the bookshelf. "I'm beginning to think the man sailed to America."

"No I've *not* conceded." A tone of irritation flavored his father's response. "I'll cover England with a fine-toothed comb. If John Everett is in the country, he *will* be discovered." His attention turned back to the map. "Now, here, in London, is where I last saw his daughter, Grace."

At the mention of the name, Stephen looked up from the book he was reading. "Grace Everett?" He hastened over to the map. In a fury, he pushed the two men aside and with a swoop of his hand, the markers went tumbling to the floor.

"Stephen! What in the world—"

"Grace Everett, whose father is John!" Stephen scanned the map in the Cornwall County area. His finger came to rest on the small print of the town of Bristlecone, near the coastline. "Of course! Father, John's daughter, Grace!" Stephen looked up and smiled in triumph at the other two. "You may search all you like, but you'll *never* locate John Everett."

"Of what are you speaking?" His father's irritated tone took on an edge.

"John Everett is now known as John Viana. His family lives where you directed me last summer—near Bristlecone!"

His father looked puzzled.

"Listen to me," Stephen said. "When I injured myself in that area last summer, I was taken in by a family that tended the lighthouse there. As you can imagine, I was a bit dazed after suffering a blow to the head. They put me up for the night, and I arose before anyone else the next morning. I left a note on the stationery of the man of the house, whom I had not met the previous night. Oh, why did I not recall this before? The name on the stationary was *John Viana!*"

"I'm following you thus far, Son, but there must be a million 'Johns' in England! What makes you think John Viana is *our* John?"

"Last summer, the week before you sent me to Cornwall County, I, too, met Grace in London. I saw her again this January, at the Huntington's ball. This time she gave me her post office address. Father, she lives near Bristlecone—Cornwall County. She was not there the day of my injury because, as you told me, she was traveling with neighbors and was still in London at the time. Is it just a coincidence that Grace Viana has a father named John and they live in Cornwall County, the very region Mrs. Boswell revealed to you last summer as the locality from which Grace was visiting?"

His father rubbed his temple as though he was getting a headache.

"Father, there were two other daughters there as well, and did not you yourself tell me John Everett has *three* daughters?"

"You may have something there, Stephen, but it still sounds a bit farfetched to me."

Stephen sighed. An instant later, he snapped his fingers. "Father, until just now I had no idea that John Everett's daughter was named Grace. Tell me again about her appearance."

"Lofty, slender, that unusual coppery hair, features fine, skin fair, and I know from the past that Grace Everett has blue eyes."

"You have just described Grace Viana."

William Sutton stared at his son. "When can you leave for Cornwall County, Stephen?"

"Tonight."

The night of the twenty-fifth of May brought a rolling fog to Plymouth. At the crest of a high bridge near the pier, John Viana watched from the shadows as a lone man approached and stood under the misty light of a street lamp. He knew that the hour must be approaching ten o'clock, and even in the dimness he recognized the man as Edward Scarborough.

For the first time in his life, John fought an anger that threatened to drive him to an action he would regret. He struggled to stifle the thoughts of vengeance rising in his heart.

John watched and waited as Edward paced back and forth, pulling a watch from his coat every few moments to check the time.

Thirty minutes elapsed. Still, John waited. A couple walking arm in arm passed under the light. Edward watched them, but, engrossed in conversation, they seemed to ignore his presence. If they saw John at all, they gave no indication of it.

Another thirty minutes passed. Edward pulled his watch from his coat one final time and returned it to his pocket. Throwing his arms into the air, he looked around and turned to leave. John followed several paces behind.

Edward's stride was quick, and at times John lost him in the shadows and the fog, but he reappeared under one street lamp after another. John kept his footfalls silent.

At last, Edward turned at a small building and dashed up an outside staircase. John quickened his pace and reached the bottom of the stairs just in time to see a door close on the second landing.

After waiting several minutes, he climbed the stairs and tapped on the door. When Edward opened it, John grabbed hold of his coat lapels, forcing him inside and against a wall of the flat.

"You have no idea what you've stumbled upon, Scarborough," John hissed between clenched teeth. He struggled to control his anger. "You'll give me the information I need, and I'll let you go unharmed. Those are *my* terms!"

The shock in Edward's eyes explained his silence, but his glance darted from John to the desk just beside them, and then back to John. With a firm grip on him, John looked for himself at the desk where a folded letter laid, a burgundy wax seal still fastened to one edge. His eyes switched back to glare into Edward's frightened face.

He threw Edward into a corner, grabbed the letter, and left the flat.

Under the hazy orange light of a street lamp, John Viana pulled the papers from his pocket and began reading the letter penned over two years before in his mother's shaky penmanship.

Shock and disbelief overwhelmed him. Tears clouded his vision. He blinked them away and reread her words, "to gain your full and unrelenting forgiveness for the disappointment I became to you." He focused on the London address at the bottom of the page.

John searched the town until he located one lone cab stopped at a curb, the light from a lamp almost lost in the fog. Its coachman was slumped over asleep atop the carriage, a blanket draped about his shoulders. John woke the man, who drove him to the train station.

He spent what remained of the night and all of the next day in the Plymouth station. It was nearing midnight the following night when, at last, he reached the station in London. He hired a coach to take him to the business district.

The fog that had blanketed Plymouth also shrouded London. It thickened the further the carriage drove, and a cool drizzle had begun. The horse plodded down the empty street of the address on the bottom of his mother's letter. When the carriage halted in front of the office, he found it as he suspected it would be—dark and unoccupied. He was willing to stay outside and wait until daybreak if need be. However, several yards away, a light from a window streamed onto the wet sidewalk. The driver agreed to wait, and John dashed toward the light, gathering his overcoat about his neck.

Peering through the glass, he could see a young man at a desk under a lamp near the back of the office. He tapped on the window. The man looked up.

"What may I do for you?" he asked when he opened the door.

"I'm a client of William Sutton, who keeps his office a few doors down."

"Yes, I know Mr. Sutton well."

"I must see him at once. It's a matter of urgency that will not wait until morning." John pulled the letter from his pocket and pointed out the address at the bottom.

After squinting, the man stepped back into the office, leaving John in the rain outside. A moment later, he emerged with a small card. On it he had written what he said was William's home address.

In the wee hours of the morning, the cab pulled up to a large home. The Sutton name arched in iron letters high above the entrance gates, which opened with a screech.

John paid the coachman. He walked up the stone pathway to the front entrance of the house while the clopping of the horse faded away. When he approached the large doors, the only sound he could hear was his own heartbeat loud and furious in his ears. The drizzling rain intensified.

He reached out for the iron knocker and rapped on the solid wooden door. He waited. The violent beat of his heart persisted.

A few moments later he pounded again, louder this time. The door creaked open. A tired face appeared in the light of a single candle.

"May I help you, Sir?"

"I am a client of William Sutton. It is urgent that I see him right away. I will not leave until I do."

With one eyebrow raised and lips pursed, the man, who John assumed to be a servant, eyed him from head to toe. "Follow me."

He led John through a large foyer and past a staircase to their right. John could only see the bottom two steps, which were of white marble. The remainder of the staircase remained hidden among the deep shadows of the darkened house. Their footsteps echoed around them. Moments later John followed the servant into a large room and paced while the man plodded around, lighting several candles. Shelf after shelf appeared in the flickering light, reaching the ceiling and brimming with books.

The servant took John's wet coat and hat.

"May I tell him who is calling?"

"John Everett," he replied. Calling himself by that name sounded strange. It had been so many years.

The servant left the room, closing the door behind him.

It was much smaller than the Winterfield library. The bookshelves were of dark cherry wood. Overstuffed chairs, an inviting couch, and a large desk decorated the comfortable room. A cabinet filled with bottles of wines and liqueurs sat among the shelves.

John's pacing continued as he ran his fingers through his hair. His deep sighs only served to intensify his anxiety.

On the far wall he stepped to two tall leaded-glass doors that opened to a small balcony. He strained to look beyond the railing but could only see the flames of the candles in the glass and his own dark shadow.

Several minutes passed. In the reflection of the doors, John caught the study door behind him opening. He turned to approach the man he recognized as William Sutton, sleepy and dressed in house shoes, silk pajamas, and robe.

"John!" William almost shouted, hastening forward to meet him in a firm embrace. "The best-hidden man in England appears out of nowhere on my very doorstep! Do you realize I've been combing the country for you for over *two years*?"

Although happy to see his old friend, John had no smile to offer, feeling only his own agitation.

"What's the meaning of this, Will?" he demanded, pulling the ruby ring from his pocket and holding it up to the barrister.

"You'd better sit down, John," he replied, staring at the ring.

"I can't sit down, Will." John began pacing again. He felt like a wild animal that had been trapped and caged. "This ring was sent to me by post six days ago. It came from a young man who attempted to bribe me with the information in *this* document." He slapped his mother's letter down hard on the desk in front of William. "Now tell me what you know of this ring, Will. What did my mother tell you of it? Where on earth did *she* obtain it—the very ring that was on the hand of my wife when she sailed to her death *sixteen years ago*?" His mind was racing, his heart burning in near hysteria.

"John, your wife…," William said in a solemn tone, "…she may still be alive."

The words hit John like a brick in the chest. He lurched forward as his breath was forced from his throat. Unable to inhale, lips gaping, he clamped his hand to his chest. Dizziness distorted his vision. Wide-eyed, he staggered toward the glass doors and burst out onto the balcony.

Several steps from the doorway, he fell to his knees, the steady rain soaking him to the skin. His lungs filled from the jolt of the cool air, and he threw his head back, closing his eyes as the rain pelted his face.

His long, deafening wail pierced the thick London fog, as sixteen years of frustration, agony, grief, and despair escaped his desperate and tormented soul. He collapsed into a heap in the rain, sobbing unrestrained.

* * * * *

The next thing John knew, he was sitting on the library couch, legs outstretched. Wrapped in a woolen blanket, he sipped from a glass of brandy, an occasional drip from his wet hair falling onto the thirsty cover. A small fire crackled in the hearth.

William sat close by on a wingback chair. Leaning forward, elbows on his knees, he kept a watchful eye on his friend. His hair, too, was damp and his clothing just beginning to dry.

"Your words always did pack a punch, Will," John said after a while, trying to manage a half grin. A sip of brandy went down smooth and warm. He released a heavy sigh. William said nothing, and John appreciated the man's patience while he recovered from the shock of his earlier statement.

"The ring was a gift to me from my parents when I was in my teens." John's voice, weak and shaky, came with shallow breaths. "It was my great-grandmother's wedding band and was intended for the hand of the woman I would someday marry." He recalled his mother's letter, too exhausted to be angry. "I kept that ring for years. It was one of the few possessions I took when I relocated to Ireland. The love I felt for Angela moved me to inscribe the scripture that is now on the inside of the ring. 'Set me as a seal upon thine heart, for love is strong as death.' Little did I know then how much those words would come to mean." He smiled, remembering her exquisite face. "The old king whose words I borrowed didn't realize that love is *stronger* than death, Will. For sixteen years I've grieved as though it happened yesterday." His head wagged. "How strange. I've lived twice as long without her than I lived with her, and yet I know she'll remain within me forever."

"She must've been exceptional," William acknowledged.

"I accepted her death long ago, Will, and now you're telling me she may still be alive?" His voice strengthened as he sat forward. "Do you mean to tell me I've lived in agony for *sixteen years*, Will, for no reason at all?"

"John, it's not my intent to raise your hopes, but there is a chance."

"Tell me what you know. Tell me *everything* you know, Will. *Now!*"

William rose from his chair and stationed himself before the fireplace, grasping an iron tool. He poked at the logs.

"Your mother appeared in my office one day over two years ago, just after she'd written that letter." The letter sat untouched on the desktop. "I never knew her well, John, only her reputation and vague memories of meeting her a couple of times when I was with you. She didn't look like the woman I remembered. In her eyes there was no anger, no pride, just empty sorrow." He turned his head around. "Were you aware of her death, John?"

He nodded, sipping more of the brandy.

"She told me of her illness and that she'd known about it for some time and had revealed it to no one. Of late she had come to accept that it would soon take her life. She was frantic to find you, John, in desperate need of your forgiveness, she said." William stood to stroll about the library. "Her purpose in coming to me was to find you, stating that I was the only person she could trust. She knew I would be loyal to my friend. I gave her my word that I wouldn't give up the search for you even after her death."

John stared at the amber firelight dancing about on the otherwise dark walls.

"Now as for the ring," William said, "more than five years after hearing of your wife's death, and several years prior to your mother's illness, a woman came to her with a small velvet box and said only, 'This was worn by a woman deeply in love with your son, but *you* are its rightful owner. It belongs to your family.' The woman left without another word. When your mother opened the box, she was shocked to find the ring she had given you so many years before. She suspected that the woman could have been your wife and admitted to putting the ring and the woman out of her mind that very day. She determined then and there that, if she *had* been your wife, Lady Margaret Everett would seek her revenge by keeping the woman's survival a secret."

John sat emotionless, feeling only his heart solidifying in his chest. How could she have so hated her own son, her only child?

"However, as she explained it to me," William went on, "her conscience devoured her from the inside out. For nine years she kept that secret, and the last year of her life she could keep it no more. She expressed the belief that it was the harboring of that secret that had caused her illness, and by the time she came to me, she felt she would pay for the consequences of her decision with her own life. Never did she try to justify her actions, and she believed she deserved what would be the inevitable outcome. She only wanted your forgiveness and to reunite you with your wife, if indeed the woman was Angela."

"Did she give you a description?" John's words sounded like they had been spoken by a stranger. Never before had he felt so cold inside, like death itself.

William stopped and leaned against the desk, facing John. He crossed his arms over his chest, and his ankles in front of him. His gaze dropped to the patterned rug beneath them.

"She said she saw that woman's face in her sleep every night. Yes, she described her. Tall and slender, with an olive complexion, and long hair as black as coal, is what she said. But it was the eyes that haunted her in the dark of the night, icy-blue that pierced straight through her. Those eyes, she said, revealed a wound of the deepest kind, that of a crushed and broken spirit, a wound from which there was no healing, regardless of the passage of time."

John closed his eyes, knowing full well that type of wound. "That description could well fit my wife." His eyes opened to the fierce stare of his friend. "However, it could also describe her sister. Angela and her sister had many years between them and had not shared a close relationship. They lost contact after Angela relocated to Ireland. Although I'd never met her sister, Angela described her appearance as very similar to her own."

"That's why we need to find her, John." William was on his feet and pacing again, no doubt in the same manner he did in the courtroom when delivering a closing argument. "Did Angela survive the shipwreck? Or was her body found in the wreckage with the ring on her finger? Did her sister come to collect the body and there obtained the ring? Had she been in possession of that ring for five years? And if so, why would she then feel the need to return it to your mother? If she and Angela weren't close, would she even have known the ring had once belonged to your mother?" William stopped and crouched down before John. "I can find the answers, John, but I need your permission and help. You see, your mother could not remember your wife's family name. I had no way of locating her or her family. With that information and your permission, I can begin an immediate search. However, there is one condition."

John nodded.

"No doubt, John, you could undertake this venture yourself without my assistance. But I feel it would be advantageous for a representative to go in your stead. If Angela's alive, she may be living with her sister and her family in Spain, the country your mother told me was Angela's homeland. That would be the obvious place to begin. But, John, there's also a chance, if she is alive," William paused for a brief moment as if holding back, then said, "she may also be remarried. That could be her reason for returning the ring to your mother."

John's gaze fell to the floor. The thought never would have crossed his mind. Without voicing it, he thought, *impossible.* He knew her well and believed in his heart her loyalty would remain intact; for if she were alive, the vow she made to him would likewise be very much alive.

But instead of arguing the point, John murmured, "Very well."

"Good." William stood. "I'll arrange to leave at daybreak."

He offered to show John to the guest room. As they were exiting the library, William stopped.

"By the way, old friend, what *is* your wife's family name?"

"Viana."

William nodded and smiled, mumbling something about his son's correct deduction.

The following morning dawned clear and bright. When John awoke, he found the time to be nearing eleven o'clock. He reviewed the previous night's events over in his mind, wondering if he had been dreaming, but as evidenced by the strange room around him, it had, indeed, been very real. He looked at the small night stand by the bed and noticed a note had been placed there.

> Have made arrangements as we discussed. Please make yourself at home until you hear from me. I'll notify you when I reach Spain.
> Will

John wanted to spend the day with his youngest daughter, *their* youngest daughter, who was safe at the Winterfield estate. He rose from the bed, but sat down again. Who was he fooling? He could not be with her and keep his hopes to himself; yet how unfair it would be to arouse her hopes for a reunion that still seemed impossible.

It could be days before William located the Viana family and had news for him. What would he do in the meantime? No, he could not be in the company of anyone. He would not be distracted from thoughts of Angela, but to stay, doing nothing, in William's home would drive him to madness.

Why had he ever allowed William to go without him?

Spain. He mulled over their conversation. With a suddenness that jolted his senses, something occurred to him. William had suggested that Angela could have remarried. John's immediate thought was that he knew his wife so well as to know that she would *not* marry another. That was it! He *did* know her well! In fact, he knew Angela well enough to know that were she still alive, she would *not* be living in Spain, as William had concluded. He had met her in Ireland. She loved Ireland like no other place.

Yes, he did know her. And had she survived, she would have returned to the Emerald Isle where they had met. And that is where she would have stayed, if for no other reason than for the hope that he might someday return.

Grabbing his few items from the bureau, he wondered how long it would take to get to Dublin.

Chapter Sixteen

Grace was grateful to have Jessica back home. Work at the lighthouse had been difficult without her, then close to impossible once their father and Alexandra had left. And she had so missed the companionship of her dear sister.

Mr. Wright had spent the night of Jessica's return and the one that followed at the lighthouse, coming home only to take his meals. The four ate together in silence.

Grace and Jessica offered to cover a shift the next day, giving Mr. Wright a needed break.

Jessica had been home for two days. With the work at hand, she and Grace had no time to discuss her adventures in France.

As their work progressed throughout the mid-morning, it seemed to Grace that her sister had been re-energized. However, Jessica's demeanor betrayed a solemnity that was foreign to the once-sparkling personality. Grace noticed her several times pausing at the railing that encircled the lighthouse dome to gaze out into the ocean. Oh, her sister often had done that over the years, but this was different. Her distress over the condition of Andrew Winterfield was obvious. Grace hoped they would soon receive word from their sister, who was at present staying with his family.

The events of two nights prior also distracted them both. Had the meeting between their father and Mr. Scarborough taken place? What had been the outcome? When would they hear from him? What was the significance of the ring?

Consumed by unanswered questions, Grace, like her sister, worked in silence.

Just after the noon hour, while they were busy polishing the lens, the voice of Mr. Wright echoed to them from inside the base of Old Stormy. "Grace, you have a visitor waiting for you in the parlor!"

She looked up from her work.

"His name is Sutton. Stephen Sutton!"

Grace's heart leaped as her gaze darted to her sister. For the first time since her return, a wide smile broke out on Jessica's lips.

"Jessie, you must help me change!" pleaded Grace.

"Please tell him it'll be several minutes," Jessica called down. "Ask him to wait where he is." She turned to Grace. "We'll sneak in through the back door and upstairs."

They hurried down the spiral staircase.

Stephen Sutton wandered about the parlor, recognizing the room in which he had awakened one dreadful night almost a year earlier. His face crinkled with the memory of the intense headache with which he had suffered that morning and the confusion that followed as he had tried to make sense of his whereabouts in an already unfamiliar area.

This visit would prove to be much more pleasant.

He stopped at the desk, noting a neat stack of stationery on its corner. The name John Viana was scrolled across the top. He smiled, grateful that his memory had at last recalled this minute detail. Grace's two sisters had been very hospitable. They had had no idea that it was their own father for whom he was searching during that visit. Indeed, neither did he himself then. How surprised they would be to see him again!

After Grace pulled a pale yellow dress with a white eyelet bodice over her head, Jessica twisted her copper hair up. Grace's eyes sparkled with anticipation.

They descended the stairs together, all traces of their frantic state concealed beneath a guise of calm.

Jessica followed her sister into the parlor, a few steps behind. Upon seeing the young man that greeted them, she stopped short and gasped.

The man stepped forward to take and kiss her sister's hand.

"What a surprise to find you here, Mr. Sutton." Grace said, welcoming him. "I gave you only a post office address. How were you able to locate my home?"

"Because he's been here before, Grace," Jessica said in a cold voice. *So, Stephen Sutton and the stranger with the ring are one and the same*, she thought.

"How nice to see you again, Miss Viana," he said, holding out his hand to her. His tone sounded genuine enough, but she stepped back, placing both hands behind her back.

"I don't understand," Grace said. "*When* did you come here before, Mr. Sutton? How is it you know my sister?" She turned to Jessica, looking for an answer.

"Last summer, Grace," she responded, glaring at the now-identified stranger. "The injured man we put up for the night while you were in Kent is none other than Stephen Sutton. Did you ever locate the heirloom you had lost alongside the road, Mr. Sutton?"

Grace looked between them with a furrowed brow.

"No, you did not, did you?" Jessica continued without looking at Grace. "And that's because a greedy young man by the name of Edward Scarborough robbed you of it long before our sister ever stumbled upon you."

"Then I find myself perplexed as well, Miss Viana," he said, his expression becoming serious. "If you knew the location of the ring, why did you not notify me, as instructed in the note I left?"

"It seems, Mr. Sutton, that the ring is a very desirable commodity, for it must represent far greater riches. Its possession, in fact, has led at least *one* greedy young man to pursue the hand of one of the ladies of this house."

"You mean you thought—"

Jessica was surprised when he began to laugh out loud.

"You believed—" he said between laughs.

She saw no reason for his humor. Grace looked ready to cry.

He drew a heavy breath and wiped the smile from his face. "Please, sit down. It appears I have some explaining to do."

Grace did so at once, followed by a reluctant Jessica.

"Is your father at home?" he asked. "This information is vital to him most of all."

"No," Jessica replied. "He's not here at present."

"My father, William Sutton, is a barrister in London," he began, "and I'm studying under him in the hopes of one day starting my own practice. Two years ago your grandmother, Margaret Everett, hired him to locate your father, knowing our fathers had been friends in their youth. She had a serious illness and knew she was dying. Your father, her only son, was the heir to her estate. I confess I do not know what the estate entails, nor have I myself reviewed any of the documents. My father promised to continue the search for your father even after her death, which occurred over a year ago."

Jessica started to speak, but at once Stephen put his hand up and looked at Grace.

"Now let me tell you where you entered the picture, Miss Viana. You'll recall that you and I met at a function while you were in London. I did not know the names of John Everett's daughters, and I had no reason to suspect you, Grace *Viana*, to be one of them. And then my father spied you at the Boswell gathering and recognized you, though he'd last seen you as a child."

"So I *have* met William Sutton before," Grace exclaimed. "I thought I recognized his name when you said it. He must be the man who was staring at me from across the room that evening. Yet he never approached me."

"That's because he obtained the information he needed from others. Although you were a vital piece to the puzzle, it was your father for whom he was searching. He felt your suspicions might have been raised had he approached you, and he had no wish to frighten you. Instead, he sent me to the area where he had learned you reside. I had in my possession the heirloom your grandmother had given to my father, that being the ring, and also a letter she'd written just before her death. The contents of the letter are unknown to me."

He then looked at Jessica. "What I told you and your sister when I awoke in this room the evening you discovered me is true. I'd been injured when my horse headed into the forest. It was pure coincidence that your sister found me, and in the end, it was by your generosity and hospitality that I was able to unveil a vital link that in time led me to the discovery of your father."

He walked over to the desk and picked up a piece of their father's stationery. "This was that link. Just two days ago I recalled the first name on the top of this stationery, upon which I'd penned that note to you. I came as soon as possible. So you see, Miss Viana," he said looking at Grace, "I'm not after your father's estate." He paused, blushing. "I was interested in you before I knew your true identity."

Guilt surged through Jessica for cornering him into disclosing his feelings.

"I'm so sorry for my hasty accusation," she said. "Can you ever forgive me?"

"I don't blame you for your suspicions," he answered. "You were right to be on guard."

"We have some of our own explaining to do as well," said Jessica.

They told him of the strange letter their father had received from Edward Scarborough just days before and that he had gone to meet him.

"Then your father may be in need of assistance," he said. "Perhaps I should notify my father of his whereabouts. He may be able to arrange some help."

Without warning, Mr. Sutton's gaze flashed to the window behind Jessica.

"What is it?" she asked.

"Where's the back entrance?" He jumped to his feet.

"Down the hallway there," said Grace, pointing. "Why?"

"Keep away from the window. Someone's out there!" He dashed down the corridor.

Grace started to follow him, but Jessica pulled her back. They heard muffled arguing and the sounds of a skirmish out front. Rushing to the door, they found Stephen gripping a disheveled man by the arm.

"Edward Scarborough!" Jessica exclaimed.

The man broke loose. The sisters burst out onto the front lawn as he headed for the forest, Stephen on his heels.

Moments later, Stephen reappeared. "You know that man?" he called out, heading for his horse.

"He's the one who robbed you!" shouted Jessica.

"He just got away on horseback!" he hollered. Spurring his horse into a run, he disappeared into the woods.

"Oh, Jessie, I'm afraid for Mr. Sutton. We've not heard from him and here it is almost three hours!"

Jessica had just returned from the lighthouse, where she had been assisting Mr. Wright. She found her sister in the parlor pacing, the mending in a heap on the sofa.

"I wish we knew where they went!" Grace continued.

"So do I. And if Mr. Scarborough is *here*, where is *Father*?"

"I don't understand any of this. But speaking of Father, this telegram just arrived from London." Grace pulled it from her pocket and read it aloud, her sister looking over her shoulder.

> "All is fine. Leaving country for short time to seek something of great value. If contacted by Scarborough, notify authorities. Will advise you later. Father"

"Now I'm more confused than ever!" Jessica exclaimed. "Leaving the country?"

"Edward Scarborough must be more dangerous than we ever imagined!" Grace frowned.

"I'm so glad Father sent Alex away."

"Do you think she was the reason Edward came here?"

"I do. Just what he was plotting, however, is a mystery." Jessica dropped the telegram on the desk. "At least we know Father is well. In *that* we can be comforted." She sighed. "But what was he doing in London? I wish he had sent news of Andrew."

She relaxed when Grace's arm slipped around her shoulder.

"I hope we hear from Mr. Sutton soon," Grace said.

Half an hour later, the sisters sat in the parlor and sipped tea. They had given up on accomplishing any work while awaiting the return of Stephen Sutton.

"Grace, I can't take much more of this excitement. Our lives were so peaceful just three weeks ago. Now everything has been turned upside down!"

"And it seems it'll be some time before we're upright again." Grace agreed. "What will you do about Mr. Winterfield? You said you think you love him, Jessie. How will you ever see him again?"

Heat rushed to her cheeks. She did not recall revealing her feelings to her sister. The morning of her return was a blur to her now.

"I am resolved that I may never see him again. He's a distracted man, Grace. His sister said his passion is for his seafaring life. Even if he conquers the illness, I doubt he'll ever overcome his love for the ocean. And he'll no doubt never know of my feelings for him."

"No, Jessica. I know you too well. Something happened between the two of you, something that had a tremendous impact on you. He would have to be made of stone to be unaffected himself. I know you've not seen the last of Andrew Winterfield."

Jessica turned away. Andrew's condition appeared worse than the only other cholera victim she had ever seen. The words she herself had spoken to Mr. McGuire about that other victim rang through her mind over and over—*the man died*.

"Now, Jess, I want to hear every detail about Paris. Was it as glamorous as we've heard?"

"Oh, yes." Appreciating her sister's attempt to force her mind to focus on other topics, she related many of her adventures. "But three aspects of France will forever remain in my heart, although I was there but a few short weeks. The natural beauty of the land; the poetic language—oh, Grace, to hear them speak with their native accent, it's music to the ears; and the music itself. The captivating melodies I shall never forget." Her eyes looked right through Grace as she relived the precious memories in her mind.

"I suppose one of us should get back to Mr. Wright. It'll be dark soon."

As the two stood, Grace looked out the window.

"Jessie, look! It's Mr. Sutton!"

They ran for the front door.

"I pursued Scarborough as far as Penzance, but lost him in the town," he said, swinging down from his horse. "My search for him lasted more than an hour before I decided to file a report against him. You needn't worry about his returning. I'm certain I scared him right onto a train out of here."

"You must be right," Jessica agreed. "I've never seen a man run so fast!"

They all laughed.

Grace told Stephen of their father's telegram. In light of the news, he informed them that he should return home at once. They insisted that he remain for the night and avail himself of a hardy dinner. Already the house was beginning to fill with aromas from Mrs. Wright's cooking.

The three rowed out to Old Stormy for a brief tour before dusk. Stephen gave Mr. Wright a hand with the fuel while Jessica completed some chores. Grace and Stephen watched from the top of the beacon while the sun descended over the water.

The meal ended all too soon. Jessica stayed up with her sister and their visitor, talking until midnight. They put him up in the parlor, where he had stayed before. He joked about the nightmares he was sure to have about the head injury.

In the morning, Stephen set off for Penzance, where he would catch a train to London.

"He promised to inquire and send word of Andrew the moment he returns," Grace said as they waved good-bye.

They walked arm-in-arm back into the house.

"You said yesterday that it would be some time before our lives are set aright again." Jessica smiled at her sister before continuing. "Since the marriage of any of us would change all our lives, I would venture to say that they may *never* be the same."

That night, Jessica knocked on her sister's bedchamber door and stepped in. She took a seat on the foot of the bed.

"Grace, there's been something very unsettling with this business of Father's."

Grace sat beside her.

"He left his family in London *and* their money," Jessica said. "Later, he concealed his identity upon returning to England. All our lives he taught us, and indeed showed us by example, that money is not the road to happiness."

"It's true."

"So why, then," Jessica continued, "would he allow a report from a deceitful man such as Mr. Scarborough to cause him to run off in hot pursuit of what he termed 'something of great value'? I find myself baffled over this action Father has taken. It's just not like him at all, Grace."

"You're right. It is baffling. I can't seem to resolve it in my mind either. How could any material possession tempt Father?" She stepped to the dressing table and returned to pull a brush through Jessica's hair. "I believe time will have to tell, as we have no other choice but to wait and see what this is all about."

Chapter Seventeen

The morning was hazy in Dublin, just as John Viana re-membered it. He awoke in a small room at the inn where he had found a vacancy the previous evening after his arrival. Be-fore retiring, he wandered through the gates of the park in the middle of town, where he had spent much time in solitude dur-ing the months before meeting Angela. His time spent there yesterday was in similar contemplation.

How strange it seemed to be back.

How would this day progress? He thought about William, who must have reached Spain by now. His search would begin at once for Angela's sister, and John expected it might take some time to locate her.

And here *he* was, back on the island he called home for more than eight years—the eight happiest years of his life. This had at one time been a place of comfort, of ease, and of concealment from the storms of his past. Yet, that ease elud-ed him this day. A dull, persistent pain had developed in the pit of his stomach, which he had first noticed that harrowing night in William Sutton's library. It would not be relieved until he uncovered the identity of the woman who had visited his mother.

Did he believe in his heart it could be Angela? That hope grew ever stronger with each day. After all, he had nothing to lose.

So where would he begin? After a light meal he headed out on horseback, trotting through the town. Not much had changed, except the faces. He found himself scrutinizing each one, searching each bonnet for the familiar black locks.

Angela had been four years his junior, just twenty when they married. She would now be the prime age of forty-four and would no doubt still have the dark tresses that Jessica had inherited. He glimpsed at his own reflection in a shop window and noted the scattered gray at his temples and the faint lines that had sneaked up around his eyes. Would she recognize him?

He stopped to send a telegram to William Sutton's house servant, informing him of his location were he to hear from William.

The music of a fiddle drifted out to the streets from a pub he passed, and it called to him. He had come to love the lively melodies, an aspect of Irish culture he missed. But today he moved on.

He stepped into a few shops and wandered through an outdoor market, but no one he asked had ever heard of Angela. What would her surname be now? Did she keep the name Everett? Would she have again taken her maiden name? Or, worse still, had she remarried, as William suggested, and taken a new name altogether? He disregarded the thought.

As his search continued into the second day, he felt discouragement setting in. He stopped to sit and watch passersby. The morning haze had given way to warm sunshine. A smile found its way to his lips as he reminisced about his wife. She had had a love for the garden and spent much time cultivating flowers and flowering bushes.

Were she still alive, they could both be very different by now. Would he find that the passing of time had caused an unbridgeable chasm between them? Perhaps she would not *want* him back.

What was he thinking in coming all the way here in pursuit of a memory? Had he run wild with the possibility of her survival? Had he gone mad out of desperation? *Why was he here?* Had not his heart suffered enough over the years? Perhaps he should leave for home, content with his life and his memories of her.

He shook off the negative thoughts and mounted his horse. It was then he decided to return to the home that had been theirs. Was it possible she could have obtained it as her residence after he had left it? He headed to the countryside, greeting those he passed, looking for her features in the face of every woman. The lush countryside bombarded him with memories of the past.

Within half an hour he approached the familiar stone cottage. He stopped at the gate. The pain in his gut intensified as he scanned the property, his memories overwhelming him at the sight of the home they once shared. He could almost see her tending the gardens no longer there and could envision little Grace playing in the yard as though it were yesterday.

The blackness of the grief he had experienced when he first lost her returned in all its fury. It had taken many years to conquer the emotions, and yet now, in an instant, they flooded over him. This was the reason he had not returned before. The pain was too great.

But now that he was here, he would finish what he came for. Prodding the horse on, he neared the house.

He swallowed hard, scanning the property overgrown with weeds. Dismounting, he stepped up to the weathered door that he had long ago painted cherry red one morning in the sunshine. Taking the hat from his head, he ran his fingers over the faded wood with its peeling paint. He knocked hard.

If he were to see her, what would he say? What *could* he say after sixteen years?

He knocked again and waited for the answer that did not come. As he looked around, he realized this house could not be the residence of his wife after all. It had fallen into neglect. Were she living here, the property would be well maintained, surrounded by thriving gardens.

His jaw clenched. He fought the onslaught of anger building in his throat. Grabbing a fistful of hair, he choked back the anguish that gushed forth in sudden tears.

That smile as she skimmed a fresh rose petal across her lips—so real now—awakened his longing. Her sweet laughter flooded his ears. The blue fabric of her dress twirled about her legs in the breeze. Here, in the place their hearts and their lives had been one, he no longer needed the sight of the full moon to envision her.

Desperate to force the image from his mind, he closed his eyes and stumbled from the porch. He opened them to a battered and rusty watering can at his feet. Snatching it up, he hurled it across the yard and shouted his pain into the emptiness.

Who was he fooling? She was *not* here! His family—his *only* family—was home…in England.

His face dropped into his palms, and he pressed the tears from his cheeks.

How long would he cling to a memory, a mere apparition? When would he ever be able to let her go? Yet all he knew now was a burning need to hang on to that sliver of hope that had come with the reappearance of the ring.

He would comb the city again…and again if necessary. No stone would be left unturned.

Several days passed with not a hint of Angela Everett. He spoke with shopkeepers, pedestrians on the street, and farmers on the road. Each response had been negative. He checked the library and public records to no avail. And he had not heard from William.

Dublin was by no means the small town he had left. How could he locate one woman in a quarter of a million people?

By the fifth day his weariness sank into utter dejection. Besides inquiring of each passerby, he knew not where else to turn. Would he be willing to search for her forever?

Thoughts of the house outside of town plagued him. Seeing it again had triggered emotions he had no desire to revive, but he knew he had to return. Even though his wife did not inhabit it, he had felt closer to her there than anywhere else. It was mid-afternoon when he turned the horse in the direction of the house.

Stopping outside the gate, he allowed his mind to wander through a maze of memories. The pain was there, yet less intense now. What a happy place it had been at one time. Why could he not stay there forever—suspended in time—reliving every day with her, every last minute?

He nudged the horse forward through the gate. It plodded up to the house. No sign of life appeared anywhere. He dismounted, stepping onto the creaky boards of the porch. His loud rap on the door echoed in his ears, and he knew full well he would be met with the same silence that had greeted him before.

Why did it happen? Why did he allow her to go? What would their years have brought had she not taken that fateful trip?

The knob turned! Someone was there! His heart pounded. He tried to catch his breath as the door creaked open.

The wizened face of an old woman appeared, framed with thin, straggly gray hair. "Sure has been a long time since a handsome stranger called on *me*." A near-toothless grin greeted him. "Who ya *really* after, Mister?" Her brogue was heavy. "How do I know ya?" Her eyes narrowed as she examined him.

"Well, Mrs…?" He smiled back.

"O'Holleran."

"Mrs. O'Holleran. We've never met before. I'm looking for a woman by the name of Angela."

"Angela?" She shook her head. "Can't say right offhand I know anybody b' that name."

"She lived here…in this very cottage…many years ago."

"Well, I've been here ten years myself, but don't…" She stopped and seemed to look right through him. "Oh, *that* Angela!"

His eyes widened.

"I *do* know an Angela. Sweetest girl ya ever want to meet, but very quiet. Keeps to herself a bit too much, if ya ask me. She's a real beauty, that one. Black hair, pretty blue eyes."

John nodded, unable to breathe.

"She sells wreaths and dried flowers from a cart in town. Ye can find her now and then in diff'rent places. She delivered one t' me one time. That's when she told me she used t' live in this cottage. Would ya like to see the wreath? She does beautiful work."

He forced a breath into his lungs. "Thank you, but what I'd *really* like is to know where she lives now."

"'Bout five miles south o' town. On a hill overlookin' the sea. House's surrounded by gardens." She grinned again. "Small house, big gardens. Can't miss it. That's where she lives, alright. Right there with her handsome young man."

"Then, she's...*married*?" The word almost stuck in his throat.

"Well, she *claims* to be married. Talks of a husband who disappeared years ago, but says she knows he'll be back for her someday. She's such a happy young girl. Hums and whistles all the time, so sure she is of his returnin'."

"But you said she lives with a man."

"Oh, I assumed ya knew the lady."

"I...I did know her...many years ago." John's head dropped.

"Then I'm sorry if I confused ya. The young man she lives with is not her husband." She paused and then added, "He's her son."

John's eyebrows rose in disbelief. "Her *son*?" He thought for a moment. "How...how old is the boy?"

"Oh, fifteen...sixteen at the most."

John swallowed hard. "And what's the lad's name?"

"Why, John Everett, o' course!"

He stepped backwards as the woman rambled on.

"She's such a proud mother, too. Says 'ceptin' for the dark hair, he's the spittin' image...of...his..." Her words trailed off as she squinted at him.

"Thank you, Mrs. O'Holleran!" He took hold of the woman's shoulders and planted a hard kiss on one wrinkled cheek. "You've just made me the happiest man alive!"

He turned and ran for the horse.

"Ye hold on t' yer wife this time, Mr. Everett! She's a priceless gem, that one!" he heard her call out after him. "Finer 'n pure gold!"

Chapter Eighteen

Young John Everett had been tilling the vegetable garden in front of the little cottage since morning. His mother watched him from the window as she wove her long hair into a thick black rope and dropped it to dangle behind her back. She shook her head and looked again. Her son often caught her by surprise when she saw glimpses of his father in his mannerisms, and all the more so as he grew into manhood. His hazel eyes, hair that fell into waves, and square jaw were so like those of her husband.

Turning from the window, she tied a white apron over her dusty-blue dress, grabbed a basket, and headed toward the front door. Her spring gardens were bursting with full color in the spring warmth.

Her son looked up from his work. She knew he was eager to complete his chores, as she had promised to take a ride with him as soon as they finished. He loved horses more than any other creature and loved riding along the green hills near the shore.

When she stepped outdoors, Angela stopped and closed her eyes. Warm sunshine fell upon her cheeks. She took a deep breath of the fresh Irish air. A soft breeze was blowing in from the Channel. Pressing a wide-brimmed hat upon her head, she waved to her son and rounded the west side of the house, climbing a set of wide stone stairs that took her to the gardens in back, a large white dog trailing behind her.

John Everett stopped to wipe his brow. Looking out upon the neat rows he had just tilled, he caught sight of a black horse trotting up the winding road. As the rider drew nearer, he set down his tools and removed his gloves.

From a distance John Viana saw a figure in the garden. He spurred the horse into a gallop. At the gate he slowed the animal and swung to the ground, running toward the young man. Within a few yards of him, he stopped, astonished by a replica of his own face from many years before, staring back at him.

The young man also stood speechless. After a few moments, he ran to his father and threw his arms about him.

John held his son, aware of nothing but the embrace of this stranger of whose existence he had learned just an hour before. He pressed his face against the dark, loose curls.

Finally, it was the lad who spoke. "My mother always promised me you'd come home."

They stood in silence for what seemed an eternity. At last John was able to utter a hoarse whisper. "I have a son."

At those words the youth tore himself from John's arms and sprinted toward the cottage.

"Mother! Come quick! He's here!"

His thoughts in a whirl, John ran after the boy.

"Mother!" the young man hollered up from the base of the stone steps at the side of the house.

He stopped two steps up, John on his heels, when the figure of a woman appeared at the top.

"Son, what—" she said in a voice that drifted into her husband's ears like a song.

She stopped short and gasped.

It was her—the face that had haunted a thousand dreams, the woman who had held him frozen in time.

How could this be? How could she be here, *alive*?

The basket she held fell to the ground, pink tulips spilling over the steps. A sudden breeze lifted the hat from her head, carrying it a few yards away. She seemed not to notice, her gaze fixed upon him.

Panting from strain and bewilderment, John ascended the wide stairway, passing the lad. With each upward step, his disbelief intensified. As he neared her, he could see the glimmer of tears welling in her eyes.

At the top, he stared but a moment before reaching out, his fingertips stroking a lock of her hair that had pulled loose, the ebony silk he had yearned to touch for so long. He stepped closer and brushed it, feather-soft against his cheek. Then he gathered her into his arms, her sweet scent of rain and flowers filling his senses.

Her arms swept in a gentle circle around his waist. She trembled against him, weeping.

He kissed her head, her temple, and skimmed his mouth across her cheek, her salty tears seeping between his lips.

Cradling her head in his palms, he searched the watery sapphire eyes and found them unchanged, but for the sorrow of too many lost years. She closed them, and he placed a gentle kiss on each one before moving his lips to hers.

Overtaken by joy, he allowed the pain of sixteen years to flow out with the tears that ran from his own eyes. He tucked his face between her shoulder and neck, rubbing his cheek over her satin skin.

"I'm sorry," he whispered. "I'm so, so sorry." They stood swaying, his cheek moving to hers, mixing their tears. "If you'll again be my wife, I'll never let you out of my sight, I promise you."

"'Love endures all things.'" The light Spanish accent melted his heart. "I've never stopped being your wife."

He winced at her words. His entire body agonized over the loss he had caused by leaving their home.

"I believe I have something that belongs to you," he said in a quiet voice. Pulling back, he lifted his hand. There, part way down on his smallest finger rested the ruby ring. When he slipped it from his hand onto hers, she wilted in his arms, surrendering to more tears.

That night John cuddled his wife in one arm, his son in the other, before the warmth of a fire burning low and gathering the room into its soft light. The white dog curled at their feet.

His son fell into a quick slumber while he and Angela talked.

During the previous hours they had discussed their daughters—how they had been raised, where they lived, what they were like now. Young John had wanted to know all about each one.

John and Angela wept for the time of which they had been robbed and laughed with the sheer happiness of the new beginning they had been given. John accepted the blame for his hasty departure from Ireland. But she praised him for placing their daughters' upbringing as his highest priority.

At last, he insisted on knowing every detail of the shipwreck. Painful as it would be, John waited, his eyes intense upon her.

"For a long time I had no recollection of that dreadful day," she said, "or anything else about my life, not even who I was." She paused as though drawing from a deep well that had been long sealed. "My earliest memories were of being in a medical institution in Spain. I was there for four months before my identity was uncovered."

John watched her eyes in the flickering firelight as a slight smile appeared on her face.

"All of us were surprised to find I was with child. I recall *that* day with perfect clarity. The nurses had suspected that it might be the case and ordered an examination. I, too, had my suspicions because of the twitches I'd been feeling as the baby moved. When the doctor completed the examination, he patted my hand and said, 'You have a little miracle in there.' He had trouble believing an unborn child could have survived the trauma that had taken the lives of so many.

"That night, a young nurse, a kind and patient person, sneaked into my room and startled me from sleep. She produced a small box from her apron pocket. I opened it to find this." She raised her hand to stare again at the ruby ring that at long last sat where it belonged. "She said she took it the day of my arrival and had been keeping it in a safe place, waiting for the right time to show it to me. Upon hearing of my condition, she felt that time had arrived, thinking it might trigger some memories, in particular that of my identity."

She stopped to release an agonizing sigh, as John watched her eyes, tied to her every word.

"It did serve its purpose," she whispered, "but not in a way either of us expected. I'd recognized the ring at once, but still could not remember anything about myself or my husband, much less the three daughters who were then mourning the loss of their mother." She looked down, twisting the ring around on her finger. "That was the beginning of the nightmares."

"Nightmares?" He watched her fight back more of the tears that had already reddened her eyes, but they flowed again.

"I'd begun seeing the distorted image of a man's face forming from a blackness around me." Her brow crinkled as she sniffled. "He began pulling on my arm. I awoke screaming." She dabbed her eyes with a tear-soaked handkerchief. "The nightmare continued, recurring so often during the night that I became afraid to sleep. And then his ghostlike face began to appear in the daytime, too.

"After a while, I decided it must be a very important memory. Instead of fighting it, I welcomed it. Then it became clear to me." She cast her teary expression upon him. "It was the man who'd pulled me from the water that terrible day. He'd seen me go under. He dived down and pulled me to the surface. I remembered being afloat on debris of some sort. For how long I don't know. Somehow he dragged me ashore." Her head dropped. "He died beside me on the edge of the water, John. We were found some time later, miles down shore from the wreckage." Her tears kept coming. "He saved my life, and I never even knew his name."

She sobbed for a long time while he held her close.

"Those are the only memories I regained from that awful day. After that, the nightmares ceased, and other memories began flooding back. Soon, I could recall the faces of my husband and daughters, my family, places, events, many things. After a while the faces were followed by names, including my own.

"My sister was located, and I was released to her care. She told me what little she knew of you and helped me to further complete the puzzle. By the time our son was born, most all my memory had been restored. That was when my sister and I began our search for you." The tears flowed again. "For *four long years* we searched, John, but you were nowhere to be found!

"As a last resort, I decided I would have to work up the courage to visit your mother. I thought I could appeal to any bit of compassion she *must* have kept for her own son." Angela stopped to wipe the tears, propping herself up on her elbow. "But when I came face to face with her, I found not even a spark of any such feeling. All I saw was cold, unbridled hatred. The most I could do was return the ring to her, hoping that someday she would begin her own search.

"When I left her home, I collapsed on the road outside and wept. I decided right then that I had to look to the future and be courageous for the sake of our son. I knew if you ever learned of my survival, you would seek first for me in the land we both loved. So I used what was left of my inheritance from my parents' estate to rent this cottage for John and me."

"I'm so sorry. I had no idea." He pulled her close again.

They sat in silence for several minutes.

"John," she said, looking into his face. "Why do you continue to apologize? You are not to blame!"

He pushed himself away and stood to pace about the room. "*I* left! *I* changed our name! *I* kept hidden from all society, thinking I was choosing the best life for our daughters, not realizing I was depriving them. *I* am the one who took them from their mother!"

"You left for the *sake* of our daughters, John! You changed your name because of your mother. *She* is to blame, if anyone, and she alone." For the first time, he detected anger in her voice. "She was a hateful woman who thrived on the misery of others." Angela pulled her knees up and leaned forward. "But despite her actions, *I* don't hate *her*. I forgive her, for I would never want to be acquainted with such hatred as she harbored.

Yet, it was *she* who gave you life and *she* who drove you to me so many years ago."

"Come with me," John whispered, holding his hand out. He walked her out into the chilly breeze, leading her away from the cottage. They followed a pathway through one of the gardens. He pointed to the horizon.

"Do you see that moon?" Its crescent emitted a dim glow. "Do you remember your last words to me? You asked me to look for that moon each night at the hour of ten. You promised that you would be doing the same. Although I believed you gone, I've looked for that moon every night, thinking of you."

"If only the moon could speak." The tears started again in her eyes. "For I, too, have searched for it every night, renewing my hope that you would find me."

They stood, wrapped in each other's arms for a long time. After returning to the cottage, they talked on until she surrendered to the slumber their son had found hours before.

But John lay awake, contemplating the consequences of this new development. Where would they live? Would he return to his work at the University? Would his daughters want to move back to Ireland, a place of which they had only scant memories? What of Mr. and Mrs. Wright and Old Stormy? His family had grown so attached to them. But he could never ask his precious wife to live the hard life at the lighthouse. So much to consider…the unknowns were many, with but one absolute—there was a family to reunite.

Before falling asleep, he kissed the heads of the two in his arms, but not the dog at his feet.

John Viana awoke to the sweet smell of baking bread and found himself alone on the floor, engulfed in blankets before a cold hearth. As his eyes focused, the first vision to appear was that of a pink sunrise through a nearby window.

It occurred to him that here the sun *rose* over the ocean, whereas it *set* over the ocean at his home.

The smiling face of his wife interrupted the view. He reached out to gather her into his arms.

"Is this all a dream?" he asked, still sleepy.

"If it is, don't wake me. John is out at the stable, saddling the horses," she said. "It seems the ride promised him yesterday somehow slipped my mind."

He could not take his gaze from her face. "We have many things to take care of today."

"John...why did you not remarry?"

"I could not bear the thought of another other woman raising your children." He recalled the lonely years. "I wanted to keep you strong in my mind and in their hearts. Anyone else would've influenced them in a different direction. Besides, I've never known anything as sweet as your love. That could never be replaced, not in a thousand lifetimes. I chose to hold onto that love."

"I've been thinking about my girls. How will I ever face them?"

"Face them?"

"John, you are almost unchanged." She skimmed her fingertips over his cheek. "This is still the face of the man I married." She touched his hair near his temples. "There is just slight gray, but overall you're still the same. But my daughters remain children in my mind, Alex just past infancy. How will I recognize them? How will I ever accept them as adults?"

He took her hand from his hair and kissed it. Standing, he led her to a mirror across the room, and stood her before it. "See that face—that beautiful woman? You're looking at the face of Jessica. She is so much like you in form, mannerisms, and viewpoints that she scares me at times. Now look at the face behind you."

Her gaze shifted to his reflection.

"Alexandra is a replica of me." He paused and then added, "But without the stubble."

She giggled.

"Alexandra is simple and innocent, a child in so many ways. She still needs you—your guidance—to lead her into adulthood. Grace is almost unchanged, just taller. How do you think it was that William Sutton recognized her after all those years?" He turned her around to face him. "There's something that a mother has which is a mystery to a father. It's her bond with her children, whether they're small or grown. You'll see. The bond you had with them will remain unbroken."

He kissed her forehead to reassure her and walked to the window. Looking out, he watched his son leading the horses out of the stable. "*There* is the perplexing one."

She joined him at the window.

"There is my son, almost a man, yet just two days ago I knew nothing of his existence. How can he respect the man who separated his family? How will he ever be able to trust my judgments as a father? Will he learn to love the strangers who will be sharing his life, his home? What have I really done to him?" He looked at her. "Indeed, to *all* of us?"

Chapter Nineteen

By the fourth day after returning home, Jessica began to withdraw, seeking solace in the family's gardens. Spending almost the entire day, *every* day, in them, she hid beneath a straw sun hat. She avoided the tower of the lighthouse, as its views only brought back thoughts of her experiences aboard *The Emerald*, which, in turn brought back visions of the ill captain.

She had much thinking to do. And she needed to do it without distraction.

Her concern over Andrew devoured her inside. Why did she feel such a yearning for him? She had known him such a short time.

But she *did* know him, even better than she herself was willing to admit at times. She had learned much of him through his family, his acquaintances, and even from the brief hours she had spent with the man himself. But most of all she had come to know him through his writings. Through those journals she felt the full realm of his emotions—his frustrations with the obstacles he faced as a ship captain, his anger when the crew disobeyed, his anxiety when facing a sudden storm, his exhaustion after working long hours, his comfort when watching the endless waves of a peaceful sea, his excitement when the ship ventured into unknown territory, his happiness in living his life at sea.

His feelings had become hers. She had learned his reactions by reading the ways he confronted and solved problems.

Yes, she *knew* him. His passion and expression had drawn her in, forever changing her. The life that had been hers would never again be the same.

Stopping her work, she sat down and looked around at the land, at the house nestled in the woods, and at the distant lighthouse crown. Tears rolled down her cheeks. Though she now looked upon the things that she had loved most in her life, something inside gnawed at her, something that had begun years before and was only enhanced during her travels—something that had charged upon her full force while aboard *The Emerald* and in the presence of Andrew.

What she had revealed to Grace after arriving back home was true—she *did* love Andrew Winterfield, and she loved what he represented. Even were she to never see him again, he had drawn from her a side that she had been suppressing all her life.

It struck her then and there that to live much longer at the lighthouse would crush her. She could no longer subsist on mere imaginings of the world and lands out there. Reading of them in books would not sustain her anymore. They beckoned to her. She did not care how many oceans she would have to cross to discover them.

But how could she? What of loyalty? She could not just uproot herself and risk hurting her father—how could she be so selfish? And where would she go?

Something Grace said the previous summer blazed through her mind. What would she find out there? For what was she searching? Would she unearth some yet undiscovered happiness?

Her shoulders drooped. Grace was right. Appealing as it sounded, a life of travel and adventure was not the key to contentment.

So then *what*? What would bring true meaning to her life?

Defeated, she let her tools drop.

It was people. Her life would have no real value without sharing it with those she loved.

She could not leave here.

On the eighth day after her return, Jessica looked up from her work to see her sister running toward her.

"What is it, Grace?"

"It's a letter!" She struggled to catch her breath. "From Kent, from Richard Winterfield! It's addressed to you, Jessie."

Jessica's hand flew to her mouth. Her heart skipped a beat. She broke the seal and began reading aloud. It must have been sent express, for it was dated just two days before.

> "My Dear Jessica,
>
> "I realize by now you must be very concerned over the condition of my son, Andrew. It was my desire to contact you only after it was known which direction this illness would take, and I asked Stephen Sutton not to write to you regarding this matter. It now seems quite certain that Andrew…"

Jessica stopped reading and handed it back to her sister. "I can't read this." A tear fell to the ground as she closed her eyes.

"Would you like me to read it, Jessie?"

She nodded, but her eyes remained closed. She held her breath.

Grace glanced down at the next words on the page, looked up at her sister, then resumed reading.

> "It now seems quite certain that Andrew…should make a full recovery."

Jessica released her breath. Tears flooded over her cheeks. The sisters embraced, laughing and crying at the same time. A few moments later Grace returned to the letter.

> "Several more weeks of recuperation will ensue, but the worst is over. I understand from his physician that Andrew owes his survival to the care given him during the critical hours before his return to England. Without the continual hydration he received, he would not, in all likelihood, have survived.

"Since Andrew is yet unaware of your services, I wish to extend, in his behalf, my utmost gratitude to the greatest caregiver he could have ever hoped for, which is, of course, you, Jessica.

"Had you not been on that ship I might have never seen my son alive again.

"My family is indebted to you for your priceless service. My wife and eldest son remain abroad, but also wish to extend to you their sincere gratitude."

"Oh, Jessie! Can you believe all this has turned out in such a wonderful way?"

Jessica sobbed as the weight of a great darkness parted just as a heavy curtain from before a bright window.

Later that evening, Jessica stood atop the great pillar, coal hair flowing in the breeze, a glorious sunset blazing on the horizon. She had been out there...with him...on these very waters. Perhaps someday soon... She turned to see her sister smiling at her.

The following day brought yet more news. This time Jessica and her sister saw the express approaching from a distance. They descended the lighthouse steps and rowed back to shore, running to the house.

Mrs. Wright had the letter. "Looks to be in your father's hand," she said.

They sat in the parlor while Grace read it aloud.

"My Dear Daughters,

"I trust Jessica had a safe return trip. I will be returning myself the fourth of June. My excursion has led me to some surprising discoveries. There is much to tell you. Alexandra's return will occur on the afternoon of the third. Please prepare Brentwood House to welcome two important people.

"I long to see you again.

"My love to you,
Father"

It had been more than a month since Jessica had seen her father, and she missed him very much. Had he only known the emotional turmoil she had experienced...

"Now I'm completely baffled, Grace," she said as they sat pondering the letter. "Who in the world can he be bringing here?"

"It makes complete sense to *me*, Jess. Remember thinking how strange it was that father would traipse about the country in pursuit of mere wealth? Well...we already know that the ring belongs to his family. It's no doubt led him to some long lost relatives."

"No, Grace, I don't agree. He left his entire family, and in all the years we've lived here, he's mentioned very few of them with any fondness at all."

"Well, then, we shall have to exercise patience for one more day."

"I'm sure that'll be easier to do with the return of Alex today," Jessica said. "She, too, will no doubt have much to tell."

"And will give us an update on Andrew," Grace teased.

Jessica smiled and rose to begin some household chores.

Alexandra returned soon after the letter from their father arrived.

"Jessie, do you realize it's been over a month since we last saw each other?" Alexandra exclaimed after they all embraced.

"And how I missed all of you when I was away!" Jessica replied.

As Alexandra unpacked her things, Jessica remembered the souvenirs she had purchased for her two sisters in Paris. She ran to retrieve them, and all three gathered in Alexandra's room.

"I'm sorry I didn't bring any gifts from Kent." Alexandra looked down.

"Oh, no. We brought far too many things home with us in January," Grace said.

"So, who do you suppose Father is bringing home with him?" Alexandra looked at them in wonder.

Her sisters admitted they had given it much thought but were unable to account for the identity of the guests.

"Father does know how to stir up a household," Jessica said, laughing. "Alex, were you able to see much of Andrew Winterfield while in their home?"

At the mention of his name, Alexandra's countenance saddened as she sat down beside Jessica on the bed.

"He was quarantined while I was there," she replied. "Even Catherine couldn't enter his room—only the nurses, the doctor, and his father. However, yesterday, Jessie, I was allowed to take one of the horses for a ride. I returned and was walking across the courtyard and there, sitting in the sunshine and wrapped in a blanket was Andrew! I thought it was Roman at first—they look so much alike. I spoke with him for a moment. He said he was feeling better and was able to move around a bit more. He knew who I was, Jessie. He asked me to relate a message to you."

"He did?" She jumped to her feet. "What was it, Alex?"

"Oh, Jessie. He appeared so ill, so weak. He had a kind and handsome face, but had you seen him, you would have wondered, as I did, how he could have survived. He was so pale."

"We heard from Mr. Winterfield, Alex," Grace said. "He informed us that Andrew will recover."

Alexandra gave Jessica a questioning look. "Andrew said to tell you he was glad that Father had appointed him as your custodian that day in the warehouse."

Jessica's head dropped, her lips parting in a smile.

"Jessie, what day? What did he mean? Jessie...is he in love with you?" Alexandra stood, casting a stern look at her.

Jessica's gaze shifted to Grace, who looked at her in silence, a grin forming at the corners of her mouth.

Chapter Twenty

Mr. and Mrs. Wright stood in front of Brentwood House to meet the carriage.

Jessica and her sisters watched from the parlor window. Their father emerged and greeted the couple with warm embraces. She saw a puzzled look form on his face when he looked around. His daughters were nowhere in sight.

They had decided the parlor would afford them a good view of the guests before having to meet them. The three crowded around the window, careful to remain hidden from view. Where were the expected guests? He spoke for a moment with the Wrights. Mrs. Wright's hands rose to her cheeks, a muffled squeal penetrating the glass of the parlor window.

Jessica looked at her sisters, puzzled.

"What did he tell her?" Grace asked.

"I don't know," Jessica said.

When they looked back the trio had begun walking toward the entrance of the house, excited chatter coming from both the Wrights. Jessica strained her ears, but was unable to discern their words.

She and her sisters hurried to a position in the middle of the room, straightening their dresses and checking each other's hair before standing in a straight row to greet their father.

The party entered the foyer.

"I can't believe it," Mrs. Wright was saying. "I just can't believe it!"

"You talk to the girls," Mr. Wright said. "I'll tend to Old Stormy."

"I'll be nearby if you need anything," Mrs. Wright offered.

Upon passing the parlor doorway, she glanced at the three. Jessica was quick to discern worry in her smile.

When the front door closed, their father stepped into the room. Rather than wait in proper stance for him to approach them as they had planned, they rushed into his arms.

But in his quick embrace, Jessica felt something amiss.

"Sit down, girls," he said, his tone almost a command. "I have some startling news."

"Father, we've missed you so much," Alexandra chirped after seating herself on the sofa. "Where have you been?"

He did not sit, but paced the room. "You'll recall the ruby ring. It belongs to someone very important."

"Let me guess, Father," Alexandra interrupted. "It belonged to our grandmother, but now that she has died, you have inherited everything that belonged to her. We're moving into a palace, just like in the fairy tales!"

"Alex, please!" Grace reprimanded. "Let him speak."

"If only it were that simple, Alexandra," their father said.

Jessica watched him with uncertainty as his steps took him back and forth before them. His fingers rubbed his temples.

"All right," he stated after a moment of tense silence. "Do you remember several years ago in the spring when Alexandra found the dead bird in the meadow?"

"Yes," Jessica said. "She brought it back here for burial."

He dropped to one knee before them. "Recall that she mourned because there was no doubt a nest of baby birds somewhere awaiting the return of their mother that would never happen?"

Jessica stared at her father. Beads of perspiration had erupted on his brow. His voice sounded almost desperate.

"But she *wasn't* dead," Alexandra said. "Remember, Father?"

He grabbed Alexandra's hands and Jessica jumped. "That's right!" he exclaimed. "She was only stunned and not dead at all. We watched her fly away, back to her nest, to her babies!"

"What are you trying to say, Father?" Grace asked as he rose to his feet. "That there is some relative you've brought to meet us?"

"Our Grandmother!" Alexandra shouted. "She's *not* dead. You've brought her home to us!"

"No, Alex!" their father cried. Jessica shrank back against the sofa at the irritation in his voice. "It's your *mother*!"

Silence filled the room like the blackness that engulfs the landscape on a starless night. All Jessica could hear were her father's words echoing over and over in her mind, *your mother*! She struggled to take a breath as her sisters erupted in a barrage of questions.

"Where is she?"

"Where has she been?"

"Does she want to see us?"

"What does she look like?"

"How did you find her?"

Each question pealed through Jessica's head like a clap of thunder. She covered her ears with her palms, but still she heard them.

"Does she remember us?"

"Does she still love us?"

"When can we see her?"

Jessica jumped to her feet and fled from the room. She stumbled up the staircase, frantic to reach her bed chamber. Slamming the door behind her, she pounded her fist against the wall. The commotion downstairs did not let up, and she then heard Mrs. Wright's voice join in, trying to calm her sisters. Her face dropped into her palms and she burst into tears.

A knock on her door was followed by her father's voice. "Jessica."

"No. Go away."

But the door opened.

"I don't have all the answers," he said in a calm voice. "But she does want to see you."

"She's dead!" Tears flushed over her cheeks.

"No. She's been living in Ireland. She survived the accident."

"How could you have been so *cruel*? How could you have taken us from her?"

"I didn't know."

"Why didn't she search for us?"

"She did—for many years."

"Then why did she stop?"

"Jessica, she's here. That's all that matters now."

"Where was she during all those fearful nights? No one was there to comfort that child when she awoke screaming from nightmares. No one even heard her because you were out at Old Stormy. Did you know that, Father? Did you know I suffered most nights as a child with awful visions of her death? Do you know what I endured because of my fear of the ocean? Why did you never go back to Ireland? We could have found her. Why have you never taken us there?"

When she felt his arms surround her shoulders, she tried to move away. His grip tightened.

"Jessica, it's time you realize your father is not perfect. Allow me to be human." He let loose of her and stepped to the door. "I never meant to sever you from your mother. Don't *you* now perpetuate that break." With that, he left. The door clicked closed behind him.

When Jessica at last descended the stairs, through the parlor doorway she could see her father sitting cross-legged on the sofa. The sounds of soft voices—those of her sisters included—and even laughter reached her ears.

At her footfall on the last step, her father looked up. On his feet at once, he led her, not into the parlor, but the kitchen. The scent of the pork roast dinner she had missed lingered.

"Jessica, there's something else you need to know."

He had taken both her hands, but she could not look into his face for fear the tears would start again.

"When your mother sailed for Spain so long ago, it was too soon to know, but…"

She then did look up and saw the troubled look in his eyes. All at once, her sorrow was for him. What he must have endured the previous weeks!

"She...was expecting another child," he managed to say. "You have a younger brother."

Her chin began to quiver. The oncoming tears were for him. The enormity of it all!

"His name is John, and I'd like you to meet him first."

Sticking his head around the door, her father called out toward the parlor. Within moments, Jessica was staring at a young version of her father, but with tousled curls as black as her own hair. The young man ran forward, throwing his arms about her.

"You're just like I thought my whole life," he said, stepping away. "Just like Mother."

His Irish brogue coaxed a little smile from her. The lanky youngster trotted out of the room, leaving her speechless and staring at her father. The door her brother had pulled closed started to creak open.

When Angela Everett entered the room, Jessica's breath stopped short. Her lips fell open as the portrait in the library she had studied a thousand times came to life before her. The sparkle in her mother's eyes revealed a kindness and love that the portrait had kept concealed for sixteen years. Jessica could only stare, feeling as though she knew her, as though they had never been apart.

Her sorrow and anger melted.

And then the portrait spoke. "Hello, Jessie."

It was a voice sweet and tender, compassionate. When a tear slipped over her mother's perfect cheek, Jessica wondered what her own expression was saying.

She tried to recall just one memory of her somewhere in the corners of her mind. Tears began to well because her recollections were no more than shadows. But her eyes and her heart could not deny the bond they must have shared for four short years.

Angela took a hesitant step forward. She held her hand out. Jessica saw the ruby ring.

The ring! All this time it had belonged on her *mother's* finger!

Rather than take the hand, Jessica fell into her mother's arms and sobbed against her shoulder while Angela rocked her. The door closed with a creak as John Viana slipped from the room.

A week later, Jessica paced her bedroom floor as her father and mother packed for a trip to London.

She ignored the soft tap on the door.

Moments later the door cracked open. "May I come in?" her mother asked.

Jessica tried to smile. "Of course you may."

"I like this room, Jessie," her mother said as she walked closer. "It must be a consoling place to be during times of distress."

Jessica looked into her mother's caring blue eyes and admitted defeat. "Time cannot take away a mother's discernment and instinct, can it?" she asked.

Her mother sat on the edge of the bed and patted the space beside her. Jessica accepted the invitation and sat close enough for her mother to place one arm around her shoulders.

"Jessie, when I met your father, I'd been in Ireland and away from my family for two years. I had some new friends. A few young men had taken notice of me, but I courted none of them because I had no interest. But when I met your father, I knew he was different. He was intriguing and intelligent, yet kind and humble, and, well, he made me laugh. Our relationship grew, and before I knew it, he proposed marriage to me."

Jessica tried to envision her father young and in love.

"What I'm trying to say, Jessie," her mother continued, "is that I don't have much experience in courtship. Ours was very short."

Jessica looked away.

"But I do understand what it is to feel true and real love. To feel a deep yearning so strong that it hurts, as if your heart would burst if you had to wait a single moment longer before seeing him, to feel the agony of not knowing if he feels the same about you."

Jessica looked over to meet her gaze. "You endured that pain for sixteen years, didn't you, Mother?"

"That pain and I are old friends. I know it better than any other human feeling. And when I look into your eyes, Jess, I hurt all over again. I see that pain in *your* eyes. May I help?"

"You and Father are leaving for London tomorrow. He is very near there." She had been growing more anxious, wanting to go along but the trip would be just a few short days, perhaps the only time they would ever find for themselves. How could she ask to intrude? She could not, but would endure as her mother had. Maybe in time her feelings would wane. "Perhaps you and Father could pay him a visit," she suggested.

"Does your father know of your feelings for him?"

"He doesn't even know of our acquaintance. I didn't wish to dampen his elation with *my* problems."

"I'm sure your father wouldn't feel that way, but you're kind and unselfish to think of his feelings first. This is a very delicate subject. I suppose there's not enough time to talk to him about it now. What's the young man's name?"

"Andrew Winterfield."

"I've not heard the name Winterfield in many years." A broad smile spread across Angela's face.

Jessica told her how they had met and about his writings in the ship's logs and how it was she had begun to know him. She related the time she spent on *The Emerald* and how she yearned to know more and more of this fascinating man.

"I'll speak with your father if you'd like," her mother offered. "Perhaps a visit would be in order."

"I dare say he wouldn't refuse *you* any request, Mother."

They laughed and embraced.

John and Angela had been invited to stay as guests at the Sutton home. A servant at the door greeted them, the same man who had met John on that momentous rainy night.

He escorted them to the north wing of the house, 'the guest wing,' the servant explained.

"Mr. Sutton will be joining you in the study in two hours," the servant said. "He has asked me to tell you that you, along with the Sutton family, will be dining at Winterfield Manor this evening. And to please make yourselves comfortable."

The servant bowed his head and left them alone in their light and spacious chamber.

"I met William's wife and sons only once when his two boys were small," John said after the door closed behind the servant. "I'm excited for you to meet them."

"I remember your talking about William Sutton in the past," Angela said. "You had only good things to say."

"We were very close in our youth, but lost contact the year before I left England."

"I'm anxious to meet the man who's responsible for reuniting our family."

They unpacked their few belongings and took a brief stroll through the grounds.

At three o'clock they returned to the study, where their meeting with William was to take place. Upon entering the room, John shook his head.

"Although seeing this study for the first time a few weeks ago," he said, scanning the room, "it's forever etched in my mind."

"Why is that?" she asked, taking his arm.

He led her to the glass doors and they stepped out onto the sunny veranda where he had dropped to the ground in the rain.

"Let's just say it's where I passed some of the darkest moments of my life, the place where I discovered I'd forfeited sixteen entire years."

They heard a noise inside and stepped back in as William Sutton hastened toward them in much the same manner he had approached John three weeks before. A smile of victory spanned his face as he grabbed hold of the pair in a rough but warm embrace.

"I can't express the utter happiness I'm feeling at this moment," William exclaimed. "Who would've ever known I could assist you in such a way?" he said, stepping back.

"Mr. Sutton, how can we ever repay you?" Angela asked.

"John, no wonder your devotion remained so solid all those years," William said, examining her face. "Is she not the sweetest, most beautiful creature you've ever laid eyes on?" His smile was beaming. "My dear, you owe me not a thing. Nothing in this world could begin to approach the reward I'm experiencing this very moment. This is payment in excess," he said, squeezing them both again. "Please sit down."

They seated themselves on the couch before the large desk behind which William then sat. Pulling a pair of spectacles from his pocket and a thick file from a drawer in the desk, he folded his hands, his elbows coming to rest upon the desktop.

"John, I realize not a single object could ever compare to this treasure before you…," he said, holding an open palm out toward Angela, "…but there's this matter of a large fortune that has been left in its entirety in your name. As your mother's barrister, I have the obligation and responsibility to distribute those assets as described in your father's will." Before John could protest, William held up his hand. "Now I know, John, you have no desire, no interest whatsoever, in this inheritance, but might I inform you that, technically, this estate has belonged to you since the death of your father. Your mother realized all those years that, at any time, you had the right to turn her out to the dower house that was her entailment."

"I never wanted any of it," John said. "Can the assets be sold?"

"According to the will and current laws, if you surrender your rights, the estate is to go to the next oldest surviving son of your grandfather, which would be your Uncle Kenneth."

"No!" John jumped to his feet, throwing his palms on the desk. "Kenneth is *not* my oldest surviving uncle, Will, and you know that!"

"John, I'm sorry about your Uncle Matthew." William removed his spectacles. "Perhaps you hadn't heard. He was exiled shortly after you left England."

For a brief moment, John could only stare in return, but then pushed himself from the desk and began pacing.

"So, they did it," John mumbled. "They convicted him." He stared at the shelves filled to the brim with law books. "Couldn't *something* have been done, Will? Was there no justice? Would no one vouch for him? I can't believe they went through with it and convicted him. *His own family!*"

"John?"

He turned to his wife. She looked bewildered. He had never told her of it. He had never told anyone—except William, who was just starting to study law at the time.

"John," said William, "I wish something could've been done for Matthew."

John stopped before a high wall of books, crossing his arms. The threat looming over his uncle when he had left had been carried out—banishment. He had been helpless then, as was William. Oh, he had tried to speak with his mother about it. But she opposed Matthew, and that opposition carried over to *him* when he sided with his uncle.

He settled onto the edge of his chair, taking his wife's hand. "I've never told you the details surrounding my decision to leave England. My father and uncles all had seats in the House of Lords. Though my father was a conservative, his brother, Matthew, was an outspoken liberal. He sympathized with the poor, but recognized their blight on the nation and proposed a plan to rid Britain of its workhouses and homeless through innovative education and employment programs. He appealed to his peers from two perspectives: the saving of monies spent to support these unfortunates and the creation for all residents of a stronger sense of community and self-worth."

"Did they reject such idealistic proposals?" his wife asked.

"Not at first. The dissension began when he espoused the cause of a young woman who had committed a crime and been arrested. Matthew stood in her defense, insisting that hers was an act of desperation. He admired her courage and contended that had the nobility of England exercised such valor, there would be little poverty in the entire realm. However, her crime constituted a national threat, and he soon lost all support for his programs. Wanting me to back him in his cause, he came to Cambridge where I was just finishing school. He believed I would soon be taking my father's seat and pointed out what great things we could accomplish together, assuming I'd agree."

"Wasn't that a year after your father's death?" Angela asked.

"Yes. And though having great fellow-feeling for the girl and admiring his efforts in her behalf, I gave Matthew no hope of my taking the title. The only certainty I had in the government—in any government—was that man's ruling himself has only proved disastrous for the majority. Indeed, I had no certainty in my own future and made that clear to him. He left disappointed. But during the short time he was with me, his brothers and their wives, including my mother, sparked an investigation into his past activities, including his associates. They exaggerated reports, and falsified accounts. When all was said and done, they charged him with subversion.

"Of course, I never knew the real reason that drove them to such an action—and against one of their own, no less. But I knew they perceived some kind of threat, either against their positions, their salaries, or perhaps even the reputation of the family. Regardless, within weeks of his return, he was arrested."

"And that's what drove you to Dublin?" she asked.

"I couldn't bear to see him convicted, and could only hope that the truth would become known and justice would triumph. But even if it did, I couldn't allow myself to live among a society and family that would turn like animals on one of their own. I would go where I could serve others in my own way in peace. When I left London, I never looked back. The last bit of news I heard came from you, Will." He looked at his friend. "Remember when you tracked me down at the train station to inform me that they were calling for Matthew's deportment?"

"Several months later, I heard he'd sailed," William said.

"I suppose I should be glad for Matthew," John mumbled. "I'm certain he's better off wherever he is."

An uneasy silence seeped through the chamber.

"What's to be done with the estate, John?" William asked. "Your father saved almost every shilling he had. And what of Candlegate?"

"They would never allow a deserter to take possession of the Earl's castle," John argued.

"I don't think they know just *what* to do with it. I can't imagine in the country's entire history a Lord ever refusing his inheritance! I doubt they can keep you out just because you decline the Seat. Candlegate was your childhood home, John. You loved Surrey."

William watched his friend pace.

"Remember, if you deny it, it'll be turned over to Kenneth."

John whipped around to glare at him. "I intend to accept the inheritance, Will." His eyes narrowed. *"All of it."*

During the carriage ride to Winterfield Manor, John and his wife chatted with Stephen Sutton about his involvement in their case.

"I understand from my daughters," John said, "that the young man who ended up spending a night in the parlor of my home last summer was none other than you, Stephen. Had I only known!"

"Circumstances don't always cooperate," William interjected.

"I told you before you needed *me* along," Stephen's younger brother, Preston, piped up. "You could've avoided all that trouble if you'd taken me with you to Cornwall, *and* we would've found Mr. Viana."

"You think so?" Stephen asked.

"You're both forgetting one thing," John said. "I didn't want to be found."

"I have some things for *all* of you to think about," Angela interrupted. "Had you not been injured, Stephen, you wouldn't have been robbed by Mr. Scarborough, and you wouldn't have left that note on my husband's stationery. Nor would you have recalled the name 'John' and made a connection to Grace. Had you not been robbed, Mr. Scarborough wouldn't even have been involved, and he would not have sent the ring to John. That man, in his greed, orchestrated the sequence of events that led to John's reunion with your father, culminating in his finding us in Ireland. Had your visit to Cornwall last summer been uneventful, none of us would be sitting here this evening. So you see, Mr. Sutton," she added, turning to William, "circumstances *did* cooperate. And quite well, I might add."

William began to laugh, and the others followed suit. "John," he said, chuckling, "I wonder if I might make an associate of your wife. She has quite a talent for getting to the bottom of things."

"I'm very sorry, Will," John said, slipping his arm around Angela's back, "but my wife is unavailable."

The comment sent the entire carriage into laughter.

"Tell us about your daughters," William replied. "Perhaps one of *them* has inherited this unique talent."

"Yes," said Preston, leaning forward, "tell us about your daughters."

Introductions at Winterfield Manor occurred in the foyer.

"Richard, this is my wife, Angela," said John.

"What a pleasure to meet you at last." Richard lifted her hand to kiss it.

"We've decided that the entire family will be known as Viana," John announced.

"And how do you find it to return to your maiden name?" Richard asked Angela.

"I like it. I feel as though I'm twenty again."

They all laughed.

"I apologize for the absence of my wife and eldest son," Richard said after introducing Catherine. "They're traveling abroad."

Angela hugged Catherine, happy to meet the young lady her daughters had befriended in the winter.

"Pardon me for being so forward, Mrs. Viana," said Catherine, "but you're very stunning."

"I've never had such a gracious greeting." Angela smiled.

"And so much like Jessica," Catherine added. "I thought you were she when you stepped out of the carriage."

After the introduction, Preston took the arm of Catherine, leading her a few steps away and talking in an undertone.

"Did you ever think the three of us would be reunited?" Richard asked, placing a hand upon one shoulder each of John and William.

"And under the very best of circumstances, no less," William said. "I'm sorry I've neglected our friendship over the years, Richard," he added. "Here we've been in such close proximity all along."

"Business," Richard replied. "A poor excuse, is it not?"

"And, John?" William asked, turning to him. "He'll just have to beg our forgiveness so we can all move on."

Laughter once again filled the entrance hall.

"The younger of my twin sons, Andrew, will be joining us for the meal," Richard said to the small group. "Perhaps you've heard of his recent brush with a severe illness. It's left him quite weak, and he still keeps to his room most of the time. He's been preserving his strength today for the pleasure of joining our gathering."

Angela had not yet revealed to her husband Jessica's feelings for the younger Winterfield son and was eager to meet the man of whom her daughter had spoken so well.

Richard began the evening with an abbreviated tour of the mansion. Angela lagged behind with Catherine.

"You must have mixed feelings about your brother's illness," Angela said. "After all, it *has* kept him at home these few weeks."

"I was so afraid for him at first," Catherine said. "I would linger around his door for any chance of glimpsing him when the nurse would enter or leave. When I did see him, he was so pale that I didn't even recognize him. He was only released from quarantine a week ago. We've been spending much time together ever since. He loves the game of chess and has been teaching me how to play." Catherine looked down. "It's as you say, Mrs. Viana—I'm truly happy to see his recovery, but will be sad to see him return to his ship so soon."

Angela offered a sympathetic smile to the young lady who displayed an obvious fondness for Andrew. "Perhaps you can join your brother, Roman, and learn the trade of buying."

"No…I would rather join Andrew, but I know there's no place for a woman on the cargo ship."

"Then perhaps he'll settle close by to raise a family some-day."

"I would like that very much, but as I told your daughter, Grace, while she was visiting in January, it would take a special woman, indeed, that could steal his heart away from his life on the ocean. I don't believe that woman exists."

Angela's brow furrowed at the comment.

The tour ended in the grandiose dining room, where all were invited to sit. The fireplace stood in darkness this warm summer evening.

John smirked when his wife took a seat.

"Why do you smile that way?" she whispered.

"Because you chose the very chair Jessica sat in for the one and only meal we ever ate in this room."

"Something so simple provokes a smile like that from your lips?"

"I'll have to tell you later of the conversation that took place at the end of the meal, involving Richard's rather arrogant eldest son. Perhaps 'thrashing' would be a better description for what occurred."

"Jessica?"

When he nodded, she smiled, too, and could only imagine what had transpired.

Soon the tall figure of Andrew Winterfield appeared at the dining room entrance. He apologized for arriving late and took a chair near the end of the table between his sister and John Viana.

"These Winterfield sons do like to make a grand entrance," John whispered to his wife.

Angela scrutinized the young man while his father introduced him to their guests. He was indeed very handsome, though appearing a bit thin.

When Richard introduced Angela, she saw he was a bit startled.

"You'll excuse me, Mrs. Viana. For a moment I thought you were your daughter."

"That seems to be a common occurrence of late."

"I also understand that congratulations are in order for the recent reunion of your family," Andrew stated to both the Vianas. "I spent some time with Jessica when she was aboard my ship. She told me much of you, Mr. Viana, and everything she knew of you, Madame. Her eyes revealed a longing to know you. I'm pleased to hear of your restoration and that of your son to the family."

Angela thanked him. He had a pleasing, gracious way about him, and she was content with her first impression of the young man.

"I understand you've been ill of late," John said. "I'm happy to see you're feeling better."

"Thank you, Sir. I hear I owe my recovery and present health to none other than your daughter."

This statement surprised Angela and her husband as well, by the expression on his face. Jessica had mentioned to her mother caring for the ill captain, but did not take credit to this extent.

"Is that a fact?" asked John. "You'll excuse me if I appear a bit surprised," he said. "I assumed your illness occurred after your return to England."

"No, Sir, but during our journey. I'm most indebted to your daughter. I remember very little of the last thirty-six hours, but the account has been related of her continual care for me. I heard it said she didn't leave my side, even depriving herself of sleep and nourishment, all the while braving a severe storm. Were you aware of your daughter's intense fear of the ocean, Sir?"

"Yes." John's reply was cool. "It's a respectful fear, considering what happened to her mother."

Angela discerned that John's response was a defensive one. Of course he knew of her fears—*all* of them.

"Yet, she also has an unusual curiosity about the sea," Andrew said, "and reported to me that she had read about many of its creatures and hidden secrets." His smile seemed to ease the tension. "I understand full well her respect for and interest in the ocean."

As the meal wore on and conversation flowed, Angela decided Andrew Winterfield was a very likable young man. He seemed a strong leader of his crew, an organized, confident, yet kind young man. His warmth and congeniality was extended to William Sutton and his family, as well.

She was discreet in her observances of Andrew, becoming ever more pleased with his demeanor, and wondered whether Jessica realized the reason she was drawn to him was the fact that he was very much like John. She appreciated the attention Andrew paid to Catherine. He seemed concerned with her every need. The young lady glowed with affection for her brother.

The later evening found the small party in the billiard room. Andrew sat with the ladies as the other men competed on the two tables. Now and then they called him over for the most difficult shots. Otherwise, he sat beside Angela, engaging her in private conversation.

"My father was ecstatic to hear of your discovery after so many years. I'm sorry you had to miss so much of your daughters' lives."

"It will take some time to come to know them well, I imagine," Angela responded.

"Yes," Andrew looked down at the floor, "I would have to agree. It will take many years." His expression brightened when he again looked at her. "My father relayed a conversation he had had with your husband when your family was guest in this house in January. He said they were in this very room. Your husband revealed the intense love he still felt for you. Father recalled being impressed by such enduring devotion, and here the most unexpected of outcomes has occurred."

"My own faith never wavered," Angela said, "although I had a distinct advantage over John, for he had no reason to believe that I was still alive."

"How you must've agonized thinking of your daughters growing up without you."

"Every new day brought greater anxiety," she admitted. "Had it not been for my son, I don't believe I would've survived."

They conversed for over an hour. She told him many of her memories of her young family and prodded him about his feelings on numerous topics.

It was well after midnight when the two families returned to the Sutton home.

"I admire your selection of friends, John," Angela said as she changed into her nightgown. "Their families are very pleasant."

"What did you think of Stephen Sutton?" he asked.

"He seems like a respectful young man," she replied. "What is your opinion?"

"He asks too many questions."

"Oh? I hadn't noticed. Questions about what?"

"Grace...during the game, at every opportunity."

"Well, they *did* meet at Brentwood when he was there. I defy any young man to be anything but paralyzed in her presence." Her comment only provoked a growl from him, but since they were on the subject, she pressed forward. "I was most impressed with Andrew Winterfield. He seems to be an exceptional young man."

"Exceptional, yes. He left me with the same impression," said John. "But I think his regard for Jessica is more than casual. It makes me wonder about *her* feelings." He shrugged. "We may never know."

"Perhaps," she mumbled.

* * * * *

Dawn gave way to mid-morning. John Viana paced about the shadowy room, looking again at his wife as she began to stir awake.

"What it is, John?" she asked.

"A letter arrived about a half hour ago from Winterfield Manor, signed by Andrew."

He handed her the letter as she sat upright, tucking the sheet around her. She read it aloud.

"Dear Mr. and Mrs. Viana,

"It was a pleasure to meet you last evening. I hope you enjoyed yourselves, as did I.

"As I conveyed to you in conversation, I feel I owe a great debt to your daughter, Jessica, and would appreciate the opportunity of expressing my gratitude to her myself.

"Since I am unable to travel at this time, I am requesting the honor of her presence for a fortnight here in Kent. I will, of course, cover the expense of her trip, and if you feel it inappropriate for her to stay at Winterfield Manor, I will also provide her with lodging at the Scotsman Inn in Canterbury. An escort will, of course, be supplied for the journey.

"Respectfully awaiting your reply,
Andrew Winterfield"

Angela placed the letter on the bed.

"I don't know what to think of it," he stated and began pacing again. He sighed, running his fingers through his hair.

Her gaze was heavy upon him as he struggled to sort his thoughts, but she remained silent.

"The past couple of years Jessica has captured the attention of several young men," he said and sat beside her on the bed. "However, she hasn't reciprocated any interest that I know of. She has set her standards high and is not tempted by just any man, no matter his wealth, station, or charm. No, she'll require a man of integrity, one who is firm and confident, yet compassionate and reasonable, one who will protect her, yet not smother her." He looked down at the letter that rested on the bed. "Andrew Winterfield is just such a man." He stood and stepped toward the curtained window. "I'm not ready for this, Angela! If I let her come..." His gaze rose to the ceiling. "...then I let her go. What shall I say to him? How shall I answer?"

"Well, that depends," Angela responded after a moment.

He turned to her.

"That depends on your goal in raising her. Was it your intent to bring up an independent young lady, an intelligent and responsible woman, one who is capable and an asset to society?" She looked straight into his eyes. "A woman will either bring honor to her parents by *her* decisions or be in servitude to them by *theirs*."

He clamped his eyes shut and turned away, pain forcing his breath through clenched teeth. He felt as though a sharp knife had just run him through. He covered his eyes with one palm. Moments later, his racing heart began to calm, and he settled again by her side.

"Of course you're right," he whispered. "After all, I've never expected any of my daughters to serve at the lighthouse forever."

"Perhaps the question is not if you, John, or any other person is ready, but if *she* is ready," Angela added.

"Well," he said after a moment, "there's one matter in which I do have a say—she'll *not* be staying at the Winterfield home!"

Angela smiled and leaned over to kiss his cheek.

Chapter Twenty-One

As Jessica stepped off the train, she looked around through the bustling crowd for the chauffeur who was to meet her at the London station. Moments later she felt the presence of someone standing close behind her.

"This is no place for a lady," came a deep voice.

Once again chills ran through her body as she recognized the familiar voice. She closed her eyes and envisioned his handsome face.

"I was feeling a bit cooped up, Captain," she responded, not moving.

"How is it you know I'm the Captain?"

"Because we've met before, Sir," she said, turning to him. With satisfaction she gazed at the sparkle in his dark eyes, happy to see for herself that he was regaining his health.

"Hello, Jessica Viana. Thank you for coming." He kissed her hand.

"It would seem, Mr. Winterfield, that you enjoy startling young ladies by sneaking up from behind."

"No, not *ladies*…just you. I hope you don't mind, but I've arranged for a chaperone to accompany us during your stay."

He motioned to his chauffeur to collect her bags and then held an arm out to lead her to the waiting coach. As they approached the white open carriage, Catherine Winterfield stood and stepped out. She ran to them and embraced her in a warm greeting.

"Jessica, I'm so happy to see you again!"

"How have you been, my dear friend?" Jessica approved of Andrew's choice of chaperone.

"I think you'll find London in the summertime to be very different from when you were here last," stated Andrew.

As the carriage rolled along, Jessica, indeed, found delightful differences. Replacing the glittering frost of January were colorful blossoms of June. The streets, empty in winter, bustled with people buying and selling, strolling and rushing about. Delightful aromas of freshly baked bread mingled with the warm summer breezes.

Before long they reached the countryside. The misty January forests had given way to lush green flora. As their carriage glided past, Jessica caught sight of birds hopping from limb to limb and signs of wildlife everywhere.

"I didn't think it possible that the countryside could be any more beautiful than it was in January, yet how wrong I was," she murmured.

"I thought you'd enjoy the sights around Canterbury," Andrew said, "so I rented a room for you there. The town's much smaller than London, yet it has much to offer."

The journey through the country was lengthy, but Jessica enjoyed every mile. At last the carriage stopped before a cozy cottage-like inn settled in the forest outside the town.

"I trust you'll find these arrangements suitable," Andrew stated, assisting her from the carriage.

A bellman unloaded her bags while Andrew escorted her to the entrance of the inn. Oil lamps lit the cozy foyer. He stepped up to a high counter.

Almost unable to believe her eyes, Jessica stood back and gazed about as Andrew spoke with the clerk. *Suitable?* she thought, scanning the vestibule. *He must think me a princess to put me up in such a place!*

The walls, floors, and high ceiling were of mahogany paneling. Oriental rugs on the polished wooden floors added to the rich, warm atmosphere. High wingback chairs of deep floral patterns were arranged around a large stone fireplace. The dark wood staircase was lined down its center with a beautiful oriental runner, held in place at the base of each step with a shiny brass bar. Paradisiacal paintings lined the walls, framed in heavy carved mahogany.

After she was registered, he joined her in the front room.

"A coach will return for you in two hours," he said. "I hope you don't mind; I took the liberty of arranging dinner this evening at Winterfield Manor."

"It sounds lovely," she said.

"Until this evening then."

The clerk walked around the desk and escorted her to her room, which was decorated much like the lobby. The four-poster bed was of heavy mahogany, its plush quilt embroidered with a dainty floral pattern. On the pillow was a single red rose. A porcelain pitcher and basin were set into a heavy table at the bedside. On one wall hung a large mirror, framed in ornate gold, above a smaller table topped with the largest arrangement of freshly cut flowers Jessica had ever beheld. Its fragrance filled the entire room. Once again, the wood floor was covered with a large round rug.

With her thoughts still spinning around her handsome host, she felt this must for a certainty be paradise!

Late afternoon found Jessica seated in the plush black coach belonging to Winterfield Manor. The sun hovered in the western sky above the lush hills when she pulled up in front of the mansion. Her heart raced when she saw Andrew standing at the entrance waiting for her.

"I thought perhaps you would enjoy a stroll through the grounds prior to dinner. Catherine has told me how you and your sisters loved to walk when you were here in the winter. I'm certain you'll find the summer views even more pleasing."

She nodded with excitement, not daring to voice her true thoughts—that it mattered not what he had planned for her. Just to be in his presence again was more than enough to satisfy her.

"Good then," he said at her response. "Catherine has decided to join us, but she'll be on horseback. She's in the stable now."

They walked across the familiar courtyard and found Catherine had already saddled and mounted the horse.

"Mr. Winterfield," Jessica said as they strolled, "I can't tell you how much I am relieved to see for myself your remarkable recovery. It's as though you'd never been ill at all. Had you only seen your face a month ago on that horrible night..."

"Indeed, I didn't know myself what had hit me." He paused for a moment and then asked, "Miss Viana, did your father state the reason for my invitation?"

"No, just that you had requested my presence."

"I've heard the account of how you cared for me."

She felt her face flush.

"I realize I'll never be able to repay you, but wished to extend a small token of my appreciation. Your father was good in allowing me to thank you in person. I understand that I might not have survived had it not been for your kindness. I owe you a great debt."

"You owe me nothing, Sir. *You*, instead, bestowed kindness upon *me* by enduring the anger of your crew and quieting my fears. To see your strength returning is repayment in excess of what I ever dared wish. Do you remember any of the last part of the voyage?"

"I remember wishing I could die," he replied. "But I also recall seeing your face at times and thinking I was dreaming. I felt your head rest beside my arm and tried to speak, but couldn't." He looked into her eyes as they walked. "I apologize for giving you such a scare, as I know you were already struggling with other fears."

"It's over now, and you are safe. Nothing else matters."

Catherine trotted up beside the couple.

"Watch what Sampson can do." She nudged the horse into a canter and jumped over two fallen limbs in the path. They laughed at Catherine's playful manner and strolled on.

Their return to the house came an hour later. Catherine trotted ahead toward the stables.

"The Winterfield grounds are an array of endless beauty." Jessica sighed, invigorated by the walk, still in disbelief to be in Kent in the presence of a healthy Andrew Winterfield.

"I've asked the servants to set a table for us on the balcony outside the library. The dining room seems a bit intimidating for two."

"I enjoyed meeting your parents," Andrew said after the first course was served. "I spent some time conversing with your mother. She seems to possess many inspiring qualities. Patience, candor, and, above all, loyalty. A few of the qualities a man wishes for in a woman." He looked away, as though embarrassed. "She praised your father for the fine young ladies he had raised, yet I saw in her eyes the sorrow and yearning for that precious lost time which will never be recovered."

"Indeed," Jessica said. "I know not how she survived all those years, knowing her family was alive somewhere, unaware of her existence, knowing they were drawing further away with every passing year. I often wonder how different our lives would have been had our mother never boarded that ship."

"I'm certain you long to know everything about her—and your younger brother."

"How can one ever make up for sixteen lost years?"

"It will no doubt be a slow and difficult process," Andrew stated, looking down.

The sun painted the horizon in pink and orange hues over the Winterfield property.

"I thought you would prefer this to the London opera," he said. "Although there's nothing more spectacular than the sun setting over the ocean, I wanted you to see it from a different view."

"It's nothing short of breathtaking," Jessica acknowledged. "Have you ever stopped to consider that the sun is always setting someplace on the earth?" she asked.

"I think you'd like to see it from each of those vantage points. Am I right?"

She smiled and thought about it. "I think I should be content to see it set over the ocean every night."

He looked a bit saddened by her comment. Why? Did he not realize that it was because *he* lived on the ocean?

At the end of their meal, the stars appeared in the darkening sky. Andrew escorted her to the balcony railing, where they stood gazing at it in the same manner they had aboard *The Emerald*. He pointed out some of the constellations that guided him at sea on a clear night. The summer air was warm, much different from their first meeting at the ball earlier in the year.

"What I find fascinating," he said, "is to stand on the ship's deck on a glassy sea at midnight and look into a cloudless black sky. With the water reflecting the stars and moon, you find yourself surrounded by the universe as though you were not on the earth at all—no interruptions. The only sound is the ship breaking the water's surface. That is the most magnificent and humbling experience in this vast world. And that's one reason I love life on the ocean. You'll never experience that on land."

"Amazing." Jessica stood immersed in his description.

"When I see the order and precision up there, I'm in awe," he said, wonder in his words. "Men set their clocks by it; birds use it to guide their paths across land and sea. Where would we be if the sun did not rise and set with such precision each day? Our very lives depend on the exactness of the universe. Men have accomplished much, but it's insignificant when compared to the unreachable intelligence behind the design in the universe."

Despite the chill that settled into the air, they talked late into the night. Catherine appeared for a brief time to join them in conversation, but then bade them a good night.

Later, Andrew escorted Jessica, by coach, to the inn.

"Our chauffeur will be here for you at nine," he said as they walked to the front entrance. "We have a special surprise in store for you tomorrow."

"Thank you, Mr. Winterfield, for an enchanting evening."

"The pleasure has been all mine," he said, turning to leave.

When Jessica returned to her room, she fell onto the feather mattress and giggled, unable to believe she was not imagining the entire experience. She drifted into sleep, dreaming of the wonders of London, Kent, and, of course, Andrew Winterfield.

The following day Richard, Andrew, Catherine, and Jessica rode in an open carriage in the country, a picnic lunch stowed away under the seat. The hillsides smelled of life itself, just as Grace had described the previous summer.

They spent the day jumping brooks, picking wildflowers, and strolling the lanes of a little town they had stumbled upon.

Jessica carried a dainty bouquet of white buttercups Andrew had plucked for her from the meadow where they had picnicked.

"These grow along the forest's edge near my home," she told him. "I made necklaces with them as a child. They're my favorite."

Once, as Andrew conversed with his sister, she hastened ahead to walk with Richard.

"This day reminds me of the outings my father liked to take when we were little," she said.

"John is a good man. I know he was the best of fathers. Does he not take you on outings anymore?"

"Now and then. We venture around the Land's End area, but not as often as we used to."

"Then we'd better make good use of our time while you're here. On to Leeds castle!" he called out to the group.

The days in Kent rushed past. After spending some time with Andrew in Canterbury, Jessica was treated to a tour of Winterfield Imports, where he showed her the spot they had played together as children. They toured several estate homes and the winery on the Winterfield grounds; he took her and Catherine sailing and fishing in the Channel; they went horseback riding along the shore at the family's beach home, where they collected seashells and swam in the ocean. Andrew and Jessica talked long into the night by a crackling fire on the beach. They watched the sunset together every evening.

The final night came much too soon. Catherine hugged Jessica farewell, as Andrew climbed aboard the coach and seated himself across from her. The carriage pulled away from Winterfield Manor in the direction of the inn. Dusk was falling when they arrived.

"Would you accompany me on a brief tour of the gardens?" he asked, assisting her from the carriage.

They chatted as they walked. It seemed there was still so much to say.

"Mr. Winterfield, I can't thank you enough for your hospitality. This has been the most wonderful time of my life."

"I'm sorry to see it end," he said, his voice heavy with sadness. "Miss Viana, I wish to be open with you." He stopped and looked into her eyes. "My intent in asking you here was to show you my gratitude for what you did for me." He looked down for just a moment, as though not wanting to go on, but said in a stern tone, "I'll be returning to my duties on *The Emerald* next week." He paused, studying her face as if to discern her thoughts, and then began walking again. "You see, when I accepted the position as Captain of *The Emerald*, I made it clear to my father that my services for him were to be temporary, until I decided what I wanted to do with my life. As time passed, however, I found I was right where I belong. For the past month I've felt as a fish out of water." He stopped. "Miss Viana, I don't wish to mislead you. My life is my ship. My love is the sea."

She gazed into his eyes for a long moment before saying, "That's no surprise to me. I discerned as much being with you on the ship, and during this visit listening to you speak with such passion about your life."

They stood in silence for several moments, eyes locked, before he turned aside and escorted her back to the door of the inn. He lifted her hand to his lips in a tender kiss.

"Farewell then, my wonderful friend," he said. "I shall never forget you or your kindness in caring for me." With that, he turned and walked to the coach without looking back.

Jessica could not speak, not even to utter a 'good-bye.' In silence, she watched the horses pull away. Before they were gone from sight, she rushed to the inn. With the door closed behind her, she backed up against the foyer wall and burst into tears.

Inside the black coach, Andrew sat stiff against the leather seat as the horses took him away from the inn. With tight fists pressed to his sides, he closed his eyes and forced the breath from his lungs. A single tear fell to his lap.

The following morning, as Jessica completed her packing and awaited her cab, there was a soft rap on her door.

"Excuse me, Miss," said a servant from the other side. "There is a gentleman waiting for you in the sitting room."

Jessica's heart began pounding. She peered into the large mirror and found her eyes puffy and red, for she had cried herself to sleep the night before. She splashed some cool water on her face, took a deep breath, and walked out of the room, head held high.

When she reached the sitting room she found the tall form of Mr. Winterfield, his back to her as he peered out a window at the front lawn. She said not a word, but her footstep announced her arrival. As he turned, she was stunned to find, not Andrew, but *Roman* Winterfield standing before her! She took a step back.

"Miss Viana." He bowed his head to her.

Jessica curtsied but made no reply. Whatever was *he* doing here?

"I heard you were in town, and desired to see you prior to your departure," he stated. "May I escort you to the train station?"

"Those arrangements have been settled, thank you."

"Very well. Then I'll state my purpose in calling. I understand you performed a heroic duty in behalf of my brother and felt obliged to offer you my sincere gratitude."

"I did what any sensible person would have done, Mr. Winterfield," she stated, her voice flat, desiring no part of the conversation. "Your family owes me nothing. Now, if you will excuse me..."

"Miss Viana, there is one other reason for my visit."

Of course there is. "Yes, Mr. Winterfield?" She sighed. Their last dreadful conversation the night of the ball in January flooded back into her mind.

He turned from her and began a slow pace about the room, hands cupped behind his back.

"It's regarding my brother. I don't wish for you to leave here with the wrong impression of his feelings. You see, I believe he may be confusing gratitude with affection. Being caught up in a wave of emotions this past month, he's struggling to sort one from another."

How dare he intrude in such a delicate matter! Although knowing better than to continue the conversation, Jessica could not resist.

"And who, may I ask, gave you the authority as keeper of your brothers feelings?"

"Perhaps you're not aware of the special bond that exists between twins, even into adulthood." The familiar anger began building in his eyes as he glared at her. "It's much more than any typical sibling relationship." His eyes narrowed as his glare intensified all the more. "I love my brother and know him through and through, better than any other person. Andrew listens to me. He often takes my advice, and my advice to him now is that he is *not* in love."

"Mr. Winterfield, it's apparent to me that it's *you* who has trouble understanding his feelings. Furthermore, your concern for your brother is not based on love at all. I am, in fact, convinced you're incapable of such an emotion. It's also apparent that you do *not* know your brother as you say. Otherwise you would have been aware that he has sorted his feelings and made a decision. Rest easy, Mr. Winterfield. Your brother has chosen to return to his duties on your father's ship."

A smile eased over Roman's face.

She turned and left the room. Entering the lobby, she found that her trunk had already been loaded onto the coach. She boarded without looking back.

Chapter Twenty-Two

Twelve men stood at attention as their captain ascended the ramp to the ship.

"At ease, men; you're not in the queen's fleet."

They relaxed at once and moved to welcome him back aboard *The Emerald*—all with the exception of one. Smiley McGuire had no smile this day and no welcoming greeting for his captain. As Andrew Winterfield looked over at him, Mr. McGuire turned aside.

"Let's get this lady on the water," Andrew commanded. "We have a long journey ahead of us." He stared at Mr. Mc-Guire, who still did not look toward him.

The men were all familiar crew members to the captain with the exception of the first and second mate, who were new to the ship.

They had sailed for several days, and Mr. McGuire still had not said two words to the captain.

On the fourth day Andrew was working in his cabin when he noticed Smiley pass by the open door.

"Mr. McGuire!" he called out.

"Yes, Captain, Sir?" He reappeared in the doorway.

"I've not had the opportunity to thank you for the cakes you brought to the house. I'm sorry I was unable to see you that day."

"Wasn't expectin' t' see ya, Sir."

"My father informed me you baked them yourself. I had no idea you were such a proficient baker, Mr. McGuire."

"Oh, yes, Sir." He seemed to perk up a bit. "I'm a fine chef, Sir. Learned as a child. Who'd ya think it was that cooked fer ye and the young lady while she was aboard, Sir?"

"It was *you* who prepared those fine meals?" Andrew's eyebrows rose.

"Every course. Wasn't hard t' get Mr. Harrison out o' the kitchen for awhile."

"At the time I couldn't account for the delicious food. I found it unusual for such quality from Mr. Harrison, in particular with his reservations about Miss Viana."

The two were silent for a moment before Mr. McGuire asked, "How ya feelin', Sir?"

"I still require rest on occasion, but am almost recovered."

"That's not what I meant." Smiley pointed to his own chest. "I meant in here."

Andrew stood up and took a few paces away. "Matthew Clark called on me two days prior to our departure. He came to give me his resignation." He turned back to Smiley. "It seems his conscience would no longer allow him to serve on *The Emerald*. He revealed to me a conversation he had had with Miss Viana the night of that dreadful storm, one he'd told to no one. It seems he was far off course and had no idea where we were. It was she who reported our location. We were in extreme danger, and she, a keeper of the lighthouse in the area, was the only one who knew it." He looked away for a moment. "She saved us all that night, Mr. McGuire. With certainty, our ship would have succumbed had she not reported to him when she did. Mr. Clark piloted *The Emerald* during my absence, but has now chosen another berth. Every man on *The Emerald* that night can thank Jessica Viana for his life." He returned to stand before the sailor. "I saw her not long ago, Smiley. We spent two weeks together, and she never mentioned a word about it. Leaving her was the most difficult challenge I've ever faced in my life, far more difficult than that illness or any storm I've ever battled."

"With all due respect, Sir, what're ya doin' here?"

"You of all people should understand that, Smiley."

"The ocean is a lonely companion, Sir; she'll turn and bite ya the first chance she gets. A man needs a woman t' share his life."

"*This* is my life, Smiley!" he shouted, defensive at the reproof, but then calmed himself. "And she is, in every sense of the word, a lady. I cannot ask her to live a life at sea. Besides, she's terrified of the ocean."

"Ya underestimate her," Smiley argued. "I saw things in her ya didn't. Many times I caught her standin' at that railin' and gazin' out across the water as if...well, I saw in her that same desire for the sea that I feel in m'self, the same one ya feel deep in yerself, too. And that night of the storm—she had no fear that night. Brave and strong, that's what she was. She knew what had to be done, and did it. She faced the fury of that storm head on. That's no woman who fears the ocean, but respects it. And there's no doubt of her feelin's fer *you*—the way she cared for ya. And when she left after it was all over—the way she *kissed* ya, Sir..."

"She kissed me?"

"Sorry ya missed it. That was some kiss. Ask yer father. He was there."

"Well, there's something about her you *don't* know, Smiley. She lost her mother at the age of four and was reunited with her just a little over a month ago. And, if that is not enough, there's a brother whose existence *was not even known*! I met her mother, Smiley. To see the sorrow in her eyes...this cruel world took something from her that'll take *years* to restore, if *ever*!" He paused, Jessica's features flashing through his mind. "Smiley, that family is now reunited. I can't just step in and separate them again. I *cannot* do that!"

"Don't ya think *she* has some say in it?" Smiley asked.

Andrew's head was down, but he looked up to cast a fiery glare upon the sailor.

"S'cuse me, Sir." Smiley turned and left the cabin.

Upon Jessica's returning home, her father announced that the family would soon be leaving for Ireland. There they would begin exploring the Emerald Isle in search of a new home.

Snatched up by a whirlwind of emotions, Jessica reeled at the news. She covered her distress under the veil of her tasks.

Darting from love to pain to grief to anger, her heart returned to the intense love she felt for the Winterfield's second son. How could he have led her on so by inviting her to Kent, just to walk away as he had? He never even looked back!

He *must* have sensed her attraction to him! And she had seen in his eyes and heard in his voice much more than casual regard for her. How could he have injured her in such a manner?

Could she have misread him? Thinking back on it, she saw that he had had no intention of starting a relationship from the very beginning.

What had she expected? He must have felt he owed her a great debt for the service she rendered him on the ship. She had to admit that to invite her to Kent and show her all the magnificence of the countryside and the beach had been a wonderful way in which to convey his appreciation. But did she expect *more*? Had he not expressed to her the entire time his passion for his life? He had never stated any intention of changing that. How could she be angry with him for his honesty, for deciding for himself the direction his own life would take, and for thanking her in such a wonderful way?

Shoving the polishing rag into her pocket, she dropped to the floor beside the lens in the tower's lantern room. She had assumed he had fallen in love with her. What a mistake!

Yet, how could she be angry with this man of integrity whose honest desire was to express his appreciation? She was certain he had not intended to mislead her.

Her mind accepted the logic of such reasoning. Her heart could not.

She buried her face in her hands until she felt her sister's presence beside her. The sorrow in Grace's eyes brought forth a fresh flow of tears.

"How can something as wonderful as love *hurt*, Grace?"

"Because it seizes your heart."

Jessica covered her eyes again. "I wish it would let mine go."

"And instead, it will make you *grow*."

"Is this how you felt when you hadn't heard from Stephen?" She looked up.

Grace nodded.

"How did you cope with it? What did you do?"

"I'm afraid you'll have to do more, Jessie. I had his promise that he would write. That's what I clung to."

Jessica stood and wandered from the glass room out to the lighthouse railing. Grace followed.

"I lost him, Grace, and to what?" She wadded the white rag and pitched it over the side. "To *this*! I hate this ocean! It's mocked and entrapped me all my life. And now it's stolen from me the greatest thing I've ever had. It's more powerful than even love, Grace. I despise it…and it will *forever* dominate me!"

"No, Jessie. It's *not* stronger than you. Don't be so hasty to give up on yourself."

"You're right. I never had him." She sighed in surrender. "All I can do is grieve the loss of what could have been. Tell me people don't die of broken hearts. Tell me my anguish will fade with time."

"I'll tell you whatever will ease your heart, but perhaps you should discuss this with Father."

"No. I'll not let him or Mother see my pain. She put forth much effort to persuade him to let me go. I'm indebted to her." She wiped the tears from her cheeks and stood tall. "I'm resolved, Grace. Our trip to Ireland will be a memorable family holiday. I'll not look to the things behind."

Neither the adventure of exploring a new land, with its unique people and culture, nor the tiny, inviting cottage where her mother had passed so many years diminished Jessica's yearning to be with Andrew.

Their outings to the house where she was born and the hillsides overlooking green valleys, rolling lush hills extending as far as her eye could see, and the cool and fresh air with its frequent fog only left her with a longing to share it all with him.

One day, while walking with Alexandra, she stumbled upon a field of wildflowers. She could imagine walking alongside him just as she did in Kent. The meadow ended at the top of a hill that tumbled down into patches of green bushes, giving way to the ocean farther below, where the waves broke upon the rocks of the untamed shoreline.

After persuading Alexandra to rejoin the rest of the family, Jessica sat in quiet contemplation, thinking how strange the setting before her pictured her own situation. The meadow and rolling hillside was much like her life, a part of nature and the elements, situated by the sea, basking in the sunshine and salty breezes, at times glowing amidst a bank of fog.

And there, at the shoreline, was his—rocky and wild, restless and ever-changing.

They had so much in common, so many interests they shared. She laughed at the irony of it. This wildflower meadow belonged right where it was, by the side of the sea.

Yet, try as they might to cross the barrier of the shore, those churning waters would never meet the meadow. Because of their differences, the two would never—*could* never—unite. Their boundaries had been set.

In late July the family returned to Brentwood and Old Stormy. Sad to be leaving the island, Jessica found a strange sort of solace in knowing that soon, in some as yet undetermined locality, Ireland would be her new home.

Chapter Twenty-Three

One warm August day, Jessica joined Grace on the bench in the garden.

"Oh, Jess, has it not been a grand summer?"

Yes, for Grace it had been grand, indeed, and Jessica knew it was enchantment speaking through her words; for even as she approached, Grace had been reading yet another letter from Stephen.

"And what does the charming Mr. Sutton have to say today?" Jessica asked, elated for her sister's growing relationship.

"Oh, this time he just talks of events in London—the parties he has missed, the balls he has declined attending."

"The punch bowl just wouldn't be the same without you." Jessica snickered, and her sister laughed as her cheeks reddened.

"After reading his letter," Grace said, "I feel guilty for attending the parties *I* have since our return. And speaking of parties, Jess, is your heart changing toward Mr. Robertson? He seemed to fancy your company above all the ladies the other night."

"It was only because of *your* coaxing that he even asked for my hand in the dance."

"Just because I'm diverted with romantic interests of my own doesn't mean I'll ever neglect my sisters'."

"Grace," Jessica said, "was it not you yourself who stated that romance often happens at the most unexpected times and places? I wasn't searching for it when I stumbled upon Mr. Winterfield, and I'm not searching for it now. I'll be content with my life am I never to discover it again."

246

"I don't believe you," Grace said.

"You don't have another choice," Jessica said as she rose to leave. "Teas and luncheons will satisfy my heart for the time being."

Despite Jessica's lack of interest or encouragement, Mr. Robertson persevered in his attempts to pursue a friendlier relationship with her, and she obliged him at times by walking with him when in town. She liked him well enough to call him more than a simple acquaintance.

She also spent much time with her dear friend, Claire, when the opportunity presented itself. They enjoyed browsing the many shops of Penzance. Afterwards, they tailored hats and dresses to replicate the new fashions they discovered there.

Late August found summer winding down. Jessica's father had posted his resignation with the Lighthouse Committee, agreeing to stay until a suitable caretaker was located, which could be several more months. The Vianas had yet to decide on an Irish locality, anyway, so her family continued in their care of Brentwood, just as they had for many years.

Still, Jessica struggled with mixed emotions. Without conscious effort, she had fallen in love with the Emerald Isle. Yet, the thought of parting with Brentwood and the Wrights was almost unbearable. Despite the hard work involved, this was home.

Even the house itself had become part of her. There was comfort in the library, where she had completed her studies; in the parlor, where she had snuggled with her family on cold winter nights before a crackling fire; in the gardens, where they had brought life to the soil; in the lighthouse, where she and her sisters had raced playfully as children; and in her cozy bedchamber, where she had watched her father disappear into the forest on his way to his duties at Old Stormy and where she had enjoyed sweet dreams under her feather comforter. Her home was modest, but it was all she knew, all she had ever needed.

And now her family had begun packing its belongings. Crates began lining the hallways, filled with items that could be stored for the upcoming winter and transported to their new home.

As Jessica approached them, she could not help but think of the day she explored the cargo area in the hull of *The Emerald*. It had been over two months since her return from Kent, and she had not heard from him. Perhaps she should have declined his invitation in the first place.

She tried to distract herself from thoughts of Andrew, but it seemed there was no mending the hollowness deep inside. Her father had often told her that the heart was vulnerable, but prior to summer, she had little comprehension of the magnitude of that statement.

Passing the crates in the hallway, Jessica hastened up the stairs, where she pulled her journal from a shelf in her room. She leafed through the pages and then turned to the back cover. There, dried and pressed, several small white buttercup blossoms were tucked away. They had belonged to the wildflower bouquet Andrew had plucked for her in the meadow where they picnicked while in Kent. There they lay, forever preserved. Perhaps someday she would be able to discard them. Now was not that time.

Her throat stiffened as tears began to well in her eyes, but she was jolted from her thoughts by her mother calling her name. She blinked the tears away, lifted her head, and replaced the book.

Angela, Grace, and Jessica pulled on their gloves and cloaks as Angela kissed her husband's cheek. Mr. Wright had brought the carriage to the front of the house.

"We'll return soon, John." A frown crossed his face as she spoke. "You don't mind if we go to Bristlecone to look at fabric for Grace's dress, do you?"

"Of course not." He followed them outside, watching the carriage pull away. "Hurry back," he called. "Be home before dark."

Half an hour later, Alexandra was in her room, packing some clothing into a trunk. Peering out the window, she spied a man in a top hat approaching the house on horseback. She dropped the clothes and rushed down the stairs to greet him.

In a little shop in Bristlecone, Jessica skimmed through fabrics with her mother and sister. Her fingers glided over a bolt of white satin. She pulled her hand away. The pain building in her heart, she walked to the front of the shop, placed her gloves atop the wooden counter, and awaited the clerk. Perhaps there had been a delivery of heavier autumn materials. She looked back at Angela Viana, who held a fabric up to Grace and then had her step over to the light of the window.

She looked back at the counter. There, atop her gloves, lay three white buttercup blossoms. She picked one up and twirled it by its delicate stem, holding it to her nostrils to take in its sweet scent. But where was the benefactor? As she turned around, she was startled by a man standing behind her. She stared into familiar deep eyes.

"Mr. Winterfield!"

"I apologize for startling you, Miss Viana," he said after bowing his head in greeting. "There's a matter I would like to discuss with you if you will do me the honor of walking with me."

Several minutes later Grace approached the counter. The clerk had returned. "Have you seen my sister?"

"She asked me to request that you meet her at home. She left a few minutes ago with a gentleman I didn't recognize."

Grace looked down at a top hat sitting on the counter beside Jessica's gloves and two small blossoms.

Outside, the couple strolled in the warm sunlight. Jessica's heart pounded so hard she had trouble catching her breath. In an instant she found herself in the whirlwind of emotions that she had spent weeks trying to sort out and control.

"Mr. Winterfield, I can't express my surprise in finding you here. You have traveled quite a distance." She looked up into his dark eyes. "And I see your health has continued to improve."

"My body has recovered," he said, "but my heart has not."

She looked away. After much effort, she had learned to guard her feelings and was determined to keep them harnessed.

"I've been sailing the west African coast these two months."

"Have you?" she responded, her voice quiet. "What an experience you must have had." The report of such a journey under normal conditions would have prompted a far more excited response from her adventurous spirit.

"The trip afforded me much time alone with my thoughts."

She felt his gaze settle upon her as they walked.

"Do you recall our last conversation?" he asked.

"Yes," she replied without returning his look.

They had drifted away from the town and were now on a footpath in the forest.

"I...I was not altogether honest with you then, Miss Viana. You see, I didn't request your visit to Kent just to thank you."

Jessica kept her eyes fixed on the path.

"The truth is I wanted to see you again."

"Oh?"

"I saw Matthew Clark two days after you left."

"You did?"

"Why didn't you tell me what occurred that night on the ship?" His voice took on a commanding edge, the captain in him now speaking.

She gave no reply.

He stopped, took her by the wrist, and turned her to him.

"Miss Viana, *I owe you my life*! Do you not realize that?"

"Is that why you came here?"

She did not want to know the answer. An affirmative response would validate his brother's accusation that his feelings for her were based on mere gratitude and obligation, and not on love.

Her head dropped. She closed her eyes, fighting hard against a tear that slipped to the ground despite her effort to stop it. She held her breath and awaited his reply.

"No." His firm answer came after a moment. "No. There's more to my visit. I was dishonest with you in another way, as well. However, when you hear my motive, perhaps you'll find a place in your heart to forgive me."

Through watery eyes, she looked at his hand, still holding her wrist.

"You'll recall that I said, 'My life is my ship, my love is the sea.'"

She squeezed her eyes shut, agonizing over the words that stabbed through her yet a second time.

He released his grip on her arm and turned his back to her.

"I was lying to myself, as well as you. You see, my life changed forever one January night when an intriguing woman stepped out onto the veranda where I sat." Turning back, he reached out to lift her chin. She refused to look into his eyes. "Later she boarded my ship…and stepped into my heart. Then I met her parents. They were as wonderful as she. But their family had been apart for many years and had just found one another again. I couldn't take it upon myself to fall in love with their daughter and whisk her away. I couldn't be the one to separate that family again. So I lied to myself. I tried to fool my heart into believing I could just walk away from her."

One tear after another seeped over her cheeks.

"But what I didn't realize was that, in my attempts to protect her parents," he continued, "I wounded *her*…and myself."

He took both her shoulders. This time she did look up at him.

"I can't live another moment without asking three things of you," he continued. "First, please forgive me for the injury I've caused you. I saw the pain in your eyes at our final meeting in Canterbury and have not been able to bear it since. After all you did for me, after the tender care *you* bestowed upon *me*, how could I have mistreated you so by leaving you in that manner? I won't blame you if you can't forgive me, but I must know if you will."

"You underestimate me, Mr. Winterfield. I see no need for forgiveness."

He shut his eyes, releasing his hold on her, his shoulders drooping.

"Yes, I was injured," she said, wiping her face, "because I allowed myself to be. But you—what crime did you commit in choosing your own path?"

His eyes opened, perplexity written across his expression.

"I have no need of forgiving you because I don't resent you for your decision."

"Thank you." He sighed with relief. "My second request, then, is related to something that I'm compelled to tell you here and now." He stepped away, and began pacing. "Words can't explain the pain I, too, felt when I left you that night at the inn. That pain has only intensified since our parting. I love you, and I *must* know if I'm too late. I must know now—do you love me?"

She could scarcely believe what she had just heard! In her nervous state she began talking, not even considering the words that rushed from her mouth.

"I loved you before I ever met you. I realize that sounds unreasonable if not outright insane, Mr. Winterfield, but please allow me to explain. It began when I was visiting Kent and heard the praises of you by your sister. She couldn't know how they were affecting me and revealed them with complete innocence, having no intention of stirring my interest, I'm sure. Then I began hearing accounts of you by other acquaintances. I found myself listening to comments that, to most, would've seemed ordinary. But then I did something unethical, and I have a confession to make."

His dark eyes grew large. "I'm sure, Miss Viana, you're incapable of acting in an unethical manner."

"Oh, dear!" It was her turn to pace. "Mr. Winterfield, I… while I was a guest in your home, I would sneak into the library after everyone else had retired for the night, and, well… I began reading your personal journals from *The Emerald*." She put one hand over her eyes. "At first I was just intrigued by your journeys to distant lands, but then I began to know you through your writings." She stopped to take a quick breath. "I began to anticipate your reactions, to think as you would think. By the time my visit had concluded, do you know with what impression I was left of you?"

"No…tell me," he whispered.

"I found in those writings a strong and adventurous man, a man with a passion and appreciation for life. One who is fair in his dealings with others, even when wronged. Your decisions were always sound, the decisions of a man of wisdom and integrity. I should've recognized you during our conversation that night on the veranda, but I confess I didn't know your identity until after I had returned inside, and by then you were embedded in my heart."

His lips had dropped open.

"So it's *I* who is in need of *your* forgiveness, Mr. Winterfield, for I intruded in a most personal matter."

After a moment, his mouth relaxed into a smile. "My father used to examine those logs in my first years of sailing. It was his way of tracking my activities. But they became nothing but mere showpieces on the desk in the library. Twenty thousand books in that library, and you chose *those*. Who would have ever known they would serve such a purpose? Furthermore, those journals were there for any guest to read. You did not intrude. Therefore, I have no need of forgiving you, either, for what crime did *you* commit?"

"Now you understand why I'm able to say that I fell in love with you before I ever met you," she said. "And what's more, you are not too late. I've put forth every effort, but have found that a love as strong as the one I've cultivated for you will not be uprooted."

"Then this leads to my third request," he said, stepping closer. "I ask that you come back into my life—forever this time; and if you cannot live in my life...I surrender to yours. You see, the life I live at sea is meaningless without you. I'll place my feet forever on solid ground if I know you'll be by my side. I love you, Jessica. Please consent to be my wife."

"I know—and will always know—how much you love the sea. Asking you to leave that life on my account would be cruel. I will *not* allow that."

Yet, could she join him in his life? She stepped back, clenching her fists one inside the other and pulling them to her lips. Her thoughts raced. Yes, she loved him...almost more than life itself. She now understood his reason for the injury, as well as his decision to leave her. And the deep wound in her heart had been soothed by his apology. She sorrowed for him, too, for he had suffered the same burning pain she had endured all these weeks. And it sounded as though it had impacted him much more so, for it was he who had inflicted the blow upon them both.

But much as she had longed to hear the words he had just spoken, she knew that the resonant 'yes' her heart was crying out would not be so simple. If she did accept him, how would they live? Could she sacrifice all she knew—her family—to live on a ship that she would be forced to share with his crew?

And would she ever gain admittance into the Winterfield family? His mother and his brother were sure to be far less than enthusiastic about their union. To accept his proposal could expose her to ridicule and abuse by them for the remainder of her life! Could she ever accept that? Was love strong enough to conquer such obstacles?

Yes, there was much to consider.

"Mr. Winterfield, I can't give you an answer at this time. There are several concerns which demand resolution."

"I'm sure they're concerns with which I myself have been struggling. May I relate to you my own conclusions?"

"No!" She would not be influenced by his view. "I must work them out for myself. There is also another man I must consider."

"Another man?" His cheeks filled with color. "You said I wasn't too late! You said you love *me*. You can't possibly care for two men at the same time."

"I can if the other man is my father."

"Oh...of course. Please accept my apology and take all the time you need. When may I return?"

"Your returning won't be necessary. I'll meet you here at this hour tomorrow evening. It's time enough."

"Please..." He reached a tentative hand toward her elbow. "Let me walk you back to town, and you can take my horse. Remember...you left word for your family to return home without you."

She stepped away from him. "Thank you, but I'd rather walk. I have much thinking to do."

Shadows had grown long, and the colors of the evening were graying by the time Jessica returned to Brentwood. She offered a subdued greeting to her family members, rushing from room to room in search of her father. The house was filled with the aroma of the meal she had missed; however, she could not give attention to her stomach at the moment.

"Father's out at Old Stormy, Jess." Grace looked concerned.

As Jessica ascended the lighthouse steps, she could hear him whistling as he worked at the top of the pillar.

She startled him when he caught sight of her.

"Jessica," he said in a welcoming tone and laid down his tools. He wiped his hands on a cloth and held an arm out to her. When she stepped forward, he guided her out to the railing of the old tower.

"It's been a long while, has it not, daughter?"

She looked up at him, not knowing where to begin. It *had* been a long time since they had talked, just the two of them. Oh, he had tried since her return from Kent, but not only did she not know what to say to him, but she had felt that what happened was no longer of any consequence. He, as well as her mother, would have to be satisfied with her response that her trip was enjoyable. Neither had pressed her for information.

With his arm around her shoulders, he looked out across the dark waters. A cool summer breeze caressed their faces as the red beam reached out over their heads.

"How is Andrew?" he asked without looking at her.

"He's well now." She was amazed at how he always knew what was on her mind. She thought for a moment before asking, "Father, how strong is true love? Can it withstand *any* assault? Can it overcome *any* barrier? Can true love conquer the treacherous waters of an angry sea?"

"You've heard the verse 'Love never fails,'" he said a moment later. "When a relationship dies, it's not the love that has failed, but the individuals. Perhaps they were not realistic in their view that there *would* be storms, so when these came, they were unprepared."

"How can one prepare for what is yet unknown?"

"Devotion will prepare you. If love is the sail and devotion the wind behind the sail, they can keep the boat from capsizing no matter how fast and furious the waves come. Then the next day brings the sun sparkling on a quiet sea. It was the wind and the sail that kept the ship afloat."

"But what if one day you find there's no more wind?"

"Love prepares one to exercise devotion come what may."

"*Your* devotion survived the most difficult tempest inflicted on any marriage, I'm sure, Father. What you and Mother faced would make most any other storm a mere ripple."

"Don't misunderstand, Jessica. You mustn't underestimate *any* potential hazard. If you know rocks lie beneath the surface, you'd be wise to take care in considering whether or not to sail that course."

"My route is fraught with danger, Father." Tears threatened again.

"Perhaps, but perhaps not. Is there not a safe channel you can navigate? Let's hear these concerns of yours. We'll talk them out, and maybe you'll see which direction to choose."

They talked long into the night, as the full moon rose, bathing them in pale light. The reflection on the water's surface sparkled and winked into the distance.

Andrew Winterfield paced on the pathway in the forest just outside of town where he had last seen Jessica the previous evening. If he had to wait just one moment longer, he feared his heart would shatter.

If she did not return, her answer would be clear. The concern in her eyes had been so severe, he knew not what to make of it. All day he had tried to prepare the words he would say to her, but had admitted defeat, thinking he had an idea as to her concerns, but not knowing for certain.

Oh, why had he handled matters the way he did? He turned to take a few paces in the opposite direction. Why had he not been honest with her while she was in Canterbury? They could have resolved the issues then and there.

He threw his hands into the air, turned around again, and came face to face with her!

"Well, it seems the tables have turned, Mr. Winterfield. For the first time it's *I* who has startled *you* from behind." He detected no humor in her voice.

"I...I didn't hear your horse."

"That's because I walked." She put her head down and strode past him. After a moment, she turned back.

His thoughts froze. No words would form.

"It appears there are many barriers to the uniting of our lives," she said.

"I believe I know what they are," he stated, his thoughts thawing. "You're concerned about my family. But, Jessica, as you get to know my brother better, you'll see he's not all bad. He would give you the shirt from his back."

"Perhaps. But not the love from his heart. How can you defend him? Did you know he came to me my last morning in Canterbury to make certain I understood you were *not* in love with me?"

Unable to help himself, Andrew laughed. "Someday you must tell me the details of your encounters with my brother. I saw the fire in your eyes after you left him on the dance floor the night of the ball. I believe that was when I began to fall in love with you, for no woman stands up to him. You have courage and boldness, and an unusual zeal for honesty." He watched a cloud cross her face.

"I'm sorry," she replied. "What I said was unkind. I accused your brother of something I wouldn't wish upon my worst enemy—that he is incapable of love. You know him much better than I, and he must have some redeemable quality. I'm just afraid he'll interfere."

"Don't concern yourself over Roman." He consoled her as he had when he learned of her fear while she was aboard *The Emerald*. "He has known for quite some time my true feelings for you and is well aware of my intentions in coming here. In fact, I made it known to *all* my family."

She looked surprised. "How did your mother respond? I'm not a favorite with her. She had quite different expectations for you."

"I believe she's happy that I may be, at long last, 'settling down.' She's right now awaiting your answer to my proposal, anxious to throw a ball at Winterfield Manor in celebration of our engagement. But I know you have one more concern, perhaps the greatest of them all—where and how shall we live?"

"At the risk of sounding redundant, I repeat that I would never dream of asking you to leave your life on your ship," she said at once. "That's not an option, and is not even a question in my mind. Do you agree?"

He was more than willing to give up that life, but would his attempts fail as Mr. McGuire's had?

"I suppose," she added, "that I'd better adjust to your life."

"You mean you'd do that for me?" Overcome with elation, he lifted her from the ground, spinning around once as they both laughed. "But what of your fear of the ocean?" He stopped laughing.

"You dispelled that fear. I admit I don't know exactly *how* this arrangement will work, but I know it will. I'm not afraid. Not of life on the sea or of your brother."

He reached out and traced the outline of her chin with the backs of his fingers. This time he would *not* let her go.

Leaning toward her, he hesitated before closing his eyes and touching his lips to hers for the first time.

Immersed in their kiss, neither noticed the sun setting behind the trees around them.

Before Andrew could assist Jessica from his horse, the front door of Brentwood House flew open. Rushing out into the shadowy evening, Grace and Alexandra raced toward the couple. Alexandra arrived first, flinging her arms around Jessica.

"I know you wouldn't have brought Mr. Winterfield back with you had you not had good news! So tell us…we can't wait a moment longer!"

The excitement in her voice made them all laugh.

Jessica looked up to see the outline of her parents in the light of the doorway.

"Let us include the *whole* family in on our news, shall we?" Jessica said, slipping one hand around Alexandra's elbow and the other around Andrew's.

John pulled a bottle of white wine from a crate awaiting transportation to the lighthouse island. "And in celebration… only the second bottle ever used at Brentwood for a purpose other than the polishing of the lens. Bring some glasses, Mrs. Wright!" he called out with joy. Before pouring the wine, John offered his hand to Andrew. "I could not have asked for a finer son-in-law were I to have made the choice myself."

The family stayed up long into the night as Andrew entertained them before the hearth with stories of his adventures at sea. Speaking with a consuming passion, he colored his descriptions with such detail that John thought he could feel the ocean swells beneath the floor.

Jessica appeared mesmerized by his deep voice, and John watched her eyes as she watched Andrew's. The young woman before him was not the same one he had sent off to France in April. She had been transformed. Oh, her appearance was the same, but in recent weeks he had noticed the distraction in her eyes, the change in her mannerisms, even a difference in her stance. She was somehow more graceful, more mature, he thought. He had also sensed her recent pain, but this night found her revived. This night her eyes revealed happiness, security, and above all, real love.

The pain of loss stabbed his heart. He felt the gentle touch of his wife beside him as her hand slipped across his back. When he looked into her eyes, she smiled. His pain subsided. It was because of her that his daughter had life, and because of her that he had allowed his daughter to grow, and because of her that he could now let her go.

Angela kissed his cheek and mouthed the words, "I love you."

He rested his head against hers as Andrew's stories forged on.

The warm September evening drifted into sunset. A small group of family and close friends gathered on a short cliff overlooking the ocean near Bristlecone.

The bride was making final preparations at Brentwood House. A white carriage outside awaited her, her mother, and sisters.

Angela looked at her daughter and smiled. The dress they had made together was white satin with a rounded lace neckline and a wide satin sash that peaked at the base of the bride's sternum and wrapped down and around her back to tie into a large bow below her waistline. Beneath the bow, large pleats fanned to the ground. The long, sleek sleeves lent elegance to the simple gown that matched well the style and figure of the bride. Her copper locks were curled, pulled atop her head, and pinned in place. Tiny flowers decked the outline of each curl, and delicate amber ringlets dangled down her back underneath a netted veil, which sprawled to the floor behind her.

"Just one more touch," Angela said, spraying a soft mist over her from a tiny crystal bottle. "Grace, I can't tell you what it means to me to be able to share in this day. For years I fretted I would not see my daughters' weddings. But I'm determined not to shed a tear," she said, "at least not until I see the groom's reaction."

"Mother," Grace said in a sad tone, "I only regret that almost since the time you arrived here, we've been consumed with the planning of this day. We've just begun to know each other."

"No tears, Grace, no regrets." She smiled. "On the contrary, the planning of a wedding is a special occasion that allows a mother and daughter to draw ever closer as they spend almost every step of the way together." Angela reached down to take her hand. "I've come to know your tastes and your styles, your concerns, your hopes and desires. I've heard your endearing expressions about your fiancé, your father, and your sisters. You've told me stories of your childhood, which I've locked away in my heart. Oh, yes, Dear Daughter, we've come to know each other—even faster, I believe, than we would have otherwise. This is an experience I'll treasure always." She embraced Grace, whose eyes began to well with tears. Holding up one finger, Angela added, "No tears now. We can't have red eyes on your special day."

The bride nodded and blinked the tears away.

Before the sun dropped into the ocean, John met the carriage that brought his wife and daughters to the small gathering. He watched Stephen, who smiled with obvious pride, as he walked arm in arm with his beautiful Grace along the satin runner.

When they reached the groom, John looked into the eyes of the man who would from that day forward be called his 'son.'

"I entrust her to your care now, Stephen. I know you'll cherish her."

"You have my word, Sir," Stephen replied with firm confidence, returning the solemn stare.

John offered Grace's hand to Stephen and took his place beside his wife.

As the two exchanged vows, he peered around at Jessica. She stood beside her fiancé, who had returned from his work for this special event. He thought of the irony that two of his daughters would be sharing their lives with the sons of his two closest friends from childhood, forever reuniting the three of *them*, as well.

How much all their lives had changed in a single year! Each day he counted his blessings as those wondrous changes brought added joy to his heart that had been so barren during the long years of his wife's absence. The full moon, just rising in the eastern sky, even seemed to be smiling its approval. Responding to an old habit, he pulled out his pocket watch and checked the time. It was not even nearing ten o'clock.

The newlyweds sealed their vows with a kiss while the setting sun spewed its last rays across the sky, the surface of the ocean smiling back in a reflection of gold.

Chapter Twenty-Four

The following weeks passed in quick succession, and the cool air indicated the approach of winter.

"Jessica," John called out to his daughter as she passed his study. "Close the door," he requested after she stepped in. "There's a matter I would like to discuss with you."

She obeyed and approached the desk where he sat.

He stood and strolled around to lean against the front of the desk, crossing his arms. "I understand, Jessica, that you and Andrew have set your wedding date for next May."

"Yes, Father."

"I'll not belittle your intelligence or mine by asking why it is you've chosen to postpone the event that means so much to you." He stepped toward her. "I know you, Jessica, and I'd like to thank you for thinking first of your mother's feelings. You knew it would cause her great pain to lose two of her daughters so soon." A smile played at the corners of his lips. "You astound me more and more, Jessica. You've acted in a thoughtful and selfless way."

"In truth, Father, my decision was not at all selfless. I'll tell you a secret—I couldn't bear to leave my mother just yet."

He hid a smile. "And how does your fiancé feel about this matter?"

"Well..." She took a few steps away from him. "It may be many months before we'll return to England after we're married. I don't know when I'll see you again once I leave. Of course, Andrew is anxious for me to join him, but we discussed it, and it was he who suggested next spring." She looked back at him. "Father, he's a wonderful man. Do you know that he didn't ask me to marry him at first because he couldn't bear to break up our family?"

"No, I didn't." He held his hand out to her, and she stepped over to take it. "Jessica, I couldn't be happier with your choice. Your mother encouraged me to allow you to make your own decisions. She believed you were a trustworthy young lady, and she was right. There was a time I stated my disappointment in you, and I'm sorry I hurt you. I just wanted you to realize your own potential. You know, there's something I recently learned about you."

Her eyebrows arched in question.

"I heard about what you did while aboard that ship. Do you realize how many lives you saved that night?"

Her head dropped.

"Jessica, you've brought me much honor. I'm very proud of you. I *always* have been."

"Thank you. And I have another secret. From the time I was small, you've shown me that I was the captain of my own life, but you were there to guide my ship between the rocks. Did you know that I have always viewed you as my navigator?"

He offered a half laugh and a nod. "The Navigator...an admirable role, indeed. But I'm afraid I must now relinquish that responsibility to your fiancé."

"No, Father. He'll become my captain. No one will ever take your place. The principles you taught will continue with me and any family we may have."

He kissed her forehead. "Your mother and I have decided to stay at Brentwood until you're ready to leave. It'll be hard work this winter—for her, in particular—but we felt it would prove more difficult to ask you to move twice."

"Thank you!" She threw her arms around him.

"Excuse me, Mother, Father." Jessica located her parents in the study before John was to relieve Mr. Wright for the night at Old Stormy.

"Come in, Sweetheart," her mother invited.

She sat down on the chaise beside her.

"Would the two of you be very disappointed if Andrew and I were to be married near London?"

"London?" Her father looked perplexed. "I believe I speak for both your mother and me when I say that we'd be happy were you to be married on the moon, but London? Jessica, you and Andrew both were about as happy there as a pig at a dinner party. Why would either of you want to be married anywhere near there?"

"I fear you may feel us both insane when I tell you. Andrew had an idea, and I've been thinking it might be nice."

"Go on," her father coaxed.

"We'd like to be married on the deck of *The Emerald*. We'd prefer an intimate group and feel the top deck would afford the perfect setting."

Her father's eyebrows rose.

"But we don't insist if you don't agree."

Her parents looked at each other.

"I think there's not a more fitting place for your wedding," her father said.

"Mother?" Jessica asked.

"Well, adjustments in plans will be in order, but I think it'll be beautiful."

"Thank you!" She jumped up to hug them. "It'll mean the world to Andrew."

She started to leave but turned back. "Oh, Andrew writes that his mother is anxious to know when our family will be able to travel there for the engagement party."

"We're still considering that," her father responded.

Jessica returned to her room to write her fiancé.

After completing her letter, she looked out the window into the darkness below at a swinging light heading toward the forest. In the glow of the lantern she could see her father's form. He disappeared when forest engulfed him. The familiar lights of Old Stormy rotated in the distance, piercing the night sky.

She curled up in her high wing-back chair to read again the last letter to arrive from Kent, where her sister had spent the last six weeks, living her new life.

My Dear Jessie,

I realize I have only been gone a few weeks, less than half the time I was in the area last year, but already it seems a lifetime. I suppose that is because I know in my heart I will not be returning to you.

Our trip to Scotland was glorious, Jess! Four full weeks exploring the mountains and glens, and still we did not get our fill. But winter is setting in. It was growing cold there when we left. Oh, Jess, you should see the little inn where we stayed! It was so quaint, over two hundred years old and such a cozy place. Someday perhaps we could meet you and Andrew there on holiday. How I would love that!

Except for missing my family, I am so happy! Stephen is a most wonderful man. I love him more and more with each passing day. He has promised we will move to the country as soon as we are able.

Did you hear, Jess? Edward Scarborough has been taken into custody! My father-in-law will be the prosecuting barrister. The charges are robbery and bribery. Father has been called as a witness. He will be needed here in London for the trial and will soon be hearing from Mr. Sutton, if he has not already.

Do you realize what that means? Father would not consider coming to London without the entire family! We will be able to be together again!

Oh, I miss you so! What will I do when you leave England? How often will I see you then?

I suppose children must grow up and lead their own lives. But, Jess, I am convinced the distance between the paths we have chosen will matter not. You and I will always be the closest of friends. Promise me we will remain close through frequent correspondence, and please notify me just as soon as you know when you will be coming.

> Yours Always,
> Grace

* * * * *

The very next day the notice of the Scarborough trial arrived from London. John was expecting it, as Jessica had read Grace's letter to him.

"The date of our trip to Kent has been decided," John said at the dinner table that evening. "I've received word from both my old friends. We've been invited as guests at the Sutton home. I'm certain the Winterfields will be busy in preparation for the engagement ball."

A few days following brought a letter from Mrs. Winterfield.

"Mother," Jessica said, finding Angela in the parlor. "May I ask your advice on a matter? This letter just arrived, and I'm not sure what to do."

Her mother read the letter aloud.

> "My Dear Jessica,
>
> "I have just received some distressing news from my son, Andrew. He states that he would like the wedding ceremony to take place on his ship! Imagine that! A wedding on that smelly ship! I certainly hope you will not agree with this preposterous idea, and are able to talk some sense into him.
>
> "After all, this is a Winterfield wedding, the first in many years. Society is buzzing with excitement, and is in expectation of Winterfield tradition. The guest list has already swelled to five hundred!
>
> "This idea of your wedding occurring on *The Emerald* simply will not do! I appeal to the sense I know you possess since your fiancé remains obstinate regarding this matter.
>
> "Sincerely Yours,
> Olivia Winterfield"

"Your future mother-in-law has no difficulty in expressing herself!" Angela put the letter down and looked away in disgust.

"I'm afraid she's accustomed to having her way. But we differ in our visions of this wedding. Only in recent days had we considered London, and here she has the guest list well under way! What shall I do, Mother? I so want to have a good start with Andrew's parents."

"Jessica, is not your wish, as well as Andrew's, to have a small gathering? It seems there's no middle ground in this matter. No compromise can be made." She patted her daughter's hand. "I know you'll be able to express your view in a tactful manner."

Richard Winterfield walked through the warehouse toward his office. He was surprised upon opening the door to find his wife pacing the floor and his son, Roman, sitting in the leather chair behind the large desk, ankles crossed and shoes resting upon the desk.

"Roman, what a surprise to see you here." Richard gave him no smile and began sorting through the mail on the desk. "I believe it was June when I saw you last. How's business in France?"

Roman did not answer. Instead his mother forced a letter under her husband's nose. "Look at this letter, Richard. It's from Jessica Viana. How can she respond in such a manner?"

Richard sighed and read the brief letter.

"What I find in this letter, Olivia, is a woman who's showing great respect in support of her fiancé regarding a decision which is theirs to make. What seems to be the problem?"

"She's determined to ruin all my plans. That's the problem, Richard. I insist that you set them straight in this matter!"

Richard ignored his wife's demand and looked over at his son. "And to what do we owe *your* visit, Roman? I didn't expect to see you until the engagement party."

Roman's feet dropped to the floor.

"Well, Father, that's the very reason I made an unscheduled stop here." He pushed the chair back and strolled to the front of the desk where his father stood. "I'll be leaving tonight, but wished to speak to you in person about this upcoming event."

Richard walked around the opposite side of the desk and seated himself in the chair his son had occupied moments before.

"Olivia, please sit down. Our son wishes to speak with us."

His wife situated herself on a chair behind Roman.

"What is it, Roman? What matter is so pressing as to bring you all this way?" Richard's voice carried no expression.

"The very matter of this engagement. I will not be attending that party. You've proven yourself a trustworthy and loyal friend to John Everett, Father, which is noble on your part, but must you form a marriage alliance with this family?"

Richard stared in silence at him.

"Father, listen. You've worked hard to uphold the Winterfield name and to carry on the pride of your father and his father before him. You've taught your children the meaning of success and the responsibility of commitment to both community and family. But what responsibility has John Everett—excuse me, John *Viana*—taken?" Roman put both palms on the desk and glared at his father. "That man abandoned his society and even his family name! So where are the Everetts now? He has taken that fine family name," Roman brought his right palm up and squeezed it into a tight fist, "and he has trampled it into the dust under his feet." He threw his arm down to his side, standing tall before his father. "The Winterfields have sat in the seat of justice and have stationed themselves before kings. And where, may I ask, have the Vianas placed *them*selves?" His lip curled. "Before the swine they raise. He had success at his fingertips, but look what he chose for himself. It's because of his decisions that John Viana is lower than the dirt he tills, as far as I am concerned. Father, how can you tarnish the Winterfield name by this union? It's a disgrace!"

Roman scowled at his father.

Richard mulled the words over in his mind. His wife raised her eyebrows at him. He could see the mockery in her expression.

"Roman, sit down please," he said after a moment of silence. He rose from his chair as Roman seated himself beside his mother.

"It's clear to me, Son, I've made a grave mistake. Your mother and I owe you a tremendous apology."

Roman smiled and turned to his mother, who looked puzzled by her husband's response.

"Olivia, I want you to take a good look at this young man. Never in my life would I have imagined that the most empty, most self-centered and pitiable man on this earth would be one of my own sons!" The volume of Richard's voice intensified. "I blame *you*, Olivia, for ruining him!"

Olivia's eyes widened at the accusation.

"And I blame myself for condoning the behavior of the two of you all these years by my silence." His voice boomed. "What a mistake I've made!" He glared into the eyes of his astonished son, who opened his mouth, but was cut short. "Do not interrupt me, Roman. I heard you out, and you will now hear me. You say the Winterfield's have sat in the seat of justice. Your father, uncles, grandfather, and great-grandfather have, indeed, done their best to administer that justice with fairness and impartiality. You, on the other hand, with your narrow and calloused mind, have nothing of value to offer anyone.

"John Everett left this community because of people like you, Roman. Rather than stay and support the injustice in this pompous society, he stood against it. He alone found the courage to inflict the severest of punishment, that of abandonment. What better way to show his intolerance of such behavior? What better way to show responsibility to this community? John Everett has a quality you will never know, Roman Winterfield—that of integrity. He faces each day with something money can never buy, and one that you are without—a good conscience. And success? Oh, you've found success, all right. You have succeeded in positioning yourself so high that you can now boast in being the only man to my knowledge who has made himself *friendless*. Well done, Roman."

Roman's florid face radiated his anger. His chin trembled.

"As far as I'm concerned, Roman, you have a choice to make, and I'll give you exactly three months to make it. Listen to my words. You will make significant changes in your attitude, you will be here in support of your brother on the first of February, you will welcome your new sister-in-law with open arms, and you will treat her and her family with the kindness and respect they deserve. Or you will choose to continue on your present high-minded course and will find yourself without a family. While I'll never threaten your livelihood, if you are not at that ball, your position with Winterfield Imports will go from heir to common employee. You will have no share in any Winterfield assets and will no longer be welcome at Winterfield Manor. If you will not humble yourself, I will do it for you.

"I will not see your face until then, Roman, but if you are not at that party, I'll never see you again. Weigh your decision with care." He then turned to his wife. "And I am giving you no choice, Olivia. You'll start improving your attitude *now* by helping your son prepare his wedding wherever and however he and his fiancée see fit. I'll no longer tolerate this arrogance in my home. I'm so ashamed of the two of you."

He walked out of the office, leaving his wife and son dumbfounded.

Chapter Twenty-Five

When the train slowed to a halt at the London station, Jessica thought she had stepped back in time a year to the day her family had arrived for their first momentous visit to Kent. The same butterflies flitted about in her stomach as they had then, but that first time they came from the excitement of the unknown. Now they fluttered in anticipation of the familiar—to see her sister again and, above all, to be reunited with her fiancé.

The bitter January chill blasted her face as her father and brother sorted through baggage, all their breaths little dissipating clouds. Her mother snuggled up to her, Alexandra joining them on the other side.

"When will Andrew arrive in London?" Alexandra asked.

"It will be at least a week, perhaps longer." Jessica's voice dragged. "Can you believe I haven't seen him since Grace's wedding? How have I survived these four months?"

"Mother," Alexandra said, "if only you'd known her two years ago. As opposed to marriage as any person I've ever heard."

"Opposed to oppression and boredom is closer to the truth," Jessica retorted, "which is only a reflection of what I've seen in others."

"I can promise you, boredom will never be an issue when you're married to Andrew Winterfield," Angela said, a smile crossing her lips.

"And if it ever so much as threatens," Alexandra piped, "you'll always have your dear mother- and brother-in-law as entertainment." She tittered.

"Yes, and through such close association, I'm sure to cultivate some of their matchless qualities myself," Jessica said. They all broke out in laughter. "I hope you're not too disappointed to discover that Roman will be overseas until the first of February. Ah, the little conveniences of running an import business."

Alexandra pulled her hand over her mouth to hide her snicker.

"Olivia Winterfield is not what I'd expected," said Angela a week later. "She seems quite the opposite of the woman who penned that letter to you in the fall, Jess—all pleasantness and smiles. Why, she's gloating over every detail of the wedding. It's all she speaks of. And how accepting of your every idea she is, praising your every wish. I must admit I'm astonished."

"I am, in fact, quite amazed myself," Jessica said, unable to account for such a transformation.

"I knew your response to her letter would be firm, yet respectful."

"That can't be the reason, Mother. I lack the persuasiveness to provoke such a radical change in that determined woman." Jessica shrugged. "But I'll not complain, and only hope it continues."

"He's here!" Alexandra burst into the room, closing the door and backing against it. "Jess, he's here. Are you ready?"

Jessica looked at her mother, who put a final pin in her hair.

"I feel like this is my wedding day. Can I be any more nervous?" Every muscle tightened as she peered one last time in the mirror. "Oh, I hope he likes my hair this way. He's never seen me in curls." Ebony tresses spilled over her shoulders.

"Of course he will," her mother said. "Besides, they won't last long. Your hair is so heavy, they'll pull out soon."

"What do you think, Alex? Is this skirt fitting? Or is it too simple? I knew I should've bought linen. Cotton is just so... dreary."

"No. I've never seen you more lovely, Jessie. He'll be speechless."

Alexandra opened the door to the balcony that overlooked the entrance hall, and at once voices drifted up the staircase. Jessica recognized Andrew's as he conversed with Stephen. A small squeal seeped from her throat as a wide grin overtook her lips. She walked to the top of the staircase, fearing she would trip and tumble down in her nervous state. She looked back at her mother and sister, who remained in the doorway. Angela waved her ahead.

Gripping the marble banister, she took the first step down.

"I've arranged for you to be with us in the courtroom, if you wish," she heard Stephen say.

"Very good." Andrew's voice carried to her ears.

About halfway down the steps, she saw the backs of Stephen and Grace. Andrew, facing them, stopped speaking as his attention was drawn upward. His gaze remained upon her, and he stepped past them to the foot of the staircase.

She forced herself to breathe, finding him even more handsome than before. The sparkle in his eyes made her heart dance.

When she reached the bottom step, he said nothing, but drew her close.

A wall of stale air hit William Sutton in the face when he entered the foursquare courtroom, followed by his son, Stephen, John Viana, and Andrew Winterfield. He looked around. The witness he hoped would shock a confession from the accused had not yet arrived.

With its musty smell and high windows, the chamber had become his second home. Chilly and silent when empty, it now bustled with people. The heat and odors generated by the numerous bodies in the spectators' gallery permeated the atmosphere, stifling the trial participants below. An occasional catcall to one of the jury or to William himself disrupted the hum of muffled chatter filtering down to the courtroom.

The lawyers from William's office awaited him at the mahogany table. Officers of the court and clerks filled the remaining seats, save the half-dozen tall podiums housing the judges' chairs, which awaited their arrival. The jury was seated across the room.

The bar stood empty. Soon Edward Scarborough would stand behind its short wall to face his accusers.

Silence fell upon the chamber when a side door opened. Several men in black robes filed in to fill the remaining places.

Behind them, a clerk appeared and placed two documents and the ruby ring on a table before the judges. The defendant, shackled and led by a jailer to the bar, was left to stand alone.

"He looks thinner...and pale," John whispered to William.

"Did you expect better after weeks in jail? Let us hope he's not carrying fever. We'll all fall ill."

The proceedings began with the reading of the charges.

"Mr. Sutton," said one of the judges, "please present your case."

William stood. "I wish to prove today that the defendant, Edward Scarborough, robbed the victim in this case, Stephen Sutton, of his possessions upon finding him unconscious on a roadside. He thereafter proceeded to send a letter of bribery to John Viana based on some information included in his ill-gotten gain."

"The witness box is yours, Mr. Sutton. Please proceed."

William looked into the eyes of the defendant, who glared back at him.

"I call Stephen Sutton," he said, turning away from Edward.

Stephen rose, seating himself in the witness box in the middle of the room. After taking the oath, he described his journey to Cornwall County eighteen months earlier and his subsequent visit to Brentwood House the previous summer. The judges began their questions.

"The day you were injured, Mr. Sutton, you had in your possession the ruby ring and the letter, both now placed in evidence before the court, and five gold coins. Is this correct?"

"Yes, Your Honor."

"You told the magistrate during his interview that you sustained a head injury and fell unconscious from your horse. Is this also correct?"

"That is correct."

"And your recollection is that, when you regained consciousness, you found yourself in a house, lying on a chaise and in the presence of two young ladies?"

"Yes, Your Honor."

"When did you first notice the absence of your personal belongings, namely five gold coins, the ring, and the letter?"

"The following morning when I rose to leave."

"Mr. Sutton, are you acquainted with the defendant in this case, Mr. Edward Scarborough?"

"Not well, Sir."

"How many times have you been in the presence of Mr. Scarborough?"

"Besides today, one time that I recall."

"And on what occasion was that, Mr. Sutton?"

"While I was visiting the home of John Viana and his family last summer."

"Let me be certain I understand your testimony, Mr. Sutton. The day the items disappeared, you were unconscious for an extended period of time, you awoke to find yourself in the home of two ladies, and it was a full year later before you ever met Edward Scarborough. Am I correct?"

"Yes, Your Honor."

"Have you ever seen this ring in the possession of Edward Scarborough, Mr. Sutton?"

Stephen hesitated. "No."

"Is it at all possible that any number of people could have passed you on that road while you lay unconscious?"

"A slight possibility, I suppose. However, most would've rendered me assistance, not robbed me. The road to Brentwood is not a well traveled route from what I understand."

"As a resident of London, Mr. Sutton, are you familiar with the frequency of travelers along that particular stretch of road?"

Stephen's gaze darted to meet his father's. William sat, arms crossed, unmoved by the questioning. Stephen turned back to the judge. "It's what I've heard from others, Your Honor."

"Mr. Sutton," said another judge, leaning forward, "you stated to the magistrate that the women who rescued you from the roadside that evening were members of the Viana family, tenders of the Brentwood Lighthouse."

"Yes."

"Would you agree that a lighthouse keeper is an occupation of meager salary?"

"I believe that the keeper of a lighthouse receives a modest income, yes."

"Would you not also agree that a ring such as the one you had dangling about your neck for all to see would have captured the attention of the ladies who discovered you? Would not a ruby of that size dazzle the eyes of a poor man's daughters?"

"With all due respect, Your Honor, I am unable to view things through the eyes of a poor man's daughter."

Subdued chuckles drifted down from the spectator gallery.

"Would you not agree, Mr. Sutton," the judge retorted, "that the possibility exists that one of the ladies who rescued you could have also robbed you?"

"I fail to understand why they would care for me after robbing me, Your Honor."

Several more laughs resounded into the high ceiling.

"Mr. Sutton," another judge spoke up, "are you not now *married* to one of the women who tended that lighthouse?"

After a pause, Stephen answered, "I am."

Gasps filtered down from the gallery.

"After your injury," the third judge continued, "when did you next see the ruby ring?"

"Approximately one year later."

"And where was the ring?"

"On the hand of John Viana's wife."

"Did you see Mr. Scarborough give the ring to Mrs. Viana?"

"No."

"So, you were injured, the ring was missing when you regained consciousness, and the next time you saw the ring was on the hand of Mrs. Viana—now your mother-in-law—a full year later. Is my assessment correct?"

"It is." Stephen's voice was almost inaudible.

"Counsel, do you have any additional questions for this witness?" the judge asked William. "Otherwise, we need to move on."

William stood and approached Stephen. "Mr. Sutton, you verified that you're now married to one of the women who once tended Brentwood Lighthouse. Tell me what you know of the moral standards of her family."

"Their patriarch is an admirable man of integrity. He has inculcated fine virtues in all his children. The Viana family may have been in material want at that time, but morally they were, and continue to be, a very wealthy family."

"Do you think it possible that any of the daughters of that family could have robbed you, or anyone else for that matter?"

"In my opinion it is impossible."

"Thank you," William said, turning to the judges. "I have no further questions."

William returned to the table with Stephen.

"Excellent testimony, Son," he whispered, glancing around the courtroom for the expected witness. "Let Edward build a bit of confidence. It will make the fall that much greater."

William stood again. "I would like to call John Viana as a witness."

After John settled into the witness box, William began. "Mr. Viana, you've heard the testimony of Stephen Sutton that he was robbed along the roadside near your home and cared for by your daughters. Since Mr. Sutton didn't see the culprit, please tell the court why it is you believe the perpetrator to have been Edward Scarborough."

"Almost a year later I received a parcel containing a letter of bribery from Mr. Scarborough himself. Enclosed with the letter was the very ring that was heisted from Mr. Sutton."

"Please explain what you encountered when you followed the directions in the letter."

"I was led straight to Mr. Scarborough."

"And upon locating him, did you find any other items reported stolen from Mr. Sutton?"

"I did. I found in Mr. Scarborough's possession a letter that had been in Mr. Sutton's pocket."

"Thank you." William motioned to the judges, then seated himself.

One of the judges began the questions. "Mr. Viana, on that table you see two letters. Are you familiar with the contents of each one?"

"I am, Your Honor."

"Are you the son the late Margaret Everett, author of one of those letters?"

"I am."

Harried whispering, followed by loud gasping, waved through the spectators' gallery. The noise grew to an alarming level, echoing in a fury across the high ceiling.

One of the judges stood, slamming his wooden gavel upon the podium. "We will have order in this room!"

The crowd hushed at once.

The judge gave John a hard look. "So are we to call you Mr. Viana or *Lord Everett*?"

"You may call me by either name. It matters not."

"It may not matter to you, but how is one to believe the testimony of a man who uses an assumed name?"

Whispers again rose from the gallery. John gave no reply.

"For the sake of simplicity," the judge continued, "and in recognition of your true identity, We will call you by your given name. Now, Lord Everett, when and where did you meet Edward Scarborough for the first time?"

"In the parlor of my home. I believe it was early August, eighteen months ago."

"What was the reason for Mr. Scarborough's visit?"

"He was there to call on my daughter."

"At that time, Lord Everett, was he wearing the ruby ring?"

"Not that I noticed."

"And on subsequent meetings with Mr. Scarborough, did you see him in possession of that ring?"

"I did not."

"If you never saw the ring in the possession of Edward Scarborough, what makes you accuse him of robbing it?"

"As I stated before, the following spring I received a parcel that included a letter and the ring."

"We are familiar with the contents of both letters," the judge said. "The one you claim was sent to you contains the name of Edward Scarborough. Is that the reason you believed the bribe originated with Mr. Scarborough?"

"It is."

"Lord Everett, what style of writing is used in the letter you claim you received along with the ring from Mr. Scarborough?

"It is written in type."

"What about the closing of the letter?"

"It's also typewritten."

"So we have no definitive proof that it was composed by Mr. Scarborough since we find no signature."

"The instructions in the letter led me straight to Edward Scarborough, and none other, Your Honor."

"Nonetheless, this letter could have been composed by any number of people, even you, Lord Everett. Is that not right?"

"That may seem so, Your Honor, but 'a man of meager salary,' as I was called earlier, would not likely own printing equipment."

Titters arose from the crowd.

Yet another judge spoke. "Lord Everett, following the episode at your home eighteen months ago, when did you next see Mr. Scarborough?"

"At a dance the following week."

"What did you observe Mr. Scarborough doing at that dance?"

"Dancing."

The spectators once again broke into laughter.

"Did you observe him dancing with any of your daughters?"

"Yes."

"Were you aware of a romantic interest between any of your daughters and Mr. Scarborough?"

"When one has three daughters, one must always consider that possibility."

"Did one of your daughters spend much time in the company of Mr. Scarborough that evening?"

"*Some* time, I would say, not 'much' time."

"So you keep a close eye on your daughters. What were your feelings toward Mr. Scarborough after you observed your daughter spending time with him, Lord Everett?"

"I felt she was too young for courtship."

"I repeat, what were your feelings toward *Mr. Scarborough* at that time? Were you angry toward him? Were you jealous of his attentions toward her?"

"I am not jealous, but am an attentive and protective father." John's voice remained calm and even. "I felt warranted caution toward Mr. Scarborough."

"Did you feel Mr. Scarborough was not good enough for your daughter?"

"As I stated, I felt she was too young to be courted. I would have felt the same regardless of the suitor."

"Lord Everett, at the time of the summer dance, were your daughters aware of your true identity?"

"Only my eldest."

"So the others were, at that time, unaware that their grandmother was Lady Margaret Everett, and that they belong to a family line of great wealth, a family of very high standing in London?"

"They were unaware of that fact."

"But *you* were aware that your daughters were in line for a great inheritance. In fact, they are heirs to one of the largest fortunes in England. Knowing this would, indeed, cause a man to be very selective in his daughters' suitors. A man belonging to an average family, such as Mr. Scarborough's, would never do for the daughter of the Everett lineage, would he now? When was it you next saw the defendant, Lord Everett?"

"In Plymouth, the following spring."

"Did you travel to Plymouth in order to meet Mr. Scarborough?"

"Yes."

"Did you visit him at his flat in Plymouth?"

"I did."

"Were you invited into his flat, Lord Everett?"

"No."

"But you entered his flat, did you not? The magistrates's report states that is where you claimed you found your mother's letter."

"That is true."

"According to Mr. Scarborough's report to the magistrate, you forced your way into his flat and threatened him. Then you hurled him into a corner before leaving the premises. Is this correct?"

"I did not threaten Mr. Scarborough."

"Is this account correct, Lord Everett?"

John glanced at William, who nodded. He looked back at the judge. "Other than the threat, your description is correct."

Gasps echoed throughout the gallery.

"I see. In other words, you sought to destroy your daughter's relationship with an unacceptable suitor, first by hunting down and assaulting him, and then by fabricating this elaborate tale about robbery and bribery. All this against a man whose only intention was to love your daughter. Clever plot, Lord Everett. A guilty verdict would, indeed, rid you of this commoner."

Edward stood tall, a smile of triumph settling over his face.

When the judge motioned, William began his cross-examination. "Mr. Viana, do you oppose your daughters' marrying commoners?"

"I could not object to such a union, as I consider myself common."

"So, Mr. Scarborough's social status alone would be no deterrent to his marrying one of your daughters?"

"It is my only wish that they marry men of integrity and morals. That is what makes a man rich in my opinion."

"Thank you. I have no further questions."

As John returned to his seat, William conferred with his fellow attorneys, hoping to stall the proceedings.

"Mr. Sutton." The judge's tone reeked with impatience. "Have you any further testimony to present?"

"I'm certain my final witness has been detained. If you will kindly grant me a few minutes more, I'm confident he'll arrive."

At that precise moment, the large double doors opened. A husky, graying man entered the room. He was dressed in worn black slacks and jacket.

The man glanced at the defendant as he passed him.

Edward stepped back, his eyes widening. William hid his satisfied smile from the judges.

The newcomer approached William, and the two spoke. Then the man pulled a document from his pocket.

"I request admission of a document, Your Honors," William said.

When one nodded, he gave the document to the clerk, who passed it to the panel.

They consulted in low tones amongst themselves, and after several minutes announced their approval.

"Please proceed, Mr. Sutton," one judge ordered.

"I call Mr. Albert Scarborough to the witness box."

Murmurs arose from the crowd as the burly man took the seat.

After Mr. Scarborough stated his name and recited the oath, William proceeded with the questioning. "Mr. Scarborough, what is your relationship to the defendant, Edward Scarborough?"

"He is my son."

"And what is your occupation?"

"I own a mercantile in Penzance."

William stepped over to the table and picked up the ruby ring. He returned to the witness. "Mr. Scarborough, have you ever seen this ring before?"

"Yes. Eighteen months ago on Edward's hand."

William heard the defendant's gasp above those of the crowd.

"At that time, Mr. Scarborough, did you inquire of your son about the jewel?"

"I did. He told me he'd found the ring in the underbrush alongside the road outside of Penzance."

"Did you believe his explanation?"

"No. He would never have seen that small object from atop his horse. When I questioned him further, he left the house in a rage. He returned later that evening, locking himself in his bed chamber and refusing to answer any more questions."

"Mr. Scarborough, will you please identify the document you handed me when you arrived?" Mr. Sutton proceeded to the table of exhibits and picked up the newly admitted document. He retraced his steps to the witness box and handed it to Mr. Scarborough.

"It's an invoice," the witness replied.

"How did you come into possession of this particular document, Mr. Scarborough?"

"I found it in Edward's desk in his bedchamber."

"And the invoice reveals the purchase of what item?"

"A hunting rifle."

"Quite an expensive commodity I would say. Please read the name of the purchaser on the invoice."

"Edward Scarborough."

"And what is the date of the purchase, as indicated on said invoice?"

"The fifteenth of July, eighteen months ago."

"What, may I ask, does the invoice say about the cost of the item?"

"Its cost was five pounds."

"Five pounds." William turned to pace toward the defendant. "The exact amount that was robbed from Stephen Sutton. And, in fact, the purchase was made just five days after that event." William looked over at the judges. "Are these facts just a coincidence, gentlemen?" He turned back to the witness. "Mr. Scarborough, could it have been possible that your son had purchased the ring and the rifle with his own funds?"

Albert Scarborough leaned forward and glared at Edward through squinted eyes. "Not unless he had *robbed* someone."

Edward averted his eyes from his father's glare.

"Now, let's return to the topic of the ruby ring. Please tell us when you next saw it."

"Several weeks after I first noticed the ring on my son's finger, we attended a dance at the home of a family by the name of Castleton. Edward wore the ring to the dance that night, flaunting it at every opportunity. I pulled him into a quiet room and demanded he tell me the truth about where he got it, but he refused."

"So what occurred after the dance?"

"It was several weeks after our conversation on that night that I gave Edward an ultimatum. Concerned for the reputation of my family, I insisted that he either enroll in school or go to Plymouth to work in my brother's shop. He chose the latter."

William stepped away. "Please tell the court what type of business your brother, Edward's uncle, owns."

"A print shop."

Loud mumbling quaked throughout the gallery. As William stood motionless, the volume in the echoing chamber increased. He glanced over at the defendant. Edward's face burned scarlet, the arteries in his neck protruding.

"I have no further questions," he said, seating himself.

The judges conferred for a few moments before excusing Albert Scarborough. William crossed one knee over the other, his hands folding onto his lap.

* * * * *

At last the time arrived to examine Edward Scarborough.

"Mr. Scarborough, did you ever visit the home of John Everett?" one judge asked.

"Yes. I visited there one time with a friend."

"What was your reason in calling?"

"To see his youngest daughter, Alexandra."

"Were you fond of Alexandra Viana? Or, I should say, Alexandra Everett?"

"I was in love with her and hoped to ask for her hand in marriage."

"On the day of your visit to that home, did you have in your possession the ring that now sits on that table, the ring of which you have been accused of robbing from Mr. Sutton?"

"No, I did not."

"Had you ever seen that ring prior to your visit to the home of John Everett?"

"No."

"Did you ever see the ring after the visit?"

"Yes."

"When?"

"The one and only time I ever saw that ring prior to this hearing was at the Castleton dance a week after that visit."

"Where did you see the ring?"

"On the hand of John Viana, Sir."

Murmurs rippled through the spectators.

"Have you ever before this trial seen the man who identified himself as Stephen Sutton?"

"Never."

"Have you ever happened upon a man lying unconscious alongside the road from Penzance to Bristlecone?"

"No."

"Are you familiar with the contents of either letter presented as evidence?"

"No, I have never before seen either of them."

"Did you compose the typewritten letter and then send it to John Everett?"

"No."

"Where did you obtain the money to buy the rifle that is listed as a purchase on the invoice?"

"My father gave me the money for that purchase."

"Mr. Scarborough, did you live in Plymouth during the time your father stated earlier today?"

"Yes, I did."

"Did you work in your uncle's print shop?"

"Yes."

"Did you ever print a letter to any person while working for your uncle?"

"No."

"Do you have any idea where that letter originated?"

"I do not."

"Did you ever receive a visit from John Everett while you were living in Plymouth?"

"Yes, I did."

"Please explain."

"It was in May, last year—around midnight, I think. I heard a knock on my door. When I opened it, I found Mr. Viana on the stoop of my flat. He offered no greeting, just stood there and glared at me. I knew he was there to harm me. Before I could close the door, he grasped the lapels of my overcoat, forcing me inside and against a wall. He said I had better stay away from his family or things would go very badly for me...or some threat to that effect. I don't recall his exact words. He then threw me into a heap in the corner and left the flat."

"Thank you, Mr. Scarborough," the judge stated and turned to William. "Proceed with your examination, Mr. Sutton."

William approached the witness box.

"Mr. Scarborough, do I understand your testimony to be that John Viana threatened you because of your interest in his daughter? Why do you think he would do that?"

"Because I belong to an inferior class from his perspective. These accounts of robbery and bribery are his clever attempts to rid himself and his daughter of me. That's what I believe."

"You said you loved John Viana's youngest daughter."

"Yes, I did."

"To what extent?"

"I don't understand."

"You mentioned marriage."

Edward shifted, clearing his throat. "I believe I mentioned that."

"Mr. Scarborough, what is Alexandra Viana's favorite color?"

"Excuse me?" Edward asked in surprise.

"Her favorite color. What is it?"

Edward shook his head and stated, "Blue? I don't know."

"And what is her date of birth?"

Edward hesitated. "I can't recall."

"Did she like poetry, Mr. Scarborough?"

"What woman doesn't?"

"Since you were so in love, Mr. Scarborough, you must have danced together often. What was her favorite song?"

Edward did not respond.

"You seem to have little knowledge of this woman for whom you claim such love—and this romance only a little more than a year ago. Has your memory abandoned you so soon?" William paused as Edward's face reddened. "Why did you desert the relationship, Mr. Scarborough?"

"After his brutal assault, I felt myself in danger from her father."

"Ah, that never stops real love, Mr. Scarborough. If you were in danger, would you not have the same concern for your lady, since she lived in the very household of this dangerous man? Any warmblooded Englishman would concern himself first with *her* safety. No, Mr. Scarborough, danger never stops true love. In fact, it enhances the excitement of the romance, would you not say? You were not in love with Miss Viana, nor have you ever been in love with her." William shuffled through some papers on his table, while Edward shifted in obvious agitation, crimson color again rising to his face.

"How would *you* know who I loved?" Edward lashed out. "You know nothing about me!"

William smiled.

"Allow me to turn to the topic of your life in Plymouth. Please describe to me your daily routine."

"I worked fourteen hours per day, six days per week for that man!" His eyes still blazed with fury.

"And what of your social life?"

"What social life?"

"So what time did you usually arrive home from work?"

"Nine o'clock at night."

"And what did you do after that?"

"My uncle worked me to exhaustion. Most nights I crawled into bed and slept until daylight."

"And what of the night John Viana called on you?"

"No different. I went right to bed."

"You were not out that night?"

"No."

"You were not standing on a bridge waiting for Mr. Viana to meet you as was requested in the typewritten letter?"

"No. I was sleeping."

"Do you have the habit of sleeping in your overcoat, Mr. Scarborough? You testified that Mr. Viana arrived at your flat around midnight, three hours after your stated bedtime. You said he grabbed the lapels of your overcoat."

Edward's only response was his grip tightening around the railing of the bar. His arms shook. Anger seethed in his eyes.

William walked to the exhibit table and lifted the ruby ring. Holding it between his thumb and forefinger, he raised it high to peer through the circle of the ring as he rolled it back and forth in his fingers. "You also testified that the only time prior to this trial you have ever seen this ring was the night of the Castleton dance on the hand of John Viana. Did I hear you right, Mr. Scarborough?"

"Yes," he hissed through clenched teeth.

"Are you certain it was *this specific ring*?"

"Yes! He has had that ring all along. He was wearing it that night."

"On which of John Viana's hands did you see this ring?"

"On his right hand."

"And on which finger did you see this ring, Mr. Scarborough?"

"On his fourth finger."

"His fourth finger?"

"Yes!"

William watched his impatience escalate. "Where on his finger?"

"At the base of his smallest finger!"

"Are you certain of this, Mr. Scarborough?"

"Yes!"

"You are absolutely certain that this ring was sitting at the base of John Viana's fourth finger on his right hand on the night of the ball?"

"I'm certain."

William turned to John. "Mr. Viana, will you please stand?"

John obeyed.

"Please hold up your right hand, Mr. Viana."

John complied. William placed the ring upon his fourth finger. He pushed it until it would go no farther. "Please show the court, Mr. Viana, where this ring has settled on your finger."

John lifted his hand up. Those who could see it gasped. The ring sat just above the second knuckle on John's fourth finger.

"The ring will not go beyond his knuckle," stated William, looking at the judges.

"Please approach, Mr. Everett," one judge ordered.

After the judges and the jury inspected John's finger and the ring, John handed it to William and returned to his seat.

"You should never assume, Mr. Scarborough," William stated, clicking his tongue. "Just because that ring fit your own slender finger does not mean it would fit John Viana's. Anyone who knows John Viana also knows he has very large hands."

William noted the tendons in the defendant's neck protrude.

"I believe we've offered proof that you are a malicious liar, Mr. Scarborough. Have you spoken a single word of truth since

290

you took that oath?" William rested his elbow against the witness box. "How can you soil the reputation of this innocent man with these foul lies?"

"Make your point, Mr. Sutton," one of the judges said.

"Yes, sir. John Viana, a respected and well-liked man in his community, has worked hard to raise his family with honor and dignity. Degrading a man of such integrity is nothing short of slander. Can we add that offense to your ever-growing list, Mr. Scarborough?"

Crimson color flushed Edward's face. *"Honor? Integrity?"* He thrust a finger out toward John Viana. "Even his own mother despised him! She was sickened by the very mention of his name!"

"Why, Mr. Scarborough, I thought you hadn't read that letter from his mother!"

The crowd burst out in loud chatter.

Edward's head turned to the gallery, the realization of his mistake written on his expression.

William stepped over to the table. The crowd hushed as he picked up the letter and read aloud. "'That is how I felt for years, John, at the mention of your name. It sickened me to my very inward parts.'" He shot Edward a wilting look. "*You* stole that ring, the coins, and this letter from a helpless man. *You* typed a letter of bribery to the owner of that ring! And when your plan failed, you returned to Brentwood Lighthouse—for what reason, Mr. Scarborough? Just what was your intention toward Alexandra Viana, whom, we now know, you did *not* love? In fact, you barely even knew her."

Edward Scarborough thrust a pointed finger at the barrister. "You entrapped me! You manipulated me! I should have sold that ring and been done with it. John Viana doesn't deserve that fortune. He walked away from it."

Several guards surrounded the defendant, who fought the restraint while screaming threats at the barrister.

The courtroom filled with loud cheering as the entire body of spectators jumped to their feet and applauded William Sutton.

* * * * *

The following morning, Jessica found the Viana and Sutton families gathered in the breakfast nook.

"That was an intriguing experience yesterday, to say the least, Mr. Sutton," she said, crossing the threshold.

"You mean standing in the cold outside the courthouse?" William teased.

"Besides that." She joined him in laughing. "It helped to have so many gathered around, giving information about the proceedings in bits and pieces. I must admit I wondered about the importance of interrogating Mr. Scarborough about his claim to have only seen the ring on Father's hand."

"The man has been lying about that ring since I first questioned him," William replied. "I wonder at his admission to ever seeing it at all. He would have done better for himself to deny it altogether. Nevertheless, I decided to catch him in his own trap by a simple demonstration."

"Very clever," John boasted.

"Ah, but showing him to be a liar does not make him guilty of robbery, bribery, or anything else. All these charges remain to be proven," William said. "It was your eldest daughter, John, who assisted me with the point of bribery."

"Tell me how she managed that, Will." John cast a proud smile toward Grace.

"Robbery was a fairly simple verdict with the invoice," William explained. "But the only piece of evidence we had to prove bribery was the letter you received from the scoundrel; yet how can one prove the origin of such a letter? Edward showed forethought in composing it in the manner he did, but any intelligence he may possess ends there, for he did not plan his defense anywhere beyond. Edward had burned behind him one bridge that would be the very source to scorch him. And none other than your daughter, Grace, revealed that source to me. Tell them, Grace."

"Jessie, Alex, I didn't mention this to you before, but the night of the Castleton dance, I happened upon Albert Scarborough and his son in a private, yet heated argument. My presence went unnoticed by either one. I turned to exit when Mr.

Scarborough brought up the subject of the ruby ring he had noticed on his son's hand. My curiosity piqued, I stayed but a few moments as he threatened Edward. That's when I took my leave. It was later in the evening that you, Jessie, located Alex and me, and we eavesdropped on Edward and James Gregory, where all was revealed to us."

William nodded. "I found Albert Scarborough willing to testify that not only had his son been in possession of the ring, but also had worked for some time in his brother's print shop, a fact unknown to all parties involved until I interviewed Albert. He was a key witness for our case. Yet his knowledge of this whole situation would have been overlooked had Grace not mentioned that brief conversation, and I thank her for that. Still, I felt all this evidence a bit inadequate. Edward had to be led into a confession of some sort. I studied his behavior throughout the proceedings and found him to be very short-tempered. It would be an elementary task to draw him into an argument, and even into revealing a portion of Margaret Everett's letter, with which I was quite certain he was familiar by that point. He followed my lead as a rat would have followed the Pied Piper. It was easier than I expected." William stretched his arms above his head and yawned. He interlaced his fingers and placed them behind his head as he exhaled and leaned against his chair back. "Yes, Edward Scarborough will serve as an example to this entire community."

William's butler entered the nook, holding a silver tray. William took from it a newspaper. A smile twitched at the corner of his lips after a quick glance at the headline, and he set the paper aside.

Jessica, who sat closest to him, reached for the paper.

"'Yet Another Victory for the Masterful William Sutton.'" She read the headline aloud. 'Sutton shot holes in the defense until, when the dust settled, the only thing standing was the truth,'" she continued. "'Sutton will preserve the reign on his long-standing position as London's leading barrister.' Your prosecution is summed up in one word, Mr. Sutton—'Artful.'"

But it was the final paragraph that caused a look of concern to becloud the expressions of William and her father. "A key witness for the prosecution was sixteen-year resident of Cornwall County, John Viana. His true identity, as revealed during the trial, is that of former London resident and the heir to the supposed unclaimed estate of Margaret Everett, he being the only son of the late Earl Ivan Everett—the elusive John Everett."

Jessica looked up from the paper to observe her father and William exchange uneasy glances.

If his presence had gone unnoticed during their previous visit, it was certain to arouse the attention of many now.

Chapter Twenty-Six

By the night of the engagement party, Jessica thought Olivia Winterfield's admittance to the local asylum was imminent. In the process of her insistence on perfection to the smallest detail, Olivia had reverted to the insensitive, belligerent woman Jessica had met the previous year.

Spending much time at Winterfield Manor during the days since the trial, Jessica pitied the servants, who were unable to escape the wrath of their mistress as she barked orders, sending them running hither and thither. The woman appeared mad with anxiety!

But perfection was the final result as the shadows of evening settled across the estate, and the hour of eight drew near. By some miracle Olivia had retained her sanity, and most of her hair.

Andrew Winterfield settled onto the cushion of a chair in his father's bedchamber, crossing one leg over the other.

"Father, please quit pacing like that. You're making me nervous."

"It's just that I expected to hear from him by now."

"But you told him not to contact you before today."

"Yes, but I was certain he would have kept in touch with your mother. No one has heard from Roman since November."

Andrew placed his foot on the floor again and leaned forward. "Do you think he'll show tonight?"

Richard stopped to tap his foot, contemplating Andrew's question. He hesitated before responding. "I don't know. But if not, he's made his decision with regard to the family *and* the business."

"What about Mother? What does she think of all this?"

"She's tried to dissuade me since November, but I'm earnest in my demands, Andrew. I'll not turn back. Not now; not ever."

Andrew looked away, certain Roman's loyalty to him would prevail.

Guests in excess of three hundred had been invited to the engagement party, and the Winterfield and Viana families formed a long receiving line to welcome each one as their names were announced.

Andrew introduced each guest to his fiancée and her parents. Thereafter, Andrew's parents and Catherine greeted each one, followed by Grace, Stephen, Alexandra, and young John Viana.

The guests were ushered into the large tapestry gallery, which had been converted into an elegant ballroom. The receiving hall resounded with the hum of conversations as the number of guests grew.

An hour later, Jessica stood tall as the final guests were introduced—nine gentlemen who had arrived together in two carriages.

As their names were called, they clustered to one side and waited before approaching the receiving line. Jessica looked at Andrew in question. She did not recognize the names or faces of any.

"And Mr. Harry McGuire."

Her hand flew to her mouth. Tears filled her eyes as each of Andrew's crew members approached her to place a kiss on her cheek. She broke out in sobs when Smiley stepped over and reached out to embrace her.

"We all owe ya a 'thanks,' Miss, and we're grateful t' be here."

"I didn't recognize you, Mr. McGuire! What a transformation!"

The black jacket with tails that reached the backs of his knees, along with the high shirt collar and cravat, gave the sailor a tall and slender appearance. The once-ragged red curls were tamed, his face shaven. He appeared ten years younger than she remembered.

"Bein' in this suit," he whispered in her ear, "helps me t' understand the meanin' of true sacrifice."

Jessica giggled, drying her eyes.

As the last guests were escorted into the ballroom, Jessica heard Richard mumble to Andrew that several of his fellow Parliament members had not made an appearance. She shrugged, thinking that might be for the better.

It was nine o'clock when the orchestra started and the dancing began.

The hour of eleven drew near. Jessica left the dance floor with Smiley McGuire to return to the side of her fiancé, who stood conversing with his father.

"I'm convinced now we'll not see him tonight," Richard was saying as she approached, "which means we may never see him again."

"I'm sorry, Father."

"Not as sorry as I am for you," Richard said with a sigh. "And I'm sorry our happy occasion has to be overshadowed by his absence. It seems his pride is more important than his own brother. My disgust over his disappointing choice is my prevailing emotion at the moment, however."

Jessica felt it best not to intrude by asking what had transpired between Roman and his family.

"Let me say, though," Richard continued, "I'm proud of the marked improvement I've seen in your mother since November. She did struggle to maintain composure these past two weeks, but she has made a valiant effort to change her attitude."

Jessica could now agree. Since the party had started, even among her uppity associates, Olivia displayed a kind manner, and paraded her and her parents among them. Perhaps Olivia Winterfield had realized a new beginning.

An instant later, Jessica was swept back to the dance floor by another sailor.

Near midnight, Andrew took Jessica's arm and escorted her through a door behind the orchestra. They stepped into the large but cozy library. Andrew closed the door behind them and shut out the sounds of the party. He lit a few of the lamps and fell into an oversized leather chair, motioning for her to join him.

"I am afraid if I sit down I'll split a seam," she said with a laugh.

Her gown, although full and flowing from beneath her breastbone, was fitted above, held tight by a train of satin buttons down her back.

"I wanted just a few moments alone," he said, standing again. He took her into his arms as they looked up at the high ceiling and the mural of the angry ocean crashing against a rocky cliff.

Jessica looked back down into his eyes.

"There will be many storms ahead of us," he said, reading her mind. "But we have the strength and the knowledge to face them."

She smiled, having full confidence in her captain. Taking him by the hand, she led him to the family portraits, which she had studied in detail many times over. "You know, this isn't your likeness at all," she teased.

As they stood scanning the faces of the Winterfield family, they heard the noise from the party gush into the room and go silent again as a man stepped in and pulled the door closed behind him.

The two spun around to find Roman standing in their midst!

Jessica stared at him in astonishment, never expecting to find him at their party.

He stood silent for a moment, but then stepped toward them, offering a hand to Andrew, who grasped it with firmness. Roman pulled him into an embrace, clapping his back.

"Have you seen Father yet?" Andrew asked.

"No," Roman said, pulling away. "I managed to escape his notice. I wanted to see you first, and I saw the two of you duck in here."

When he turned to Jessica, she took a few steps back. This was the first time she had ever seen the two together. Although not identical twins, they bore a striking resemblance to each other in the subdued lamplight.

"Miss Viana…Jessica…may I have a word with you in private?" Roman requested.

"Mr. Winterfield," she replied, lifting her chin, "I'll not be drawn into another argument. Whatever it is you wish to discuss can be said in the presence of my fiancé."

"It's not my wish, nor my intention, to argue," he said in a softness she had never before heard from him. With eyes fixed on her, he held his arm out toward the balcony doors. "Please?"

Jessica looked at Andrew, who nodded. Looking back at Roman, she saw in his eyes, not the familiar anger and resentment, but kind pleading. She released a sigh, turned, and walked toward the balcony doors, fearing she was stepping into a trap. Oh, would there ever be peace between them?

Andrew followed her, removing his jacket and placing it over her shoulders. He kissed her cheek. She watched him cross the library floor and disappear through the door leading back to the ballroom. Dropping her head, she stepped out onto the veranda.

In the ballroom, a servant approached Richard Winterfield. "Excuse me, Sir. Several men have arrived out front, requesting that I summon Mr. Viana."

"Is that a fact? Thank you. I'll see to the matter at once."

Richard scanned the room and beckoned to Andrew, then to William Sutton as well.

On the library balcony, Jessica stopped just over the threshold while Roman took several paces ahead of her.

"Jessica, I...It has been brought to my attention by someone who means a great deal to me that perhaps I have not treated you with much respect in the past."

"*Perhaps?*"

"Please...If you only realized the great difficulty with which I am struggling at this moment. You see, I've not been accustomed to considering the feelings of those around me. Although it's no excuse, my work requires...that I treat others with indifference. As a result, it seems I have become rather condescending and now find myself not well-liked among my peers." His head dropped down. "As well as my own family."

Jessica remained quiet. He began pacing.

"I've been thinking for some time now how I might arrange for a few changes and decided to begin with you, if you'll permit me." He looked as though he were waiting for her approval. She offered no response, so he continued. "I came to you last summer, the day you left Canterbury, intent on injuring your feelings. You did not seem a good match for my brother. I thought he deserved someone...better, and I hoped I would succeed in driving you away.

"But now I see it's not my right to make that decision for him. I wish first and foremost for my brother's happiness. He's my closest—and perhaps my only—friend. We may be opposites in many ways, but he shows true loyalty to and confidence in me, even when I fail in his eyes. I am most concerned about his decision in this matter of choosing a wife, and if you are the right choice, then..."

Why had he paused? Would he never accept her?

"Then I congratulate you, and...I welcome you into this family."

She was not quite sure how to respond.

"And what is more..." He walked toward her. She took a step back. "I apologize for the manner in which I have treated you in the past," he blurted, "and ask for your forgiveness."

His words, spoken in great haste, seemed to include 'apologize' and 'forgiveness.' Had this been what he said?

He stood in silence, awaiting her response.

All at once his father's earlier words made sense to her. Richard must have put him up to this. Could Roman not even apologize on his own? Was it so hard to treat others with dignity? What was more, would his repulsive behavior have ever become plain to him had his father not stepped in? She wanted to scream out, *how much has he paid you to humiliate me in this way?*

And yet, there was a certain tone of modesty in his voice, she had to admit. Would she ever know whether he was trying to right his wrong or just placating his father?

"Mr. Winterfield." Annoyance rising in her throat, she forced herself not to be argumentative. "I do realize your effort and sense your concern. I also appreciate your expressions. Yet, I believe true sincerity is proven over time as shown by one's deeds. I so wish for peace between us. The forgiveness you request may be granted at some point in the future, but I fear that the pain you've inflicted upon me has been so great that now is not that time." She prepared herself for the familiar anger to flare up into his eyes.

He looked toward the veranda floor, and, to her surprise, a slight smile formed on his lips.

Just then the library doors flew open.

"Jessica!" Alexandra stopped short when she caught sight of Roman. "Oh! Excuse me. How do you do, Mr. Winterfield?" she said with a quick curtsey. "Jessica, Andrew told me I would find you here. You are wanted inside. Come at once!"

Jessica glanced back at Roman and excused herself. He bowed his head to her.

Alexandra took hold of her hand. They hastened through the library and into the ballroom, passing through the crowd and up the large winding staircase near the front entrance to a second-floor window of leaded-glass. Their mother and Grace sat in shadows on the window seat and peered down upon the front porch of the mansion.

When her mother saw her, she pulled her to the window. Outside, several men had gathered. Six were poised before a row of carriages, whereas Richard and Andrew Winterfield and William and Stephen Sutton were standing on the porch. The women could discern only a few of their words, yet the angry tone of their voices could not be mistaken.

"What do they want, Mother?" Jessica asked.

"I'm not sure. But Richard asked your father to remain inside, so I assume this has something to do with him. I'm afraid the mention of him in the society paper has stirred up some contentions."

It seemed to be the night for confrontations, Jessica thought, looking up at the frame of the high window. Stepping on the cushioned window seat, she stretched to reach an iron latch. Her mother and sister helped her from the seat as they pushed the narrow window open. Cool air seeped in along with the voices.

A gray-haired man of slight build stepped toward the group that had gathered on the porch, "Send him out, Winterfield. Our words are for *him*."

"Malcolm Winslow," Richard responded, "I believe you received an invitation to our gathering. Come in and join the festivities."

Another man stepped forward. "Do not trifle with us. We're here to make it known that we have no intention of accepting the daughter of a traitor into this society. John Everett has brought ostracism upon his family name. Do not make the same mistake, Winterfield, by uniting your family with his!"

Jessica feared for Andrew when she saw him step forward. His father grabbed hold of his arm.

The second man spoke up. "And William Sutton, 'London's leading barrister.'" Sarcasm saturated his voice as he quoted the article that had praised William just two weeks earlier. "Rumor also has it that you yourself have also approved of such an alliance involving your own family. Why is it you would malign your own fine reputation?"

"It would appear, Eastman," William answered, "that you and your band are a minority in your cause." He stretched out his arm behind him. "Do you hear the music, the cheerful sound of a large crowd rejoicing with us in this happy occasion? Why, I believe I even saw your wife joining in the celebration."

"You're on dangerous ground, Winterfield!" Malcolm Winslow pointed at Richard. "This entire community will turn against you. You'll be driven from your business and your home. Your name will be detested wherever you go."

"And this coming from a man who, weeks ago, praised me and my business as a valuable asset to this community," Richard replied in a calm tone, "a man who has entered this very home and who has sat to enjoy a meal with this very family, and on more than one occasion. Who's acting the traitor now?"

The door behind the four men on the porch opened and out stepped Jessica's father. Her mother gasped when she saw him.

"All this commotion because of me?" John stepped in front of the men on the porch. "I'm flattered. What can I do for you gentlemen?"

"John Everett...," Malcolm Winslow said, disdain dripping from his words. "You would make a mockery of this society. You spurn your very roots only to return two decades later to claim one of this city's greatest fortunes. Don't deny it! Why else would you have returned here a year ago? As if that's not enough, you then wedge your way into one of its most influential families through this pretense you call a marriage. I knew your parents well, Everett. They were the finest of people. They worked hard to maintain the family's reputation as a long line of great lawmakers. For generations Everetts have played a significant role in the building of this community, indeed of this fine country. The only mistake your parents made was in producing an only son, one who would bring that family name to ruin. Your daughter is *not* an Everett."

"That's the only truthful statement I've heard thus far," John replied.

Jessica smiled with pride.

"She will not be accepted by this society," continued the man they called Eastman. Jessica recognized him as the one who had confronted her father at the ball the previous January.

"To save the Winterfield family the pain of such rejection and probable future discrimination, we stand as one in contesting this marriage."

"So now you wish to protect me?" Richard piped. "You, who just moments ago threatened to drive me from my home and my business? Which will it be, Eastman—friend or foe?"

The man did not respond. The two groups stood in silence.

Jessica feared Andrew's anger was at its pinnacle. She saw her father lean over and say something to him.

All at once a man stepped out from the shadows. He walked tall, hands clasped behind him, stationing himself between the two groups, his back to the porch.

"At least there's still *one* sensible Winterfield!" exclaimed Malcolm Winslow.

"How nice to see you again, Winslow. I believe it's been several months," Roman replied.

Jessica watched Richard. She felt sure whatever had been simmering between father and son in recent months would impact what happened next. How unexpected that the outcome lay in the hands of the unpredictable Roman Winterfield!

"You've no doubt overheard this discussion." Winslow glared at him. "I know your disposition, Roman. Set your father straight on this issue."

Roman turned toward the porch and looked up at Richard. "Father...I'm sorry."

Jessica's heart sank. How could he do this to his father, a noble and loyal man?

"You see," Roman continued, "I'm well acquainted with the Everett name. Though not being associated with Margaret Everett, I knew her reputation and heard accounts of her husband's dealings."

Jessica was surprised at the calmness in his voice. She saw his head turn to address her father.

"It's as Winslow says, Mr. Everett. Your mother did, indeed, work with vigor to build that family name. She wielded great influence on this people."

304

Roman turned to the side, looking between the two groups.

"But," he continued, "the devices she employed to build this community were not the same as the instruments chosen by her late husband. Ivan Everett has been painted as a man who possessed honesty, integrity, and inner strength, among other fine qualities. These were the tools he used to build the foundation on which he stood. But can the same be said of his forefathers, his brothers, and his wife? You tell *me*, Winslow. You knew her well. Was she a woman of moral integrity?"

Malcolm Winslow remained silent.

"Or did she employ forceful manipulation?" Roman asked. "Did she stand on honesty as her foundation, or secret bribery? And can it be said she possessed inner strength? My recollection is one of a woman who relied on oppression and intimidation of those beneath her. She and her husband became to this society two opposing examples. And which pattern did *you* choose to follow? I think I can answer that question for you...for myself...and for many of the leaders in this society." Roman turned his attention to Richard. "I repeat, Father, I'm sorry. I'm sorry that, instead of displaying integrity and choosing to follow the example of men like Ivan Everett—and like you—I've followed the example of the prideful in this community."

Again, he looked at John.

"I believe there was something about your mother, Lord Everett, that my father hadn't the heart to tell you. While men the likes of Eastman and Winslow claimed loyalty to her, they were nowhere around during the final stages of her illness. Nor were their wives there to comfort her, console her, or care for her at her most dire hour. From what I've heard, Margaret Everett suffered and died unaided by any of her acquaintances."

Jessica watched her father's head drop.

"Can such a woman be called successful?" Roman asked. No answer came from even one of them. "I would call that shameful." He looked from one to the other. "I am learning that true success can only be the product of fine qualities such as those possessed by you, John Everett, and by you, Father."

Jessica looked at her sisters, whose expressions told of the same surprise she herself felt.

"What are you saying, Winterfield?" Malcolm accused.

"What I'm saying," Roman said, his tone changing to anger, "is that you are not welcome here. Remove yourselves at once from my father's property."

"Ye heard the man!"

Jessica gasped when Smiley McGuire emerged out of nowhere, followed by several of the sailors. "Off with the lot o' ye, or we'll be removin' ye ourselves."

She began laughing when the opposers slithered into the shadows and disappeared.

Over an hour later most of the guests had dispersed, and the hosts were bidding farewell to those remaining. Afterward, the three families gathered in the parlor.

"This is all my fault," John said. "Whatever was I thinking in bringing my daughters back here last year? I knew full well they would never be accepted into this society."

"*Whatever were you thinking?*" Andrew spoke up. "Mr. Viana, the happiness of most in this room has been the direct result of your decision to bring your daughters here. You've brought three families together, and two of your daughters will be happily married because of it. Also, your presence here has brought an important issue to the fore, one that demands an answer from each of us. Will we stand for integrity? Or will we side with insolence? Look how your example has already affected *one*." He cast a look of pride Roman's way.

His brother raised his eyebrows. "Just because we agree on this issue doesn't mean it'll happen every time."

"But we *do* agree on this," Andrew answered, "and that's all that matters at the moment."

Jessica was astonished to see a smile, not only on Roman's lips, but in his eyes. It almost wiped away the uneasiness she had felt with his last words.

"However," Andrew added, "this society will never agree. I've been no part of it for several years now, and neither will I raise a family here."

Jessica looked at her father. He winked at her. Yes, it was just as her mother had said—Andrew Winterfield was very much like him.

Richard moved to where Roman was seated and extended his hand.

"Welcome home, Son."

Chapter Twenty-Seven

"No tears, Mother, no regrets." Jessica repeated her mother's words, spoken to Grace eight months earlier.

"You're the bride I only dreamed of being when I was your age," her mother stated. "We were married in the courthouse. I wore a simple blue dress."

Jessica stood before a mirror. Her mother had tailored white Persian silk Andrew had sent in the fall into a gown that draped across Jessica's torso in crisscross fashion and gathered into countless little folds. Flowing around to the back, it crossed again to meet a large bow of white lace just below her waist. The gown trailed into a long train several feet behind. Tiny pearls lined the folds across her torso, around and down into the train, and when the light hit them, Jessica thought they resembled the sparkling spray of a trickling fountain. Her hair had been twisted into a tight knot on the back of her head and sprinkled with more of the tiny pearls. The remainder of the silky lace had been gathered and tucked beneath the shimmering coal knot. Its pleats opened into a soft fan streaming to the floor.

"You're the most beautiful bride I've ever laid eyes on," Catherine said, a twinkle in her eye.

Grace and Alexandra nodded their agreement.

Olivia Winterfield stopped short after stepping into the room. "My goodness...Andrew will faint in the presence of such beauty." She placed a kiss on her cheek. "Jessica, I know we had a rough beginning, but I want you to know I have every reason to be proud of my son. He's a good man...and he has made a good choice."

"Thank you," Jessica whispered. She had been surprised by her mother-in-law's recent kindness, but this was the first time she had been a recipient of her affection. She fought to control impending tears.

"The coach is waiting," Olivia said before leaving the room.

"Jessica, you've made my family so happy," said Catherine. "I once believed there was not a woman in the world that could succeed in diverting my brother's attention. How happy I am I was wrong. It could have been no ordinary woman. Did he tell you how he felt about you while you were here last summer?"

"Not then, no."

"So I knew before you did! The night before you left, Roman had made an unexpected stop home, as is his usual way. I overheard him and Andrew talking in the library. Andrew said he was very much in love with you, and, although Roman had his objections, I was so thrilled. At last he had found true happiness, and I would have the sister I've longed for!" Catherine, too, kissed her cheek.

The ladies filed out of the upper bedroom suite of the Winterfield mansion. Catherine and Alexandra trailed behind, carrying the yards of fabric of the train. Jessica glanced at the indoor garden as they passed by. Busy servants readied the feast that was to follow the ceremony. They, one and all, stopped mid-task to watch her as she passed.

Andrew's nervous foot tapped the floor of his cabin below the deck of *The Emerald*. Smiley McGuire pulled the last button through the hole in the elongated cuff at Andrew's wrist. White sleeves flared above the cuffs to the ivory double-breasted vest. He stepped to the mirror to examine the cravat. His father draped a black waistcoat with long tails across the bed.

"Father, I've seen no trace of Roman," Andrew said. "No one has heard from him since the party."

"Andrew, please sit down and stop worrying."

"What if, at the last minute, he has decided to contest the marriage?" Andrew sat on the bed, drumming his fingers on one knee.

"Your brother may have made some dramatic changes of late, Andrew, but two qualities in him remain the same—determination and stubbornness. He's in support of your decision. That hasn't changed, I'm sure." Richard gave him a reassuring pat on his shoulder. "He'll be here. Now, are you ready for your bride?"

"Father, I've been at sea for nearly four months. I haven't seen her in all that time. My nerves are in shreds!"

"Good! I'd be worried otherwise. Shall we go?"

Andrew, Richard, and Smiley reached the upper deck, where more than fifty family members and friends had been greeted by Andrew's crew members. Olivia strolled over to him as though she were walking on a cloud. He kissed her cheek.

"You look stunning, Mother."

"I always do, Andrew. The day your brother and you were born, I would not even see your father until I was absolutely radiant." She smiled at him. "Son, you had better stand close to your father. I've prepared him to brace himself so he can catch you when you faint."

"What?" he asked with a laugh.

"You're so handsome." She put her palm on his cheek. "The most attractive man on land or sea, but take care, Son. You think you've swept that bride of yours off her feet, do you? Just wait till you catch sight of *her*." She winked and turned away to take her place as two Winterfield carriages arrived on the dock below.

Jessica looked up into her father's eyes and thought she saw them water. Arm-in-arm they ascended the ramp to the deck of *The Emerald*. To her utter amazement, she felt as calm as the breeze that fluttered the white ribbons on the arch at the top of the ramp.

Stepping through, she held tight to her father's strong arm and at once was looking at the face of her fiancé just a few short yards away. The glimmer in his eyes took her back to the morning she had met him in the hull far below, the moment he had stepped into the dusty ray of sunlight. She felt this day as she had on that momentous morning. Without a doubt, his was the most handsome face she had ever seen.

Every wish, every hope in life—everything right and good that could be—was summed up in him, every question answered. She knew now how wrong her view of love and marriage had been when she was young. Her father's words rushed back upon her with renewed meaning, words he had spoken so often over the years. 'A wife complements her husband,' he would say; 'she completes him.'

She fought the urge to release her hold on her father and run into Andrew's arms. At that instant, she recognized that her role as daughter had come to an abrupt end. All her father's instruction would carry through to her new life with her husband.

They took one last step together, and as Andrew reached out, her father joined their hands and cupped his around them.

"Honor…dignity…respect," he said to Andrew, too quiet for anyone but them to hear, "this is how she has been raised. This is what she expects and deserves."

"May the day she receives anything less be the day I die, Sir," Andrew responded in earnest.

John placed a light kiss upon her cheek and stepped back.

A movement from the corner of her eye caught her attention. She looked over to see Roman appear to take his place on the other side of Richard. She watched a quiet smile brighten Andrew's face and forced back her own feelings that tried to surface.

"Before I invite you all to the manor in celebration," Richard said when the ceremony had ended, "I would first like to announce the couple's first wedding gift." With that, he motioned to Smiley, who produced a small package wrapped in white fabric and tied with a satin bow. Richard handed it to Andrew.

Beneath the soft fabric were three brown leather books. In gold embossing on the front of each book were the words, *The Sapphire*. Puzzled, Jessica opened the cover of one and fanned through its pages to find them blank. She looked with curiosity at Richard.

"Jessica, Andrew," he said, "your parents could not bear the thought of you raising a family on this old cargo ship. It simply will not do. Therefore, Andrew, I'm releasing you from your duties at Winterfield Imports for the time being, and you and your wife are ordered to leave this area and enjoy your new life together. You're not to return here until at least next spring, when we'll discuss further your obligations to the business."

Holding one arm out, Richard guided them to the starboard railing, where they looked out into the harbor.

They stood speechless, watching a double-masted ship dock beside *The Emerald*. The schooner paled in size next to the tea clipper, but sported long, sleek lines and rounded sails. Her name was spelled out in large letters across the hull, *The Sapphire*.

"Father!" Andrew gasped.

"She's an Italian Parenzello. The extended wedding date gave us the time needed to have it custom built. I expect a full account of her journeys in those books," Richard said with a wink.

The group broke out in applause as Jessica and Andrew kissed their parents. The guests surrounded them in congratulations.

In all the excitement Jessica had forgotten the presence of Andrew's brother until he approached them. He embraced Andrew and turned to her.

"My brother deserves real happiness. With you he declares what you once referred to as 'genuine love.' May nothing ever come between you." Taking her shoulders, he kissed her cheek. She was stunned when he embraced her and had not even the chance to return the gesture when he pulled away and disappeared into the group of guests.

Wide-eyed, she looked over at Andrew, whose contented smile warmed her overflowing heart.

"Have my two best friends at last found peace with each other?" he whispered.

Chapter Twenty-Eight

Andrew Winterfield stood to drag his sleeve across his perspiring forehead. He reached for a drink of water and gazed out over the pier of the harbor where they had ported to rest for a few weeks and complete some minor maintenance on *The Sapphire*. Even in January, the sun bore down on the Greek islands.

They had spent the summer months sailing along the Scottish coasts. Andrew had taken his new wife to some of his favorite coves and port towns, which he himself had not seen since childhood.

Afterward, they had sailed to the Emerald Isle, where they had spent several weeks along the northern coast. Once, the fog was so dense they were forced to dock for several days in the fishing village of Donegal. There they became acquainted with the friendly locals and enjoyed the tastiest of seafood, which Jessica had to admit surpassed even that prepared by the expert, Mrs. Wright. They visited other villages of the western coast, and before long *The Sapphire* sailed south, burdened with Irish wares.

The cold and unpredictable fronts of the forthcoming winter forced them to the place Andrew had planned to introduce to his new wife—the ports of the Mediterranean.

He set the water down and reached for a rag, recalling one warm night on their journey when he had awakened her from sleep around midnight. Beckoning her to follow him up to the deck, he cupped his palm over her eyes. In the crisp night air, he led her in silence to the railing of the bow. Standing behind her, he dropped his hand.

"Behold…the universe," he whispered.

Thousands upon thousands of stars sparkled and winked, not a single one obstructed by even the smallest cloud. Across the glassy surface of the sea, thousands more reflected the night sky in perfection.

"Where's the horizon?" she asked.

"There is none. It's you and I suspended in the universe."

She gazed in all directions, astonishment and moonlight reflecting in her eyes.

"It's as though God took his mighty hand and scattered a million perfect diamonds upon an endless satin veil," he explained. "He gave all this to us, Jess; the Giver of perfect presents."

"The most magnificent view I've ever beheld," she whispered. "It's as if they're twinkling all for me. The heavens do indeed declare the glory of God."

They had stayed on the deck that night, basking in the rare and majestic experience until sleep had overtaken them.

Pulling himself from the memory, Andrew caught sight of his wife running along the dock toward the schooner, waving a white page.

"Andrew!"

He laughed at her, shaking his head at the manner in which she had gathered her yellow dress up with one arm, her legs exposed as she ran.

"Jessica Winterfield!" he reprimanded her with a smile as she neared. "Do take care. I wouldn't have another man coveting my lovely wife." He pulled her close to kiss her cheek.

She giggled, out of breath.

"Andrew, it's a letter from my father. Let me read it to you."

It had been several months since she had heard from her family. The last correspondence had been weeks old by the time it reached them.

They had also received an occasional word from Andrew's family. The most recent letter had reported the sobering news that after many long years of service, Richard Winterfield had been voted out of his chair in the House. Jessica had been

314

upset by the news, knowing full well his expulsion was due to her union with their family. But Richard expressed great joy in having the opportunity to focus on more important matters, such as his daughter. He had also conveyed firm conviction in his son's choice and reassured Jessica that she was not to blame for the intolerant attitudes of others. His letter had assured her of his deep love for her.

Andrew sat down to draw another sip of cool water. He splashed some on his face as his wife read the news from England. The letter had been written two weeks prior.

"My Dear Children,

"How we miss you and hope all is well. We have some exciting news. First, I would like to announce that we have settled on a location for the future Viana residence. It has, indeed, required more effort than once thought, but your mother and I have at long last purchased a small island off the southwestern Scottish coastline. You will no doubt be surprised that we are not returning to the Emerald Isle as we had discussed, but after much consideration, we decided that a new home in a new place suited us both. You will be happy to hear, Jessica, that it is forested, with the potential for many a footpath.

"We have consulted with your father, Andrew. His advice in the matter of building has been priceless and has led us to the decision to begin the construction of a replica of the Bavarian castle Reiswyck on the island. This, we realize, will be an enormous undertaking, which may well span several years. Every stone and piece of lumber will be imported to the island, not to mention the equipment that will be necessary."

"Oh, Andrew, are you not thrilled?"
He nodded, waiting to hear more.

"For assistance on this project to begin in the spring, we have consulted numerous architects from all over Europe. The castle will be built for the purpose of housing any or all of our children and their families as they grow, on occasion or on a permanent basis, as they see fit.

"Since the castle will house the Viana, Sutton, and Winterfield families for generations to come, we feel the construction should also be a family project. As such, for added assistance I call upon my children. Richard has approved our use of *The Emerald* for the importing of materials, if you, Andrew, would be willing to captain the ship for this purpose. It would require your sailing to various ports for materials and could span the next several years. Of course, you would be compensated."

His wife could have only imagined the excitement that began building in Andrew's heart. He felt like a child in a candy store! Jessica beamed at his expression and resumed reading.

"Please consider with care whether to join us in this venture in whole or in part. Your decision, either way, will be welcomed and respected. Please notify us at your soonest opportunity so we may commence with our plans. At this time we are also awaiting a reply from Stephen and Grace."

"There's more, but what do you think?" asked Jessica, bouncing on her toes.

"Your father's advice is to consider our decision with care, and I think we should do just that."

"Oh," Jessica groaned. Her shoulders drooped, and a tiny pout crossed her face.

"So I think," he said, rising to his feet, "that we should appear in person to tell your parents we'll be there every step of the way!"

Throwing her arms about his neck, she let out a excited shout. "What an adventure it'll be! Thank you!"

After a few moments she calmed enough to return to the letter.

"Our second and most important announcement concerns the arrival of the Sutton baby! Your sister delivered a healthy boy on the twenty-ninth of December. Your mother had been with her the previous month in London to assist in the preparations. She reports that the baby favors his father in looks, with the exception of his mother's, grandmother's, and aunts' blue eyes.

"The remaining Vianas will be leaving tomorrow to join them in London. I know you, too, will be excited to return there as soon as possible. We all look forward to a reunion.

"With Love,
Father"

"A nephew!" Jessica leaped around, laughing. "We have a nephew!"

Her zeal for life and adventure always amused him.

"Smiley!" he called out, still staring at his wife.

The head of Smiley McGuire appeared through an open hatch. "Yes, Captain, Sir? Just puttin' the finishin' touches on tonight's meal. Roast duck with all the trimmin's," he said and kissed his fingertips. "Wait'll ya smell the aroma!"

Andrew did not look at the sailor, but kept his gaze on his wife.

"Smiley, after that delectable meal, we'll prepare to cast off for Chatham, England…first thing in the morning."

"Yes, Sir!" he said with enthusiasm and disappeared again.

Andrew wrapped his arms around Jessica's waist, pulling her close.

"Do you realize what today is?" he asked.

"One of over two hundred of the most glorious days of my life since our wedding. And even more special because of its being the fifteenth of January, two years to the day from the night I first met the most intriguing man in the world."

He smiled, certain she had not remembered. Then another thought occurred to him. "The letter didn't say what they named the baby."

"No, it didn't," she said, holding the letter up again, turning it over. "Oh, there's a post script here."

> "Much to the delight of both your mother and me, the baby is to be called after our family name—Everett Sutton."

"After all," she said, "my grandfather was a man of impeccable reputation and unquestionable integrity."

Taking his wife in his arms, he looked out over the sparkling waters of the Mediterranean.

Despite the frigid January wind whipping around one corner of the house, John and Angela Viana left the grandfather clock bonging ten and stepped into the shadows of the veranda outside the library of Sutton Manor. He scanned the dark sky for the familiar luminary, his hair tossed by the winter gale.

He recalled when he and his daughters visited Kent the first time together and the dread that overcame him as he realized that their road was soon to fork. Rocky and twisting, those branching pathways gave no hint of the forthcoming gratification for them all. And now their roads would soon run parallel. A smile of satisfaction settled onto his lips. His cheek rested against the softness of his wife's hair.

"Did you know, all those years Jessica considered me her navigator?" he said over the wind.

"That comes as no surprise. She's one of the fortunate few privileged to view life through *your* eyes."

Far above their heads the bright sphere of the full moon glowed. Upon its carved surface, he could almost discern the soft lines of her cheeks, the arch of each delicate brow poised above eyes as deep as the sea. He still found it difficult to believe that the face for which he had anguished night after night, year after year, was now beside him.

His palm ran the length of her cloaked arm, and he pulled her to him. His eyes closed. No more would he be a prisoner of his memories. No more would he agonize for her touch.

Feeling her arms slip into the folds of his coat, he focused again on the luminary. It faded away behind a cloak of ashen clouds.

And he whispered to his wife, "Never again will I let you go."

𝕿𝖔 𝖇𝖊 𝖈𝖔𝖓𝖙𝖎𝖓𝖚𝖊𝖉...

Be sure to get your copy of the next
exciting book in The Viana Memoirs!

The Journey
Available May 2008.
See excerpt beginning
on page 321.

Chapter One

Footsteps intruded upon the stillness of Simone's bedchamber. She was startled out of a restless sleep.

Her husband stood beside her bed. He held a finger before his lips and beckoned her to follow him. For a moment she hesitated. Rarely did she venture outside her bedchamber at night.

Taking her hand, he pulled her along the shadow-cloaked corridor. In silence they passed several oil lamps burning low. Shadows stretched like crooked fingers across textured walls dulled to a curry yellow by the lamplight.

She looked down. They both walked barefooted. He, however, wore his outdoor wrap. She shivered in the thin nightshirt that served her well under her coverlet but proved woefully inadequate in the drafty hallway.

Somewhere between her still-drowsy state and her husband's recent peculiar behavior, she felt a growing sense of foreboding. For the first time since their wedding eight years before, she knew fear in his presence. Was it for her own safety? Or was her alarm in behalf of him?

He halted at a closed door. Before turning the curve of the handle, he placed a tiny brass saucer over the lamp flame nearest them on the wall. The deepening shadows enfolded her, and she shuddered. In haste, he pushed the door inward, nudging her into the dark parlor.

Moonlight filtered through the tall leaded-glass window on the opposite side of the large room. His warm hand gripped her cold one. They crossed the thick wool rug toward the window half draped by a heavy red curtain. Easing it aside, he motioned for her to peer out at the courtyard washed in moonlight. Between the stone carvings and the flower gardens, two figures stood talking.

The full moon played hide-and-seek behind a gauze of clouds and for a moment lit up the men's features. She recognized the taller, Pashur, her husband's closest general, who had served him for the past eight years.

Though their features were clear, their words were muffled through the glass. Simone strained to understand them, but could only shake her head.

She peered up at her husband. Worry lines furrowed his forehead. He raised one fist to his lips. The thick gold of the signet ring flashed in the moonlight.

Moments later, he motioned her back to the bedchamber in the same silent manner. He lit a single lamp, and her marble dressing table glowed in the soft light. She watched his reflection in the tall, gold-framed mirror hanging above it. He turned and stepped toward her.

Eyes burdened with pain now stared at her. And her anxiety escalated.

In some inexplicable way, he had changed in the previous weeks. A stranger peered out from the familiar dark eyes, once lustrous and abounding with life, but now dreary. His gaunt face seemed to grow paler each day. In mere weeks, he seemed to have aged a dozen years. Even the strength in his touch had waned. He was withdrawing into a seclusion from which even she—with all her exuberance and laughter—had been unable to draw him.

"Did you recognize those men?" he asked in a language that was all but unheard in the European nations that lay to the northwest.

"Only Pashur," she replied in the same tongue. "Of what were they speaking?"

He looked away. "Conspiracy. The other man is Addon, the leader of a powerful revolutionary group. They have been meeting in secret every night for the past week. And now they convene right under my nose. In the courtyard of my very castle!"

"You need not be concerned." Simone raised her chin. "One word from you will silence them—all of them."

His eyes squeezed shut as though her words had stabbed him. "Not when my generals are against me."

"Sabiir, you are a mighty king with a strong military. Rulers from surrounding nations shudder before your army. You are victorious in all your campaigns, and your people cherish you. They would never allow injury to you."

As though burdened with a weight too heavy to carry, his eyelids opened slowly. Through his dull gaze, he studied her face. "In your eyes I have always found strength and loyalty." He looked away. "I will be leaving you soon."

"You will be back. You have always returned to me." When he did not respond, she added, "Or I will accompany you."

Taking both her hands, he pressed them against his lips. But his eyes hardened. "This is a journey from which I shall never return. I must face it alone; no army before me, no subjects to back me; even you—my sweet and trusted companion—cannot follow me."

"What are you saying?"

"I am faced with my most formidable enemy—one I cannot defeat. I am dying, Simone."

She pulled her hands from his and turned away. Chills skirted her body. In her heart she had known, but to hear it from him—in his own voice—was to be run through with a dagger.

He had faced death many times. And each time he had prepared for battle, she had prepared to face life without him. But he had cheated death. He had always returned the victor. Even now, a strange semblance of his past strength filled his eyes and his voice. She turned back, her countenance falling.

He lifted her chin. She straightened her back to stand tall.

"You were always strong. And you will be strong now." His approving nod reassured her despite his frightening words.

He dropped to his knees and placed his cheek against

her belly, which had grown ever rounder over the past several weeks. She coiled his hair, the color of pitch, around her fingertips. A quick thrust from within her abdomen was followed by his sad smile.

"I may not live to meet my child. He will carry my name and be heir to my throne. When he is old enough and strong enough, the people will be told of him." He groaned, pushing himself to a standing position; her hands flew to cover the sorrow in her face. "I erred when I spoke to Pashur of my illness," he said, stepping away. "Now he seeks to use my death to his advantage the moment I am gone. But you will be the key to the throne. Follow my orders, and all will be right again in time."

"Tell me what I am to do."

"Upon his birth, the child will be given to Rios, who will conceal him. Rios was loyal to my father. He tutored me from the time I was an infant. My father entrusted both my education and upbringing to his care. Rios taught me to be more than a king. He taught me to be a ruler. And he has been loyal to me all my life. He will teach my son of his lineage, of his responsibilities to this people."

"How am I to hide such a thing as the impending birth of a child?" she protested. "Already my servants know of it. I'm certain Pashur knows of it, also, at this late hour."

"I trust you to find a way to protect our child."

"He will have me executed."

"Indeed, Pashur is not a man to be trusted. However, he will not be your executioner. He will treat you with respect and dignity after I am gone. Yes, he will put you under guard, but he will not harm you. Of this I am confident because of the manner in which he has dealt with our enemies. You are not his enemy."

"Perhaps not, but I carry his enemy."

"That is the reason the child must escape."

Pulling an object from his pocket and the signet ring from his hand, he placed both in her palm, wrapping her fingers around them.

"Now listen carefully to what I tell you."

324

Weeks later, a rare drizzling rain cooled the arid region.

A woman, cloaked and hooded, kept to the shadows in the wee hours before daybreak. Making her way against the protection of the low structures along the empty stone street, she reached a darkened doorway underneath a simple sign that advertised the town's glazier. She slipped inside.

In the dimness, her footfall brought forth a man from the rear of the shop. Reaching up, the woman pulled back the black hood.

"Your Highness!" The man dropped to one knee. "The king sent word that he would be sending a servant."

"I had to be satisfied in the knowledge that these items have reached your hands." From underneath the cloak she produced the two objects the king had given her and a small scroll. "The future of this kingdom has been entrusted to your care." Her gaze upon him was stern.

"I will not rest until it has been accomplished. You have my word of honor, Your Highness."

CPSIA information can be obtained
at www.ICGtesting.com
Printed in the USA
FSHW011412060120
65788FS